# MINDMASTER

## BLACKWING PIRATES, BOOK 4

## CONNIE SUTTLE

Print ISBN: 1-63478-021-3
**Print ISBN-13: 978-1-63478-021-6**
eBook ISBN: 1-63478-020-5
eBook ISBN-13: 978-1-63478-020-9

Published by:
SubtleDemon Publishing, LLC
PO Box 95696
Oklahoma City, OK 73143

Cover art by Renee Barratt @ The Cover Counts

*To Walter, Joe, Larry, Lee, Dianne, Sarah, Mark and Denise.*
*Thank you.*

For my sister, Barbara,
until we meet again.

# ACKNOWLEDGMENTS

As always, this book is the result of collaboration. If it weren't for the support of my editor, my cover artist and my beta readers, it would be less than it is. All mistakes, as usual, are mine and no other's.

About the Author:
Connie Suttle lives in Oklahoma with her husband and a conglomerate of cats. They have finally banded together to make their demands, which has proven disconcerting to all humans involved.

You may find Connie in the following ways:
Facebook: Connie Suttle Author
Twitter: @subtledemon
Website and Blog: subtledemon.com

Demon Revealed

Demon's King

Demon's Quest

Demon's Revenge

Demon's Dream

*God Wars Series:*

Blood Double

Blood Trouble

Blood Revolution

Blood Love

Blood Finale

*Saa Thalarr Series:*

Hope and Vengeance

Wyvern and Company

Observe and Protect*

*First Ordinance Series:*

Finder

Keeper

BlackWing

SpellBreaker

WhiteWing

*R-D Series:*

Cloud Dust

Cloud Invasion

Cloud Rebel

*Latter Day Demons Series:*

Hot Demon in the City

A Demon's Work is Never Done

A Demon's Due

*Seattle Elementals Series:*

Your Money's Worth

Worth Your While

*BlackWing Pirates Series*

MindSighted

MindMage

MindRogue

MindMaster

*Black Rose Sorceress Series*

The Rose Mark

Rose and Thorn

Black Rose Queen

Queen of Thorns and Roses

~

*Future Wars Series*
Buffer Zone
Black Zone*

~

*Other Titles from SubtleDemon Publishing:*
Malefactor
Transgressor
Underhanded*
by Joe Scholes

*Forthcoming

# CHAPTER 1

*Queen's Palace, Le-Ath Veronis*
*Lissa*

"At least the hub worlds are safe, now." I allowed a sigh to escape while I shook my head. Travis, Trent and Vik had come with Randl and Dori—not just to visit, but to take half the prisoners out of my dungeon.

Randl and Dori had taken the opportunity to visit Niff's for a treat, leaving me to talk in private with my sons before they transported the prisoners.

Any prisoner who'd had contact with D'slay or the Prophet was about to be relocated to a secure facility on Sirena, the most well-hidden planet in the universes. The prisoners included the bodies of Akrinn and Lorvis, whom Kooper had brought back when X and XIII's crews disappeared following A'pelur's destruction.

"We'll be using Akrinn and Lorvis again—like canaries in coal mines," Vik grinned when I asked him about the bodies.

"So you'll be taking your ships back," I crossed arms over my chest.

"That's the plan," Travis chuckled. "And the Alliances can charge Randl with the thefts. Eventually."

"Kooper is still on probation," I dropped my arms and turned away.

"We know. He'll either earn his place or he won't."

"I think Ildevar is trying to coax Lendill out of retirement to help, but I don't know how that's going. In the interim, Kell and Opal are continuing to act as co-directors with Kooper, because he trusts them most. That puts Lok as a vice-director, but they need at least two more. Don't know who will fill those spots, yet."

"Mom, I think Randl and the rest of us on Sirena have left all that behind. We're different. Sure, we're still willing to work with the ASD and CSD, whenever their goals align with ours. As for taking orders—those only come from Randl."

"You're saying you're a separate entity?" I wasn't sure how I felt about it.

"Ask Jett. He'll be the first one to tell you that."

"How is he? Teeg is having trouble coming up with a suitable replacement."

"Jett would be hard to replace, no matter what."

"There's something you should know," I said. "About the applications Teeg is looking at." Yes, Teeg was my son Gavril, but this decision belonged to his alter ego—and to his identical associate, Tybus. Both would have to agree on a selection.

"What's that?" Trent frowned. "What's bro up to?"

"Well, it's more like what your great-grandfather is up to. Griffin has applied for the job."

"What the bloody, foot-scraping hells for?" Vik cursed.

"I have no idea. I'd have tossed the application in the trash first thing, but Teeg and Tybus are considering it."

"Did he get tired of being on the run with Wylend?" Travis snorted.

"Maybe he feels guilty, finally," Trent suggested.

"What is he using for experience?" Vik asked.

"A hundred thousand years of working with the Saa Thalarr," I shrugged. "Of course, Teeg can't pass that information along to just anybody—knowledge of the race protects itself."

"Convenient for Griffin, I guess," Vik frowned. "Although he did save us, once—you, me, Gavril, Nissa, Toff and Trik."

"I think somebody else held his feet to the fire." Probably my sister, Breanne, but she'd never admit it. Gavril was still in the womb at the time, too, so there was that.

"What will we do if he gets the job? He's a citizen of Karathia—through Wylend, and that makes him a viable candidate," Travis said.

"I don't know. He just needs to stay away from me whenever possible," I grumped.

"He'll be forced to tell the truth—no matter what," Trent grinned.

"Well, that's something to think about," I agreed.

"What can he bring to the table that other candidates won't have?" Trent asked.

My shoulders sagged. "He has the ability to *Look* into the future—through his mother's Elemaiyan side of the family," I admitted. "If he focuses on the right things, he'll know something is coming before most other people will."

I didn't say that's why I existed—he'd planned my birth long ago to take care of a big problem he foresaw in the future.

I just wasn't expected to live over it.

"Dori and Randl are back," Travis announced, breaking me away from thoughts of my father and his machinations. "They're waiting for us in the dungeon."

"You can't stay longer?" I asked my sons, after Randl and Dori transported their chosen prisoners to Sirena.

"Mom, you know we have to find the Prophet. If we don't, we'll have more incidents like the hub world takeover attempts. Next time, we may not survive."

Travis was right—they'd been targeted by the Prophet, and he'd almost pulled them into his army. Only Tenigar's sacrifice, and the power Randl and the rest of us wielded against V'dar, the Prophet, kept them from being subjected to his slavery.

"Keep us posted on Jett's replacement," Vik pulled me into a tight hug. "I know he's concerned about who takes his place."

"I will," I mumbled against his chest. "Stay safe, all right?"

"That's the plan." Vik moved away so I could hug Travis and Trent. *Reah told me the same thing,* he sent, giving me a lop-sided grin.

*She's not wrong,* I replied.

*Randl*

"You think they'll have any use for us other than perking up whenever they're close enough to the Prophet?" Dori asked me as we studied several of our new prisoners. Until now, the dungeon in our palace had gone unused.

"I'm hoping we can find the Prophet's weak spot," I confessed. "But to find that, I have to get past his obsessions."

"Good luck," Dori shuddered. "I wouldn't want to see into these heads—or his."

"Neither do I, but after the hub-world battles, when we saw how strong he was with only five of his pet rogue gods with him, we have to find an edge or we'll lose this fight."

"Without those rogues, it would be a fair fight," Dori grumped, before putting both arms around me and laying her head on my chest.

"There's never been anything fair about the Prophet—he was made that way."

"Not only do we have to find him again, we have to figure out how to defeat him once we find his new lair."

"I know." I leaned in to kiss the top of her head. *"The god who always comes at the end. Damn; why didn't anybody see that coming?"*

*We were waiting for the right one to carry us into battle—Reviendus, Soul of the Universes,* Kev'Ril, my Chief R'pex, noted.

*I think you're giving me far too much credit,* I told him. His coin—my most prominent, rested on my shoulder. Bennall, Kev'Ril's Second-In-Command, was next to him. My entire back was covered with the rest of the coins I carried, each of which represented a planet—a world destroyed too many times to count by the one they'd named *the god who always comes at the end.* This time, that god bore the name V'dar.

"When will we take our ships back?" Dori mumbled against my chest.

"Tomorrow," I said. "Tonight, we'll have a meeting to decide how to accomplish that."

~

"My question is this—do we take our ships all at once, or one or two at a time?" Travis asked later. We'd convened for the meeting after dinner.

"More dramatic to take all of them at once," David said. "That will leave a few folks scratching their heads and settle a bigger bounty on yours, don't you think?"

"If you want drama, then take half the ships, and when they send in an entire flotilla of investigators to go over the site with every tool they have, take the other half right in front of them," Susan suggested.

"Do we even want drama?" Vik asked. Denevik, who sat on his right, nodded in agreement. *We're with Vik on this,* Cudworth sent. He and Ocenosek, the other two High Demons on the roster, dipped their heads once to confirm their choice in the matter.

"How often do they check those ships?" Jincus asked.

"Good question," I replied.

"A botguard makes rounds every hour or so, roughly," Dori consulted her comp-vid. "If anything seems out of place, a message is sent to the crew on duty. They make a decision whether to physically check the inventory, so to speak."

"You want to leave an illusion behind, don't you?" Ilya Ironsmith grinned.

"I think we can work an illusion that may fool a standard botguard —at least for a while," I said. "We can slip into the evidence space station and past Alliance security easily enough."

"Are we planning to relocate all of them, or fly them out of there?" Trent asked.

"If you relocate, you'll have to get them past the sensor range of the space station—and that means as far as Veridium Prime. The ships are tagged you know, and until we find and destroy those tags, we'll be sending signals to any Alliance space station. Veridium Prime is non-Alliance, so it shouldn't matter if we're in orbit around their planet."

"We could park there, find and destroy the tags and then relocate again," Zanfield pointed out. "Whose idea was it anyway, to put spelled tags on those ships?"

"Uh, that would be Uncle Erland," Travis cleared his throat. "He suggested it long before the BlackWing Pirates came along, so he wasn't targeting us. The Alliances used those things sparingly, though, until the Prophet—and we—came along."

"I can probably find the tags fast." Perri, who sat beside Zanfield, spoke up. "I'll set my hands on the ship to lead me to the power-scents on board."

"We can probably help Perri with that," Nari and Tiri offered. Jett, who sat between the twins, agreed with them. They could find anything if they knew how it vibrated, and a spelled tag would certainly vibrate differently than the rest of the ship.

"What about Veridium Prime?" Chief Markus asked. "Should we be prepared for them to attack us while we're in orbit around their planet?"

"They don't have the capability—they can't travel beyond their own atmosphere, yet," Travis reported. "As for weapons—they're barely experimenting with nuclear power. That's where they are, technology-wise, right now."

"They have some lessons to learn," David leaned his head on a fist and frowned. "Let's hope they don't destroy themselves while they're learning."

"So, we're all for relocating to Veridium Prime, ridding ourselves of the tags and then relocating here?" I asked. "Any objections?"

No hands were raised. "All right, that part's out of the way. Now we decide who's going with me and who will fold aboard ship once we're in Veridium Prime's orbit."

"Take us with you, then," Denevik raised his hand.

"That will only protect four ships," I pointed out.

"That's four more than you'll start with," Vik said.

"So. We have four High Demons, to nullify four spelled tags. Which ships are most important to us?"

"X," Travis said immediately.

"XIII," Dori said.

"I think we should consider XII, too," Zanfield offered. "It's our science vessel and important because of the research."

"Agreed. What's the fourth one?"

"IX," Ilya said. "Zaria says IX."

IX wasn't even on my radar at the moment, but Zaria thought it was important. "All right, IX it is. Who else is going with me to get the ships out?"

"I'm going," Ilya said. "I can transport several to Veridium Prime, even if they have spell magnets on those tags."

"You think they'd go to that much expense?" I focused on Ilya.

"Depends on how devious they are about thwarting us," he shrugged.

"I thought they were on our side," Perri grumped.

"They are—but not all of them know we're on the same side. If it's protocol to put spell magnets on spelled tags to prevent a most-wanted criminal from stealing from their impound, then they'll set spell magnets," Travis explained.

"What do spell magnets do?" Jincus asked. He was the least familiar with spells laid by wizards, witches and warlocks.

"Spell magnets lock onto spelled tags, and, if they get too far apart, prevent the evidence—in this case, our ships—from leaving the area. It's like a tractor beam formed by a spell rather than engineering."

"How strong are they?" Jincus asked.

"Depends on the strength of the one or ones building the spell," Perri replied. "I doubt they're messing around, here; criminals have access to wizards and warlocks, just like anyone else, and they generally pay better. These will be the best spells the Alliance can afford."

"*A weak shade of loyalty can be bought, but the price is steeper than a great mountain,*" Tamp quoted an ancient Falchani philosopher.

"*And, as shadows do, it fades when exposed to sunlight,*" I finished the quote for him.

"Somebody's been reading Falchani philosophy," Travis chuckled.

"I've had plenty of time to do so," Tamp agreed. Turning back to me, he said, "We need a Captain and a pilot for BlackWing IX, remember?"

"We do," I agreed. "Let me think on that, all right? Now, unless somebody has something else to discuss, we're done for the night. Get some sleep—we have work to do tomorrow."

*Le-Ath Veronis*

*Cassie King*

I wiped down my practice blade and returned it to its place on the wall of the palace dojo. While only six months had passed here since I'd been transported away from Earth IV, Zarigar had taken me back in time five years, to receive weapons training with pistols, rifles, blades, knives and anything else that could be employed as a weapon. Salidar de Luca had also taught me strategy and many other things before he declared me proficient, then Zarigar arrived to bring me back to Queen Lissa's palace.

I'd passed my last test moments ago, when Travis and Trent's uncle, Crane, invited me to a sparring match. At the time, I hadn't realized it was a test. I thought it was an exercise.

I preferred fighting with my fire—I was a fire demon after all, but Sal told me several times that I could find myself in situations where fire should be the last weapon to employ.

After I cleaned up, I was invited to lunch at Avii Castle, where Destiny was having lessons with Pauly Ironsmith. And, in the time I'd been gone, I hadn't heard from Denevik once.

He was aboard BlackWing X, according to Lissa, working for Randl Gage and searching for Ver'Dak's new hiding place. One thing was certain—if Ver'Dak didn't want to be found, he was deadly serious about it.

As for my sprite guards, Rob, Zephyr, Ebb and Blaze, they'd been invited to the Elf King's domain to learn new secrets and teach a few of their own.

Chet, his ginger tabbiness, stood near the door, waiting for me to finish cleaning my practice equipment and notice him again. Meowing loudly, he reminded me that he was hungry, too. "Come on —I need a shower," I told him. "Somebody will feed you fish afterward, I'm sure of it."

He was used to my relocation trick and didn't ruffle a whisker when I lifted him in my arms and hauled him to the guest suite Lissa provided for me in her palace.

Sal said my trick was more like folding space than *skipping*. He said *skipping* was the technique most demons used to relocate, so I wondered how I'd come by my alternative talent.

He suggested I ask Zaria, if I met her someday.

Half an hour later, I was dressed well enough for lunch in a glass castle, when *he* appeared.

Things got weird after that.

~

*ASD Ship Impound Facility*

*Randl*

*Everybody is in place,* Vik reported, meaning all four High Demons had *skipped* aboard the proper ships. Ilya and Tamp were with me on BlackWing XIII, the flagship and largest of our fleet.

Ilya and I were about to move eleven ships; VII and VIII had yet to be replaced. *Ready?* I sent to the High Demons.

*Ready,* they replied.

*You'll be in Veridium Prime's orbit in three—two—one.* Ilya and I transported the ships to an agreed upon location far above the planet. I was ready to call the others in to take over their ships when things went sideways.

*And sideways meant the new Director of the CSD was already there, waiting for us.* When he appeared on the bridge of BlackWing XIII, I knew who he was.

My heart skipped a beat because of it.

# CHAPTER 2

*BlackWing XIII*
*Randl Gage*

"First day on the job, and look who I've captured," Griffin strode around the bridge of my ship as if he owned it. "I'm sure the Founder of the Campiaan Alliance will be appropriately impressed."

"Not likely," Ilya muttered.

"You're the warlock—who lived and fought with the Falchani, right?" Griffin turned narrowed, hazel eyes on Ilya. If looks could kill, they'd both be dead in that duel.

"Has Teeg briefed you on ah, everything?" I asked.

"We have an appointment later today," Griffin sniffed. "Why aren't you trying to kill me? Go ahead, I can defend myself."

"We, uh, know that," Ilya coughed.

*Zaria, we have a problem,* I sent, along with the image of Griffin pacing on my ship.

"I thought you knew things," I said, hoping that Zaria—or someone with authority—would come and remove this one before he caused us more trouble.

"How do you think I managed to get three CSD ships here in time to stop you?" Griffin smiled. He was more than satisfied with his trick; I could read it on his face as easily as a bird flies.

*Everything okay?* Dori sent.

*We have an uninvited guest,* I replied. *Stay where you are. This could turn into a problem.* I sent her the image, too.

*Holy shit—is that?*

*Why yes, yes it is.*

Zaria, Zarigar and Teeg San Gerxon arrived then, cutting off my silent conversation.

"Jumped the gun, did we?" Zaria became her Larentii self, crossed arms over her chest, unfolded her white wings and glared down at Griffin.

"Get back on your ship and leave, or this will be the shortest period of employment you've ever had," Teeg growled at Griffin. "I asked you to wait until the briefing before going out to hunt criminals. This is one of the reasons," he swept out a hand to include Ilya and me. "Randl is working with us, if you haven't figured that out, yet."

"He was pissed when he left," I told Vik later, as he and I sat in my study aboard XIII having a beer. We were still in Veridium Prime's orbit; Perri and her crew were going through every ship to find the tags and get rid of them before we moved the ships to Sirena.

"Wait until Mom hears about this," Vik shook his head. "They already don't get along. Teeg says that Griffin thought you'd stolen the ships, just as the wanted listings say, and managed to override the crew's good sense, convincing them to follow you."

"I'd like to say it was an honest mistake," I blew out a sigh. "I don't think that's it."

"What makes you say that?"

"I get a strange vibe from him, that's all."

"Jett will be pissed."

"He's a long way down that line already," I said. "If that was Griffin's objective, then he did a hell of a job."

"Any beer left?" Travis and Trent folded in.

"Help yourself," I jerked my head toward the cold-keeper in my office. "Still a few bottles in there."

"This is the best reason to steal a ship from a criminal," Trent opened the cold-keeper, which was disguised to look like every other cabinet in my study. Tossing a bottle to Travis, he pulled one for himself and shut the door.

"Ah, good to find all of you here," someone new arrived.

"Wisdom," Ilya rose and dipped his head respectfully to the Mighty Mind.

"Don't get up," he held out a hand when I began to rise from my chair. "I just wanted you to know I've found the crew for IX. They're already on board."

"What?"

"I argued with him. I lost." Zaria and Zarigar appeared, but Zaria was the one who spoke as she frowned at Wisdom.

"Grandfather, I question your motivation in this. You understand how dangerous this will be," Zarigar's brow creased as he also frowned at Wisdom. Wisdom had arranged births, so he could lay claim to Zaria as his daughter, and Zarigar as his grandson.

Something in Zarigar's words made me think he had more than a passing interest in the crew Wisdom chose for us. I hoped he'd tell me what it was sometime.

"Will somebody please tell me who is working for me now?" I interrupted. "I've already decided to give Jett the Captain's chair."

"Of course," Wisdom turned toward me and smiled. "Jett is a good choice. Come. I will make introductions to his crew."

"Perhaps I should do that," Zarigar suggested, his tone filled with irony.

"Well, perhaps you should. I did conscript them," Wisdom admitted.

"You mean they didn't have a choice in the matter? How much smoothing over will this entail?" I demanded.

"Oh, they're ready to work with you, Randl. They just dislike how it came about, without being consulted, that's all," Zaria huffed. "You even have a chef for the galley, who can also handle part of the ship's operations. If you'd like to keep everybody happy, then make sure not to upset Beverly."

"She's not that bad," Wisdom scoffed.

"Hmmph. Get one of her kids killed, you'll see what I'm talking about."

"Her kids are here?" Travis asked in disbelief.

"Relax, they're all grown, not her children by birth, and all of them are well-trained in their duties. All can handle weapons, and all of them have a few—special talents," Wisdom explained.

"I stand by my statement," Zaria snapped.

"Where are they from?" I asked as congenially as I could.

"The future," Zarigar turned toward me. His words were loaded with a weight even I couldn't measure.

"Are ah, all of you from the future?" Ilya spoke cautiously.

"Yes," Zarigar replied. "We must go back soon; I merely wanted to ask my grandfather to reconsider his choices."

"They won't remember," Wisdom began.

"And I have an enormous problem with that," Zaria argued.

"As do I, for many reasons; not least of which is that it will be unfair to us—and to them," Zarigar said.

"Then I hope it proves worthwhile," Wisdom snorted and disappeared.

"Great," Zaria lifted a hand in surrender. "Come on, we have people to introduce."

"Captain Jett Riffler," Zaria introduced Jett and me to Rob Newbourne, Jett's Second-in-Command. I gripped Rob's hand and my head swam with visions.

"Earth sprite?" I asked as we shook.

"That's right. Zarigar said you'd know," he added.

"Your pilot, Zephyr Seabreeze," we went to the next in line—an air sprite.

"Navigator, Ebb Tidewater." I shook politely with the water sprite.

"Weapons master, Blaze Fireglow." I blinked—a fire sprite? That sounded interesting.

"Lieutenant Cassie King." I touched her and my mind was filled with visions of fire. I froze while images of her life flashed through my head.

"Randl?" I didn't come back to myself for a while, and only with Zaria's and Zarigar's help did I blink and realize that I was still on the bridge of BlackWing IX rather than Earth IV.

"Cassie saw what you were seeing—at the same time. She's in the galley, having tea with Beverly," Zaria said gently as I blinked a second time. "You brought up some bad memories for her, as you've probably realized by now."

"Yeah. That's ah—wow. She's grateful that she and the others are alive though," I drew in a painful breath and let it out again.

"Small compensation for a great deal of sacrifice," Zarigar grumped.

"Agreed," I said. "Might we join her for tea? I'd like her to know I didn't mean for that to happen."

"I'd say that's a good idea," Zaria told me.

*Did you know her father is,* I sent to Zaria as we made our way off the bridge.

*That is something for her to know later, when she returns to the future she came from,* Zarigar heard and intervened.

"That important, eh?"

"Most certainly."

"Wait until Vik hears we have a fire demon," I said.

"Hmmph. Wait until Denevik *sees* her," Zarigar snipped.

"If you have concerns, dearest, you may speak with Randl," Zarigar told Cassie later. We sat at a table in the ship's galley, having tea.

Zarigar had transformed himself to a more suitable size for the available seating.

"You mean about Denevik? About not realizing we've met—in the future?"

"I doubt he will remain a stranger long," Zarigar soothed.

"We can't discuss anything that happened—to any of us. What if I slip up?"

"Don't worry so much, all right?" Zaria leaned in to hug Cassie. "Once this is over, we'll see how things stand."

"At least Rob and the others are with us." Cassie shivered.

"Now, don't you start that," Beverly pretended to scold her. I liked Beverly already, and wondered how she hadn't attained the rank of Admiral yet. I'd seen how the young men and women she called her kids rushed to do her bidding.

I'd seen some of their history in Cassie, too, and marveled at how far they'd come—from little more than slavery within their Shakkor Agdah race to living freely on Le-Ath Veronis, attending schools there and learning how to master various positions on a star cruiser.

Beverly, dark-skinned, not yet middle-aged and with a smile that could light a universe, had attended classes with several of her charges —those who'd needed her presence and encouragement most. As a result, she'd earned degrees alongside them. Sixteen young men and three young women were eager to serve under Jett, Cassie and the others, but they'd always answer to Beverly first.

"The ability to bend time is a wondrous thing—and a two-edged blade," I lifted my cup of tea to Cassie and Beverly.

"Ain't that the truth," Beverly spoke in English, and tapped her cup against mine.

"I'm giving Beverly temporary mindspeech," Zaria said. "She and everyone else aboard this ship have medallions, too. I think it's necessary for anyone who's in this fight."

"Thank you," Cassie breathed, turning toward Zaria.

"How is Eli?" I asked, changing the subject.

"Very well," Zaria beamed. "He's having fun learning."

"We should go back, Mother," Zarigar told Zaria. "The tags have been found and destroyed. The ships and their crews must return to Sirena and regroup."

"You'll let us know if anything is needed?" Zaria rose from her chair.

"Of course."

"Regular updates, too," Zarigar requested. "If help is needed," he didn't finish.

"I'll keep you informed," I said.

He and Zaria disappeared.

*Prepare all ships for transport to Sirena*, I sent to everyone who could hear mindspeech.

*BlackWing IX is ready, Commander*, Rob reported.

"Where are they now?" Sabrina asked. She, Travis and Trent sat inside my study in the palace, asking about our newest recruits.

"Either marveling at their quarters or wandering through the palace grounds," I replied. Of all those who worked with me, Sabrina was having the most difficulty accepting our newest members.

"You don't argue with Wisdom," Travis told her gently. "He brought them. If they weren't trustworthy or up for the job, they wouldn't be here."

"I just don't understand," she argued. "Weren't we enough?"

"An old proverb on Falchan says, *refusing a willing hand is often the same as removing one of your own*," Trent quoted.

"I hope there won't be trouble between you and the new ones," I placed a warning in my words. If there were trouble, I doubted it would be initiated by our newest recruits. I wouldn't hesitate to put a stop to it, either.

"I'll be nice," Sabrina muttered, lowering her eyes.

"Thank you. Is there anything else?" Sabrina shook her head. Frankly, at that moment, I wanted to have Tamp's trick of becoming a cactus and standing in the sun, my sharp spines a warning for all to stay away for a while.

"Where is Rajeon right now?" I asked Travis as my three guests rose to leave.

"Want me to send him in?" Trent asked.

"Yeah. I think I'll assign him to BlackWing IX, along with Nari and Tiri."

"You want Rajeon to act as liaison, and the others to look for traces of the Prophet, don't you?"

"A liaison who can size up a situation in less time than it takes to blink," I agreed. "Jett, Nari and Tiri know what they're doing. We're looking at a maiden voyage for all the others, and Rajeon is well suited to watch over them."

"He fits in well anywhere—good choice," Travis complimented me. "He can morph himself into any situation."

"Are you saying they have no battle experience?" Sabrina snapped in outrage.

"They have battle experience—most of them. Just not aboard a star cruiser," I pointed out. "Those sprites can give Travis and Trent a run for their money in a blade fight. You don't want to know what Cassie can do."

"What can she do?" Sabrina demanded.

"Don't be the bad guy, here," I barked at her. "We already have an enemy, if you haven't noticed. I expect every crew member to behave in a professional and civil manner. That will be all."

*She's still upset that she didn't get to go with us while we were on assignment to Murazal,* Travis informed me.

*A part of me understands that, although she would have been in more danger than the ones who did go. I hope she understands that and soon. We don't need dissension in the ranks.*

*We'll do what we can.*

"How much of a problem do you think Griffin will be?" Ilya tapped on my door while I waited for Rajeon to arrive.

"I hope he *won't* be a problem," I said, realizing that I was likely fooling myself. I'd seen the look in his eye when he left—he wasn't happy. We didn't need roadblocks from previous allies set in our path. Yes, I was grateful for Jett's presence in the Formidables, but his giving up the position of CSD Director came at a steep price.

"I ah, heard that Lissa is refusing to speak with Teeg, because he hired Griffin as CSD Director," Ilya added.

"Understandable," I sighed. "Seems like there are more than a few rough edges and ruffled feathers to smooth over—in many places."

"And at a time when we need it least," Ilya said.

"You wanted to see me?" Rajeon tapped on my open door.

"Come in," I told him. "Shut the door behind you."

"I know to be straight with you," I told Cassie, Jett and Rob later in my study. "I'm adding Rajeon to your crew as a liaison, since you're the newbies on the roster. Rajeon is a pod'l-morph. He can shift into anything, including rocks and plants. He is also a good fit in any situation. I expect you to treat him as one of your own."

"No reason not to," Rob drawled.

"Your accent—is very similar to Winkler's," I said.

"It is similar. He's from Texas; I've spent too much time in Alabama. Those are both Southern states where we come from."

"If you ever go to the South—on Earth III or IV, I suppose, you'll understand better," Rob explained.

"The food is good," Cassie told me. "I think we can have Rajeon speaking the language—accent included—in no time."

"Who knows—it could come in handy," I said, grinning at Cassie. "I'll introduce you at dinner tonight; it'll be served buffet style in the garden, according to the folks in the kitchen. I'll have uniforms for all of you in two days. I'm also open to any suggestions on where to begin our search for the Prophet."

"There's plenty of unrest going on; I've discussed this with Ildevar and Teeg already," Jett said. "The Prophet could have a direct hand in some of it, or it could be a smokescreen, just to distract us."

"What would you do in those cases, then?" I asked.

"Do as much research into the unrest as we can, drill down to the underlying causes, if there are any, and decide whether to put feet on the ground," he replied.

"That's what we did with the hub worlds recently. It paid off, for the most part," I nodded. "It also revealed to us how daunting and dangerous the Prophet is. He has rogue gods that he's swallowed whole and claimed their power as his own. If that doesn't worry you, it should."

"Oh, we had a taste of something similar just before we left Earth IV," Rob snorted. "Zarigar explained a few things to me when I asked. It's not something I can talk about now," he held up a hand.

"You've seen blowback, haven't you?" I breathed.

"I really can't answer that question. Sorry."

"You don't have to. We have an enemy to focus on now, and that's what we're going to do."

What I understood at that moment was why, even with seeing events around Cassie, I couldn't read some things from the past in those before me. Wisdom had blocked certain people and events from getting through.

They'd been through a war, though; I knew that much. They were fighting the same war now, perhaps, but from another side of it.

Sabrina was foolish to think of them as inexperienced. In some ways, they could be more familiar than we might imagine.

"I learned from Lendill Schaff that the Prophet is something of a necromancer and can reanimate the dead," Rob began. "As an Earth sprite, I think I'd like to test the ground where he raised some of them."

"Why?" I asked.

"To see if the ground will tell me that tale," he replied.

"Rob sticks his bare toes in the dirt," Cassie explained. "He can tell if somebody or something has passed over or through it—or is still connected to it."

"I thought that only worked on your home planet," I said.

"I tested it on Wyyld II—it worked," Rob shrugged. "If the Prophet has a way to cover his tracks, so to speak, after pulling bodies from the soil or disturbing graves, I'd like to test that ground to see if he left any traces behind."

"I'm not sure that's a good idea, what with the Prophet's disease," I began.

"I'm immune. We all are," Rob indicated Jett, Cassie and himself. "We were immune to the, ah, disease Shakkor Agdah came up with on Earth IV, too."

"Is it similar? Do you know?"

"I can't say," Rob coughed into his hand, reluctant to discuss the topic.

"The one on Earth IV killed within three days, so that much is different," Cassie said. "There was no cure and no way to prolong the lives of any victims. They were highly contagious, too. Any contact with a carrier would ensure another victim—unless you had natural immunity, like my kind did."

"I'm beginning to see why Wisdom brought you to us," I shook my head in wonder. "Rob, I can get you to a place where the Prophet pulled bodies from graves. I'd like to hear what you can get from that."

"Problem," Zanfield walked in with a comp-vid in his hand.

"What problem would that be?" I held out my hand to take the tablet from him.

"You made the headlines on Cadrile III."

"I don't recall volunteering for anything of the sort," I tapped the comp-vid.

"You didn't have to. No idea how they found out, but they sure got a quote from the new CSD Director. He is certainly not pleased with this turn of events."

"Who does your hair?" Cassie examined the yellow-to-flame-red gradation in Zanfield's coif. "That's so creative," she added, admiring the cut and color.

"You like it? Perri does this for me with a spell."

"What in the name of the stars is this tripe?" I bellowed. The headline was huge and to the point. *New CSD Director Captures—Then Loses—Most-Wanted Criminals in Both Alliances.*

# CHAPTER 3

*S*irena
   *Randl*

"We don't know how the information was leaked," Wyatt San Gerxon, Teeg's son, stood in my study looking more than apologetic. "We've questioned everybody on the three ships Griffin had with him, and none of them breached protocol."

"How did the information end up on a Reth Alliance network a thousand light years away from Campiaa?" I asked, after struggling to calm myself and speak coherently.

"Dad says we ought to investigate Veridium Prime—maybe they found a way to transmit information," Wyatt said. "He certainly wants to investigate the news network that released the information."

"But he has to work with the ASD to get permission to question their sources," I acknowledged.

"He says you could send someone to investigate and get around the usual citizen protection laws."

"Because nobody expects the worst criminals in both Alliances to look into the matter." My sarcasm wasn't lost on Wyatt—he understood it could be a trap. If the Prophet hadn't seen those headlines—which were now all over both Alliances—he would soon.

*If he wasn't neck-deep in causing them in the first place*, I reminded myself. It was possible—after my most recent experience with him, *anything* was possible.

"Has your grandmother weighed in on the situation?" I asked, turning away from more morbid thoughts.

"Gran is furious," Wyatt sounded uncomfortable. "Of course, Drake, Drew, Dragon and Crane aren't happy either, because this is beginning to paint targets on a lot of backs, Travis and Trent's included."

"How the hell did they get the information that we have Falchani among the BlackWing Pirates? They have some information on me, most of it false, but to start tossing out descriptions of my crews? That infuriates me."

"And places my uncles in danger. Dad knows that. He's already apologized to Drake and Drew and promised to get to the bottom of this if he can. Is there someone else we can send to Cadrile III? The only silver lining in this, as Gran says, is that nobody knows that Dad ordered Griffin to leave you guys alone."

"Because that would blow this thing wide open," I agreed.

"Yeah. The Prophet doesn't need to know that his number one rival is working with both Alliances to get him out of the way. Maybe we can find somebody to investigate this mess—somebody who isn't recognizable in either Alliance," Wyatt sighed. "Besides, Cadrile III is beginning to experience political unrest—their presidential election is coming up, and the differences in the candidates is ah, polarizing."

"You mean the media turned away from the politicians for five minutes to post the story about us?"

"Somehow, they tore themselves away," Wyatt nodded. "Surprisingly enough, even without images attached to the story, it's still the biggest headline in both Alliances."

"Those candidates must be pissed."

"No doubt about it."

"I think I may have a few folks to send to Cadrile III—they're from the future, and on nobody's radar at the moment."

"Shouldn't take long, I imagine, to get to the bottom of this."

"Let's hope so. We'll be meeting later today to select the worlds to investigate for evidence of the Prophet's interference. For now, it's the only way we have to track the bastard."

"Don't tell me who you're sending to Cadrile III. We don't need more information being released into the ether," Wyatt said. "I'll tell Dad you have somebody looking into it, and he'll have to be satisfied with that."

"You can stay for dinner if you'd like," I offered.

"Nah. I've asked Ilya to take me home after we're done, here."

"Do me a favor, then?"

"Sure."

"Keep an eye on your great-grandfather for me."

"I'll do my best."

"I know this is last minute, but I'm sending you out tonight," I told Jett. He, Cassie, Rob and Rajeon sat in my study, having an after-dinner drink. "Rob, I'll have to keep my promise on the necromancy locations later; I'm sending BlackWing IX to Cadrile III."

"You want us to investigate who leaked the information to the media about us and the new CSD Director, don't you?" Rajeon asked bluntly.

"That's it in the smallest of nutshells," I agreed. "All CSD agents and employees involved have been questioned extensively, and there's no evidence that any of them released the information. I'm sending you because you're a new, unrecognizable entity as far as the Alliances go. Neither they nor the Prophet know anything about you, yet. Right now, that's a plus in this investigation."

"We can sniff around," Jett said. "With Rajeon's and Cassie's help, I think we can get in just about anywhere."

"Do you have someone on board who is good with tracking electronic information—and breaking into said information to begin with?"

Cassie and Rob looked at one another before turning to me and saying, "Baarkann," at the same time.

"Stay safe while you're doing this," I warned.

"If I let Baarkann get hurt, I'll hear it from my sister—they're good friends," Cassie told me. "He's found a way to message her without anybody being able to track where or who he is. It's genius and perplexing at the same time."

"Did she come back in time with you?" I asked. "Your sister?"

"Oh—no, sorry, she's only fourteen and still with Quin at Avii Castle. She's getting lessons with Pauly. We were promised that we'd be transported back to the time we left, with no interruptions."

"Is she a fire demon too?"

"Ice demon," Cassie said. "And a good one."

"Ah." I knew then that Cassie's father was not her sister's father. But, as Zarigar had pointed out, that wasn't my secret to tell.

"We'll gather the crew and be underway in an hour," Jett said.

"Good enough. Rajeon, keep me informed."

"Will we know where the other BlackWing ships are sent?" Rajeon asked as he rose from his seat.

"Only if it's necessary," I said. "The reason you're going to Cadrile III in the first place is that classified information was leaked to the media. You can't tell what you don't know."

"True enough. Commander," Jett dipped his head to me before leading the others from my study.

*BlackWing IX*
*Cassie*

"Last minute addition to the crew," Jett informed me as Zephyr and Ebb readied the ship for the journey to Cadrile III.

"Who?" I asked.

"A High Demon. I heard you know him in the future."

So far, we hadn't run across Denevik anywhere. He and the other

High Demons had private dinners in someone's suite—Vik's, or so I'd heard.

"How and why?" I asked.

"No idea. Ask him yourself."

"You know that's not going to happen. It's probably better if I avoid him altogether."

"This isn't a big ship," Jett reminded me.

"I just don't like the idea of having memories messed with after we're done here," I said.

"I think it's a safe bet that Zarigar's memory won't be affected."

"What makes you say that?"

"Call it a hunch. You think there's any tea to be had in the galley?"

"You'll get some if I have to make it myself."

"Hyperdrive is ready to engage, Captain," Baarkann announced on Jett's communicator.

"Zephyr, Ebb, take us out," Jett said. "Hold on, Cassie, we'll be there in four days."

⤳

"Tell that man to slow down on the tea and go get some sleep," Beverly told me later as she prepared a second pot to send to the bridge. "If he were a werewolf, his tail would be bushed out twice its size."

"I'll tell him, for as much good as it'll do," I reminded her. "You have enough help in the galley?"

"More than enough," she sniffed. "They want to try every recipe they ever heard of, I think."

"You think it was because they spent most of their life on Earth IV hungry?" I asked her.

"I think so. Their royalty didn't give a damn about how or when they were fed—just that they run out and die fighting for their foolish power grabs."

"Don't forget the poison sacs they were forced to carry," I said.

"Hmmph. If we hadn't had help from the Larentii, they'd still be scarred top to bottom. That stuff was neutralized when it was removed, too, or I'd worry about it getting passed along."

"I worry about it getting passed along where we came from."

"Those people do have a tendency for foolishness," Beverly agreed. "I think my kids are happy now. At least that's what they tell me."

"Good. Now it's our job to keep them safe."

"I think they might help you with that," she dimpled. "They have their own ways of doing things, and some of them may surprise you."

"Then I'll look forward to seeing them in action."

"It started when they learned how to play hide-and-seek," Beverly's smile turned into a grin. "They never got to play games like that when they were little. I told them how it was done and they put their own special spin on it. It amuses them to hide from their brothers and sisters."

"I'll have to ask about that," I said. "I'll get this to Jett," I lifted the thermal carafe Beverly prepared for him.

"Tell him what I said. We don't need a sleep-deprived Captain."

"I'll tell him. No idea how much good it'll do."

*Sirena*

   *Randl*

"Is there anybody who wants to volunteer to poke around Veridium Prime?" I asked, before sorting assignments for the rest of the crew. I'd called everyone still here to a breakfast meeting, to get things going.

"Science vessel volunteers," Bear Wright, Captain of BlackWing II, lifted a hand. "With the equipment on board, we should be able to make a pass to detect the use of new technology."

"Sounds good," I agreed. "You have that assignment. Now, who wants to go to Phume? Ever since the trouble on Galk, Phume's nearest hub world, there have been rumors that someone transported prisoners from Evensun to their world, to destroy their government. As you know, Phume is in the nearest solar system to Evensun, but there's really no reason for them to worry about escapees. There's contention between factions in the government, and plenty of strikes going on because of it, but that still doesn't justify the rumors."

"We can look into the rumors," Travis said. "It doesn't make any sense, so we should be able to get to the bottom of it soon and go on to other things."

"Good enough. That's your assignment for now. Who wants to go to Mardir?" I named the planet where D'slay had hidden himself in a mountain retreat. If he'd caused other trouble or gone there at the Prophet's bidding, I wanted to know about it and why. Were there others on Mardir, now that D'slay was dead?

"BlackWing I, I take," Nenzi announced.

"Good. Who wants to look into the famine and unrest on Voriss?"

By the time breakfast was over, everybody had an assignment, except BlackWing XIII.

*My ship.*

I wanted to study a certain Sirenali woman in the dungeon before selecting my target. I'd asked Gerrett to come with me. She knew things about the Prophet; I was sure of it.

Getting those things from her, after the Prophet laid his own obsessions, had been impossible to do.

So far.

There had to be a way to get information—surely. We just hadn't found it, yet. Without that information, I'd be forced to go back to the last place we'd seen the Prophet; P'loxett. It was nothing more than blasted rubble, now, thanks to the Prophet.

The spirit of P'loxett was also dead—it had aligned with the Prophet's goals and helped him attain them. If Tenigar hadn't sacrificed himself, the Prophet would have succeeded in taking many of us.

*And destroying the rest.*

We'd gotten past the matter of possessing sufficient power to overcome him—it was evident that we didn't have the strength, even with many of the most powerful helping. That meant we had to rely on cunning and talent, instead.

"Fuck," I breathed as the dining hall cleared out. Ships would be leaving in two hours for their assignments. If XIII were to stay on schedule, I needed to get to the dungeon now.

"I'm ready," Gerrett appeared at my side.

"Yeah. Let's go." I rolled my shoulders to release gathering tension. *Cunning and talent. Did we have enough of those things to win this battle?*

*We are with you, Reviendus,* Kev'Ril informed me. *Never forget that. Do not doubt yourself—or those who stand beside you.*

*I don't doubt the resolve of those with me and around me,* I told him. *The preservation of all lives is a weighty matter and has become my greatest concern. If we fail, all will be destroyed by the Prophet, as you well know.*

*The god who always comes at the end,* Kev'Ril confirmed. *We are with you, no matter who is victorious. If you fall, all fall. At once. The Prophet will have nothing to gloat over and control, Reviendus. If I and the other world spirits die, all is gone in an instant.*

Now I understood fully what was at stake—and why the R'pexi hadn't joined with anyone else to fight others like V'dar. I needed to have a conversation with Zaria and the Wise Ones, but not now. Time was needed for me to assimilate this new knowledge, and what it meant to all of us.

*We cannot fail, then,* I told Kev'Ril.

*No, Reviendus, we cannot.*

~

She stared long and hard before blinking, as I studied her. She'd never changed from her scaled persona, either, to become more humanoid in appearance.

In fact, she'd shed some of her scales; no doubt attempting to push herself through the narrow bars of her cage. With power, and while she watched, I narrowed the space between bars even more, while her fury grew. She hissed at me when I finished.

Gerrett leaned down to pick up three scales she'd stress-sloughed. Stuffing them in a pocket, he gave her stare for stare as I did my best to get past the obsession laid on her. Using my strongest will, I searched her face, hoping to reveal the tiniest bit of information.

"Do you even have a name?" I asked, when I was unsuccessful.

"Fuck yourself," she hissed around the fangs in her mouth. The obsession was strong but ineffective against Gerrett and me.

"Did he tell you to say that? V'dar?" I asked.

"Fuck yourself."

"He told her to say that," Gerrett turned toward me with a lift to his chin. "He probably screwed her, too."

She hit the bars hard enough to scrape more grayish scales off her skin. A few of those scales clung to the thick, steel shafts when she backed away with a hissed, "Fuck yourself."

"Keep this up and you won't have any scales left," I reached out to carefully lift away the small flakes.

Perhaps I should have known. Or, perhaps it was for the best. Visions swam through my mind—she couldn't stop me from seeing images left behind in what she'd torn away from herself.

V'dar couldn't command or obsess scales. He could only command and obsess minds. "Well, we're done here," I said after coming back to myself. "The soundproof barrier will be placed again, so it won't do you any good to try to obsess those who bring your food and water. See ya, Y'ariel."

Gerrett and I folded away while she screamed in frustration.

"What did you get?" Vik took a seat in my study aboard XIII an hour later. "Besides her name?"

"Images, mostly, some I didn't recognize. Others I did recognize, most of them dead. I suppose it's a good thing she doesn't have the Prophet's disease—or is immune to it. She couldn't keep him from obsessing her, though."

"Any images that concern you?"

"She saw a lot of D'slay, plus the vampire assassin. We know they're dead. The one that worries me most looks Krelk—or part Krelk. In the images, he always wore dark goggles over his eyes."

"That sounds weird. You think he has a light sensitivity?"

"No idea. Y'ariel didn't know much about him, other than he helped the vampire assassinate targets. Plus, he appeared to be a favorite of V'dar's."

"Anybody else?"

"Perri's relatives—Alken, Gillen and Qatti. I figure they're still out there, somewhere, causing trouble on V'dar's behalf."

"Filth," Vik growled.

"Keep that information from Perri if you can, although you can tell Zanfield if you want. It wouldn't hurt for one of them to know they're still out there."

"I'll talk to Zanfield."

~

*G'margis*

*Alken Wilker*

"Is there no relief from the fucking cold?" Qatti fumed. "Why can't we create a warming spell?"

"Because the Prophet didn't have time to move enough Sirenali bones here to embed in all the walls. The parts of the compound where we work aren't included, and the lack of that protection could reveal the compound to those who hunt us," Gillen snarled at her. "I've explained this already."

"Why can't he get more bones?" Qatti asked the same question she'd asked a dozen times or more.

"Because that's not important right now," Gillen glared at her. Another loud argument was in the works; I attempted to defuse it.

"The Prophet still doesn't know for sure that Randl Gage is dead—or if he's in hiding," I pointed out. I was dressed in two sets of thermals, in addition to my outer clothing, a coat, heavy boots and thick socks. "The only places to get warm are the sections near the tree and plant farms, where the bones and bone dust were already incorporated into the walls. The Prophet has the other areas shielded well enough that no trace of it will be evident to a casual observer. If we employ our spells, however, there are power sniffers available to the enemy and they could detect us if we use warming spells."

"Why can't we work near the tree farm, then?" Qatti was still inclined to complain.

"Because we don't know a damn thing about trees," Gillen lost patience and snapped at her. "P'loxett was the one guiding the arborists. Now that he's gone, they're doing their best to keep the trees thriving, using whatever knowledge he passed on."

"Why didn't he move us to F'margis instead?" Qatti ignored Gillen's outburst. "It's covered in volcanoes. Hell, you can see rivers of lava from the surface of this planet."

"Because there wasn't a safe space large enough to carve out of the underground," I explained. Gillen wanted to zap Qatti; I could read it easily in his expression and the stiffness of his shoulders.

"I'd prefer the warmth."

"F'margis is the opposite of G'margis—it's so hot it's melting—an ocean of fire rather than ice. Two blinks there and you'd be begging for the cold," Gillen derided Qatti's statement. "Put on another layer of clothing."

Qatti walked away, mumbling about looking fat already.

"Fat or frozen, your choice," Gillen raised his voice so she'd hear. The entire exchange made me glad I'd never considered marriage. I had other ways of getting sex, and so far, hadn't been held accountable for any of it.

"You're wanted in the control room," one of the Prophet's inner circle approached Gillen and me. We'd started calling his kind drones, because they were bound to his rule and locked into the job of delivering messages throughout the warren built underground on G'margis.

*What does he want now?* I sent to Gillen.

*No idea. Come on. We have to go.*

Following the drone dutifully, we began the journey toward the center of the hive, where the Prophet's control room lay.

At least it would be warmer, there.

~

*BlackWing IX*

*Cassie*

"They always look so peaceful from this distance." Rajeon breathed. He stood with Jett and me as I got my first look at Cadrile III.

The planet rotated as it should, as if nothing troubled it. I suppose the predicaments and misfortunes of the tiny creatures on its surface didn't extend to the planet's general functions; it traveled its way around a binary star system at a predictable rate.

"Are we asking to interview anyone at the media company that released the information?" I asked.

"They've already refused to name their source, and blocked requests for interviews from more legitimate entities," Jett said. "That means we use alternative methods to get in. They have tours of their facility, so a few of us might go in to see if we can find a weakness."

"Or we could pull the fire alarm," I suggested. "I can be a contained fire long enough for somebody to get in and out."

"That may take a bit of careful planning," Rajeon warned. "Security cameras are everywhere in that building. That means getting in using alternative methods. I can look like any employee or any piece of equipment—at least on the outside."

"Unless you can match an eye scan, good luck," Denevik joined us on the bridge.

I stiffened at his presence—mostly I'd avoided him during our four-day journey. Avoidance was no longer an option, I realized. This close, he didn't have to speak to announce his arrival to me—I *felt* it.

As if we were connected, somehow.

"Not sure I could pass an eye scan," Rajeon shook his head. "Although I'm pretty good at copying someone."

"I can get you in through the ground beneath the complex," Rob offered. "Then Cassie can burn through the floor to get us inside the building."

"Rob has the best option," Zephyr turned in her seat to tell us. "I can get in through the air, but I can't take anyone else with me."

"I can go through water pipes, but I have the same problem as Zephyr—I can only get myself in that way," Ebb said.

"Unless you want part of it to burn, first, I'd be no help at all," Blaze shrugged.

"I think I can help," Baarkann said. "Once the Earth sprite and Cassie get us inside."

"Are there plans of the complex available?" Jett asked.

"I have them on my comp-vid," Rajeon passed him the tablet in question. "We can put them up in the meeting room and decide the best route to get in."

Fifteen minutes later, we sat around the meeting room table while a three-dimensional image of the network's main complex emanated from Rajeon's comp-vid. It consisted of an oblong cluster of buildings with a courtyard at the center, complete with trees, plants, walkways and a fountain.

"Laser security screens between buildings," Rajeon pointed out. "Cassie and Denevik can transport past those, but they'd still be visible on the other side, and there are security cameras everywhere throughout the courtyard."

"We should go beneath the building where information is stored," Baarkann suggested. "Although it is likely to have the most security within."

"That makes sense," Jett drawled.

"How long will it take security to get to us if I melt the door shut?" I asked. "It has to be metal or anybody could break through it."

"Excessive heat will cause the fire prevention system to activate, and you'll be sprayed with foam," Rajeon pointed out.

"This is getting us nowhere fast," Rob drawled.

"Baarkann, how long will it take you to shut the security system down if I transport you to a terminal?" I turned toward him.

"If you can get me to a terminal, I can insert a program that will accept us as employees and allow us anywhere. I only have to get eye scans and fingerprints from anyone going in, myself included."

"Is there a terminal in the records vault?" Rob asked.

"There usually is," Rajeon agreed.

"I say we transport inside the vault, then, Baarkann loads his program, we get the information we need and transport out again," Jett tapped the table with a finger.

"That sounds like the best idea," Denevik agreed. "Who's going in with Baarkann?"

"Call me Barry," Baarkann said with a modest shrug. "Destiny shortened my name and I like it."

"Good enough. Barry, get eye scans from Cassie, Rajeon, Denevik and yourself," Jett ordered. "You're the ones going in."

"If anything happens, you and I will get Barry and Rajeon out," Denevik told me as we geared up for our attempt at espionage. "You take Barry, I'll take Rajeon."

"Sounds good," I said, although my voice cracked from being so close to him. He smiled and patted my shoulder.

"Don't worry, we'll get through this," he promised, misinterpreting my wobbly speech. "Just don't kill anybody."

"I'll remember you said that," I replied tartly.

He grinned; my heart melted just a little.

We'd already had the eye scans and fingerprinting done; Barry promised that the information would destroy itself in a matter of minutes, so it wouldn't remain in the network's system.

That meant we were on the clock to get in, get the program loaded before the alarms went off, find the information and get out before Barry's program dissolved.

*No pressure.*

*BlackWing XIII, One AU from P'loxett's Former Position*
*Randl*

*We're about to go in,* Jett reported.

*Who?*

*Cassie, Rajeon, Denevik and Barry.*

*Will that work?*

*If Barry's program does what he says it will.*

*Interesting. Keep me informed.*

*I will.*

～

*BlackWing IX*

*Cassie*

"Ready," Barry held up the smallest information chip I'd ever seen. I knew computers in the here and now could scan information chips set on a flat Portal, but this one wasn't big enough to cover a fourth of my smallest fingernail.

"If this doesn't work, be ready to get hauled out of there in half a blink," Denevik warned. "Ready, Cassie?"

"Yeah. Let's go." I transported our group straight to the records vault at the network. Without hesitation, Barry went to the comp station at the center of the room and dropped the tiny chip onto the equally small scanning surface.

Then, I blinked when his hand emitted light above both. Staring in shock, I watched as the chip disappeared into the scanner, leaving nothing behind.

The computer woke immediately from its power sleep. Barry used his other hand to pass a wave of light across the screen.

"Good afternoon, sir," the computer greeted him as if they were lifelong friends. "What may I do for you?"

"I'd like all the information you have on the recent broadcast regarding the CSD Director and the capture of the most-wanted BlackWing Pirates."

"Of course, sir. Only a moment." It was only a moment before information was displayed on the screen. "Will there be anything else?"

"Download the information to this chip." Barry placed another chip on the scanner.

"Information downloaded. Do you have another request?"

"Is the information regarding the originating source included in the download?"

"As much information as exists, sir."

"What do you mean?"

"The information originated from this network, and was downloaded on this terminal in this room, sir."

Denevik's hand gripped my arm—hard.

"Can you tell me who downloaded the information?" Barry asked.

"I am prevented."

"Time's almost up—we have to leave," Rajeon hissed.

Barry carefully lifted the chip from the scanner, before turning and nodding to me. I hauled us out of there just as the security alarms began to sound.

# CHAPTER 4

lackWing XIII
      *Randl*

"It actually said *I am prevented?*" Jett and I held a comp-vid call on a secure line.

"Four witnesses say exactly that," Jett told me. "They were able to get out before their images were recorded by the comp in question, too, but it was close."

"Send a copy of what they recorded; I want to look at it," I said.

"Sending now."

"Have you looked at it?"

"I have, as have Cassie, Rob, Barry and Rajeon. What's there is pretty much what was reported, too."

"Are you worried that the Prophet is behind this? Because I am," I admitted. "It sounds exactly like something he'd do—place obsession and then have the information inserted into the network's records system."

"Any number of employees could be obsessed to believe whatever was downloaded," Jett agreed. "But how did he come by the information? If he knew where we were, we'd be dead by now, or in a fight for our lives."

"What if he has spies on Veridium Prime?"

"That's possible, I suppose, but they'd still need the technology to pass along the information."

"I'll have Bear Wright and BlackWing II take a closer look. Ilya can go with them."

"Now that we've got what we went after on Cadrile III, we could help with that," Jett offered.

"I'll consider it. Chart a course for a rendezvous with my ship near P'loxett's former location, and we'll have a discussion. I think I'd like to ask Barry a few questions, too."

"We'll be there in three days."

"Jett, let's move up that schedule. I want to be away from here tomorrow. I know you have the power to fold space—move the ship here now."

"We'll be there in ten."

~

"They're here," Dori announced as BlackWing IX appeared on her viewer. "In less than ten."

"Good. Would you like to come with me while I discuss the information with Jett and the others?"

"Do you want me to come?"

"Yes. Bring Zanfield and Perri, too. I have some theories about Barry and the others of his kind. I'd like Perri to tell me what she gets from them, power-wise."

"I'll uh, let them know."

"You're having misgivings about this. Why?" I asked.

"These people are our allies. I hope you don't intend to single them out and make them feel like outsiders."

*Wait—was that what I was doing? Marking them as different, when we were all different in some way?*

"Cancel Perri and Zanfield, then. It's just you and me."

"All right."

"Need anything before we go?"

"I'm ready."

I grabbed her hand, impulsively kissed the back of it, and folded space.

~

*BlackWing IX*
*Cassie*

The second Beverly heard that Randl wanted to question Barry, she was on her way to the small meeting room adjoining the captain's cubby. I hoped Randl was prepared to have his ass handed to him if he mistreated Barry in any way.

Beverly took the seat next to mine at the round table, waiting for Jett, Barry, Rajeon and our visitors to arrive. Randl folded in with Dori, his mate, before Jett and the others came in.

Randl lifted an eyebrow as he turned toward Beverly. His eyes, nearly white, didn't see. His mind did all the work, and that meant he saw things normal people couldn't.

"I see I should mind my manners," he offered Beverly a smile. "Don't worry—I merely want to ask Barry how he was able to communicate so well with the comp on Cadrile III. This is a talent that could make a great deal of difference in finding the enemy."

"So you're saying you're pleased with his work, then?" Beverly's arms crossed as she held Randl's penetrating gaze.

"Extremely. I'd like to know whether any of his brothers and sisters can do the same thing."

"They can, but none are as good as he is," Beverly relaxed her stance a bit. "The rest of them have other talents—different talents—where they shine."

"It's one thing to see an expertise with computers in someone, and quite another to understand that they may be able to meld with the technology itself."

I nodded slowly at Randl's words—I felt he was right; I just hadn't known how to explain what I'd seen on Cadrile III. The computer had addressed him as if he were an old friend or a beloved superior.

*Until the absorbed chip had expired, breaking the connection.*

I still wasn't sure how the chip was absorbed in the first place; I'd never seen anything like that before.

"Commander," Jett walked into the meeting room with Barry and Rajeon behind him. Although he hadn't been requested, Denevik strode in, looking as if he were in protective mode.

I wanted to shiver as he took the chair on my other side, placing me between himself and Beverly. Being this close, I felt a pull to touch his arm or hand but held back. He hadn't made a single overture; therefore, I was obligated to hold myself to the same standard.

"Barry, if you can, will you explain the connection you can make with a computer?" Randl began after everyone was seated. Barry's chair was between Rajeon's and Jett's, so I hoped he felt safe enough where he was.

"I, ah, just feel them," he floundered for the right words. "I can close my eyes and see all the connections it makes while it thinks or processes a request."

"Tell me about the chip you made—that was absorbed into the machine."

"It's a type of gel—I'm sure you're familiar with, that is meant to vaporize once it's exposed to the proper surface."

"But that sort of thing generally won't hold anything else within it, much less a comp program."

"It does what I ask it," Barry replied. "I'm not sure how else to explain it."

"Rajeon?" Randle turned toward the pod'l-morph. "Will you become diamond or crystal? After that, I'd like Barry to touch you—to see whether he can get any information just from that connection."

"All right," Rajeon sounded hesitant, before turning to crystal while still in his seat.

"Barry?" Randl urged.

Barely daring to breathe, I watched as Barry touched his fingers to Rajeon's crystal arm. The contact was short, before Barry jerked his hands away.

"He didn't want me to pry," Barry turned back to Randl.

"You felt that?" Rajeon became himself again and blinked in surprise at Barry.

"Yes. It was quite—forceful, actually. I understand privacy, sir, as I like my own. Very much."

"Can you put your hand on people and determine the same thing?" Randl asked.

"Not really. If you want that talent, you should speak with Annie."

"He means Aanaani," Beverly said. "She prefers Annie, though."

"What can Annie tell me if she puts hands on someone?" Randl asked.

"She knows how they're feeling—happy, sad and so forth. She can also tell if someone is ill, and sometimes what the illness is. That's from limited exposure to regular humanoids, though, and she hasn't had any medical training."

"Do you think she'd like medical training?" Randl asked.

"Perhaps, but she chose what the rest of us chose, because she didn't want to be alone in her studies."

"One more question, Barry," Randl said. "How did the nineteen of you get together and escape the others of your race on Earth? I've spoken with Zarigar, and he tells me that was a very difficult feat. He also says you rescued human captives, too, which made things even more difficult."

"Siivaar, who prefers to be called Star, can bring others to him. Together, he and Annie found the rest of us. We felt the same, you see, and Annie knew it. Star drew us in, and the rest you know."

"You think of Beverly as your mother?"

"She has been the best mother any of us could ask for."

"Beverly, your children are exceptional," Randl gave her a smile. "Barry, will you put a list of talents together and send it to me? This will help in making future assignments according to individual and combined strengths. No, I don't intend to separate you, not without your permission," he held up a hand.

"Then we will do this for you, Commander," Barry dipped his head to Randl. "We understand all too well when power and the desire to

42

destroy go hand in hand to cause widespread suffering. We have seen enough of that already, although we are still young."

"Thank you, Barry. You made a difficult assignment much easier," Randl told him. "I'm raising you to the rank of Chief of Engineering. I'll assign ranks to the others as their talents are revealed."

"Thank you, sir."

"You deserve it. Dori, are you ready?"

Dori hadn't spoken yet, but she'd listened, fascinated by what she'd learned from Barry. "Thank you for hosting the meeting, Jett," she said.

"No problem," Jett gave her a radiant smile.

*You know, don't you?* Randl pointed mindspeech in my direction as he and Dori rose from their seats.

*That you intended to invade their privacy at first? I got that idea. This was a much better way to handle it, Commander.*

*I understand that, now. These young people are special, in ways I hadn't guessed.*

*They've been forced all their lives. Don't let that happen here*, I said.

*That will be my command from now on,* he agreed. *Thank you for being here and providing a safe environment for Barry to answer questions.*

*He's best friends with my sister. I will certainly not be the one to go back and tell her I let someone bully him.*

*Good to know.* I watched a slow grin light his features.

"Should we join BlackWing II around Veridium Prime?" Jett asked Randl.

"Yes. Actually, if they've found anything, perhaps we can put boots on the ground to check out leads?"

"I'll talk that over with Bear and Ilya, then consult with you first," Jett replied.

"Good enough. Keep me informed." Randl and Dori disappeared.

"Well, folks, get ready for another relocation; we're on our way to a non-Alliance sector in fifteen."

"I'll make sure the engines are online and ready," Barry said. He and Rajeon left the room first.

"I'll have tea sent to the bridge," Beverly told Jett before following

Barry out the door.

"Thank you," Jett called after her.

"Well, nothing like relocating to prevent jet lag," I sighed as I rose from my seat.

"Jet lag?" Denevik chuckled. "I haven't heard that in a while."

"Are you dissing me?" Jett turned and smiled.

"Um, no."

"I know. I'm just teasing, Lieutenant. Will you inform the rest of the ship we're about to relocate?"

"Sure thing, Captain."

"Good. Denevik, if you'll assist the Lieutenant."

"Sure thing, Captain," Denevik parroted my words with a grin.

I drew in a breath as he lightly touched my elbow to steer me toward the door.

"We'll meet with II's crew after we eat and go through a sleep cycle," Jett told us once we were in orbit around Veridium Prime. He'd called most of us to the dining hall, where dinner was ready to be served.

Only Ebb remained on the bridge; he and Zephyr would spell each other for eating and sleeping. Rob, who'd come in shortly after I did, now stood near a dining hall window, looking out at Veridium Prime as the ship circled the planet.

"If Cliff were here, he'd be watching this with a cup of coffee in his hand," Rob sighed.

"I know." Just the mention of Cliff's name revealed the empty spot in my soul—the one that only Cliff occupied and now ached at his absence. I cursed Black Myth and whomever it was that killed my friend. I didn't equate Barry and his chosen family with Black Myth—I figured the Shakkor Agdah hadn't always been the evil that Black Myth became.

"I will never find the words to describe how much I miss him," Rob sighed as he continued to watch the planet below us.

"A missing piece of us," I agreed. "Something that can never be replaced."

"Something amiss?" Denevik asked, as he and Rajeon walked up to us.

"Just thinking about a good friend we lost," I mumbled. If this were the Denevik of the future, he wouldn't have to ask who it was. This version had never met Cliff.

"I'm sorry," Rajeon said, his voice low.

"He was a werewolf—the Grand Master and a fierce protector," Rob said. "He died saving my life—again."

"Those deaths are often the hardest to deal with," Denevik said. "Come. Eat now, then rest. There may come a time when you will avenge your friend. You cannot do that if you are hungry and tired."

"Cassie, he's right." Beverly had arrived and caught the last of our conversation. "Mr. Cliff won't mind if it takes a while longer to get that bastard. Come on, now, before it's all gone."

"All right." I followed Beverly toward the food, laid out buffet style so we could serve ourselves. Rob, Rajeon and Denevik followed. We ended up sitting at the same table to eat, too.

"This is the best," Rajeon said after tasting the jambalaya.

"It would be better if I could get real andouille sausage, but this is the closest thing available," Beverly smiled at him. "I'm not into watery soup courses, but you'll learn that fast enough."

"Beverly says that broth by itself is for making gravy," I teased her.

"Well, it's the truth," she laughed.

"Rob?" Randl appeared in the dining hall and pulled a chair to our table to sit with us. "How do you feel about making a trip to the ground where the Prophet raised the dead?"

"I'm good with that," Rob said.

"Perfect. When you wake, I'll come for you—and anybody else you'd like to bring with you."

"I'd like to go." Beverly surprised me by offering first.

"If I can take everybody at this table, I'd be good with that," Rob replied. "If more zombies show up, Cassie can take care of them for me."

"While I hope the zombies are long gone, I'd still like to see how you do that," Randl turned in my direction.

"Only if it's necessary, trust me," I told him. I had troubling memories of the last time I'd set my fire free, and it was terrifying. Rob verified my answer with a quick nod. He'd been at a safe distance when it happened; I decided to ask him sometime what it looked like from his vantage point.

"What did you do—to be this reluctant to do it again?" Rajeon asked.

"Hmmph," Beverly sniffed. "Some people may never get over that melted pile of granite."

"It's a melted pile of Rhyolite now," Rob observed. "Any Earth sprite would know," he added.

"Geological terms notwithstanding," Beverly said, "It was well-deserved."

"Can't argue with that," Rob lifted his cup to toast Beverly.

~

*BlackWing XIII*
*Randl*

I knew something was wrong the moment I got back from BlackWing IX. Rather than telling me, Dori gave me her comp-vid.

*Initially Undetected, Break-in at Media Solstice's Main Office on Cadrile III May Be Work of BlackWing Pirates. Report says nothing was taken after alarm system triggered.* The information originated from Farixx Media, the premiere news service on Morik.

"Fucking, ear-twisting hells," I cursed.

~

*Cassie*

We didn't learn about the news from Morik until Randl came for us after our sleep cycle and breakfast were over. I appreciated the wait, because most of us wouldn't have slept if we'd known about it before.

I worried that it would upset Barry most, but he took it in stride, saying it was a plausible conclusion. My concern was that Randl would send us to Morik next, instead of letting us investigate Veridium Prime as intended.

Everyone asked to visit a zombie-raising site were now sitting in the Captain's cubby, while Jett and Randl held a private conversation outside.

*Cassie?* I was surprised to hear from Barry, who was in his engineer's office, working with two others at the moment.

*You need something?* I asked right away.

*Do you think Randl or Jett will object if I attempt to hack into Farixx Media's computers from here?*

*I can ask.*

*Would you? I can guarantee that no connection or trail will lead to us or the ship, even if we're not successful,* he said.

"We're considering a visit to Farixx Media," Jett walked in with Randl behind him.

"Barry thinks he can hack them from here," I said. "He says he can do it without leaving a connection to us or the ship."

"Even from a power sniffer, or a talented warlock?" Jett frowned at me.

"I'm not sure about either of those things, but I have faith in Barry's talent. Besides, what if we find the same thing we found last time—that the information was planted in their computer system by someone we can't get a lock on?"

"If it's the Prophet, do you think we can trace this to him or his compound?" Jett asked.

"I'm not that familiar with Barry's process; you'll have to ask him," I replied. "Last time, we expected the information to come from an outside source, not to originate within Media Solstice. Employees usually leave their signature or another kind of marker on whatever they enter. Barry says all that is missing. I'd say we weren't the only ones breaking into Media Solstice, but we were the ones setting off the alarm."

"Could you have shut down the alarm system—if you wanted to?" Jett asked Randl.

"It would be difficult—those alarm systems have backups of their backups. If any of those systems go offline, the others start ringing alarm bells."

"I imagined they'd have multiple layers of security," Jett agreed. "Is the Prophet that powerful and canny?"

"Remember the rogue gods he holds?" Randl reminded him.

"Yes. I recall that clearly."

"Tell Barry he can do it, but not before we get back from our field trip," Randl told me.

*Barry, they say yes, but not until we get back. I think it's to keep you safe.*

*I'll be waiting. Be careful where you're going.*

*We will.*

I blinked when Zarigar arrived the moment I finished my conversation with Barry. "Zarigar will be bending time to get us to A'pelur at the appropriate moment."

"The planet that no longer exists?" Rob asked.

"The very one," Zarigar agreed. "There, the Prophet pulled more from the grave than in any other place. I'll take you to the most remote cemetery, where you may do your exploration, Earth sprite."

"We didn't want to overwhelm you, but A'pelur is the most recent place the Prophet did necromancy—that we know of," Randl explained. "Only a few were taken from this particular site, though."

*Are you ready, dearest?* Zarigar sent to me.

*As ready as I can be. I don't think reanimated dead will scare me as much as they do others.*

*This pleases me. We will go, now.*

*Randl*

The stink of the Prophet was all around the remote cemetery Zarigar brought us to, but only three graves had been disturbed. This ancient cemetery belonged to a farming family, three of whom had died only a few months earlier in an accident.

They were the only bodies V'dar wanted—the others were skeletons crumbling to dust. I waited for Rob to remove his shoes and dig his toes into the ground; I didn't point out the graves the Prophet targeted.

Soon enough, I'd know if Rob would be useful in finding ground disturbed by V'dar, and if so, how sensitive he was to it.

Denevik stood between Cassie and Rob, as if he anticipated having to protect both. *He's High Demon*, I reminded myself. Any spells placed by warlocks in V'dar's employ would be negated roughly fifteen to twenty feet around him.

I hadn't felt any evidence of a warlock's or witch's spell, but Denevik wasn't leaving anything to chance.

Rajeon, too, stood at the edge of Denevik's protective circle, ready to act if anything popped out of the ground or transported in to disrupt our exploration. Beverly, on the other hand, wasn't far from where I stood, watching intently as Rob sunk his feet into the dirt as easily as if he'd stepped in water.

"Commander, I've never felt anything this evil," Rob gasped as he spoke. "Or this angry. It's coming from that area of the cemetery." He twisted around to point toward the freshest graves. "If it's all right with you, I'd really prefer not to get closer to it, because it's stronger there."

"Very well. Shall we take you to a place where the evil may be less disturbing? I know of several older places that the Prophet vandalized."

"I'll do it, but I think once more will be enough for today," Rob confessed. He was distressed by what he'd felt, that was easy to see.

A moment passed; I realized Randl was having a mental conversation with Zarigar. Zarigar nodded, and folded us to another location on another planet.

"Bornelus," Denevik hissed at once. Randl raised a hand, stopping anyone from speaking again. Nearby, a square pit lay, as if something of exact dimensions had been pulled from it by a giant hand.

With reluctance, Rob's feet melted into the ground like before. And then he visibly shuddered.

"Even the trees are tainted, here," he hissed through clenched teeth. "Filth is leaching through the ground, beginning at the edge of that hole." Shuddering again, Rob collapsed.

The only thing keeping him up at that point was Denevik's quick action; he became his smaller Thifilathi and jerked Rob away from the poisonous soil.

"Can you purify what's clinging to his feet?" Denevik turned a haunted look in my direction.

"I think I can do this without burning his skin," I agreed, concentrating while I formed fire with my hands. Closing my eyes, I focused on the soil covering Rob's feet, and released a cleansing fire upon the dirt only.

Rob's skin wasn't even warmed by what I released, but the soil was now clean of what infected the rest we stood upon.

Rob woke, found himself being held by Denevik and breathed a relieved sigh. "Don't put me down on that shit again," he begged.

"Cassie?" Randl called out.

I turned toward him.

"Will you stay here with me for a few?" he asked. "Zarigar, will you return the others to the ship?"

"Of course," Zarigar agreed and folded the others away.

"Do you think you can do the same thing with the ground here—purify it of the Prophet's filth?"

"I've never tried anything like this before," I admitted. "Can't hurt to try, though. I've never seen Rob collapse like that."

"What do you think might be the perimeter of the cleansing, if it's successful?" Randl's sightless eyes studied me; I understood that he was seeing me in another way, but he'd developed the uncanny habit of behaving as a sighted person would, narrowed eyes and all.

"No idea. How much would you like me to attempt?"

"Well, how about a two-ship diameter, using BlackWing IX as a guide?"

"Well, that's the length of six football fields," I said.

"Since we were trained by the same one with blades and weapons, I understand what you're saying," a wry smile tugged at his mouth. "Do you need time to prepare?"

"I think I can do this," I shrugged. "You ought to get out of the way, though."

"My shields should hold up," he argued.

"I'm not taking any chances. Either move out of range or I don't do this."

"For your own peace of mind, then," he said, before disappearing.

I built fire in my mind—fire so hot nothing I knew could withstand it. Fire so large it would cover six football fields in every direction. For the focal point, I chose the center of the square hole I stood beside.

And then I released what I'd built.

*Randl*

Cassie was right in asking me to leave. Not because my shield wouldn't hold—that had yet to be tested.

What I witnessed that day will remain with me all my life. I watched a cleansing fire remove every trace of the Prophet's sickness in the soil around the hole. The affected trees were also incinerated, so they wouldn't carry the disease another way to unsuspecting creatures.

I hoped that somewhere, V'dar felt that part of his influence dying. I wanted him to feel it.

*I wanted it to hurt him.*

I found myself wanting him to know who'd done this to him. A new opponent had entered this battle, and he had no idea who she was. And, as I'd sensed her parentage, there was a good chance he'd never know unless she walked up to him and introduced herself.

I had some questions for Zarigar, now. Questions I hoped he'd consent to answer.

# CHAPTER 5

*B*lackWing X
*Randl*

"Soil samples from Bornelus," I set two containers on the desk in the Captain's cubby. Trent was Captain for the day, and he stared at the containers before lifting dark eyes to me.

"Before and after?" he frowned.

"Before Cassie did her thing, and after. I wish you could have seen it. I know you breathe fire when you're a dragon, but she *is* fire."

"What do you want me to do with the samples?"

"Test them. Tell me if there's any difference. Take all precautions on the before sample. I doubt it will matter on the after one."

"You think she burned the Prophet's disease out of it, don't you?" Trent began to rise from his chair.

"I know she did. The dirt around that hole is no longer tainted by him. We can't test for its presence; I just want to know if there are other differences now."

"Do you think the Prophet felt what she did?"

"No idea."

"You want him to know, don't you?"

"I think I do."

"Will this work on the concrete that he's mixed with infected bones? Last I heard, they were transporting that stuff to hidden locations until somebody found a way to destroy or neutralize it."

"I don't see why not, but it's worth testing. It makes me wonder whether the fire demons from Earth IV had the same ability to purify that stuff—albeit on a smaller scale," I mused aloud.

"*Had* the ability?"

"Cassie is the last of her kind. All the other fire demons were systematically destroyed by an enemy, because they were far too dangerous—for the enemy, of course."

"Forced extinction?"

"Yes."

"Hey, boss," David greeted me as he walked in with a comp-vid in his hand. "Engine test results," he handed the tablet to Trent.

"Everything okay?" Trent asked.

"How else would it be?"

"Thank you."

"Vik and the others were due back half an hour ago," David told Trent.

"Did you send mindspeech?"

"No. That's why I'm telling you."

"Who else is with him?" I asked.

"Travis, Zanfield, Perri and Ilya."

"Want to go have a look at an ancient, abandoned quarry with me?" Trent rose from his seat and pulled his ranos pistol from a desk drawer.

"What's going on there?"

"At first, a few robberies. Then, more recently, an abduction. Authorities are still investigating, with little evidence."

"How little?"

"As in no evidence," David snorted. "They've found nothing, and the abduction was six days ago. Even the girl's family didn't report her missing; her school did that."

"How old?"

"Sixteen."

"Damn. Yeah. I want to go. Let me call some backup, first."

~

*Cassie*

"Gear up, we're going to Phume," Blaze announced after calling Rajeon, Denevik, Zephyr and me into the weapons storage aboard ship. If Rob hadn't been incapacitated by his earlier brush against the Prophet's evil, he'd have come with us.

After stuffing blades into the sheaths at my back, I slid my ranos pistol into the holster and nodded at Blaze. Zephyr's single blade was strapped to her right side, a ranos pistol on the left.

Rajeon and Denevik carried pistols, but no blades.

"I'll get us to X, Randl will take us after that," Denevik said.

"Go," Blaze jerked his head in a nod. Denevik *skipped* us to BlackWing X.

~

"We can't reach them with mindspeech," Randl told us when we arrived. "We can't get a response through their medallions, either."

"Do we have the location where they entered the caves?" Zephyr asked. "If you do, it will be easier for me to use air or wind to search for them."

"We have a general location, before they dropped off the grid," David growled. He was ready to take someone apart; I wasn't gauging his determination or ability to do so according to his height.

Amterean-trained dwarves tended to be fierce warriors—Salidar taught me that by bringing someone he knew to spar with me. I'd never believe I had the upper hand again, simply because I was taller.

"Is everyone ready?" Randl asked.

"Ready," Trent replied.

Randl folded us to a solid rock wall, pock-marked with dark openings from its base to the top. "Damn, looks like somebody defaced Uluru," David whispered as we stared at the red, sandstone monolith.

"Uluru is bigger," I whispered back. "This place reeks of foul play."

"There are bones at the entrance to the lowest cave," Denevik said. "Not animal bones, either."

"Why didn't they report this going in?" Trent hissed.

"Maybe they couldn't," Randl suggested. "Something is definitely going on here. It feels like—like," he hesitated.

"Like split-time," Trent snapped, stalking toward the cave where the bones of some unfortunate victim lay.

There wasn't time to ask what split-time was—the air around Trent shimmered as he walked away, and then he disappeared completely.

"Fucking, closet-snatching nightmares," Randl cursed and raced toward the spot where Trent vanished.

The rest of us ran behind him to catch up. Just before the air around me shimmered to swallow us, Denevik gripped my hand and leapt toward Randl's disappearing form.

*Randl*

Denevik and Cassie were the only two to come through with me. Had the others gone to different locations on the same planet?

"Where are we?" Denevik's gaze swept the empty, open plain around us. He knew as well as I that we were no longer on Phume. It was summer there, and hot. Here, bone-chilling gusts whipped tufts of sparse, winter-dried grasses around our feet, accompanied by the keening sound only a bitter wind can make when crossing a deserted prairie.

"We're on Evensun," I hissed, as a hard gust of air blew Cassie against Denevik.

"I guess it's not hard to see why there are rumors of prisoners from Evensun appearing on Phume, then," Cassie grumbled, as Denevik's hands gripped her shoulders and steadied her in what looked to be an oncoming storm.

"I'd say they're no longer rumors—they're facts," Denevik confirmed.

"Agreed. And, since we didn't gate through to the same place, there are multiple gates to escape through," I said.

*Randl? Can you hear me?* Trent's sending was tentative.

*I can hear you,* I replied. *Are you alone? Are you safe?*

*David is with me. We're safe enough, but boss, I think we're on Evensun.*

*We are on Evensun,* I replied. *Try to contact the others. Tell them to send mindspeech to me so I can find them. I'll come to you in a few seconds, I just have to mark this gate so we can find it again.*

*Gates? Mom outlawed gates,* Trent began. *What the hell is going on? It's like the laws of nature have been turned upside down.*

*We'll be there in a few,* I told him, trying to force my brain to sort our conundrum while holding a mental conversation. Trent was right, though. Nobody should be able to create or enable gates—not without a great deal of power.

*I've placed a marker,* Kev'Ril informed me. *We can go anytime.*

"David and Trent are safe; we're going to get them now," I announced, before relocating to their position.

The wind was fiercer there, almost forcing us to collide with David and Trent as they hunkered beside jutting rocks, conserving their body heat. "We need to get out of here," David shouted, to make himself heard over the screaming wind.

Flakes of snow began to fly past; a blizzard was coming. If I hadn't known it for myself, Bennall's warning would have let me know that a terrible storm was brewing. Forming a bubble shield to protect us from the cold and screeching winds, I took several deep breaths before asking Trent if he'd heard from anyone else.

"Nothing yet, or they could be busy fighting off hordes of murderers and other filth," Trent mumbled. "Thanks for the shield."

"If you'll include the rocks inside your shield, I'll keep us warm enough while you consider what we should do next," Cassie offered.

"Yeah. Good idea," I said, expanding my shield to include the outcropping. Cassie placed her hands on the surface of the granite and warmed it enough that it would radiate gentle heat for hours.

"Much better," David released a heavy sigh. "Thank you." he fist-bumped Cassie.

*Randl?* Vik's sending sounded like an old radio transmission, attempting to break up between us. Static was getting worse as the storm grew stronger.

*Vik? I'll be right there*, I told him, noting his position through his mindspeech and folding space.

~

*Cassie*

"Where did he go?" Trent sounded frantic.

"He went after Vik," I said. "Didn't you hear him?"

"I heard nothing," Trent shook his head. "I hope Travis is with him," he added.

*Is anyone there?* The voice crackled, as if hampered by static.

*Travis?* I replied.

*Yes.*

"Travis is in trouble," I said. "We need to go help him."

"Avilepha, connect with me. I can find him if I can hear his mindspeech," Denevik's words were urgent.

"How?" I asked, as Denevik locked his eyes with mine.

I discovered how—Denevik was in my mind, somehow, as if we were connected at a cellular level.

*Travis?* My mindspeech sounded inside my brain before echoing back from Denevik's.

*Here.* Travis' voice cracked.

Denevik gripped my arms and *skipped* us away from our warm bubble.

*Into a place far less hospitable.*

~

57

*I can't fold away*, Travis sent as he fought off four attackers wielding long, machete-like knives. Denevik and I had landed in a cave, where Travis' blades flashed furiously to fend off his adversaries. Light from the nearby entrance was the only illumination allowing us to see what was happening.

Bodies of those who'd attacked Travis and died in the attempt, were piled high behind the next four trying to kill him.

Beyond the pile of bodies, others waited for their turn at the man who'd landed in their cave by accident. None of them were armed—they waited for those ahead of them to fall so they could snatch up the blade and present a fresh opponent against the Falchani.

*Could be a spell, then*, Denevik sent, before becoming his smaller Thifilathi and rushing toward the four knife-wielders.

Rather than take a risk that they could cut him, I tossed fire at their blades, melting the sharp metal from rough, bone handles.

The four attackers screamed and ran from Denevik, then, forcing those waiting behind them to turn and retreat into the cave, too.

"Thank you," Travis nearly collapsed where he stood. "I landed here, tried to fold away and couldn't. I've been fighting them off forever, I think."

"You've been gone a while," I agreed, pulling my canteen from a cargo pocket of my pants. "Here. Take it slow, okay?"

Travis sipped water, forced himself to stop, and turned toward me. "Not enough room to become dragon," he whispered, before lifting the canteen to his mouth again. "Not nearly enough room," he said, after swallowing more water.

"And nobody could hear your mindspeech, is that right?"

"Not until you heard me."

"It's weird—it sounded almost like a bad radio connection, instead of mindspeech," I told him. "Denevik says maybe a spell is keeping you from folding space. I suppose it could affect mindspeech, too."

"They're scattered in the cave, now," Denevik returned, brushing cave dust off his sleeves. "You have no idea how much I appreciate Zaria's gift of remaining clothed after I come back to myself."

"It's the medallion, I'm sure," Travis said, before emptying my canteen.

"Need more?" Denevik unzipped his own cargo pocket.

"Maybe," Travis said. Denevik handed his full canteen over, while I accepted my empty one.

"Randl says these are gates that somebody set up," I said. "Can you get us back to Randl's bubble shield?" I pointed my question at Denevik.

"Gates? Mom destroyed the gates," Travis, like his brother, insisted.

"Something sure as hell opened these up," I said.

"Move closer to me; I'll see if we can get out of this place before our cave-dwellers return," Denevik ordered.

He and I pulled Travis in before Denevik *skipped* us back to Randl's bubble shield.

"Definitely a spell," Randl confirmed when he arrived with Trent and David. "I'd say it layered confusion with the blocking of mindspeech."

"Is that why I was fighting with blades rather than firing my ranos pistol?" Travis asked. He was almost back to normal, though still exhausted from fighting so long.

"I believe so," Randl agreed. "Now we have to find Zephyr and the others, then figure out what the hell is going on and who caused this mess."

"We need to shut down these gates, too," David grumbled. "We don't need criminals showing up wherever those gates lead."

"I'm surprised they survived the gates," Vik said. "Only certain ones should be able to use them—in the past, only the Elemaiya and others with sufficient power could step through them."

"Evensun's prisoners are getting through—that's a given," Denevik growled. "Some of them, anyway."

"Those who just happen to wander in?" I asked. I had little knowledge of the gates in question; this was a learning experience for me.

"It's possible," Randl spoke absently. I could tell he was deep in thought—or perhaps in communication with one or more of his spirit coins.

Denevik had a spirit coin, centered on his chest; Randl was practically covered in them. I hadn't seen them; Denevik described them for me. *Randl has a tattoo on his back, from the Falchani,* he'd explained. *Spirit coins cover every bit of that tattoo, making the sun gold, the moon silver, and the eye—it is so carefully crusted by coins that it's a work of art on its own.*

I wanted to see it, but asking would be awkward. *You'll see it if you're meant to see it,* I told myself, quoting one of Aunt Shelbie's favorite sayings. For now, I had to be satisfied with that.

*Cassie?* Zephyr's voice filled my mind.

*Zephyr? Where are you?* I gasped aloud at her sudden mindspeech.

*The wind is blowing so hard, I had to become a part of it to survive,* she told me.

"I can get a fix on her, then extrapolate where to land to draw her in," Randl said, his words urgent. "Come with me; we'll catch her."

Before I could squawk in surprise, we were gone from the bubble, landing in knee-deep snow in the middle of nowhere. Visibility was limited to a yard. Maybe two at most. Snow came, heavy and fast, hurled by a high-pitched, howling wind that made me want to cover my ears. *I see you,* Zephyr shouted, before Randl and I were knocked off our feet by Zephyr's physical impact. Before I could spit out a mouthful of snow, Randl transported us to his bubble.

*Randl*

"That was brutal," Zephyr shook out her clothing before looking at Cassie expectantly. She wanted to go back to the ship, that was easy to see.

"We still have to find Blaze, Rajeon, Zanfield, Perri and Ilya," I sighed. "No word from any of them yet."

"We were hijacked?" Zephyr asked.

"Looks like it," Cassie confirmed. "Most of us ended up in different places, too, or so it appears."

"Perri and Ilya can likely keep themselves warm, as can Blaze. Rajeon and Zanfield may not have that luxury. If they're in this blizzard, we have to find them fast," I said. "Cassie, if you and Denevik will search for Rajeon, I'll start hunting for Zanfield."

"Can somebody trade me a full canteen?" Cassie asked.

"Here," David handed his over. "It's almost full."

"Thanks." Cassie closed her eyes, sending mindspeech to Rajeon, I'm sure. A deep intake of breath later, her eyes popped open. Grasping Denevik's hand, both *skipped* away.

*Zanfield?* I sent. *Where are you?*

*Queen's Palace, Le-Ath Veronis*

*Lissa*

Desperate mindspeech from a future daughter-in-law is never easy to deal with, especially if the two sons she's engaged to have been missing for hours, in addition to another son who'd gone on the mission with them.

Sabrina and I were now having a comp-vid conversation, while Winkler sat with me in my suite and Jincus sat with Sabrina aboard BlackWing X.

"Trent, Vik and a few others went to Phume. We didn't hear from them after they went. When the time came for them to report back, David and I were already worried," Sabrina reported.

"Travis, Randl and a few others went down to look for our missing squad. Now we haven't heard from them, either, and mindspeech doesn't work."

"You say Randl's with them?" Winkler attempted to calm Sabrina, who was wiping tears away.

"Yes. I've contacted Jett and the other captains; they're doing what they can to locate them, but so far, there's no sign they were ever on Phume."

By now, Jincus had put an uncomfortable arm around Sabrina, and patted her shoulder. She leaned against his shoulder and sobbed.

"I'll be right there," I told the distressed Second Engineer and ended the communication.

"Want to go to BlackWing X with me?" I asked Winkler.

"Sure thing," he said, taking my elbow. He folded us so I wouldn't have to.

*Cassie*

We hadn't gotten mindspeech from Rajeon.

No.

What I'd gotten before passing it on to Denevik was an image—of what Rajeon had become to combat the storm and survive it. His ten-foot, crystal formation was half-buried by snow when Denevik and I arrived.

With barely a thought, I melted the snow around the crystal and around Denevik and me. "Rajeon," I screamed, trying to make myself heard over the screaming winds. "We're here to take you to safety."

Nothing happened.

*Has he gone into hibernation?* Denevik sent, while becoming his smaller Thifilathi for the second time that day. His scales would protect him better from the cold than the clothing he wore.

*Do pod'l-morphs hibernate?* I asked, placing my hands on Rajeon's crystal and warming him gently.

*If I were him and I could, this would be the perfect time to do it,* Denevik pointed out.

*Rajeon,* I shouted into his mind—wherever that was located at the moment. There was no reply.

*How deep do you suppose he's buried below the surface?* Denevik asked.

*No idea,* I said, while expending energy to warm myself, now. If Destiny were here, she'd be perfectly fine in this weather. Ice demons loved extreme cold. They could play in it while the rest of us looked for warmer places.

*We may have to take him back like this,* Denevik pointed out.

*Damn.*

*My thinking exactly.* Denevik drew himself to his larger Thifilathi—eighteen feet of full, obsidian-scaled-and-winged High Demon, before putting his hands on Rajeon's crystal and prying it out of the snow and frozen ground.

*Ready, avilepha?* he sent.

*Get us out of here,* I confirmed.

~

*Randl*

Zanfield was almost frozen stiff, and half-buried in snow when I found him. Actually, Bennall found him, after connecting his medallion with mine. I hadn't known it was possible, but she and Kev'Ril thought it worth a try.

If we'd taken any longer, he may have died in the blizzard. Throwing a warming spell around him, like a light blanket so he wouldn't warm too quickly, I transported him back to the bubble shield.

There, I found that Cassie and Denevik had been forced to bring Rajeon back in crystal form, because he hadn't responded to any of their pleas to wake and change.

Also, I found that Zephyr was now forcing warm air to circulate throughout the bubble, after Cassie warmed the rocks again.

That, in itself, would help warm Zanfield, who was now beginning to shiver slightly.

"I sure hope Perri and Ilya are together, wherever they are," Trent and Vik approached me as I knelt beside Zanfield, checking his hands for signs of frostbite.

"We still have Blaze out there, too," I reminded them.

"I hate to ask it of them, but I think Cassie and Denevik should go looking for Blaze, while you take us to look for Perri and Ilya."

"I'll take Vik," I told Trent. "High Demons seem to have a better handle on this than anyone else," I added. "I think most of this is spell work, and these are powerful spells."

"Meaning High Demons are impervious," Trent nodded thoughtfully. "Damn."

"I only stayed here because I couldn't find the others," Vik confirmed. "And with the storm coming on, I wasn't about to leave anybody behind."

"Thanks, bro," Trent slapped Vik's back.

"Solidarity, bro," Vik fist-bumped with Trent.

"Cassie, have you tried to reach Perri or the others?" I asked, while Zanfield began to shiver harder.

"I'll do that now," she said, closing her eyes.

*Damn. She turned out to be useful,* Vik sent.

*More than useful, I'd say,* Trent agreed, cutting his eyes briefly to Travis.

∼

*Cassie*

*Perri? Ilya? Blaze?* I sent.

I jumped and squeaked when all three tried to answer at the same time. Again, their replies were crackling with static, but they were there.

"Where?" Denevik's hands landed on my shoulders.

*Are you together?* I sent.

*Alone,* Blaze replied.

*Perri and I are together,* Ilya informed me. *We have a shield up, but the cold is seeping in, no matter how strong a heat spell we cast.*

*Get them first,* Blaze said. *I'm all right for now. Just—hurry.*

*On our way,* I sent, while Denevik *skipped* us to Perri and Ilya first.

∼

*G'Margis*

*V'dar*

"Destroy the information or destroy the place. Both, if you can—I want them to learn they can't fling my name about without repercussions," I tossed the comp-vid to Gillen.

My team of hackers had given me the information; it appeared on a particular media company's system earlier in the day and was scheduled for release on their morning news programs.

How they'd come by the information I had no idea, but only a small portion of it was correct. Along with naming me a most-wanted, second only to Randl Gage and the BlackWing Pirates, they'd also called me cowardly, and less powerful than I was. A false term I disliked greatly was sprinkled throughout the communication; I was called *delusional*. It had no relation to me. In truth, this entity had no business reporting anything about me, as they knew nothing.

*At all.*

"It will be done," Gillen nodded briefly.

"You can take one other with you, if you desire," I said. "Choose wisely. Any failure in this will result in less than desirable consequences. On your part, of course."

"I'll see it done." Gillen stalked out of my laboratory, his shoulders stiff and set. I waited to see whether he took his wife or his brother with him. It was always useful to know who meant more to someone —in case leverage were needed.

As for those who thought to spread information about me and mine, they'd learn quickly enough that I was off-limits. They could blame everything I did on that fool Randl Gage if they wanted.

*As long as they left me out of it or painted me in a far better light.*

*Cassie*

Perri and Ilya were easy enough to collect. Blaze—his predicament was worthy of a Jules Verne tale.

A ring of prisoners surrounded the circle of fire Blaze created to protect himself. Warmed enough by the flames to become active in the snowstorm blowing around them, the prisoners flung rocks and anything else they could find to use as weapons, attempting to kill the interloper, then steal his boots and clothing.

They didn't realize if they killed Blaze, the welcome fire he'd built would die with him. They would freeze to death before reaching sufficient shelter to save their own lives.

*What do we do?* Perri shivered as we stood inside an invisible shield Ilya had erected around us. Blaze was weary from fending off thrown rocks; several had hit him, because there was a trail of blood down the left side of his face.

*Stay here; I'll handle this,* Denevik sent, before *skipping* beside Blaze and pulling himself to his Full Thifilathi. The roar, accompanied by widespread, leathery wings scared even the bravest attackers so badly they all scattered with terrified cries.

Wasting no time, Denevik hauled Blaze against his chest, *skipped* back to us and then *skipped* us to Randl's bubble shield. Perri's cry of "Zanfield," as she knelt beside his shivering form was immediate and frightened. She loved him more than even she knew until that moment.

"Thanks for coming to get me," Blaze dropped to the ground, exhausted.

"We need a med kit," I said, kneeling down to look at the wound on his left temple.

"It's not bad," he said as Vik dropped to his knees beside us and flung open a small kit of medical supplies.

"It's still bleeding," I told Blaze, as Vik cleaned the wound and placed a temporary bandage over the jagged cut. "When we get back to the ship, we'll make sure there's no permanent damage."

"We heal fast," Blaze grumped.

*Cassie?* Barry's sending tore me away from helping Blaze—he sounded upset. *Cassie,* he went on, *someone just destroyed the computer system at Media Solstice on Cadrile III. I felt it die.*

# CHAPTER 6

*B*lackWing X
        *Randl*

"They didn't just destroy the computer system—they destroyed the entire complex," Lissa handed a comp-vid to me the moment we returned to X. She'd come to help calm Sabrina after learning of Travis and Trent's unexplained absence, so she was waiting for us when we returned.

"What destroyed it—or who?" I asked, studying the first images to come from an alternative news agency.

"At least it was in the middle of the night, so there was only a minimal number of deaths connected with it," Winkler growled. "Nearly thirty reported dead as it is, and that's a preliminary number."

"This was no accident," I said, as I studied more images of the devastation. "Somebody did this, and not *something*."

"I get the same feeling," Lissa said. "It's making me itch, and that's never a good thing."

"I say we go do some sniffing," Winkler said.

"I'd like to speak with Barry, first," I said, surprising Lissa and Winkler. "He felt the computer die. Maybe he has information that can point us in the right direction."

"Let's go visit Barry, then," Lissa sounded determined. "If that doesn't tell us what we want to know, then Winkler and I will make a visit to Cadrile III."

"Did you get anything else with that knowledge?" I asked Barry. He, Beverly and Cassie sat in Jett's cubby while I asked questions. Cassie was tired, but she'd come anyway because Barry asked her to. She and Beverly—he and his chosen siblings trusted these two women more than they trusted anyone else.

Barry was still upset—as if a friend had died rather than a machine. Perhaps to him, they *were* friends, but that wasn't relevant at the moment.

"I have what may be a final image," Barry admitted, while Beverly rubbed his shoulder in a comforting way.

"Can you show me?" I asked.

"Give me your comp-vid," he said.

Pulling my tablet from a cargo pocket, I slid the device toward him. He touched the surface with a hand—it came to life without a password or a fingerprint from me—as it shouldn't have done.

"Here," Barry gave the tablet back to me. "The image is your latest entry in your personal log."

"How the hell?" I muttered as I was forced to enter my code to get into the desired file. My feelings of confused anger dissolved instantly when I saw two faces pictured in the latest file—the exact likenesses of *Alken and Gillen Wilker.*

"Why would the Prophet order Alken and Gillen to destroy Media Solstice? They didn't write anything about him," Lissa said. She and Winkler sat in my office aboard BlackWing XIII, while I paced behind my desk.

"Do you suppose they had information about him—that they

hadn't published?" I stopped pacing to ask.

"No idea, and unless Barry knows, we may not be able to find out. All the information was stored there at the main office. I doubt any of the satellite offices have anything on the Prophet. My worry is that they'll blame this on you, after the news broke that you were behind the recent break-in."

"I'll ask Barry to check, just in case," I sighed. Generally, I didn't mind taking the blame for something that wasn't my fault, as it shored up my reputation as the most-wanted criminal in the Alliances. Something about this, though—it burned my soul to be blamed for it.

"Sit down; you've had a long day," Winkler indicated my desk chair with a hand.

"Yeah. That's for damn sure," I said and followed his advice. "First, we deal with the strangest and strongest spells I've ever encountered on Phume and Evensun, gates that are open against all odds, criminals getting through to wreak havoc on Phume, and then the Prophet sending his warlocks to destroy a media conglomerate's main office. None of this makes sense."

"Do you know how many gates are open?" Lissa was only now hearing about this aspect of the day's troubles, and she wasn't pleased about it.

"There are at least eight—Denevik, Cassie and I landed in one place, and we rescued the others from seven more. As far as I can tell, there's only one corresponding gate on Phume, outside that monolith where stone was quarried and caves carved out of the surface. That means we have to find the prisoners who've already invaded Phume and stop any others from coming through."

"Did you have a gut feeling that the Prophet was behind that, too?" Winkler asked.

"I didn't get his scent from any of it, but we may not have been in the proper place to do that."

"I've never known him to be interested in gates before, but that doesn't mean he hasn't turned his hand to this sort of thing. Those rogue gods with him could be feeding him all kinds of information, and I don't like it one little bit," Lissa said.

"I keep hearing that you closed all the gates," I told her.

"I did close the gates. It pisses me off to know there are gates open again, especially on Evensun."

"No surprise that there were so many gates there," Winkler added thoughtfully. "It's how the Bright Elemaiya got off the planet to begin with."

"Do we know anyone who actually lived there—who'd know where all the gates were?" I asked. Elemaiya were immortal, unless they managed to get themselves killed.

Winkler and Lissa exchanged a look. "We can ask," Lissa said, although she didn't sound as if she liked the idea.

"Go around him and ask Rabis," Winkler spoke softly and nudged Lissa's shoulder with his own. "You're related to him too, you know."

"Yeah." Her sigh was definitely on the relieved side. "I'll ask Rabis, as soon as we get home."

Finally, I understood. She was prepared to ask Griffin, although she'd rather have her vampire fangs yanked out. Rabis, Great-grandfather to Ashe and Great-great-great-grandfather to Lissa, was by far a more palatable choice.

I felt a pang of loneliness for my own father, who'd loved me a great deal and raised me on his own, after my mother's untimely death—a death I still blamed on V'dar and his rogue-god father. Only V'dar remained, and I intended to have justice against my half-brother, who'd murdered so many already.

I hadn't spoken to Pap recently. I was determined to remedy that oversight quickly. Any meeting or correspondence with my father required the utmost secrecy, because V'dar was still a threat to him. My hands clenched in a moment of anger; V'dar threatened the very existence of every world in every universe, and I wanted him dead.

*You must accept help wherever it is offered to take V'dar down,* Kev'Ril wisely informed me. *V'dar has certainly added to his strength; we both know this.*

*You have added to mine,* I retorted.

*And you must accept more; we feel this, Bennall and I. No matter the source, if help is willingly offered, take it.*

*Then I'll let you be the judge when those offers come*, I said.

"We should go," Winkler helped Lissa to her feet. "We have things to take care of, as do you."

"You're right about that," I nodded to Winkler. "I'll be sure to keep you informed."

"Thank you, and we'll do the same," Lissa nodded. "Tell my boys not to get lost again. I can't physically have a heart attack, but sometimes it sure feels like it."

"I'll let them know," I said. "Thank you for your help."

*Dori*, I sent, *can you come see me for a second?*

*On my way*, she replied. Moments later, she was inside my office.

"You got here fast. Were you lurking?" I teased.

"Maybe. Who wants to know?"

"Can we find some time to have dinner with my pap soon? I haven't seen him in a while."

"I think we can squeeze that in. Tomorrow, maybe?"

"I'll contact Wyatt, so he can reach Pap and set it up."

"Sounds good. Casual?"

"I think so."

"Good." She stalked toward me, like a cat pursuing its prey, before pulling my face into her hands and kissing me. There was so much emotion in that kiss; she'd been worried when neither she nor the others could reach us by mindspeech during our visits to Phume and Evensun.

"I love you," I told her when the kiss ended and she pulled away, her gaze moving across my face. I smiled, which kindled a light in her eyes and an answering smile.

"I don't deserve you most of the time, either," I added.

"I'll be the judge of that," she said and kissed me again.

*BlackWing IX*
   *Cassie*
"Need anything?" I found Rob and Blaze having a glass of Falchani

beer in the galley. Beverly kept an eye on them while putting lasagna together for dinner.

"Both of 'em wore out, yet there they sit, drinkin' beer," Beverly spoke English, with her old, southern accent coming through. "Men. Never did listen to sense."

I tried to stifle my snicker—it didn't work.

*You might check on Barry*, Beverly sent. *He's still upset.*

*I'll find him*, I said. *Is there anything I can take to cheer him up?*

*Hot chocolate. Give me a minute, I'll get it ready.*

Soon enough, I had a generous cup of hot chocolate in my hands, with whipped cream and tiny chocolate chips sprinkled on top. I transported it to Barry's quarters and knocked softly on his door.

"Come in," he called out.

I walked in to find him wedged in the corner, where his bunk jutted out from the wall. "Beverly sent hot chocolate, and she's making lasagna for dinner." I crossed his small room and handed the cup to him.

"I love her—she's the mother I should have had," he sighed and accepted the cup. "I love hot chocolate made this way."

"She's the mother you have now," I pointed out. I sat on the chair next to his desk and watched him sip hot chocolate. "I'm sorry about the comp at Media Solstice. I have a feeling you were connected to it more than we know, and that you're grieving."

"I feel as if I led those filth straight to it," he grimaced, lowering his cup with a heavy sigh.

"Barry, I can't really explain how or why I feel this way, but I don't think that's true. Somehow, something strange is happening, and I can't even begin to describe it properly. You didn't have anything to do with this—I swear. I know it's just my gut feeling as opposed to a lot of others who may know better, but it is what it is."

"I'd trust your gut feelings over most people's facts," Barry said.

"Grieve for your friend," I said, standing up and stretching. "If you want to talk, you know where to find me. Trust me when I say this, too—we'll get to the bottom of this, and vengeance will be had."

"Thank you. For the hot chocolate and for being here," he said. "I'll be okay, I just need some time."

"No worries, little brother," I smiled at him. "Don't forget, I'm here if you need me."

~

I was supposed to be resting—Captain's orders, but I sat on my bunk instead, going over the events of the day. I'd transported from Barry's room back to the galley, to ask Beverly for a cup of hot chocolate for myself.

I'd already warmed it twice while I picked through my experiences —on Phume and Evensun. I almost spilled hot chocolate when the knock on my door interrupted my thoughts.

"Come in," I called out. I'm not sure who I was expecting, but Rajeon surprised me as he walked inside.

"I just wanted to stop by and thank you," he said. "And Denevik, of course. Without both of you, I might still be a crystal stuck in frozen ground and buried in snow."

"Actually, it was gratifying to watch Denevik's Thifilathi pull you from the ground like a huge, crystal spear," I said, giving him a weary smile. "At the time, we were both worried you'd gone into hibernation because we couldn't reach you, but it still turned out all right."

"I do have a way of shutting things down if they become overwhelming," he admitted, taking a seat on my desk chair. "And that was certainly overwhelming. When you provided warmth, I woke from my shutdown."

"Glad I could help," I shrugged. "It was nothing heroic, I assure you."

"Well, I'm just happy I'm not stuck in crystal form in a blizzard," he told me. "I had no idea where I was."

"Neither did I, but Randl knew. Denevik was right to follow him through the gate."

"Denevik told me that he's learned a thing or two in his long life."

I blinked—I'd never considered Denevik's age before. I knew High

Demons were immortal unless they were killed, but that hadn't occurred to me regarding Denevik. "Did he say how old he was?"

"He didn't say exactly, but it's in the thousands. If I remember correctly, he said he'd learned a lot during the thousands of years he's lived."

"And here I am with only twenty-six years of experience." I sagged against the wall perpendicular to my bunk.

"It isn't the years; it's what fills those years," Rajeon advised as he stood and squared his shoulders. "I'm off to bed. Hopefully, we'll both sleep well."

"Amen to that," I saluted him with my hot chocolate. "May our sleep be uneventful and uninterrupted."

"When I'm not so tired, I'll ask you what that word—*amen* —means."

"It's an Earth term," I said. "Ask Beverly—she can explain it better than I can."

~

*Founder's Palace, Campiaa*
*Wyatt*

"Opal and Kell are asking for help with the Media Solstice bombing," Dad said. He'd called Griffin, who was not only my great-grandfather, but also newly-hired Director of the CSD, into his office to tell us the latest that he knew of the matter.

I couldn't bring myself to call Griffin anything other than Griffin, although his real name was Brenten Arden. And, although a member of the family, we had nothing in common. I knew enough of the stories of how he'd used Gran in the past to achieve a desired result, so I knew not to trust him.

I merely hoped he wasn't planning to fall into his old habits of inserting family members into dangerous situations to get his new job done.

"What kind of help do they want?" Griffin's hazel eyes narrowed as he studied Dad. There was a depth in those eyes that none could penetrate past the surface. Even Dad couldn't lay compulsion on Griffin; he was also a King Vampire and eons older than Dad. In fact, it was a good bet that the reason Gran was a Queen Vampire and Dad a King Vampire was because they inherited that gene from Griffin.

Gran always said he'd plotted her birth, and that her mother died because of it. That was clearly a painful story and one I hadn't pressed her about. All I knew (because Grampa Gavin told me once), was that Griffin, as a member of the Saa Thalarr, was supposed to be sterile.

He'd managed to get around that restriction somehow. He'd fathered Aunt Bree, too, but I knew little of that story. Now he was here, after convincing Dad to hire him to take Jett's place. Except for nabbing Randl when he shouldn't have, Griffin had already brought in three of Dad's most-wanted.

"It wouldn't hurt to meet them on Cadrile III and investigate the site. It's already been combed through by forensics," Dad held up a hand to stop Griffin from protesting, "but they're hoping to get some kind of feel from it. We know Alken and Gillen Wilker are responsible, but what I want to know is why—and whether they left any kind of trail to follow."

"I thought your BlackWing Pirates were supposed to be on their tail," Griffin frowned. "If they're so good at this, why are you sending me?"

"Because even the slightest bit of information could help," Dad snapped. I realized I had no desire to be in the same room with two King Vamps going after one another. "Besides, it's good press to see cooperation between the ASD and CSD," Dad pounded his desk so hard I worried the antique wood might crack.

I was ready to call for Tybus to help calm the situation when Griffin capitulated. "Then I'll go," Griffin said. "When are Opal and Kell expecting me?"

"Tomorrow morning. I'll have Opal send a schedule."

"Is that all?" Griffin stood from his chair.

"For now." Dad fidgeted with a comp-vid on his desk, as if he weren't satisfied with its position.

"Very well. I'll provide a report afterward." Rather than walking out the door, Griffin folded away.

"Damn," Dad blew out a heavy sigh. "I hope it won't be a fight every time."

"He doesn't like taking orders," I said. "He's done what he wanted for so long, I have no idea why he thought this job was a good idea."

"You have to admit he's efficient," Dad rose from his chair to look out the window. Night was falling, with the last of the sunset glinting off the bay beyond the palace grounds.

"Jett was efficient, too, and not nearly as grumpy."

"Jett isn't nearly as old."

"You're saying it's an age thing?"

"Son, neither of us know what he's seen or been through. I only know part of his story, from Mom and Dad. That's only one side. If I've learned anything at all during my life, it's that people tend to have many sides, and most people only see one of them."

"You're giving him a pass for what he did to Gran? And for what he did to Toff and Roff?"

"I'm not giving him a pass for that. I'm giving him an opportunity to help instead of harm. So far, he's done a good job."

"Are you prepared to fire him if that changes?"

"I am." Something about that statement troubled me.

"Good," I replied, as an answer was expected, and I couldn't think of a better one right then. "I need some time to think," I said more honestly, rising from my chair. "If you need me, send mindspeech."

I followed Griffin's example and folded away from Dad's office. Frankly, I itched to ask Travis and Trent to let Jayna and me travel aboard BlackWing X for a while. Hunting the Prophet couldn't be more stressful than it was at home—*could it?*

~

*SouthStar, Avendor*
　　*Lissa*

"Here, here, and here," Rabis pointed out the last three gates on

Evensun. I'd brought him a map and my request; he'd complied without argument.

"All seventeen are currently buried by a huge snowstorm," Ashe said as he studied the map and *Looked* at the same time.

"I often wondered why all the gates were in the far north," Rabis said. "Although winters usually weren't so harsh. You can't gate in or out if one of the gates is covered in snow."

"That gives us a reprieve, to hunt escapees on Phume," Merrill said. He'd come with me to visit Rabis; Winkler was at home watching our twins.

"Do you think others may have gone to different destinations?" I asked. "Why would they all go to Phume? It doesn't make sense."

"I'd suggest closing the gate on Phume," Rabis lifted his eyes to meet mine. "If you want to ensure that none can use it again, I'd set something formidable in its place, just to make sure."

"Like a pile of boulders or something?"

"Yes. In later years, many of our gates were covered by buildings or manufactured lakes. Those were marked as non-operational and were no longer shown to the young ones. It was the main reason we didn't visit some worlds after a while—the gates there were no longer accessible."

"The Prophet's rogues may know the locations of all those gates," Ashe advised. "While Randl didn't detect the Prophet's hand in forcing those gates open, his rogues may have done it for him and left no sign of their presence behind. I worry that this is only an experiment, and that his true purpose for opening gates will be revealed at the same moment he strikes a terrible blow against us."

"If you're trying to scare us, you're doing a good job," I frowned at him.

"We can't discount any theory where the Prophet is concerned," Ashe shrugged. "He won't pull his punches, I assure you."

"While we're hampered with efforts to save innocent lives, I suppose," I blew out a frustrated breath.

"Pretty much," Ashe agreed.

"Rabis, can you give me locations of all the gates? Even the non-accessible ones?" I asked him.

"My lady, there are tens of thousands at the very least."

"Fuck," I mumbled. Both Ashe and Merrill heard, however. Both had sharp hearing.

"What about giving us important ones—those you feel are important, anyway?" Merrill suggested.

"That I can do, but there will still be many of those, and it will take days, if not weeks."

"Do what you can," I told him, "and get the results to us when you can. I doubt the Prophet is ready to move tomorrow, or next week, even. All bets may be off after that."

"I will work as quickly as possible," Rabis dipped his head respectfully.

"I'll make sure you get the information when he's done," Ashe agreed. "Thank you, Grandfather. You've been a great deal of help."

∾

*Unnamed Dwarf Planet*

*Griffin*

"What did Gavril want?" I asked, pouring tea for the both of us. My father, Wylend Arden, dropped the disguise he wore and settled wearily on his chair at the table. He'd taken the meeting with my grandson, who was also his great-grandson, to find out what was going on.

"He wants you to go to Cadrile III tomorrow morning, to meet with Opal and Kell. A joint Alliance effort to solve that conundrum, I believe." Wylend pulled the pot of honey to him and poured a generous amount in his tea before drinking.

"I'm still hunting that sex slaver on Orkos," I said. "It's irritating when they can cover themselves with bone dust or surround themselves with Sirenali bones to remain undetectable. That means I have to employ more mundane means to track them."

"I can go in your place again," Wylend offered, sipping tea. "Good as always," he lifted his cup in a salute.

"If you wouldn't mind—I'm getting close, I can feel it."

"Just make sure not to arrest him publicly until I'm away from Cadrile III."

"I will certainly avoid that mistake," I grinned at my father.

"I find this refreshing—being able to go about our business without being followed everywhere, and then coming home where only I and my son live, and he's made tea."

"Works for both of us," I agreed and sipped my drink.

*G'Margis*
   *V'dar*
"Where are those records?" I demanded.

W'dell, his back bent from years of slumping in a chair staring at a desk comp, jumped; I'd startled him.

"My lord, I am nearly finished." W'dell's voice quavered as he stood and dipped his head to me. "I had to work diligently to break through many passwords; it wasn't only one source selling bones and bone dust acquired from Paricos II."

At least Vardil Cayetes was dead. If he weren't, I'd eliminate him myself. Prior to his destruction by the enemy, Toad had moved time to retrieve these and other records for me. He could have gotten past passwords easily, but I no longer had his services to command.

The list of bone and bone dust buyers was being compiled; once it was complete, I'd have names and locations of the best and worst of them. After that, they and their illegally-obtained supplies, ships and slaves would become mine.

I'd recently lost a bid for better commanders of my armies; therefore, I was on a quest to obtain the next best, plus their already-formed criminal empires. The enemy had a weakness—a reluctance to destroy what they believed to be innocent lives.

In my experience, nobody was innocent, and they'd all die eventually, anyway. "I want those lists the moment they're finished," I told a trembling W'dell. "For now, I'll see to it that your quarters and workspace are kept warmer—in exchange for a task well and quickly executed."

"It will be so, my lord."

~

*Queen's Palace, Le-Ath Veronis*
*Lissa*

After Opal sent a request for a quick meeting, I invited them to my private study. "Any suggestions on dealing with Griffin?" Opal asked. Kell, his hands on her shoulders as if to steady her, stood at her back.

"Nowadays, I only want to yell at or punch him, so I'm not much help, I'm afraid."

"Teeg says he was reluctant to meet with us on Cadrile III," Kell's deep voice didn't reveal his own reluctance to work with Teeg's new CSD Director.

None of us spoke about our desire to have Jett back in that position. Jett had moved on and was now more than he was.

*Like many of us before him.* "Once upon a time," I pointed Kell and Opal toward the sofa in my study as I took the chair behind my desk, "I thought I was an orphan. The most excitement I'd expect was coming home from work and digging through the fridge and cabinets for something easy to make after a long day. Now, I worry my own father will fuck everything up by just being his usual, asshole self."

"It does present a problem," Opal agreed. She and Kell took the offered sofa, sat close together and clasped hands.

"Let me guess—Ildevar asked you to cooperate, didn't he?"

"Yes. He suggested Griffin, because in the past, Griffin was successful in hunting Ra'Ak in hiding. Alken and Gillen are in hiding, too; most likely behind the Prophet's robe. If we can provide any information to Randl and his bunch, Ildevar wants it done. Like yesterday." Opal grimaced at the thought of doing an investigation with Griffin. I could tell she'd prefer working with anyone else, including a few criminals.

"Don't let him take advantage of you," I told her. "Because he's famous for doing that. Just ask Merrill. Or Toff and Roff."

"Because you don't want to talk about what he did to you," Kell said softly.

"Bingo," I tapped my nose. "From what I've seen, he's never gotten into a fight if he could send someone else instead."

"I suppose we'll see how this works out then," Kell sounded resigned.

"Need a drink?" I asked.

"I'd take one," Opal nodded. Kell agreed with her.

"Let's go to the arboretum, then. It's more peaceful there."

*Bexis, Orkos*

   *Griffin*

Laddus talked and laughed with five from his harem—two young men and three women, all barely of legal age. No doubt he took them long before they were of legal age—he was famous for that sort of perversity.

All five pretended to hang on his every word—it was far safer for them to do so. They tended to live longer if they stroked their master's ego. Nobody walked away from a sex slaver after they became too old to cater to his tastes; they were disposed of discreetly, unless they proved useful in another capacity.

Six bodyguards were placed inconspicuously about the private room at an exclusive restaurant; the table there was just large enough to accommodate Laddus and his guests.

Should I only take Laddus? Should I take all of them, guards included, so nobody would sound the alarm immediately? If their servers found them gone, would they even report the incident?

Ah. There it was—the solution. Compulsion on the servers first, and then I take them all with me.

Yes. That ought to capture the attention of the other criminals I sought.

*And mostly swiftly, too.*

# CHAPTER 7

*C adrile III*
    *Vice-Director Kell Abenott*

"Alken, Gillen and Qatti have a price on their heads set by the King of Karathia," Griffin snorted as we stood at the edge of the devastation that once was Media Solstice's headquarters. "The amount was raised after this debacle."

"I wasn't aware that the King of Karathia was given the information that Alken and Gillen were responsible," Opal frowned.

"Teeg is the King's brother. Of course he passed the information along. I am family, too, if you recall, although I would have advised against it, had Teeg asked."

"Of course." Opal still wasn't pleased with Griffin's haughty attitude. Griffin was reminding us that he was Teeg's grandfather, in a manner similar to that of inflicting a paper cut.

In other words, it stung after a moment's reflection.

Most people in both Alliances had no idea that the Founder of the Campiaan Alliance was brother to the King of Karathia. Or that both were sons of the Queen of Le-Ath Veronis.

Plus, with recent events being what they were, several others connected to that family were also linked to vital hub worlds and would know in an instant if anything were to go wrong—because the planet's spirits had aligned with them.

Randl Gage held most of the others, with a few exceptions. I hoped he'd get the message if the Prophet interfered with those worlds more than he had in the past.

Already, there were uprisings here and there; I had to assume that Randl was carefully looking at all of them, searching for signs of the Prophet's interference.

"Give me a moment," Griffin interrupted my thoughts as he stepped across the laser barrier onto spell-blackened ground. Once there, he leaned down and drew a circle in the dark ash.

Then, he shut his eyes and held his hand over the circle, emitting light.

*A trick my father taught me*, he sent mindspeech to Opal and me. "Ah, yes. There's the power tag—definitely Gillen's work, although he may have pulled some energy away from Alken to achieve such isolated devastation." Griffin dropped his hand and opened his eyes.

Griffin's father was Wylend Arden, the former King of Karathia. I suppose they'd had plenty of time to trade secrets after their self-imposed exile.

"How should we report this for the official files?" Opal asked.

"I suggest we say it is the work of an unknown warlock and leave it at that. It will be easy enough to suggest that we are still searching for an identity, will it not?" Griffin's hazel eyes settled on Opal's face.

"Yes, I suppose that's the best way to report it—officially," Opal sighed and turned away from Griffin's intense gaze. "We still don't know the reason they destroyed this place."

"I'm sure they did something the Prophet didn't like," Griffin shrugged. "I can't imagine that the Wilker brothers have the free will remaining to do this on their own—and there's no real reason to do this, other than at the Prophet's orders."

"Why do you say that?" I rounded on Griffin.

"Because there's no money in it," he snapped at me. "They're all about the money, in case you haven't delved into their history. Alken only stayed with the children until Perri was old enough to go out on her own and the opportunity came for him to sell Pauly. Otherwise, he was happy enough abusing both of them. If the Wilkers were able to do so, don't you think they'd have sold everything they knew about the Prophet to Media Solstice instead of destroying it?"

I couldn't argue with his logic. Gillen and Qatti had taken a job with one of the biggest criminals in both Alliances, and when the Prophet took over his compound and his fleet of ships, he'd taken the witch and warlock, too. Then, after Zanfield, through an intermediary, offered to buy Pauly, Alken had sold the boy willingly and gone to join his brother.

All three were now caught in the Prophet's web.

"Did your father teach you any tricks to find out what made the Prophet order this destruction?" Opal swept a hand toward the flattened rubble of Media Solstice.

"Sadly, he did not. No matter how I look at this, I cannot determine a reason." With a wave of his hand, he made the circle he'd drawn in the ash disappear. "We will use all our resources to search for the reason, but for now, the records in the Campiaan Alliance will reflect *Reasons Unknown.*"

His choice would force us to do the same, although I had no idea how diligently he'd search for the reason after leaving here.

*He's too busy locking up more mundane criminals to spend much time or resources on this,* Opal echoed my thoughts. *I'm beginning to think he's only interested in making himself look good to the media.*

*Well, one of those outlets took a massive hit, here,* I pointed out grimly.

*Point taken.* "Griffin, would you like to join us for lunch?" Opal did the polite thing by inviting him.

"No, thank you. I have plenty of work to do in my own Alliance." He nodded before folding away.

"Well, that wasted our morning," Opal grumbled.

"For the most part," I agreed. "I'm buying lunch. Where can we go to get the taste of Griffin out of our mouths?"

"Sushi?"

"With plenty of wasabi, please."

*Unnamed Dwarf Planet*
  *Griffin*
"You brought them here?" Wylend croaked when he landed in our shared kitchen. Laddus and his guards were eating lunch inside a powerlight cage, while Laddus' sex slaves were eating lunch at the kitchen table.

"I have to keep them for another day, to be on the safe side," I said. "We're having roast chicken and vegetables," I added. "Want some?"

"Of course. I see you have a shield around all of them so they won't escape or hear us," he added, sounding relieved.

"That shield will remain up, too, as long as they're in custody. I've already gotten information from Laddus, and I'll go about emptying all his compounds and seizing his assets after I finish eating."

"Gavril should be more than pleased—that should add to his coffers nicely," my father grinned. "Nice work, son."

"How did the meeting go?" I asked as he began filling a plate at the kitchen counter.

"As you suspected—nothing was revealed that they didn't already know. You were wise to spend the time in a more productive and satisfying way."

"Will you write your thoughts on a comp-vid to add to the record?"

"Of course. I can do that while keeping an eye on our guests."

"Well, they can't escape. Even if they do, there's nothing here that will enable them to leave the planet, except us."

"True enough. Chicken is delicious."

"Thank you."

*BlackWing IX*
  *Cassie*
"I'm doing better today," Barry told us. He'd sat at my table during

breakfast; Beverly had joined us to have coffee, since she'd already eaten. "I did have a thought, though," he added.

He wore an expression of grim determination; he'd carefully considered what he was about to say.

"What is it, hon?" Beverly asked him.

"What if one of the satellite computers at Media Solstice was in communication with the main comp at the moment of destruction? It's reasonable to think that, and, well, maybe I can get something from that comp about the purpose behind the destruction."

"Maybe we should ask Jett if we can follow-up on that," I agreed. "It's worth looking into."

"If I'm given permission to link with Media Solstice's other comps, I'd like Star and Annie to connect with me when I try this. Once I'm connected to one comp, Star and Annie can pull the others in, too, so I can communicate with all of them at once."

"That sounds amazing," I breathed. "I'd be interested just to see that part of it work."

"Will you present it to Jett? I'll answer questions if he has any, to the best of my ability."

"Of course. In fact, I may ask to have a meeting with Jett and Randl. I can't imagine that they won't be interested in finding out if linking all these comps together and talking to all of them at once is feasible."

"Are you sure this won't overload your mind?" Beverly asked gently.

"I think I can handle it—with Star and Annie's help."

"We can monitor the situation—Randl can probably disconnect you if you appear overwhelmed," I suggested.

"I'd prefer that," Barry said. "And that you and Beverly be with us, too, when we try it."

"We'll be there," Beverly promised. "If Jett and Randl agree to this."

～

*BlackWing XIII*

*Randl*

"He thinks he can connect with all the satellite comps?" I asked.

"With Star and Annie's help." Jett sounded unconvinced as he and I conversed in his Captain's cubby. "There could be a huge downside in this," he added. "Especially if we risk those lives—or their identities—for absolutely no reason. There's always the possibility that this is another trap laid by the Prophet, to draw us in."

"True enough, and I agree with you—plus the likelihood of finding the information we seek is infinitesimal. We already know the Prophet is behind this—why risk lives over the smallest possibility of finding a reason?"

"Then the answer is no," Jett nodded.

"No for now," I qualified my answer. "I don't want to risk lives in something that hasn't been attempted before, especially if the Prophet hopes to destroy us this way."

"I'll tell them that. I hope they understand."

~

*Cassie*

"Barry, I still think it's a good idea, but Jett and Randl worry that the Prophet could be laying a trap for us. They don't want to risk lives over something that may or may not help us."

"I understand that they could think that—they have more experience with him than I do," Barry said, although I could tell he was disappointed.

"We'll get to the bottom of this," I told him. He, Beverly and I sat at a small, corner table in the galley, while I told him Jett and Randl's decision.

"I know you'll keep your promise," he lifted downcast eyes to meet mine. "I want to help."

"I know you do, and we'll get this done together," I said. "It just may take a while longer."

"Patience is a virtue?" He surprised me by smiling.

"That's what my Aunt Shelbie always said."

"Destiny talks about Aunt Shelbie now and then. You miss her, don't you?"

"I do. Destiny knows, now, that our father and grandfather were responsible for her death."

"And for the death of your mother," Barry sighed. "It troubles her. At least she has Chet to talk things over with," he added.

He was right—I'd been forced to leave my ginger feline friend with Destiny at Avii Castle—he'd be safer there and could go outside whenever he pleased. I couldn't hold the door to BlackWing IX open while he decided to go in or out.

Chet was also a good listener—I knew that from personal experience.

"We're being sent to Orkos," Denevik strode into the galley and approached our table. "It appears that the Prophet has left some damage behind."

~

*G'margis*

*V'dar*

W'dell cowered as I tossed things about in his cubicle; at the top of my list of criminal kingpins to acquire was one Laddus Giele, who'd hidden himself successfully in Bexis, the capital city of Orkos.

W'dell's records had led me straight to his compound, which was empty by the time I arrived. Moments later, I received the message from W'dell that Laddus had been arrested by the new Director of the CSD.

Laddus' information regarding his slave holdings, compounds and fleet of slaver ships were now in the hands of the CSD. I'd seen images of slaves being freed and taken to shelters, while the slavers under Laddus' control were hauled to lockups.

"Fucking, head-splitting, brain-splattering hells," I cursed and swept W'dell's comp off his desk with an angry expenditure of energy. W'dell reacted by cringing in a corner of his tiny office.

I'd been so angry at finding I'd been beaten to Laddus' empire, I'd leveled his compound in Bexis.

I didn't care whether anyone knew it was me, I was so furious. "Quickly," I barked at W'dell. "What is the second name on the list?"

"I, ah," W'dell sniffled as he crawled toward the damaged comp on the other side of his cubicle.

Of course, the information was on the comp I'd just destroyed. "Fix it and get me the information," I shouted, before folding space to get away from the craven, weeping moron.

*Founder's Palace, Campiaa*

*Teeg San Gerxon*

"Eight ships are now in the secret location, and I've taken the liberty of employing some of the bone dust we recovered to hide them," Griffin reported, laying a memory chip on my desk.

This was information that wouldn't go into the official records. I'd ask Reemagar to send a copy to the Larentii Archives after Griffin left my office. "Well done. I assume the rescued slaves are being cared for?"

"Yes, but it could take a while to reconnect some of them with reality."

"Drugs?"

"In many cases, yes."

"Are there any who would be of help to us—in providing information, that is—if they were healed?"

"Perhaps a handful."

"Get their names and images to me and I'll approach Quin."

"She could be of help," Griffin agreed. "I'll see you get the information right away." He turned to leave.

"Griffin?"

He turned back to me.

"Excellent work," I said. "Thank you."

~

*BlackWing XIII*
    *Randl*

IX and XIII were in orbit around Orkos. Jett had already communicated with Teeg San Gerxon, who'd given permission for us to investigate Laddus Giele's former compound. It made sense in a twisted sort of way; V'dar was probably looking to take Laddus' ships, only to find they'd already been confiscated by the CSD. He'd expressed his displeasure by leveling the place.

"Shall we survey the damage?" I asked. Jett, Cassie, Barry, Denevik, Rob and Vik stood around my desk, waiting for me to take them to the planet's surface.

Travis would fold in with Ocenosek and Cudworth to help us. X was still orbiting Phume, looking for escaped prisoners to return to Evensun while Lissa, Reemagar and Connegar went looking for open gates to block.

"Ready," Jett agreed. He was more familiar with Orkos than anyone else present; it was a member planet of the Campiaan Alliance.

I folded the crew to the pile of rubble that used to be Laddus' home in Bexis.

~

*Cassie*

Denevik and Barry stayed close as we combed our section of Laddus' compound. "Looks like the kitchen," Denevik mumbled as he lifted this piece or that in his glove-covered hands.

He was correct; I pulled a bent, gold-plated silver tray from the mess around me and studied it before setting it down again. It had dried food on it, making me grateful for the thick, forensics gloves I wore.

At least the CSD had gotten all the evidence and the inhabitants out before the Prophet went on the rampage. "Cassie?" Barry's voice had gone breathless.

"Barry?" I jerked my head around so I could see him to my right.

"I, uh," he began.

"I'm coming," I said, wading through rubble to get to his side. Denevik followed, wary and ready to protect both of us, I think.

"These were outlawed," Barry hunkered down to touch what he'd found. Denevik's indrawn breath let me know how serious this actually was.

"A serve-bot," Denevik reached out to pull Barry to his feet. "Barry, we have to turn this over to the CSD—immediately."

"Turn what over?" Randl had folded space to see what we'd discovered. "Oh," was all he said for several seconds.

"Barry, this is important," Randl said. "I'll get a carry-bot down here. Make sure you collect every piece of this serve-bot you can find and place it in the carry-bot. I want you to see what you can do with this—enough to communicate with it, anyway. Once you have all the pieces, Denevik will transport you back to the ship so you can go to work."

Barry's eyes widened in surprise, before he nodded eagerly. In moments, the carry-bot arrived; Denevik and I helped Barry place the largest pieces into the carry-bot and then went searching for every scrap that belonged with them.

"This was an interesting implosion," Denevik muttered as we combed through debris for more pieces. "You see that none of the rubble goes past the original outline of the compound itself?"

"I saw the hole the Prophet dug on another planet," I responded. "I think he has OCD."

"I think I agree with you," Barry carefully placed a few twisted wires inside the box. "All of the parts and pieces are within a seven-foot radius. A normal explosion wouldn't have been this neat."

"So, even when he's pissed, his OCD has control?" Denevik asked.

"Looks that way."

"Weird."

"You think Laddus had more of these?" I asked Barry.

"No idea. I hope Randl asked everyone else to look for some."

"All of them were outlawed centuries ago and gradually phased out of existence, so this one may be a fluke," Denevik said.

"Phased out of existence?" I asked.

"Nobody could legally manufacture them, or their replacement parts. Once they wore out and their carbon nanotube microprocessors died, they were disassembled and the parts destroyed."

"And now that technology has been replaced, as of two centuries ago," Barry said. "Nobody can fix this unless they create each individual part by hand."

"Then you've got your work cut out for you," I told him.

"I look forward to it," he replied. "I think we have everything that hasn't been pulverized," he told Denevik. "Will you take me back to the ship?"

"Absolutely. I'll be back to help," Denevik grinned at me before he *skipped* Barry and the carry-bot away.

I continued my search for anything important when I touched a sliver of marble tile. Even through the glove I felt it—and shuddered. It was the same feeling I'd gotten from the ground surrounding the square hole the Prophet created. *Before* I'd cleansed the ground of his taint.

*Randl*, I sent. *I think he stood here.*

Randl didn't need to ask who I meant. He was beside me in less than a blink. "Yes," he steered me away from the marble shard. "His stink is especially dense there."

"Do you think the serve-bot tried to stop him?" I asked. Randl's expression was grim but gave nothing away.

"I hope Barry can tell us that," he replied. "It's why we're breaking the law by attempting to put that bot back together temporarily. It may have images and information we need. One of Sabrina's machines can create the parts Barry will need for it, and the sooner, the better."

*He's more than powerful, isn't he—the Prophet, I mean?* I sent to Randl. I was afraid to say those words aloud for some reason.

*Terrifyingly so, now that he's stuffed himself with rogue gods and consumed their power and abilities. We may be fighting a losing war, here.*

*Then we'll go down fighting,* I said. *Better that than living under his thumb until he decides to kill us all.*

*You know about that, don't you?*

*I do. My father sold me to one of the worst demons ever; one who intended to use me for his own gain. I decided to take myself out of that equation. Barry and his family did the same—they were under someone else's thumb when they decided to break free. They'd had enough of blind slavery and chose to rebel, even if they died in the attempt.*

"Bravery comes in many forms, and often at the most unexpected times," Randl sighed aloud. "I think we've found what we came here for. If San Gerxon asks, will you cleanse this ground?"

"I'd be happy to get the slimy feel of it off the planet," I agreed.

"It does have that feel, doesn't it?"

"It does."

"If he wants the clutter moved elsewhere, I can do that," Randl turned his face into the breeze that blew across the compound, moaning its way around the tallest piles of wreckage. Above us, gray clouds roiled, predicting rain.

"Weather's changing," Rob approached. "The ground has a bad feel to it—as if it's filled with hate. If the rain hits, do you suppose it will leach into surrounding areas?"

"We have to move now, whether San Gerxon wants it or not," Randl hissed. "Rob, get the others away. I have to figure out how to handle this mess."

～

*Randl*

*The sprite is correct,* Bennall's terrified voice spoke to me. *Orkos is screaming at me now—we've somehow wakened whatever the Prophet planted here. V'dar wants revenge against those responsible for taking what he wanted for himself.*

*It's a trap*, I sent to those who hadn't left already. *Get out. Cassie and I will deal with this.* Raindrops hit me in the face as Vik, Ocenosek and Cudworth disappeared last. In a frenzy, I lifted all the rubble away from the site to allow Cassie clear access to the ground beneath our feet.

"Hurry, Cassie," I shouted at her as the rain became a roaring downpour.

"Get away," she shouted back, her dark hair already hanging in strings around her face.

If I hadn't covered myself with the strongest shield I could conjure, she may have singed me with the power of her conflagration.

∽

*Cassie*

Aunt Shelbie would have said I looked like a drowned rat when I set foot on BlackWing IX after cleansing the ground beneath Laddus' compound for nearly an hour. I'd walked away from it dry because of my heat, but once I passed the perimeter, the rain hit me.

Actually, it felt good at first, as the drops hissed and spit from the radiating heat. I'd been so hot after the cleansing, I think I could have melted the metal walls of the ship just by being close to them. I stood in the rain for twenty minutes, while it cooled and then soaked me to the skin.

At least Randl had provided boots and clothing for me after I finished my task. Now, I was wet, tired and hungry. My boots squelched as I strode down the passageway to my cabin, thinking only about a shower, something to drink and a meal afterward, followed by a protracted sleep period.

"Avilepha? Are you all right?" Denevik rose from the side of my bunk as I swung the door open.

"I'm fine," I said. "Just tired, hungry and drenched."

"That may well be," he agreed as he approached, before lifting my chin with a gentle finger. "But I have been here, fretting, for more than an hour. *I* need a hug."

"You'll get wet," was muffled into his shirt, as he folded me in his arms.

"Shhh," he murmured against my hair. "One does not interrupt the hug."

One did not interrupt the hug, which continued until I was nearly asleep in his arms. I was then led to the shower, while he left me alone to undress and stand in vaguely warm water. When I came out of the bathroom later, wearing a robe, Denevik and a tray with two plates of food waited.

"How did it go?" he asked as I settled on a chair to eat.

"I think it's all gone, now—whatever the hell the Prophet did to the compound," I said, slathering butter on a roll. "I wonder if he'll notice."

"Where the Prophet is concerned, I have no advice or absolutes to offer. He changes tactics with the wind, at times."

"He sure was pissed about this—the longer I stood there, the worse it felt to me. I think Randl was about to blow the entire place, just to get rid of the waves of hate coming off all of it. Rob was about to have a cow."

"A cow, you say?" I watched as a slight smile formed on his lips.

"Well, you know what I mean."

"Becoming quite upset?" He was now grinning as he cut into his rare steak.

"That's much too mild to equate with having a cow and fails to relay the true force of Rob's impending projectile vomiting-slash-meltdown-slash-hissy fit."

"Aren't you exaggerating?" He grinned before stuffing a chunk of steak in his mouth.

"Maybe a little." I cut into my own steak. It was medium-rare and perfect. Beverly knew exactly how to prepare it for me. *Steak is delicious*, I sent to her. *Thank you.*

*I heard you needed the protein*, she replied. *Enjoy.*

"How's your steak?" Denevik asked.

"Perfect. I already thanked Beverly. Were you the one who ordered it for me?"

"I may have been involved."

"Thank you. It's just what I needed."

"Randl says he wants a meeting after you sleep. He's pulling in some of the other captains and crews to discuss recent events."

"All right. How's Barry doing?"

"We have one of Sabrina's parts printers on board now, and he's having fun remaking that serve-bot. I'm sure we'll have a functioning bot when he's finished, but it's all in what remains of its memory, I think. If the memory was damaged or wiped, we may be no better off."

"If the bot is useless to us, tell them under no circumstances are they to deactivate or destroy it. He gets emotionally involved with the machines he works with, and this one will be no different."

"I'll pass that along. Eat your food before it gets cold."

～

*Unnamed Dwarf Planet*

*Griffin*

"I used some of the bone dust found at Laddus' compound to hide him and his minions from other criminal factions—in case they get the urge to either kill or rescue him," I told my father as we ate dinner together. "Teeg and a handful of others know where they are, and that will do until they come to trial."

"Who's next on your list—the current most-wanted?"

"Actually, it's number four on the list," I shrugged. "I think I can find her easily enough, while I'm sending out feelers for two and three. Teeg allowed Randl to move the debris that was left of Laddus' compound elsewhere."

"Debris?"

"Did I forget to tell you that the Prophet, for some reason, disliked my taking of Laddus and destroyed the whole thing? Since the Prophet was involved in the destruction, Teeg allowed Randl and his pirates to take a look. Evidently, he found the debris dangerous and sent the whole mess someplace safe, before using a spell to scorch the ground."

"You think the Prophet left some of his disease behind?"

"I suppose it's possible, although I didn't think fire would so easily destroy it."

"Will you quarantine the area, then, just to make sure?"

"Already done," I said.

"These rolls are delicious," Wylend complimented my baking skills. "When are you planning to take down number four?"

"Probably in two days, if things fall into place and I locate her new hideaway. Laddus' capture sent her flying, so to speak."

"Ah. She worries that someone could find her through him?"

"Most likely." I couldn't hold my grin back. My father barked a laugh at my amusement.

## CHAPTER 8

*G* *'Margis*
*V'dar*

"Geeva's residence is empty," Alken set a comp-vid on my desk. "It appears she took ship after learning about the destruction of Laddus' main residence. Gillen and I recorded images of all her belongings—if there is anything you wish to take, we will retrieve it for you."

"Did this comp-vid come from there? Were there any comps or comp-vids left behind?"

"No, my lord. We searched, both with spells and our eyes. She was very thorough and took her servants with her."

"Then we must find her before the CSD bastards do," I hissed at my chief warlock. "Her information was the only useful piece gained from Laddus' serve-bot before I destroyed it and the compound. I have no idea why it wasn't taken by the CSD—the other useful items were cleaned out."

"Perhaps it hid from them?" Alken suggested.

"It's possible, I suppose. It did cringe away from me when I discovered it. Destroy Geeva's place," I handed the comp-vid back to the warlock. "We'll find her and her ship and take both."

"Of course, my lord." Alken shoved the comp-vid in a pocket and walked out of my study.

After Alken left, I considered my goals and what—or who—was preventing me from reaching them. Randl Gage and the CSD were now my biggest enemies. Across both Alliances, I had thousands upon thousands of graveyards, cemeteries and catacombs under my control, waiting for me to set a suitable command system in place before the real takeover began.

My anger became so hot at the obstacles set before me, I blasted a perfectly round hole in the side of a nearby wall, sending minions scattering throughout my compound's tunnels.

*Gillen Wilker*

"He said to destroy it?" Qatti thumbed through images of expensive furniture and baubles Geeva had collected.

*And we will,* Alken informed us in mindspeech. *But not before we take what we want for ourselves.*

*Where will we hide it?* Qatti asked as she mentally made notes of everything she wanted.

*I have a few ideas,* Alken replied. *Tag everything you want and we'll take it for you.*

*I want it all,* Qatti replied instantly.

I wasn't surprised in the least by her answer. *Easy enough to do,* Alken agreed with her. *I'll bring you a small bauble when we return. Will that do?*

*For now,* Qatti smiled at him.

*Where will we drop what we're taking?* I sent only to Alken.

*E'margis,* he answered, giving me the name of the third planet beyond F'margis. While F'margis was volcanic in nature and too volatile to accommodate anyone or anything, E'margis was once inhabited and then destroyed by those same inhabitants. We'd have to cover everything left there with protections spells to keep the poisoned air away from it—and from ourselves.

*Good idea*, I told Alken. *Let's get going.*

"We'll be back," Alken told Qatti. "Soon."

*Founder's Palace, Campiaa*

*Wyatt*

"Not only was the compound destroyed on Vebellix II, but damage was done to adjoining properties," Dad told Griffin and me.

"Then the Prophet didn't destroy this one. Could be his minions again, though."

"The same ones responsible for Media Solstice?"

"That would be my guess. They weren't neat there, either. Laddus' compound, on the other hand, was so neatly leveled you could have laser cut the outline."

"I've ah, heard he's OCD about everything he does," I agreed.

"Was there anything important left behind to indicate who the compound belonged to?" Dad's eyebrows drew together in a frown.

"I believe it belonged to Geeva M'ramel," Griffin said. "I found only evidence that the walls were destroyed, nothing else. No bits and pieces of furniture or other belongings."

"Was it empty before the Wilkers brought it down?" I asked.

"I doubt it," Griffin turned toward me. "I believe the Wilkers are now putting their own wealth together. Geeva was notorious for admiring expensive things. As this was probably her main residence, she may have had many priceless items inside it."

"All stolen goods, no doubt," Dad grumped.

"No way to tell, now, unless we find the Wilker's stash." Griffin turned back to Dad, leaving me to breathe a soft sigh of relief. I hated when he leveled that consuming gaze on me, as if he were stripping me bare of my every thought.

"Where do you suppose Geeva is now?" Dad asked.

"Flying through the stars if she's smart," Griffin shrugged. "Don't worry, I'll find her."

"I'll leave you to it, then. I have meetings this afternoon."

"I'll keep you apprised," Griffin said and folded away.

*BlackWing XIII*
*Randl*

"What now?" I gave Zanfield a wary look as he held out a comp-vid. His expression relayed a mild level of disgust. That, combined with lime-green hair, wasn't the best look I'd seen him wear.

"You're being blamed for destroying Laddus' compound, and for confiscating his ships and holdings," Zanfield replied as I read almost the same thing from headlines released by a second-tier news agency. "They're saying the CSD is taking credit, when there's no proof they had any part in it."

"These images were taken before Cassie cleansed the grounds," I said, flipping through the article.

"Exactly. Do you suppose this will give other criminals a heads up, and force them to hunt us rather than tending to their own illegal activities?"

"It's possible, I suppose. Here's my question—this is a Reth Alliance news agency. Where did the information come from? Are they inclined to report on pure speculation?"

"I've looked through the records—nothing like that has been released before. They're trying to crack first-tier status, and printing lies or suppositions won't support such a move."

"Do you think the Prophet may be behind it?"

"No idea."

"Damn." I leaned back in my chair. "If it's not one thing, it's another. Ask Vik to come see me. We need to discuss this before the big meeting takes place in two hours."

"I'll send him in." Zanfield left the comp-vid with me and strode out of my study to search for Vik.

Ten minutes later, Vik sauntered in. "You rang?"

"I rang," I confirmed. "How do you feel about a split-time visit?"

"Well, if it's necessary," he agreed.

"Good. We'll do it after the big meeting and we've both had some sleep."

"Because it's better to face potential Armageddon fully rested," he nodded.

"Exactly."

~

*G'margis*

*V'dar*

"Is Gage planting this information?" I shouted. "Taking credit for what I've done?" I flung the comp-vid across my office, where it smashed against a wall. "If I find that he took those ships from under my nose, I'll torture him until the end of time."

Gillen and Je'Dik witnessed my anger, but Gillen was the only one to duck when I threw the comp-vid. Je'Dik, in his usual animal-hide garb and goggles, didn't even breathe harder at my anger.

That made my anger hotter. He *should* be afraid of me. "Je'Dik," I snapped at him. "Randl Gage is your next target for assassination. Take whomever you want to accomplish this."

"I'll have to find him, first," Je'Dik sniffed. "But I'll take Gillen, here."

"No. I need Gillen. Take Alken."

"Fine. I'll take Alken, but tell him to mind his manners."

"I'll make sure of it," I said. "Go. Get the warlock and hunt this nuisance down. Start with Laddus' compound. Perhaps he'll have left something behind for Alken to track."

"I'll see to it." Je'Dik turned swiftly and stalked out of my office.

After dismissing Gillen while I stewed over destroying this news source, I sent a message to W'dell on my spare comp-vid to get the status on the rebuilding of his desk comp. I had criminals to find—and their armies, wealth and ships to take.

*Nearly finished*, W'dell replied quickly. *You'll have the information by the end of the day.*

*Good. Send me everything you find on Geeva.*

*Yes, my lord.*

"There is a problem," Je'Dik and Alken were back, landing in my office uninvited.

"What problem is that?"

"This." Je'Dik carefully set a container of dirt on my desk.

"What in the name of all hells is this?" I demanded.

"The scorched ground left behind at the site of Laddus' compound."

"If you're lying, I'll cut you into strips," I declared, touching the dirt carefully. "There is absolutely nothing in this dirt," I shouted at Je'Dik. "Not even bacteria. *All* dirt has something in it."

"Here are the images," Alken held out a comp-vid with shaking fingers. I glared as I thumbed through time-and-location-stamped recordings. There was no doubt this was Laddus' compound— except something had destroyed the virulent disease I'd left in the soil to attack unsuspecting encroachers. I was hoping to attack the CSD and infect every last one of them. Afterward, they'd belong to *me*.

"Find Randl Gage and murder him," I screeched. "Do I have to do every fucking thing myself?"

*BlackWing XIII*

*Randl*

"I think the Prophet was aiming to infect any CSD agents who came to investigate the site after he destroyed it," I announced to the crowd seated in the ship's dining hall. "It would certainly be a coup for him to have moles in the CSD. They could feed information to him, and he could collect seized ships and other assets—he's gone after those things before."

"Why does he want ships? Can't he fold space?" Ocenosek asked.

"He can, but most of his minions can't. They get from place to place in more mundane ways, and they can transport people, carry containers of used concrete and other things that have been infected with Prophet's disease. Since the disease is undetectable to normal scans, the recipients believe they're getting legitimate shipments, when nothing could be further from the truth."

"We've thwarted the Prophet on several occasions in his search for ships belonging to criminals. We've even kept him from building more ships with parts and pieces, by policing all the salvage yards," Vik explained. "Once we discovered that's what he was doing."

"This means he's going after the ships that criminals own again? Like he did with the Big Three?" David asked.

"It looks that way. The Big Three had huge fleets and were easy targets for him. He took their ships and attacked Campiaa. Fortunately, we got wind of the attack in time to counter his stolen ships with those belonging to the CSD and ASD."

"We believe that ramped up the sale of available bone dust," Dori took up the tale. "Every criminal anywhere was crazy to buy the stuff no matter the cost, just to keep the Prophet away from them. D'slay may have sold his stash from Old Earth, but we feel the Prophet already has a line on those criminals. Many have dropped off the grid, in more ways than one. Since the Prophet and D'slay were connected, the Prophet has already gotten his claws in all of those. What he doesn't have are the names and locations of the ones who'd bought bone dust while it was still the main export on Paricos II."

"Then he only has an army of petty thieves and smaller criminals," Rajeon said. "He wants bigger fish, now, and somehow managed to find Laddus—only to discover that the CSD got there first."

"And now he's pissed," I agreed. "If we don't see a bigger target painted on the BlackWing Pirates, and a much larger reward for any of us, dead or alive, I'll be very surprised. After all, I'm sure V'dar's gotten the same news release we have—falsely claiming that it was us, rather than the CSD, who took Laddus out."

"That doesn't sound good," Sabrina shook her head. Travis rubbed her back absently.

"It isn't good," I told her. "The news released by Media Solstice had some of our descriptions included in it. I don't want anyone going anywhere unless they're heavily shielded, all right? Those who can't provide a shield for themselves should be with someone who can."

Murmurs of assent traveled through the dining hall.

"What are we going to do about all this?" Travis asked.

"We'll go hunting criminals, just as the Prophet is doing. I'll ask Sabrina to compile a list of petty criminals who've dropped off the grid. They're probably still out there, somewhere, either causing trouble at the Prophet's command, or waiting to cause trouble. I'm putting Mae, Lev and Miz in charge of searching for the criminals on the Alliances' most-wanted lists. They'll work from Sirena, of course."

"What will we do with the Prophet's petty criminals if we find them?" Zanfield asked.

"I'm glad you asked that," I said. "We'll deal with this on a case-by-case basis. If we're forced to kill them, then the problem is solved. If captured, we have a holding facility on Sirena, now, where the Prophet's commands shouldn't reach them."

"Has anyone picked up any sign of the Prophet? Other than Alken and Gillen Wilker destroying Media Solstice, and the destruction of Laddus' compound? Have we found anything else on Phume?" Nari spoke, but Tiri, sitting next to her twin sister, was nodding emphatically. Jett, who sat adjacent to Nari, waited for me to answer her question.

"We've apprehended two escapees from Evensun on Phume, but there are probably others. We're still investigating possible sightings," Travis answered part of Nari's question. "Mom and Connegar have closed the opened gates on Evensun, after getting a map of locations from Rabis. They're keeping an eye on the situation, too, in case any others pop open."

"There's no evidence that the Prophet was on Phume or Evensun," I said. "His stink was all over Laddus' compound, though."

"I thought I was going to be sick, it was so bad," Rob offered. "I had to clear away debris before I could test the soil, but once that was done, I didn't even get my toes all the way in the dirt before it affected me."

"At least it's clear of that now," I said, dipping my head in Cassie's direction. "If the Prophet has learned of it, I'm sure that added fuel to the fire of his anger."

"Will he take hostages? To force our hand?" Rajeon asked.

"He's tried that—but there's no reason he won't do it again."

"Then we need to get in front of that," Cassie stated.

"What do you mean?" I said.

"We need to let him know, in some way and in no uncertain terms, that we don't *care* if he takes hostages. Let him know that he can burn down an entire planet if he wants to. We're pirates. Why should we care?"

There were gasps around the room, but I blinked in understanding. "He has to think we're in this for ourselves," I nodded slowly. "And that we're determined to be the alpha bad guys in the Alliances; that we intend to beat him at his own game and win the race to control everything, plus all the slaves and booty he wants for himself."

"Fuck the god who always comes at the end," Vik rose from his chair and lifted a fist. "The Formidables are number one."

*Yes!* Bennall whispered into my mind. *We draw him in, rather than the other way around. We will choose the battlefield—and the advantage will be ours.*

*This means we need a new base of operations,* Jett sent.

*An inhospitable planet will be best,* I replied. *Where we can set traps and build defenses.*

*I'll check our options.*

*Bring a list tomorrow, if you can. We'll put it to a vote. In the meantime, I need to have a word with Zaria.*

*About bone dust?*

*Got it in one.*

~

*Queen's Palace, Le-Ath Veronis*

*Lissa*

"You don't need bone dust," Zaria explained to Randl. "You have volunteer Sirenali, who are ready to take up the cause."

I'd set up the meeting for Randl, and invited Zaria to have tea with us. The idea he'd brought to us was a sound one, but Zaria had suggestions of her own. "You mean the Sirenali saved from Paricos II before its destruction?" Randl lifted his cup to drink.

"Those are the ones," Zaria replied. "Although I've handpicked some from the dozens of volunteers. They're trustworthy and fully dedicated to the cause, believe me."

"I would be too, if I were born sickly and left to die so somebody could grind my bones up to put in their fucking walls," I said. "They're more than grateful to Quin and Zaria for their healing and subsequent care and education."

"All of them communicate by mindspeech," Zaria went on. "When you choose the moon or planet to set up your base, Valegar and I will be happy to construct it to your specifications. We'll bring your new recruits when it's finished. They're trained to help in engineering, communications and other areas. They'll have medallions when they arrive, too."

"Sounds good. I'll look into putting a stockpile of food together," Randl nodded.

"I'll help with that," I said. "Zaria can transport it when we're done —Roff will be more than happy to help. If there are special requests, just send a message."

"I'll ask Beverly and Susan to handle that," Randl agreed. "How long will this take? I need to get back to the ship; Vik and I have a jaunt planned. Then, we'll put another meeting together to work out our plan of becoming the biggest alpha criminal in all the universes, and then taunt the Prophet with it. He's already pissed; we'll merely rub salt in his wounds."

"Do you have an idea on how to track all the criminals that bought bone dust from D'slay?" I asked.

"I have some ideas. I also have someone on IX who is adept at communicating with comps and comp-vids. We may be able to find them easier than the Prophet believes and can work on getting rid of them and taking anything the Prophet hasn't already purloined."

"Make a big deal of destroying what's left," I suggested. "Since he started that trend."

"Good idea. Thanks. I should get back, now."

"Take care on your jaunt," Zaria told him as he rose and stretched.

"Oh, don't worry," Randl gave her a tired smile. "We'll be more than careful."

~

*BlackWing XIII*
*Randl*

"Don't disturb me unless something important is blown up," I yawned as I spoke to Dori. She was better rested and preparing for a stint on the bridge while I was getting ready to sleep for a while.

"I'll make sure of it," she leaned in for a quick kiss.

"I love you," I mumbled as she drew away and smiled.

"I know. I love you, too. Happy dreams." She walked out of our suite and shut the door behind her.

Flopping face-first on the bed sounded like an excellent idea. Instead, I crawled in properly, repositioned my pillow several times and then convinced my mind to shut down so I could sleep.

~

*BlackWing IX*
*Cassie*

Zanfield, Perri and Jincus came back to IX with Denevik and me. They wanted to see the serve-bot Barry was rebuilding.

"It's almost ready," Barry said as he stood beside the serve-bot. "I haven't tried to turn the power on—I'm still checking the memory circuits and I don't want anything to blow because I was too hasty."

The serve-bot resembled a young man, actually, and could easily be mistaken for the real thing except for the opening at the back of the head, where Barry was still working.

"Human hair," Perri nodded after studying the bot for a while. "Synthetic skin—they use the same thing for burn victims."

"My parents talked about one my grandfather had long ago,"

Zanfield said. "Her name was Pelia. According to the story, Grandfather really liked her. *Way* too much."

"Too much information," Perri bumped her shoulder against Zanfield's.

Jincus walked around the bot, however, studying it closely. "Bits and pieces would sometimes show up at the salvage yard, but not nearly enough to put together. Nobody ever wanted that stuff, so it was destroyed after a while. Never thought I'd see a whole one."

"Will he have a name?" I asked Barry.

"If his memory works, we'll find out."

"When will we know if it works?"

"Probably tomorrow. I've got a few things to do before I go off rotation. Besides, it's time for dinner and Beverly made gumbo for the soup course. There's fried laka fish for dinner."

"Gumbo?" Jincus hadn't heard of it.

"Stay for dinner; I think you'll like it," I said.

"Laka fish is close enough to catfish," I explained as Denevik, Barry and I ate dinner with Zanfield, Perri and Jincus. "Beverly always knows the exact amount of cornmeal to use to make it crisp and tasty."

"Catfish? Do they look like cats?" Jincus was curious.

"They have whiskers," I gestured to imitate whiskers on each side of my face. "Otherwise, no resemblance to any cat I know."

"I loved catfish," Barry sighed. "We didn't get it often. It was always dried meat or something out of a can."

"Barry, that's behind you," I rubbed his back. "You're having laka fish with friends, now."

"And I have a mom, who cooks the fish for me." He cut another piece of fried fish and stuffed it in his mouth with a happy grin.

"Will you send updates on the serve-bot?" Jincus asked him. "We probably won't get to come back for a while to see it here."

"Sure," Barry agreed. "In real time, if you want."

"Any ideas on where our new base will be?" Zanfield asked, changing the subject.

"Someplace easy to hide," Denevik said. "I'll be interested in how many people Randl will send there, and how big it will be."

"It will be as big as we need it to be," Perri offered. "Especially if Zaria lends a hand. She rebuilt Sirena."

"That means she had to put the planet back together," Denevik lifted his glass of wine in a toast to Perri. "It was destroyed, long ago. And, as the planet is now exactly as it was before its destruction, she had to pull every atom of it together again."

"How do you know this?" I asked.

"Corez told me. She knows."

I didn't know much about the spirit coins; only that they represented entire planets. The soul of the hub world, Corez, was fused to Denevik's chest. Apparently, she spoke to him at times.

"Who holds the soul of Sirena, then?" I asked.

"Randl," Denevik replied. "Corez says she is quiet, having come back to herself not that long ago. She does speak now and then, but only to Randl and a few other spirits."

"Have you been in contact with the Queen of Corez?" Zanfield asked, feigning idle curiosity.

"Twice. Both times it was to warn her that someone was dumping poison into two mountain lakes. Both lakes provide water for villages farther down. Action has been taken."

"What kind of poison?" I asked.

"A low-level radioactive waste dumping was the verdict, although the perpetrator was never caught. It could have been dumped by slaves of the Prophet before getting away from Corez, after we fought against him last time."

"Has anyone else reported that kind of thing?" Perri asked. "Larentii can neutralize that filth, but they seldom interfere like that."

"If someone fixes every wrong and every mistake, no lesson will be learned," Denevik said. "There will be no incentive to care for anything Corez and her sisters and brothers give to all of us, if we believe that someone will clean up after us every time. We must take responsibility for our actions—and our mistakes. Besides, Larentii are the gatherers and keepers of the records. We cannot ask them to turn away from their work to help us every time we do something foolish."

"To the caretakers," Zanfield held up his glass.

"I'll drink to that," I said, and lifted mine in response.

~

*BlackWing XIII*
*Randl*

"Ready for split-time?" I asked Vik as he walked into my office and shut the door.

"As ready as I'll ever be," he shrugged. "Where are we going again?"

"We're going to visit a certain second-tier news agency, that's where."

"And it'll be right before their big release of blame for the BlackWing Pirates, I take it?"

Rather than a verbal answer, I tapped my nose.

"I think I'm looking forward to this," Vik grinned. "Almost."

*Bennall?* I sent.

*Ready.*

"Let's go."

~

The edges of my vision shimmered as Vik and I walked through a news agency's offices where time had come to a standstill. With Miz's help, I'd pinpointed the exact moment the speculative news was released by Media Gem, on Wroope. Vik and I arrived in split-time only a few moments before the news was sent out.

Intending to check every office from the head of the company on down, we stalked through the top floor, searching for Media Gem's President's office.

"This looks promising," Vik turned to the right, passing through an open door where a man sat behind a very large, antique wood desk, while three others stood before him. His mouth was open—he'd been speaking to his underlings when we interrupted.

*Release the time slowly, to hear what he has to say*, Bennall suggested.

*On it*, I replied.

Salidar Deluca, who taught me how to fight with blades and hands, would have likened what I did to letting the air out of a tire slowly. I recalled that he'd explained the expression to me, as I wasn't familiar with tires made of rubber that had air in them—or tires in general.

"Go—with—the—flooding—story—in—the—north," the President said. "It's—more—important—to—get—the—word—out—to—surrounding—areas," he added. His underlings began a slow turn.

And then things stopped dead still. Nothing I did forced the time forward again, for fifteen seconds. Everything remained frozen.

And then—he spoke again, as if his previous statement had been wiped away like dust from a table. "Make—sure—to—give—credit—for—destroying—Laddus'—compound—to—those—BlackWing—Pirate—scum."

"What the actual flying-on-a-broomstick-with-a-black-cat fuck?" Vik turned wide eyes in my direction.

"I have no idea," I breathed. "Let's get out of here. This is giving me the willies."

"What the hell?" Vik exploded when we landed in my study aboard BlackWing XIII. "It's like something was inserted in his head, and we missed the first part of it. Can the Prophet do that?"

"I felt absolutely nothing connected to the Prophet in all that," I complained. "If he can do this now and leave no evidence behind, we are really screwed."

"But you knew he went to Laddus' compound," Vik pointed out. "He didn't bother to hide that from you. Why would he try to hide this? Don't you think he'd want you to know he's behind this, too?"

"Well, that makes sense, I suppose."

"I don't think your Prophet detection is on the fritz. Maybe someone or something else is playing with us instead."

"But who or what?"

"No idea. You got absolutely no feeling in any of that—who could be responsible?"

"None. There was nothing for a while, and then invisible gears shifted and we didn't even see it."

"I hope the rogue gods he's swallowed haven't taught him new tricks," Vik shook his head.

"Damn. Them again. I suppose it's possible. I do hope that's not the case."

*Commander?* Zanfield sent.

*Zanfield?*

*Oh, good, you're back. Barry on IX says the serve-bot is functional, if you'd like to ask questions. He does say the memory is spotty, however.*

*Thanks, Zan. I'll check it out soon.*

"The serve-bot is working, but the memory may be damaged," I told Vik. "Want a beer before we visit IX?"

"Maybe two or three," Vik replied. "High Demons have a higher alcohol tolerance, and now *I* have the willies."

# CHAPTER 9

*G'margis*
*V'dar*

*We have located Geeva's ship, B'alus, my chief rogue,* informed me. *Shall we order Gillen to take it, or do you wish to do so yourself?*

*Show me,* I insisted.

The vision appeared in my mind; I saw the ship, flying through the stars at a very rapid pace. *It is in real time, as your saying is,* B'alus said. *We expended much power to find it, as we could not reach past the vast amount of bone dust carried on board. We were only able to track a single transmission from the ship. The capture must be undertaken soon, or we may lose the vessel again.*

"Then we will take it now," I breathed aloud and gathered my power.

*Only to see the ship disappear from the vision.*

"Where is it?" I shouted. "Where did it go?"

*It has been torn away from us,* B'alus howled. *We cannot track it!*

"Find Randl Gage," I screamed. "He did this to me."

*BlackWing IX*
  *Randl*

"My name is George." The serve-bot would have fooled almost anyone. I could sense the circuits and wiring that formed his synapses, rather than the biological ones in a humanoid brain.

Zaria and Quin would likely know what he was easily enough, too. For everyone else, the movement and speech were seamless and humanoid in every way.

"How are you, George?" I asked.

"I have a cloudy memory," he admitted. "I didn't recognize this place when I woke," he gestured with a hand at Barry's makeshift lab in engineering. "Barry says I'm safe here. Is that true?"

"Why do you ask?" I said.

"Because you're the Commander. And I—am not legal."

"You're safe here," I replied, as George was actually fearful—the vibe came from him in electronic waves. It would take a bit of adjustment, but I imagined I could read George as easily as anyone else after getting used to him.

"Thank you." He rubbed his forehead with a sigh of relief.

*Damn, he may as well be human*, Vik sent.

"Do you remember Laddus?" I asked, ignoring Vik's mindspeech.

"I remember him, yes, but my memory only extends to the past few days—before *he* came."

"Do you recall anything about that one?"

"He was angry. Shouting that Laddus and his wealth were taken away before he could take those things for himself. He kept blaming someone—Randl Gage was the name, for thwarting him in his plans. I don't recall much more—only a bright light and then darkness, until I opened my eyes to find Barry looking at me and asking if I felt all right."

"Will it frighten you if I say that I am Randl Gage?"

"Are you Randl Gage? Should I be frightened? Did you take Laddus and his wealth?"

"I am Randl Gage, you don't have to be afraid and no, I had

nothing to do with Laddus or his wealth. We found you when we came to investigate after the Prophet destroyed Laddus' property."

"Is this true?" George turned toward Barry.

"It's true. I can replay time-stamped recordings if you want of our arrival on the scene after the destruction."

"Perhaps later." George understood that he and his parts had been among the rubble we'd examined. That bothered him a great deal. Like humans, George was afraid of dying—of un-being. The loss of memory troubled him, too, just as it would a humanoid or any other sentient creature.

That's when the realization hit me. George was different. Different didn't mean inconsequential. In this case, it probably didn't mean not alive—at least in some sense. He survived on an alternate fuel source, but then so did Larentii. Larentii were definitely alive.

*And different.*

Fear had likely been behind ridding the Alliances of those like George, because it was either do away with them, or recognize them as a separate race which had achieved sentience.

"Let my people go," I whispered.

Serve-bots had awakened into slavery, and they'd been kept there until they'd been outlawed—because they'd finally understood pain, fear, and eternal servitude.

"What does that mean?" George was now curious, as he'd heard my statement.

"Barry, do you have room for an assistant?" I asked.

"I could use another hand," Barry admitted.

"George, would you like to work with Barry—until you decide what it is you'd really like to do aboard ship?"

"You'd allow it?"

"I will. Understand, though, that you'll be expected to follow the rules, just like anyone else. Barry will let you know about those things. Also, if you remember anything else about Laddus and your time with him—or any other information about the Prophet, I'd appreciate it if you let me know."

"I'll do that. Thank you, Commander."

"You're welcome, Ensign. Barry, put George on the payroll, and find him a uniform." *Cassie, I'd like a meeting with you, Rajeon, Denevik and Jett in an hour. In my office.*

~

"Is this about George?" Cassie asked when everyone arrived, including Travis and Trent. She was concerned, not just about George, but Barry, too.

"No—while I live, George will be safe," I replied. "We're pirates, remember? It's our job to flaunt the law. This is about our base, and a planet we've found that may be suitable," I said. "And I'd like everyone here to see what Vik and I did when we went into split-time to Media Gem on Wroope."

"You went to check on how they got the information—the *wrong* information—about Laddus' compound?" Travis asked.

"We did." Vik, his head down and arms crossed, leaned against the wall to my left. He'd ducked his head to hide the grim slash of his mouth and dark eyebrows drawn together in frustrated confusion. David, stoic as ever, stood in solidarity beside his friend. I considered ordering a round of beer, but decided against it.

"I'll form a three-dimensional image and play it back exactly as we saw it," I said, rising from my desk chair and pushing it back. Moving the desk with power to the back of my office, I cleared the center space for my projection.

I played the entire scenario Vik and I had witnessed at Media Gem to a silent, stunned group inside my office. My shoulders sagged as I terminated the visual images afterward.

"That was like shifting from third to first," Cassie breathed while shaking her head. Vik supplied the mind-spoken explanation—that it involved changing gears on Old Earth automobiles, and in a way that could damage the machinery.

"It's like they didn't even remember what they were discussing only a second before," Travis agreed. "I've never seen anything like that."

"Barry found some evidence of the planting of information at Media Solstice," I said. "It's as if the culprit learned of it and bypassed the comp this time."

"Who could do this—besides someone belonging to the Hierarchy, and a very high-ranking one at that?" Jett frowned.

"I don't think anyone in the Hierarchy had anything to do with this," I said. "I also had no indication of any kind that the Prophet managed it, either. Perhaps one of his rogue gods achieved it, but we can't say that for certain without some kind of evidence. I felt absolutely nothing when it happened."

"What do we do, then?" Rajeon asked. "We can't fight an enemy we can't see or sense."

"I suppose we'll have to wait and see if it happens again," I sighed. I felt defeated in this—like someone had pulled a trick on a child, who had no understanding of how the trick was accomplished. I certainly didn't appreciate being the child in that scenario.

*At all.*

"The second topic of discussion is the planet we've found, that could serve as our base of operation," Jett began.

"Which one?" Travis asked.

"D'Margis," Jett replied. "Every planet in that solar system has problems and is generally deemed uninhabitable. D'Margis is prone to hot, acidic rainfall, a by-product of contamination by the now-extinct population from a thousand years ago. Anything landing on the surface will be corroded in only a few minutes by the moisture in the air, which is also extremely acidic. Plus, the stench is overwhelming, if you attempt to breath the air. If we build bunkers and tunnels beneath the surface and set up a multi-layered air-filtering system, however, we should be fine."

"So, you're saying the whole place stinks?" Dave quipped.

"That's what he's saying," I said. "In other words, anyone would be foolish to set up a compound on D'margis. That's why it's perfect for us."

"Will it be safe enough?" Cassie asked.

"If Zaria and a few Larentii put it together for us, it'll be more than safe."

"Where will we berth our ships? We can't build a space station there," Rajeon pointed out.

"I'm glad you asked that," Jett grinned. "We'll be disguising the ships as we used to do and berth them with the CSD's fleet. They'll be legitimate ships in every way while they're in Campiaan Alliance space."

"So we fold onto Campiaa, take a shuttle to the military space station, fly out of official berthing, and take down our disguise once we hit hyperspace?" Dave asked.

"Exactly," I said. "Wyatt and Teeg will have things set up for us whenever we need a ship."

"Will they be the only ones to know about it?" Cassie asked.

"I'll check on that." She was right to ask—after one run-in with Teeg's new CSD Director, I was reluctant to have any further connection with him or anyone who worked with him.

"I have information on D'margis, for those of you who'd like to read up on the planet before we vote on it," Jett offered.

"If Randl says it's good for us, then I'm on board," Vik said immediately.

"I agree with Randl and stretch, here," Dave pointed upward at Vik.

"Well, then let's rephrase this—is there anyone here who has reservations about D'margis?" Jett asked.

"I have no reservations, but I'd still like to read the information," Cassie said.

"I'll make sure you get it," Jett grinned at her.

"How long will it take to get the underground compound built?" Travis asked.

"Probably not long, if I know Zaria at all," I told him. "I think it will be a matter of a few days, if that long. They already have plans for everything that is needed; the execution is the only thing left to be done. And, with Larentii involved, that can happen in no time at all."

"What do we do in the interim?" Rajeon wanted to know.

"We fly our disguised ships to CSD spaceport outside Campiaa.

You should all be ready to embark in two hours. That will give us time to put all the disguises in place and switch uniforms. While on this journey, we're all officially CSD supply ships and employees."

~

*Founder's Palace, Campiaa*
*Wyatt*

"Are you going to tell Griffin?" I asked Dad.

"Not unless I have to." Dad's mouth was a grim, straight line. "They're coming in as supply ships, returning empty after a routine supply run to a few outposts. They shouldn't draw his attention. I'll only tell him if he demands an answer."

"Because if he goes *Looking*, he'll be blocked by the bone dust Zaria placed aboard all their ships," I finished for him.

"That's right." Dad's mouth curved into a deep frown. "They'll disembark, disperse, then meet at the mountain retreat. Once the compound on D'margis is finished, they'll fold directly there, before beginning the hunt for the criminals under the Prophet's sway."

"They can probably start doing research on that while they're here," I suggested.

"True. If you would, act as liaison with them. Make sure they have everything they need."

"I will. Jayna and I may stay at the cabin, too. It was nice of Zaria to add to it and include an underground section for us."

"Completely off the radar, too," Dad grinned. "It's perfect for getting away for a while, where nobody can find me—except for you and Tybus."

"Jayna loves it," I said. "It's a hideaway when she feels too confined by schedules and plain old, everyday crap."

"They'll start arriving late tonight and continue into tomorrow," Dad said. "You're in charge of all that." He made a shooing gesture with his hand.

"Thanks, Dad," I told him and folded out of his study. I was on my way to tell Jayna that we'd be staying at the mountain retreat with friends very soon.

~

*Luxury Space Cruiser Margreet*

*Korvus Katergáris*

"You're sure that worm won't find me?" Geeva wasn't accustomed to fear; I could hear it in her voice. She'd seen what the Prophet had done to Laddus' compound after he'd been arrested by the CSD.

Then, her ship had shuddered and its engines reached the breaking point when the Prophet latched onto the vessel to pull it from the heavens. I snatched it away, transporting it to safety.

"He won't find you now. You are fortunate that I felt it when his minions located your ship. That's why I moved so quickly—to keep you away from him before he could take you."

"I still can't believe you saved me," she gushed. "Until now, I had no idea you existed, Mr. Katergáris."

"Many are ignorant of my talents—and of my existence," I said.

"Where did you acquire your talents? Am I mistaken in assuming that you are a wizard?"

"That is indeed a part of my heritage, Lady Geeva."

"Then you know of my heritage as well."

"I do. Your father was wrong to deny you a proper title and an inheritance."

"I've done well enough without him. Tell me; how much of what I have will you demand of me for saving my life and that of my crew?"

"I only desire information."

"Information can be worth far more than riches," she said.

"I know it well," I agreed. "Tell me what you know and you will be hidden away while your enemies search for you in vain."

"Enemies? Are there more than one?"

"It is not just the one who leveled Laddus' compound. There is also Randl Gage and his BlackWing Pirates. Already, one or the other has emptied your home and leveled the husk of it to the ground."

"Where will you hide me from these outrageous criminals?" She was quite indignant, forgetting for perhaps a moment that she was also a criminal.

"Not to worry; you'll be safe enough and have everything you need to provide comfort in your temporary exile."

"When will you require information?"

"Soon enough. I warn you, however. Give false words to me and you will feel a wizard's wrath."

# CHAPTER 10

*ountain Retreat, Campiaa*
*Cassie*

"I like this. Very much." George, who'd followed Barry inside the huge cabin, looked about him with satisfaction. Almond-painted walls rose above honey-stained natural wood wainscoting in a family room of sorts, with a wall of windows on the opposite side, looking down upon acres and acres of tall evergreens.

"It isn't anything compared to Laddus' riches," Denevik said.

"Laddus was far too gaudy in his tastes," George countered. "This— it feels restful to me. Laddus hated greenery of any kind. There were no plants in his house, or wood. Everything was made of hard, unforgiving surfaces, and kept sterile by his orders."

"You're starting to remember more," Barry smiled at George. "Good for you."

"So far, none of it is useful," George said. "Only superficial in nature."

"Sounds like Laddus was superficial," I said. "George, why don't you and Barry take advantage of the scenery? I'm going to find tea or coffee somewhere, then come back here and stare out the window while I drink it."

123

"I'll help. We'll bring something back for you, too," Denevik grinned at George and Barry before gripping my hand in his and pulling me from the room.

"Does he know I don't drink tea?" I heard George ask Barry before we were out of hearing range.

~

"Found the kitchen, eh?" Wyatt San Gerxon, the Founder's son, sat beside his wife, Jayna, at a large kitchen island. Both were sipping tea when Denevik and I arrived.

"Wyatt, Jayna, good to see you again," Denevik nodded at both.

"I've heard about you," Jayna smiled at me and extended her hand. "Wyatt tells me you sterilized the ground beneath Laddus' compound, where the Prophet left a surprise behind for unsuspecting investigators."

"It was an experiment," I said. "I'm glad it worked."

"At least we know now that the stuff can be killed in some way," Wyatt toyed with his tea mug. "Want tea? We stocked enough for a siege, I think."

"Tea sounds great," I said. "We need to take a cup to Barry, too, but I don't want George to feel left out."

"George?" Wyatt frowned in confusion.

"The ah, serve-bot," Denevik shifted uncomfortably.

"Not to worry, that secret is safe with us," Wyatt said quickly. "Hang on, I may have something for George, too." He rose from his seat and turned away to search in a nearby drawer.

"Here it is," he held up a small, rectangular box.

"What's that?" I asked.

"It's a spelled recharger," Wyatt reached across the island to hand it to me. "Uncle Ry built this cabin to start with; we've added to it to accommodate more visitors. Ry devised these chargers in case the power went out. This will charge several devices, just by setting it on them, and the charge will last for days. George may find it useful, perhaps."

"The King of Karathia is truly a warlock of many talents," Denevik examined the small object after I handed it to him.

"The cool factor is that it will regain its charge without a power source, after being disengaged for only half a day," Wyatt explained. "It may not seem like it, but the spell is a powerful one."

"Kudos to the King of Karathia," I breathed. "He's a genius."

"I'll get your tea," Jayna stood and walked toward a counter where a teapot waited, next to a mug tree. "Want honey, lemon, milk or something else?" she asked, setting three mugs on the counter to fill.

"Honey," I lifted my hand.

"I'll have the same," Denevik said. "Barry also likes honey."

"Oh, I didn't know anyone was here," Sabrina, Travis and Trent's fiancée, walked into the kitchen.

"Want tea?" Jayna asked with a bright smile.

"I need two mugs of Falchani Black if you have it, and regular with lemon," she said. I noticed she didn't return Jayna's smile.

I knew why. She didn't know I knew, but she disliked me for some reason. I had no idea what she thought or the reason she felt that way, but I could feel angry vibes washing off her.

I wondered if she knew I could feel it.

"I'll brew some Falchani Black—it'll be ready in a few. Want to sit and talk while you wait?"

"Are you staying?" she turned toward me.

"I'm taking a cup of tea back to Barry, and then sitting down to look at trees."

"I'll sit and talk," she nodded at Jayna, then pulled a chair out to take a seat.

*She's jealous,* Wyatt informed me. *I can sense it a mile away.*

*What does she have to be jealous about?* I returned. *I don't have a zillion credits or a tech company with my name on it or a line of patents attached to my name.*

*Most of us don't have the jealousy gene,* he replied. *She still has it. I think a few folks are waiting to see what she's really made of before offering more gifts.*

*At least we're not working closely together,* I said. *Getting this close to that kind of anger throws me off.*

*Want me to mention it to Randl?*

*I'm sure he already knows.*

*He probably does.* I watched as Wyatt sipped more of his tea. He was an absolute diplomat—nobody else knew he was having a private conversation with me about Sabrina's rudeness.

"Hey, why don't we go shopping, while you're here?" Jayna set Sabrina's mug of tea in front of her. "You, Cassie and I can go. I've been waiting to go to the new shopping center at the southern end of Campiaa Bay."

"I wouldn't mind shopping," Sabrina said quickly.

"What about you, Cassie?" Jayna turned toward me.

"I think I just want to relax here, but thank you for the offer," I said.

"Oh, come on. It'll just be us girls and a few, distant, discreet guards," Jayna coaxed.

"You should go—I don't think you've been on an outing in a while," Denevik told me.

"But," I said. I wasn't in the same league financially as Jayna and Sabrina, and Sabrina certainly didn't want me there—that was a no-brainer.

"I think you should go, too," Wyatt said. "Treat yourself—I think the Founder's private bank account can spring for an outfit or two for all of you."

"There, all settled," Jayna beamed. "We'll go in the morning."

"You can't let someone treat you like that and then run from them," Denevik told me softly as we left the kitchen to find George and Barry.

"That's easy for you to say. I guess she's expecting me to remain civil. If I lose my temper, she could lose her hair. Do you know how fast that stuff burns?"

"I do. You have more class and more patience than she ever will. I know that's small satisfaction, but it's something."

"What is she jealous of?" I stopped walking and turned on Denevik.

"Well, ah, well. Have you uh, looked in a mirror?"

"Huh?"

"Don't get me wrong, Sabrina's pretty, in a spoiled-girl sort of way. But mouths drop open when you walk by."

"That cannot be it," I argued. "That's the dumbest thing I've ever heard."

"May be dumb, but it's true." Denevik motioned for me to continue our journey to what he called the man-cave. Frankly, it was about to be a woman-cave, too, because it was an awesome room.

"Here we are," Denevik announced when we reached our destination.

"Tea with honey," I handed Barry's mug to him.

"This is for you," Denevik handed George the spelled charger. "I'm told that it's a spelled charger that will renew its power after running down and should last for a few days if your devices run down."

"A gift?" George sounded breathless as he accepted the charger.

"A gift from the Founder's son, who says it was created by the King of Karathia himself," Denevik grinned. "Since you don't drink tea. Enjoy."

"I am beside myself with happiness," George said. "Thank you."

The idea hit me then. *Barry*, I sent, *will you send George's clothing sizes to me? I'm going shopping tomorrow, and I may as well do something useful with my time.*

*He could use a pair of shoes and boots, too,* Barry informed me. *I'll get the sizes to you for all those things.*

By the time I was ready for bed, Dori, Perri and Zanfield had also joined our shopping group. I felt far more comfortable with Zanfield, Perri and Dori than with Sabrina. I barely knew Jayna, but felt she'd be a friend without Sabrina's interference.

I also had George's shoe and clothing sizes tucked away in my comp-vid, so I could shop for him. At the moment, he had two sets of clothes he could wear that weren't uniforms.

He and Barry declined the shopping trip when invited, too, and I felt more than miffed that I wasn't allowed to say no in the beginning, like I wanted.

*Want me to come with you tomorrow?* Rob sent.

*I thought you wanted to rest and relax,* I said.

*I do, but gossip gets around, you know.*

*I can fight my own battles, but thanks for the offer.*

*Randl*

"I have no idea where this is coming from," I told Wyatt. He'd asked for a private meeting with me, so currently we were hiking down a narrow, evergreen-crowded trail away from the cabin. The darkness didn't bother me; Wyatt wore lighted hiking boots to light his steps.

"It was completely rude," Wyatt replied. "Jayna was shocked speechless for a moment."

"So her solution was to invite both on a shopping trip?"

"It was a distraction, and an attempt to defuse a tense moment. Not from Cassie's point of view," he clarified hastily. "I think she was just as stunned as Jayna at such blatant disrespect."

"I got mindspeech from Denevik shortly after it happened," I confessed. "He thinks it's jealousy. Either way, we don't need this kind of division in the ranks, especially when we'll be living and working together underground on D'margis."

I didn't tell Wyatt that Sabrina and I had already held a meeting on this topic. Perhaps she imagined that this incident wouldn't get back to me—or that I wouldn't see it in her eventually.

I didn't want discipline to come through Travis and Trent, either. That was my job, not theirs, to keep peace in the ranks. It would also drive a wedge into their relationship, and I wanted no part of that.

"Maybe the shopping trip will work out," Wyatt said, although his voice betrayed little hope it would happen.

"I don't need a bully working in close quarters with the rest of the crew—it sours everything."

"Dad calls it a hostile working environment. He hesitates to place compulsion, but it's happened a time or two."

"If she continues, it's either that or I send her back to Sirena for the duration."

"If I were sure about the jealousy, I could ask Uncle Nefrigar to remove it temporarily."

"You're forgetting about the second part of the equation, here," I said.

"Cassie?"

"Yep. She's already been on the receiving end of all this. We need to be able to trust one another. Even if that were done, would she trust Sabrina in any way? I don't think so. Cassie has been betrayed too many times in her life already. This is another betrayal of sorts, and it could poison an entire crew."

"Maybe this is why Sabrina didn't get a spirit coin," Wyatt countered.

*It is why she didn't receive one—she has certain—flaws—that she must resolve,* Bennall informed me.

*What do you suggest, then?*

*If she cannot get past this destructive emotion on her own, she cannot be allowed to stay.*

*What about Travis and Trent?*

"I have an idea," Wyatt interrupted.

"What's that?"

"Aren't Nari and Tiri still working on locating the Prophet's gold?"

"Yes."

"Does Sabrina have a problem with either?"

"No."

"Allow Travis and Trent to sail X under an official disguise, while Sabrina continues to work with Nari and Tiri on a solution to find the vibrations from the gold they're hunting. Jett can go with them if he wants, although Travis and Trent will remain as ship's captains."

"Disguise X as a science vessel, perhaps?"

"Works as well as anything else," Wyatt replied.

"I want to make sure Sabrina knows this isn't a reward," I cautioned.

"Then tell her that. Until she can play nice with all the others, she won't be welcome on D'margis."

"Unless she can cure herself of whatever this is and apologize to Cassie in the next two days," I countered. "Otherwise, I'll send X into another sector and they can begin their hunt for the Prophet's gold again."

"Sounds like a plan. Ready to go back?"

"Yeah. I need a drink before going to bed."

"I'll join you."

～

*Cassie*

*I'm not in competition with her.* I kept telling myself that as we were shuttled to the new shopping center Jayna suggested. Sabrina had dressed as if she were going to a cocktail party instead of shopping, while I'd worn comfortable pants, a pullover and flats. Her heels were so high I had no idea how she managed to walk in them.

Except for Jayna, we were all disguised so nobody would recognize us. Even Zanfield was dressed in a subdued, casual manner, as was Perri. I pretended I didn't see him lift her hand to kiss it while we were driven through heavy, beachfront traffic.

Jayna sat in the first row of seats with Sabrina, while Sabrina chattered about high-end makeup, shoes and lingerie.

All her topics concerned things I couldn't afford.

*You're shopping for George,* I reminded myself. I didn't want to go to the same shops Sabrina did. I hoped I could separate myself from her and go elsewhere.

*What are you planning to buy?* Zanfield sent.

*I'm shopping for George. He has two outfits that Barry scrounged for him. He needs other things.*

That initiated a flurry of mindspeech between Perri, Zanfield and Dori.

*We're coming with you—there's no reason we can't shop for George and ourselves at the same time.* I could detect a bit of humor in Zanfield's sending.

*Thank you.* Relief leached some of the stiffness from my body; I hadn't realized how tense I was until that moment. I felt bad for Jayna, though. The poor woman could only nod at Sabrina's continuous chatter.

Once we arrived at the shopping center, the vehicle with our discreet guards unloaded first and positioned themselves—some walking toward the entrance, others spreading out in a random, nonchalant manner.

Our doors opened automatically, and we stepped away from our hover-shuttle, moving as a group toward the entrance. Sabrina walked directly toward the first, high-end clothing shop she spotted. Jayna was forced to follow.

"I think we can find shoes and boots this way," Zanfield said, pointing toward the opposite courtyard.

"Lead the way," I smiled at him. He tucked Perri's arm in his and walked casually in the direction indicated. Dori and I followed.

*Randl*

"I'm glad Jayna suggested this, rather than someone else," I told Vik. Jayna's clothing had been equipped with microscopic cameras—for both audio and image recording.

"Who knew jealousy could cause this much trouble?" Vik shook his head as we watched the images sent to a monitor from Jayna's cameras. So far, Sabrina had criticized and belittled Cassie three times, and she and Jayna were still in the first store, looking through dress racks.

"No wonder she only wears flats—she walks like a Neanderthal down the passages," Sabrina imitated a hulking, unstable creature for a moment.

"I haven't seen that," Jayna said quietly.

"Well, you don't work with her."

"I thought she was on a separate ship."

"She is, but it doesn't take long to get a feel for what she is."

"What's that?"

"A pretender."

"In what way?"

"She doesn't belong with us. It takes a special person to sail with the BlackWing Pirates. There's nothing special about her."

"Did she just say BlackWing Pirates out loud? In public?" Vik rose from his chair in disgust.

"Time to cut this shopping trip short," I agreed, and folded both of us to a discreet location outside the center. I had Sabrina's words and her image recorded in which she revealed a secret she should never have told outside safe confines, or with approved personnel.

*Cassie*

"You should have that, Cassie. It suits you," Dori insisted.

*That* was a designer scarf—with a stunning black dress that glittered with gem dust.

The cost?

Five thousand credits—for the dress alone. The scarf was another seven-fifty.

*We're shopping with the richest man in either Alliance,* she sent. *He wants to buy this for you.*

*But he's with Perri,* I argued.

*Perri is the one who asked him to buy it for you. Besides, he's already spent twenty thousand—at least—on her today.*

"I don't know," I moaned. The dress was gorgeous, I wanted it, and had no idea where I'd ever wear the thing.

"Look, George has enough stuff to fill two closets, now. Time to get something for you," Perri came to stand beside me. "You'll look amazing in that dress."

"Fine. But this is it for me. Nothing else, and I mean it."

"Well, that's settled, then," Zanfield turned to summon a sales clerk, who'd pull the dress and scarf for me and wrap them for transport.

"Where do you suppose Sabrina and Jayna are?" I asked as we walked out of the shop. Zanfield had rented a hover-cart earlier, just to carry everything he'd insisted on buying for George.

"There you are," Jayna and Wyatt stepped out of a coffee shop as we were about to walk past.

"Where's Sabrina?" Dori asked.

"Well, she had to leave earlier," Wyatt said. "So I came to keep my love company and buy her a few trinkets."

"See?" Jayne held out her right hand. A new, square-cut emerald ring sparkled on a finger.

"That's gorgeous," I said, admiring the ring.

"Want one?" Wyatt grinned.

"I've already said no more for me, and I mean it," I told him. "But I appreciate the offer."

"Ready to go back, now, or would you like something to eat, first?" Jayna smiled.

"Eat. Definitely," Zanfield replied.

"Very well. Shall we?" Wyatt took Jayna's arm and led her toward the door. "I have just the place in mind," he added.

At least we were far enough away that the blast inside the high-end dress shop only knocked us down. Twenty-two people inside and close to the shop died, with another thirteen wounded.

Wyatt folded us directly to the mountain retreat, leaving the smoke and chaos of the scene behind.

*Randl*

"It won't happen again." Sabrina hung her head after I'd presented the evidence of her breach of security.

"I could have you removed from service completely," I reminded her.

"I know."

"What was this over, I ask you? Are you that petty and jealous? Really? I've seen you make great strides in improving your attitude, among other things. And now this happens. I don't understand it in the least."

"I don't know why I feel so hostile toward her."

"Then you'll have plenty of time to consider that. I'm sending X out with Nari and Tiri to continue the hunt for the Prophet's gold. You're now a part of that investigation, so you'll be traveling with them rather than going to D'margis with the rest of us. Until things change, your home base will be Sirena only."

*Randl?* Wyatt's sending sounded frantic.

*What is it?*

*The dress shop where Sabrina mentioned the BlackWing Pirates has just been blown to bits. Dad thinks nexus echo may have played a part.*

"Fucking, ball-burning hells," I snapped aloud. "The dress shop where your little slip happened was just blown apart," I shouted at Sabrina. "Now do you see how dangerous all this is?"

She didn't cry in my presence, but I heard the sob as she closed the door behind her. "Fuck my life," I sighed. *Wyatt, how many are dead?* I asked. *Are any of ours hurt?*

∾

"I don't believe this."

Teeg, Wyatt and I stood outside the cordoned-off section of the shopping center where the blast occurred. "Griffin is on the way," Wyatt said after I'd spoken with Perri.

As a power sniffer, Perri told me that Gillen Wilker, her father, had been the one to bring about this devastation, no doubt on the

Prophet's orders. If Zanfield hadn't sat with her when she told me, she may have broken down completely.

*You think the Prophet can now employ nexus echo?* Teeg sent.

*Either he can, or his rogues did. That's why there was a lag in the execution; it had to follow a path of communication, no doubt.*

*Does Sabrina know how many people died here?*

*Not yet.*

"This is fucked up," he said aloud.

"I concur."

"We have more bad news," Vik walked up to me. He'd *skipped* in from elsewhere, so it was important bad news.

"What is it?" I gruffed. I truly wasn't looking forward to the day becoming worse.

"There's a news release that's showing up in the vids, right along with this mess," he jerked his head toward the blasted rubble.

"They're saying I'm responsible for that?" I thumped my chest with a fist while anger threatened to consume me.

"Not that, no. They're saying that you've kidnapped Geeva, and now have access to all her contacts and records."

"What in the actual fuck is happening?" Teeg cursed while I stared at Vik as if he'd grown another head.

"What's this about Geeva?" Griffin strode toward us, frowning at the devastation left behind by Gillen Wilker.

"The news media is now saying that Randl has kidnapped Geeva."

"Did you?" Griffin turned his penetrating gaze on me.

"Hells no, and thanks for asking," I growled at him.

"Then where would they get that information?" Griffin turned toward Teeg.

"You're asking me? I suppose it's the same place all the other false information came from."

"Could be, I guess," Griffin shrugged. "I hear this destruction is Gillen Wilker's work."

"It is," Vik confirmed.

"Well, that's your priority, not mine," he turned back to me, lifted an eyebrow and stalked off.

"Grumpy old cuss," Vik muttered.

"Cuss?"

"Just a euphemism for cranky old bastard."

"I'll check which media agency released the information," Wyatt offered.

"Let me know when you get it," I told him. "I'll be quite interested in how this came about."

*Great. Another visit to split-time,* Vik grumbled in mindspeech.

~

*G'margis*

*V'dar*

Two things happened simultaneously. The news of Randl Gage kidnapping Geeva, my next target, precipitated so much outrage that I failed to listen for several minutes to one of my rogues, who informed me that someone with intimate knowledge of the BlackWing Pirates had spoken their name aloud.

My anger about Geeva's capture was so hot, I argued with him about how he knew it was intimate knowledge. By the time I understood that his nexus echo search was for certain key words, it was too late to find the one who'd spilled the words to begin with.

Nevertheless, I asked Gillen to level the place where the words were spoken because I was angry, and only deaths would assuage my fury.

"Now," I straightened my robes as Gillen bowed his head before me, indicating that my will had been done. "Go directly to W'dell and ask for the next three names on his list."

"Of course." Gillen turned and walked out of the tree nursery where I stood. I wouldn't destroy the saplings; I'd worked too long to create and nurture them, before transporting them to unsuspecting worlds.

Once there, they would be planted, along with deposits of the fungus that enabled them to connect with other trees through their root systems.

My will would be passed from one tree to another, to another, until any humanoid touching those trees or eating their fruit or carving their branches would also be under my sway.

"Prophet's disease. Faugh. My will, my desires are not a disease," I hissed. "Once I have control of all others, Randl Gage will most certainly die slowly, and as I will it."

# CHAPTER 11

*Unnamed Dwarf Planet*
  *Griffin*

"I thought you were going after Geeva. Everybody's talking about how the BlackWing Pirates have her, now," Wylend informed me.

"They don't have her," I said, my voice sharper than intended. "And now is not the time to discuss my many failures."

"Another false report, then?"

"Yes." I slung my uniform jacket over the back of a kitchen chair and went to the sink to fill the kettle for tea.

"I could have gone to Campiaa for you," Wylend said as I set the kettle to boil.

"Not with Randl there. He sees too much for a blind man."

"So that's how you know he doesn't have Geeva."

"He said so himself, and Teeg confirmed it."

"Was it Teeg or Tybus?"

"Tybus is on Kifirin, lending Queen Reah a hand with new legislation," I said. "Teeg will be handling all business for the Campiaan Alliance until Tybus returns."

"You had to say her name, didn't you?"

"It wasn't intended to reopen old wounds."

"I suppose it isn't the time to discuss my many failures, either."

"I say we go out to dinner tonight," I told him.

"I like that idea. There's a seafood restaurant in Prakelia I'd like to try."

"Lobster, then—or their equivalent, with a good wine?"

"Of course."

~

*Mountain Retreat, Campiaa*

*Travis*

"It's up to you two whether you take X out, or allow Jett to captain the ship," Randl told Trent and me. "Sabrina will be on that ship with Nari and Tiri, whether you choose to go or not."

"Two captains are company, but three are a crowd," Trent shifted uneasily on his seat. He, Randl and I sat around Randl's makeshift desk at the retreat, trying to come to terms with Sabrina's jealousy and breach of security. As of now, the death toll stood at twenty-seven, with more possible.

*She knew not to say anything and she did it anyway,* Trent sent to me. As of now, we knew the Prophet was employing nexus echo, so it wasn't only spies or casual observers who could release our information—the Prophet himself was listening.

I felt relieved that D'margis would be heavily shielded and impermeable to nexus echo—Zaria would see to it herself. I'd sent a warning to Mom, who'd get the word out to others regarding the same thing.

*Loose lips sink ships,* Uncle Tony always said while teaching us about the business of spying.

His lesson had been brought home with a sharp and deadly landing.

"I think I'm too angry to go with the ship right now," Trent admitted.

"I can let you go later, if you want," Randl agreed.

"Same here—later for me, too. Maybe we can switch out with Jett or something, after things cool down."

"X still requires a crew. They need an engineer, a pilot and several other positions filled. I want Barry, Rajeon, George and Cassie on D'margis."

"Ask for volunteers from the other crews," I said. "Vik will stay with you; that means Dave wants to be wherever Vik is."

"I get that," Randl appeared thoughtful. "I'll ask for volunteers, then, and see if we can put a crew together that Jett can live with. I'll have another talk with Sabrina, too. Working with Nari and Tiri will give her a chance to save lives. Perhaps this will lead to some kind of redemption for her. In any other case, I would have dismissed her outright."

"We understand that," Trent and I spoke in unison. We'd already held lengthy mindspeech with Mom, who said the same thing. Whoever said words never hurt anyone was the biggest fool ever.

We also needed a conversation with Sabrina, which would involve a break in the relationship. Whether temporary or otherwise—she would ultimately be the source of the outcome.

It wouldn't mean we didn't love her—but sometimes love became toxic. She failed to come to us about her dislike of Cassie, which was unacceptable. We could have worked with her to get through this, or at least asked for outside help from Kevis.

"I see you're both trying to work through this whole mess," Randl said after Trent and I'd gone silent.

"When will the ship sail?" Trent asked.

"Tonight—at midnight. Will that give you enough time to do what you need to?"

"Yes." Trent rose with a weary sigh.

*Right there with you, bro,* I sent. *Right there with you.*

*Sabrina*

Nobody would talk to me.

*Nobody.*

I was afraid to watch the news vids—afraid to hear that more people had died from their injuries. Still, I couldn't explain the hateful jealousy that consumed me every time Cassie's name was even mentioned.

*Had a terrible disease infected me, and this is how it manifested?*

"I thought you had better sense," I told myself in the bathroom mirror. "I really, really did."

"Sabrina?" I heard Travis call my name.

Here it came—I knew with a certainty that I couldn't explain that neither he nor Trent would go with me on X. I was officially in exile.

*Fuck.*

*Cassie*

"Maybe if I'd said no, she wouldn't have gone off like that," I told Denevik. I'd withdrawn to my bedroom at the mountain retreat and stuffed myself into a corner of an overly-large, soft chair to mope.

"Avilepha, not one bit of this is your fault," Denevik sat on the empty portion of the chair and took my hand. "You have no control over her, her reactions, jealousy, or any other thing in this."

"Then why do I feel like crap?"

"For the same reason all of us feel like crap. Innocents died, and there was no need for it to happen."

"I didn't ask to come on this mission—I was drafted by someone else," I sighed.

"I know. And already, you have proved invaluable. Do not take responsibility for these events. This burden is not yours to carry."

"At least George likes his clothes and shoes," I said, leaning my head on Denevik's shoulder. "He was so happy—until the rest of the events unfolded."

"One never knows how happy one truly is, until tragedy comes and we wish to crawl out of our skin and into another's," Denevik whispered against my hair.

"I've wanted to be somebody else at least six times today."

"I know. All will be well—eventually." He laid a kiss on my temple and pulled me closer. *I know where the liquor cabinet is*, he sent.

"You're only now mentioning that?"

"Let's go see what they have," he said and *skipped* me into the people-cave.

~

*Founder's Palace, Campiaa City*
*Wyatt*

"I've called Griffin in; we'll see if he has any clue whether the Prophet has Geeva or if she's merely good at hiding," Dad motioned me toward an empty chair in his study. "Want something to drink? It's the day for it, I think."

"Definitely that. The media is having a field day with our report that a rogue warlock, high on Ry's most-wanted list, is responsible for the hit on the shopping center. They're speculating now on what could have caused it, rather than believe the press release that this was an odd, random act of violence."

"It tends to make me think the Prophet doesn't have Geeva," Dad said, uncorking a bottle and pouring two drinks. "If he had Geeva, I can't help but think he'd be too busy interrogating her to be bothered with hitting a shop long after the words he looked for were actually spoken."

"You think this was anger on his part, after that lie was released about Randl kidnapping her?"

"Look at the timing, son. The words are spoken. Nothing immediate happens. An hour goes by, the media is swamped with the rumor of Geeva's capture and suddenly, boom. A shop full of people is reduced to rubble."

"When you put it that way," I said, accepting the glass of bourbon and drinking a healthy portion of it.

"My thoughts exactly," Griffin folded into the room. I deliberately avoided direct eye contact.

"You have any idea where Geeva might be, then?"

"None whatsoever. Frankly, she could be almost anywhere by now. May have even switched ships and doubled back. The possibilities are mind-boggling."

"I assume you'll continue to look for her?"

"As often as I can. I understand how important she could be."

"I'd appreciate updates," Dad told him. "Is there anything else to report?"

"Nothing, other than I'll keep hunting the biggest and worst on our most-wanted list. We have Laddus. I'm still attempting to get information from him."

"What I heard is that he only had stuff on other slavers," Dad lifted his glass to drink.

"That's what we've gotten so far. We're in the process of tracing all those leads to shut them down."

"Keep up the good work, then," Dad saluted Griffin with the last of his drink, indicating dismissal. Griffin didn't bother saying good-bye —he folded away.

"Well, that was particularly unproductive," Dad observed and poured more bourbon in his glass.

*Cassie*

"Once we heard about nexus echo and what it was, George and I started formulating a plan," Barry said.

Barry had a half-finished beer sitting on a side table; George held the charger Wyatt gave him in his hand. He claimed it was a top-off of energy and made him feel good.

"What's the plan?" Denevik asked.

"Searching for key words and phrases that may mean nothing to someone else, and everything to the criminals involved," Barry explained. "If the Prophet is involved, they have to have a name or code word for him, don't you think?"

"Well, that makes sense, but how are you going to find it?" I asked.

"In all the information flying through the air, how will you sort that out from all the rest?"

"We will search for an uncommon word used among all the petty criminals we intend to track," George explained. "They will use more mundane methods of communication—either between themselves or with the Prophet's base. If we find even one, I believe Barry can connect with their machine and convince it to spy on its owner for us. He has unique talents, you know."

"I do know," I lifted my glass of wine to Barry and George.

"We have snacks," Beverly, Star and Annie walked in carrying trays of food. "If someone will pour wine for us, we'll share."

"I'm on it," I said, setting my wineglass next to Barry's beer and rising from my seat. "What kind of wine do you want? They have plenty to choose from."

"These are excellent," Denevik put a second tiny sandwich in his mouth and closed his eyes in pleasure.

"Shrimp salad—my recipe," Beverly beamed at him.

"One of my favorites," Barry collected two from the tray. "Thanks, Mom."

"Here you go," I set a glass of white wine on the low table in front of Beverly, and two reds for Star and Annie, who'd sat on an adjacent sofa.

"Look, it's starting to rain," Star lifted his glass and nudged Annie, who sat beside him.

"I love watching rain drip off evergreens," Annie sighed.

"I do, too," I smiled at her. "It's so peaceful."

"I think we all need some peace after this day," Beverly said.

"You got that right," I agreed.

*Travis*

"That felt wrong, somehow." Trent, Randl and I, in disguise, had gone to see X off. We'd gotten plenty of volunteers from the other ships, most of whom didn't want to live in a cave, or so one of them had said.

Sabrina had boarded the ship looking defeated, even after we'd told her we hadn't stopped loving her—just that we needed a break to deal with the backlash, then come to terms with the mistake and its deadly aftermath.

"I hate this," Randl sighed as the ship uncoupled and slowly left its berth behind.

"None of us can *Change What Was*," Trent breathed. "As much as we might like to."

"None of us has the ability to pick through the minutiae of time, to determine whether it will affect everything going forward," Randl replied. "Frankly, I wouldn't want that responsibility. I feel it would be harrowing in nature, to have that much riding on a single act."

"When you put it like that," I mumbled.

"Come with me; Zaria says our new abode on D'margis is finished. We'll inspect it tonight and move the others in the morning."

∿

*D'margis*
   *Randl*

"This doesn't feel like a cave at all," Travis stared at the ceiling, which was at least twenty feet above our heads. "I thought it would be low ceilings everywhere and feel cramped and claustrophobic."

"Larentii always know the proper proportions," I said, craning my neck to view the clever, recessed lighting above us. It looked like stained glass—something you'd find in an old train station, perhaps. The light behind the glass gave the impression that the sun was shining through beautiful designs.

"The plans resemble a triskelion," Trent said, tapping the comp-vid Zaria left for us to find. It held a map of the entire compound, which was quite large. "Does that make sense to you?"

"I think it may confuse the enemy. If we're attacked, we know the layout. If you look here, at the end of every coil, there are escape pods." I tapped the map on the comp-vid to enlarge the areas in question. "Unless all the enemy can fold space, there are steel doors in every coil, that will shut before the enemy can enter. They'll have to blast their way in, and that may give everyone time to get away if the order comes to abandon the facility."

"It has a self-destruct option, doesn't it?" Travis nodded grimly.

"It does. Zaria asked if I wanted it. I said yes."

"That's a long walk down each coil to get to the berths," Trent shook his head.

"Not really. Come on, I'll show you." I led them toward a large painting on one side of the grand hall.

"That looks like a Vermeer," Travis said.

"It's an enlarged copy of a smaller painting Lissa has in her study," I explained. "I've always liked it. Vermeer had a way with light. Now, tell the girl in the painting it's time for bed."

"It's time for bed," Trent frowned as he said the words. The painting slid aside quickly to reveal a trans-vator.

"The three trans-vators can only be activated with the proper voice accompanied by the proper eye scan," I explained. "If anyone else were standing here with us that the micro-cameras and audio detectors in the painting didn't recognize, it wouldn't work at all. Every authorized guest has to be entered into the main comp before they're allowed to use the trans-vators."

"Damn, that's genius," I breathed.

"Zaria suggested it. She says she got the idea from a series of books on Old Earth. She also says that the other two original paintings are in the Larentii Archives—one is by Raphael and the other by Rembrandt. Both were famous artists on Old Earth."

"What are the originals doing in the Larentii Archives?"

"Well, it seems as though they were intended for destruction by short-sighted individuals in a time of war, or something like that. She says the originals were rescued by Nefrigar and his sons, and what was destroyed were copies, exchanged at the last possible moment."

"That sounds like Nefrigar," Travis conceded. "To exhaust every possibility until the reality has arrived."

"If we get any sleep tonight, we ought to leave now," I said. "If you want to stay here, I can bring your things tomorrow with everything else."

"We'll stay," Travis nodded at Trent. I figured they'd choose to stay here. They were still feeling the effects of the day and wanted privacy. I didn't blame them at all.

~

*McAlester, Oklahoma*
  *Old Earth*
  *Korvus Katergáris*

"You haven't been here in a while," my grandmother smiled at me as I pulled out a chair at the island and accepted a cup of coffee from her.

"Only once since I moved you here, and I'm sorry about that," I apologized. "You make wonderful coffee," I complimented her after taking a sip. "Where's Grandfather?"

"He's out checking garage sales. He wants one of those buffalo sculptures to put in our yard—he's quite taken with the local mascot, you know."

"I had no idea he wanted one. I can get one for him, easily enough."

"No—let him do this; he finds it entertaining," Grandmother laughed. "He unearths all sorts of little trinkets to work on at these sales and sells the restored pieces to some of the antique shops."

"Jewelry?" I hurried to hide my frown at this turn of events.

"You worry too much," Grandmother flipped her dish towel at me, dismissing my concern.

"Have you gotten to know the neighbors?"

"You must be joking. The woman next door has a black, standard poodle named Bubbles that she dresses for all the major holidays, and she brings us delicious cakes, rolls and brownies whenever she bakes. We really like Barbara, so don't do anything to mess this up," Grandmother warned.

"Not to worry," I held up a hand. "If you like it here, who am I to tell you no?"

"You're the best grandson anyone could ask for," she walked around the island to give me a hug. I leaned into it like a child who'd been lost and then found again. I refused, however, to release the tears pricking my eyelids.

~

*Mountain Retreat, Campiaa*
*Cassie*

"Need help packing?" Jayna knocked on my open bedroom door as I held a pair of boots in my hand. There wasn't any room left in my duffel, and I was already wearing one pair of shoes.

"Hi, Jayna. I think I can hand-carry the boots," I told her as she walked in.

"There are a few extra bags in the hall closet—I'll go get a small one for you."

"Let's just get it on the way out," I suggested.

"Even better. Saves an extra trip. That leaves us time to talk about yesterday."

"It follows you like a dark cloud, doesn't it?" I said.

"It'll take a while to get it out of my head," she agreed. "I keep thinking that I should have slapped a hand over her mouth."

"Hindsight," I shrugged and invited Jayna to sit on the bed with me.

"Wyatt says that someone once told him that mistakes of this type have five categories and are ranked like this; mildly stupid, are you drunk, how dumb can you be, completely bone-headed, and fatal."

"So yesterday was a category five mistake on her part?"

"Yes, only it didn't result in her own death. The count is now thirty."

"Damn." I covered my face with my hands, hoping to stave off a feeling of nausea.

"Wyatt and his dad are speaking with family members today, offering condolences and assistance with funeral arrangements. Seven of the women killed have small children at home."

"This whole thing is a fuck-up of massive proportions."

"You have that right. I wanted to see you before you left—to let you know that we're in this together, if you need to talk. If I could, I'd go back and forget about the shopping trip altogether. This isn't your fault, Cassie. Wyatt says it isn't mine, either. Sabrina, the Prophet and Gillen Wilker own this, first, last and always."

"Thank you for that." I dropped my hands and blinked at her.

"We'll get through this," she leaned over to hug me. "There are more important things we have to do—like finding the Prophet and making sure he and his rogues and pet warlocks never do this again."

"I'd like to see that warlock try to throw a spell at me," I muttered. "I appear to be immune to that crap."

"What would you do if you ever came face-to-face with him?"

"Burn him to cinders before he could open his mouth."

"That's what I like most about you—no hesitation to do the right thing."

"Let's hope I get the chance, then."

"Ready to go find that small bag?" Jayna managed a weak smile.

"Yeah. Let's go."

*Randl*

"All of your belongings on the ships have been transferred to our new compound already," I announced to the crowd gathered outside the mountain retreat. "After yesterday, everyone here should understand how important it is to never speak the name of our host planet aloud, unless you are sure that you're shielded properly against nexus echo."

"I think we've learned that lesson the hard way," Dave said.

"Now is your last chance," I went on, "to tell me if you no longer wish to engage the enemy. We see how dangerous he is to us, now. From the lies spread by the media, who are operating under some sort of cloud and believe they are dispensing truth, to his disease which he continues to spread, to our very words being turned against us, we are all in terrible danger. We may not have enough strength among us to defeat him. If you wish to be sent back to Sirena, nobody will say a word against you. Our quest is terrifying at the very least and could end up requiring all our lives."

"I stand against the enemy," Vik raised his clenched fist. "I seek vengeance for the innocents."

"Vengeance," Cassie raised her fist.

"Vengeance," echoed from every mouth as fists were thrust skyward.

With that, I folded all of them to the new compound on D'margis.

"Here is where the Geeva kidnapping story originated," Zanfield handed a comp-vid to me. I'd brought everything from my study aboard XIII, including the massive desk, and still had room for shelves, furniture, books and plants.

"Miz sent the information after tracking it down," Zanfield added, taking stock of all the empty space around us. "I hear plants are good for helping freshen the air," he added.

"I was thinking about that," I said. "Any suggestions?"

"We'll have to add sunlamps or grow lamps," he tapped his chin while frowning at several spaces in corners and such.

"Easy enough to do."

"Right. Something tall and leafy there," he pointed to the largest space. "Maybe something short but full next to it. Then, maybe one of those delicate, flowering things on a table next to a comfy chair over here," he pointed in another direction. "Perri and I can do some research. She likes plants. Had one in college but had to give it away when she graduated. She called it Esmeralda."

"She named her plant?"

"Esmeralda deserves the utmost respect," Zanfield held up a hand. "We still don't know if she survived the move and transition."

"Look, if you can locate Esmeralda, then bring her here for Perri," I said. "And ask her to find other plants for my office, all of whom she is welcome to name."

"I'll get to work on it right away."

"You do that."

As Zanfield left my study, Travis and Trent walked in. "We may have a line on some of the petty criminals the Prophet may have taken over," Travis said. "Trent and I couldn't sleep last night, so we started pegging thefts of food and the like—the Prophet still has to feed his people."

"Go on."

"There've been a rash of raids on canning and processing plants— the kind that are situated right next to the fields where vegetables or livestock are grown," Travis explained. "Many of them have reported shipments that have disappeared, with very little evidence to go on."

"It may be nothing," Trent shrugged. "But even the Prophet has to eat. Plus, we haven't heard of ships being pirated lately—I believe we broke him of that habit by destroying his fleet and preventing him from getting more ships."

"It's worth checking out. Make a list of all the processing plants in question and ask Barry and George to find out what they can through comp-sleuthing. If they find anything that warrants investigation, we'll go in person to look into it."

Travis and Trent fist-bumped, then strode out of my office in a hurry. They wanted their efforts to pay off; I could see it quite plainly —as if they'd shouldered some of the blame for Sabrina's mistakes.

*What happened in Campiaa City isn't your fault*, I sent to them. *But your reasoning is quite sound in this, I believe. The Prophet doesn't want to risk his key people just to steal food, so he'll let someone else who doesn't matter so much do all the work.*

*Our thinking exactly, and thank you for having confidence in us*, Travis replied.

*Cassie, Rajeon, Denevik*, I sent. *I need your cooperation, along with that of Barry and George, for a project Travis and Trent have devised.*

*We'll be ready*, Denevik responded.

*What he said*, Cassie echoed.

*On it*, Rajeon replied.

~

*Cassie*

Denevik and I arrived in Barry's lab to find Rajeon, Travis, Trent and George already there.

"We won't be going out today, but we'd like to get the ball rolling on this," Travis gave us a weary smile. I could tell neither he nor Trent had slept well the night before. Understandable, under the circumstances.

"Here are the maps of all the canning and processing plants that have had shipments go missing—before they reach their intended destination on the same planet. We think the Prophet's petty criminals may be involved in this, to supply the Prophet's new compound with food and other necessities. His last compound did meet with an untimely end," Trent explained before handing Rajeon a comp-vid.

"So you think he didn't have time to transport supplies before he was forced to move?" Denevik glanced at the comp-vid screen in Rajeon's hand before turning back to Travis and Trent.

"He may have moved some things, but face it, I figure he had more important things there to save than foodstuff."

"Makes sense," Rajeon agreed. "These facilities you've marked are scattered—most of them nowhere near one another."

"As the petty criminals would be scattered so they won't infringe on another's territory, I think," Travis said. "Randl says we can investigate this. We need to get moving on it, too. We've targeted twenty-seven stolen shipments so far, and Barry and George will be searching for more throughout the day. Be prepared to leave first thing tomorrow. Trent and I will decide which theft to investigate first."

"Will you send that information to us?" I asked Rajeon, who was still studying the list of locations.

"I'll send it to you," Barry grinned. "Plus anything else we find."

"I love this sweater, Cassie," George tapped his chest. He wore a light, knit sweater over a collared shirt I'd picked out for him in Campiaa City.

"You look good in it," I told him. "It matches your eyes."

"May I hug you?"

"You bet," I told him and strode forward to hug him first. He chuckled as I squeezed him tight.

"I enjoyed that," he smiled as I pulled away. "First hug was a good one. Very good."

"Nobody ever hugged you? That's criminal," I said, hugging him again.

*We'll send what we find to you, first,* Barry informed me. *Travis and Trent need sleep.*

*Thanks. I'll ask Denevik and Rajeon to meet in the library and go over what we have so far.*

*Send your findings back to us; there has to be a pattern in this. From everything I've seen so far, the Prophet is consumed with OCD. Everything must be neat and orderly. I believe it's why he sends his warlocks to destroy things most of the time—because he doesn't like the mess and asymmetry.*

"Holy cow," I said aloud while blinking at Barry. "You're right. That's—exactly right."

"What's right?" Travis and Trent were interested immediately.

"Barry says there has to be a pattern in all this, if the Prophet is responsible," I explained. "Because the Prophet has OCD."

"Damn, dude, you're right," Travis high-fived Barry. "Cassie, if you, Rajeon and Denevik will look into that while bro and I get some sleep, we'll look at your findings when we wake."

"We're on it," I told him. "Go to bed. You look like warmed-over roadkill."

"I feel worse than that," Trent admitted. "Make notes on everything." He and Travis folded away.

153

# CHAPTER 12

*R*andl
I found Cassie, Rajeon and Denevik in the library, working through the list of processing plants which had experienced loss of shipments. They were recording dates and locations of thefts, what, exactly, was stolen, and how much.

"I see you're breaking this down," I pulled out a chair next to Rajeon.

"Yeah," Cassie replied. "All of it is packaged, canned or frozen. Nothing fresh was taken."

"Show me the log of food items," I said. Rajeon scooted his comp-vid toward me.

"You'd need a lot of storage for all this," I scrolled through the list.

"That narrows down his location to nearly any empty planet," Denevik sighed.

"After we finish here, I want to get into the records of what we know the Prophet has pirated in the past," Cassie said.

"Because it could verify that these thefts were done by his command," I nodded at her. "We already know that in the past, he never took anything fresh—it was always something that could be stored for a long time. Good work, Lieutenant."

"You should never buy what can spoil before you eat it," Rajeon agreed. "With the Prophet's OCD, I don't believe he'd steal what he didn't have space and proper storage for, either."

"Now that's good thinking," I said.

"Oh, don't thank us—Barry pointed it out," Cassie said. "We're following up on his suggestion while he and George search for more thefts. When we leave tomorrow to investigate the likeliest target, can Rob go with us?"

"I don't see why not. He's quite efficient when his toes are in the dirt."

"Somebody say my name?" Rob walked in, followed by a hover-cart laden with covered plates. "These three forgot about lunch. Beverly sent me to find them."

"Busted," Cassie laughed.

"Do you mind going out with this bunch tomorrow?" I asked Rob as he handed out plates of food.

"No. In fact, I think it's a very good idea."

"Then take a seat and talk with us while we eat," Denevik invited, pulling out an empty chair.

"Here," I pushed Rajeon's comp-vid toward Rob as he slid onto the offered chair. "You can read up on what they've compiled already. I'm going to find Vik—he and I have a bit of sleuthing to do ourselves."

"What's our destination this time, boss?" Vik asked. He'd joined me in my study, where I discovered Perri and Zanfield had been busy already. In a corner stood a flowering zaka palm, and beside it was a squat, midwinter succulent, whose pot bore the name *Esmeralda*, written in decorative script.

"Welcome, Esmeralda," I dipped my head to the plant in question.

"Who knew Perri and Zanfield liked plants so much?" Vik grinned.

"I think their early years may have had something to do with that. Neither were allowed to have pets," I said. "Zanfield often hid from his parents in their garden and was raised by the gardener and the household staff."

"Is that why there's no taint of extreme wealth on that man?" Vik asked.

"I believe that's much of the reason, yes. Plus, he watched how his parents treated others they considered less than themselves—and he himself was neglected by them. He had no desire to be them at the end of the day."

"Too many people turn into what they despise," Vik agreed. "I saw plenty of that happen on Kifirin."

"Maybe we all need a great gardener—if we don't have good parents."

"We all need good people around us," Vik confirmed. "Where are we going, again?"

"Havek," I said and folded us to a minor media company on that world.

～

*Cassie*

"The biggest difference in these thefts is the frozen items added to the usual stuff the Prophet's taken in the past." I handed my comp-vid to Travis, so he and Trent could see a comparison between older thefts and more recent ones.

They'd slept for ten hours, then got up to see what we'd accomplished.

"I figure he's expanding the menu," Travis shrugged. "People get tired of the same thing over and over."

"Or he stole somebody's freezers," Rob replied.

"Anybody who took this much in frozen food would be forced to have suitable ways to store it," Trent agreed as he read over his brother's shoulder. "Or, maybe they stole it to throw us off."

"We've found no evidence of it being dumped anywhere, or that the container bags went anywhere to recycle," Rajeon reported.

"Where do you think we should go first, then?" Travis asked.

"Where the biggest shipment came up missing," Rob said. "On Havek."

Travis and Trent exchanged glances, then turned back to us. "Not that this doesn't sound fishy, as Mom says, but it definitely has the smell of three-day-old rotted carp."

~

*Randl*

"We have questions," Travis and Trent walked into my study. "Nice plants," Travis remarked.

"About?" I looked up from studying my comp-vid. Vik and I had returned from Havek hours ago, after finding an almost identical set of events at the media company as the one we'd investigated before.

The information appeared in the minds of those in charge of the media releases, as if by magic. We'd watch the mental switch of gears, as Vik put it, with growing frustration.

One moment, another story had been the headline. Then, in a blink, the kidnapping of Geeva by the BlackWing Pirates had taken its place.

"Didn't the news report about Geeva originate on Havek?" Trent asked.

"It did."

"Guess where the biggest theft of food occurred?"

I went still. "Tell me it's not Havek," I breathed, although I could see it in both their faces. That's exactly where the theft occurred.

"It's Havek," Travis confirmed. "About a hundred miles from the media company involved."

"You think this is all tied together? I didn't see anything in those faces that indicated they had anything to do with food theft."

"There was little media coverage of it," Trent pointed out. "An entire shipment, hover-trucks included, vanished, and the story was effectively buried."

"Interesting. Are you planning to investigate it first?"

"Yep."

"Good. If you need to stay there, be sure to let me know. I can send one or two of our new Sirenali troops with you."

"Are any of them good at sleuthing?"

"I think I can find someone with that talent."

"Ask them to be ready to go at eight bells. I'd like to take George and Barry with us, too."

"Then be careful. Your new investigation company is one we can't afford to lose."

"Understood, Commander."

*Cassie*

"I don't suppose I need to tell you to look out for each other," Beverly, her hands on both hips, looked from Barry to me and then back again.

"You don't have to tell us that—it's a given," I said.

"Well, then. Take care and eat right."

"We love you, too, Mom," Barry grinned. "Besides, if we solve this fast, we'll be back for dinner."

"Hmmph. Go on, the others are waiting," Beverly gestured us out of the kitchen.

"Thanks, Mom." Barry hugged Beverly and kissed her cheek.

I didn't miss the sniffle as we walked away from her.

"Randl will take us in—there's a safe house that Teeg procured for us on Havek," Denevik fell in step with us as we left the kitchen behind. "Although all of us will have a roommate or two—not enough bedrooms to go around."

"No problem; George and I can bunk together," Barry said. "We could even add Rajeon or Rob, if needed."

I almost stopped in my tracks; I was the only female in the entire group. *Who would I bunk with?*

*If you don't mind my snoring now and then, we can share a room—all of them have separate beds,* Denevik offered.

*If you're okay with that,* I replied, feeling nervous all of a sudden.

*It's just me, Cassie. There's nothing to be worried about.* He'd sensed my discomfort, somehow.

*It'll be fine. I'll be fine,* I amended.

*Good. Randl's waiting for us.*

~

Safe House

Portal, Havek

Randl

"The shipment disappeared somewhere between here and here." We'd gathered around my three-dimensional image of a stretch of a hover-way not far from where we were. I touched the two locations where the last pings from the trucks registered, and when the next pings should have occurred, but didn't. It was a space of two miles, gauged by the speed of the trucks between previous pings.

"I'll need to walk the ground beginning where the last ping was registered," Rob said. "After we look over the local law enforcement reports."

"There isn't much," Barry reported, handing Rob a comp-vid. "They didn't appear concerned about the shipment; insurance covered the cost for the company—both for product and trucks, and that's pretty much it. They didn't find any evidence at all."

"Or weren't looking. Could be compulsion, obsession, whatever," Denevik observed. "It did happen at night—so vamps or anyone else could have been involved."

"You think a local, petty criminal may have a vamp on the payroll?" Trent asked.

"Or it could be a vamp who is the petty criminal. We can't rule anything out at this juncture," I said.

"One of the Prophet's vamps killed on Hraede had a protective suit he could wear in daylight," Rajeon reminded us.

"So we really could be dealing with anything, here," Cassie agreed. "What a mess."

"It's up to you to find anything you can to determine whether the

Prophet was involved in this," I told the group. "I expect to be briefed every day, no matter what. Lyrill, this is your first investigation," I turned toward the mute Sirenali who was most qualified to serve with the others. "If you need anything, don't be afraid to approach anyone here. They will support you, just as you will support them. All right?"

*Of course*, he sent with a nod.

"Any problems, let me and the others know immediately," I said. "Good luck." I folded away.

*Cassie*

"There's no forensics data, no evidence, and no documentation that they even looked for evidence, according to this report," Rob shoved the comp-vid toward me in frustration.

"Another vote for the obsession or compulsion thing," I agreed.

"We need to go to the site and get there in a normal way, unless somebody can shield all of us," Travis said. "Another thing we need is a legitimate reason to be there, snooping around."

"Snakes," Rajeon said.

"Snakes?" Travis stared at Rajeon.

"Or another dangerous creature on the loose," he shrugged.

"How do snake chasers dress?" Denevik asked. "We need the proper clothing and equipment."

"What kind of snake?" Trent joined the conversation.

"Oh, the worst kind—one that'll make anybody drive past as fast as possible," George suggested. "That means a lion snake, or some such."

"Some of my best friends are lion snakes," Travis grinned. "I think we have a winner."

*Hover-way M-799, Portal, Havek*
   *Travis*

Chazi, Bekzi and Darzi volunteered to help with our ruse, and folded themselves to our safe house.

Teeg then worked through the proper channels to place a warning that three dangerous lion snakes had been dumped in the area by poachers looking to sell the illegal creatures. The explanation was that the Planetary Wildlife Protection Agency, or PWPA, had gotten too close, so the poachers dumped their snakes. Local authorities then advised all local traffic to be rerouted if at all possible.

A team of snake-catchers would be sent quickly, before the snakes escaped into more populated areas. The idea was excellent—it would give us the best of reasons to examine the entire area for the theft site.

And, as our lion snake shapeshifters had mindspeech, it would be no problem to avoid finding them until we were done with our other work.

Wyatt had joined us; he'd brought the proper clothing and equipment to search for poisonous snakes.

"I've only had these on for two minutes and I hate the boots already," Trent grumped.

"Sorry, bro. Have to look official in case our images are recorded." All of us were now dressed in official PWPA labeled clothing, and thick, bite-proof rubber boots.

"At least we'll be disguised to the outside world."

"I'm with you on the boots," Rob agreed with Trent. "I'll be taking mine off as soon as we get there—I have to be barefoot to set my toes in the dirt."

"I suppose it's a really good thing that lion snakes are considered an endangered species now; capture and release on the proper homeworld is now the order of the day," Denevik said.

"Well, who knew that a vendetta against lion snakes would result in their favorite food, savanna lizards, getting out of hand after their population exploded? That increase in numbers resulted in the little buggers eating crops, small animals and everything else within reach."

"Savanna lizard hard to kill. Lion snake poison make it easy," Chazi grinned.

"Those lizards are hardy little assholes," Trent said.

"Know that. For sure. Taste good, though. Fried best," Chazi teased Trent.

"I'll take your word for it," Trent chuckled and slapped Chazi on the back.

*Is he kidding?* Lyrill, our Sirenali investigator, asked.

"He's kidding, Lyr," I replied, shortening his name as he'd asked. "About the fried part, anyway. Now. Is everybody ready? Yes? Let's go."

*Cassie*

*Still nothing,* Rob sent. I paused a moment to survey the acres and acres of wind-blown grasses beneath and surrounding the hover-way. Everything was allowed to grow naturally, and on any other day, the scenery would be lovely—with wildflowers interspersed here and there.

Rob and I were working together; Denevik was with George and Barry, who were working parallel to our location. Rob was barefoot and stopping every few feet to dig toes into the soil.

We'd worked in a grid pattern across our assigned section, which had turned into something akin to an endless search for the metaphorical sewing implements in tall piles of dried grasses.

Everyone was keeping us updated, although nothing significant had been found, other than a few bugs, worms and two harmless snakes.

That's when we received mindspeech from one of the reptanoids. *Earth Sprite, come,* he begged. *Not right with ground here.*

*Where?* Rob responded quickly.

*Here.* Rob and I looked around frantically, until we saw a large snake head poking above the tall grass of the hover-way.

A few vehicles had swept past us now and then, but traffic was down dramatically from what it ought to be.

*We're coming, Chazi,* Travis sent to all of us. Rob and I ran in the proper direction, our snake-catcher poles in hand.

*Hold back*, Rob sent once his feet touched the ground where Chazi was. I could see his face go pale.

"Get back," I shouted to the others, who'd also come running.

"It's the same, but worse than Laddus' compound," Rob breathed and began backing away. "The grass is poisoned, too."

"Chazi, come away," I called out to him. "This ground has been poisoned by the Prophet. It's in the grass as well as the dirt."

Chazi didn't waste time—he slithered past my boots, retreating toward Travis, who'd arrived with Trent and Lyr right behind him. Farther down the hover-way, Denevik and Rajeon were holding Barry, Wyatt and George back. Two more snake heads popped up near them; Darzi and Bekzi had held back, too.

*I've called Randl*, Travis sent. *This place will have to be cleansed, Cassie.*

*How will we explain a fire?* I asked him.

*Don't know—yet.*

"What do we have here?" Randl appeared and sidled up to me. "Oh, yes. It's here, all right," I watched as a deep frown marred his features. "It appears that the poison has seeped into the grass, and then spread to the other grass. Yes. It has grown, most certainly. No wonder there was little investigation. I'm sure those who arrived at this site were infected quickly, and then convinced their work was done."

"And they're still infected," I nodded as a sudden gust of wind rippled the grasses and pulled hair loose from my braid.

"Exactly. Cassie, we have to cleanse this ground before this spreads even farther. Teeg is on the way; we'll ask him to devise a reason for the burning."

"Can you tell how much ground needs to be cleansed?"

"I can feel it. We'll work together to get this done."

"So we need a burn, eh?" Teeg arrived with Astralan Starr, one of his warlock guards. Astralan was keeping him shielded from sight, no doubt, as another hover-truck rumbled past on our left.

"We really need Cassie to burn this—it's gotten into the soil and the grass—and has had plenty of time to spread since it was planted here," Randl said.

"Then we'll need three faked deaths—it's the only reason to destroy an endangered species," Teeg replied. "I can provide bodies, but one of our reptanoids will have to bite them for us."

"Sounds nasty," I made a face.

"They've been forced to do worse in the past," Teeg sighed. "Don't worry; we'll get that part sorted." He pulled a comp-vid from a pocket and began tapping a message. "There—they've been notified to close the hover-way and re-route all traffic. I've reported the deaths to the authorities and asked the fire departments to stand by in case they're needed."

"I can stay here with Cassie and Randl—the fire won't harm me," Denevik came forward to join us.

"All right. Everyone else come back to Campiaa with me," Teeg said. "Randl, wait half an hour, then have Cassie burn it down. We'll bring the others back to the safe house when you're done. Our job has turned into this; how many people were infected by this—and how many others have they infected?"

"I knew this wouldn't be a simple job," Randl said. "I would have bet money on it. I just hadn't expected it to be quite this bad."

"And if all the other theft sites are the same," Teeg grimaced.

"Just what I was thinking," Randl breathed a troubled sigh.

*You see the boundaries?* Randl's mind connected with mine, sending me images of how much ground needed cleansing. He and I stood at the center of the poisoned ground, where the theft had likely taken place. He'd searched for evidence while waiting the half hour for traffic to be rerouted.

We'd found nothing, so if there were a mess left behind, the Prophet had tidied up afterward.

*This is a much bigger job than Laddus' compound,* I responded. *If we'd found it right after the theft happened,* I didn't finish.

*Will it be a problem?* Randl asked.

*No. I'll take care of it. You should shield yourself and stand beside Denevik outside the burn area.*

*I'm there.* He'd folded away from me. *Start the cleanse, Cassie. Now.*

~

*Safe House*
*Randl*

It had taken a while to cleanse the ground, but it had been done and the fire was out, thanks to Cassie's control over that volatile element.

After getting her and Denevik back to the safe house, I'd asked Vik to join me. We had another jaunt into split-time looming. Since I knew the date and location of the theft, I wanted to see for myself who'd performed that feat for the Prophet, and I hoped to catch him in the act of poisoning the area.

Vik and I sat at the kitchen island having tea and contemplating our journey. Denevik walked in, freshly-showered and dressed in clean clothing. He searched through the cupboards to find a cup for tea.

"Cassie resting?" I asked him.

"Yes."

"Good."

"You'll be all right going back to that time and place?"

"He won't know we're there—the spirit coins can guard us against him for a short time."

"Hmmm." Denevik poured a mug full of tea and sat nearby. "Can you feel him in split-time like you could earlier?"

"That hasn't been firmly established, yet," I said.

"The last two times at the media companies, there was nothing," Vik said. "I'm waiting to see if this trip is the same. If so, then the Prophet's learned new tricks."

"If nothing else, I hope we're able to get information on his local, petty criminal," I added. "If we do that, then we can take the operation down."

"What are the odds that the infected investigators are now a part of the criminal operation?" Denevik asked.

"I'd say there's a good chance of that," I told him. "Although it may not be obvious. I'd leave them in law enforcement and let them look the other way on my criminal activities."

"Nice setup," Vik said and sipped his tea. "A solid, albeit a contemptibly criminal, plan."

"The Prophet does like everything neatly tied up," Denevik shrugged.

"You ready?" Vik turned to me after draining his cup.

"Ready. We'll be back," I said and stepped us into split-time.

*I can recreate all these images*, I sent to Vik as we watched a crew go through two hover-trucks, taking inventory.

*They're local, for sure, and that one, there*, he nodded toward the one who held the drivers inside a shield—*it takes a third-level warlock to do what he's doing.*

*He has the ability to relocate the trucks, too*, I pointed out.

*True. Wait—is that?*

*That's Gillen Wilker*, I gripped Vik's arm—hard. *What the hell is he doing?*

Gillen had folded in, bearing a small box and what looked to be a glass jug of dirty water.

"Move aside," Gillen ordered everyone around him. We watched as the thieves gave him plenty of space. When he opened the box, first, I understood it was spelled, because the stench of the Prophet spilled out with the grass seeds Gillen dumped on the ground.

He then opened the jug of brownish water, and I almost went dizzy at the reek of the Prophet pouring out of it as he soaked the seeds he'd dumped.

Once both containers were empty, he nodded at the third-level warlock, who folded the drivers and the crew away. Gillen then transported both hover-trucks elsewhere.

*I've seen enough*, I told Vik, taking us out of split-time and back to the safe house.

~

"This one—in his most recent arrest warrant, was listed as a possible employee of Wilz Brak, who has since disappeared from everybody's radar," Barry handed his comp-vid to me. I'd sent the mental images to him; he'd connected directly to the comp-vid and in no time, he had the latest criminal investigation on what appeared to be the crew chief of the theft ring.

"This means we may ultimately be dealing with Wilz Brak, whose specialty in petty theft, systems hacking and credit diversion has been upgraded somewhat," Vik said. "We just have to track him and his den of thieves, plus one third-level warlock."

"All of whom are probably hiding behind walls filled with bone dust," I said. "I think we're going to need all the sprites working on this project—not just Rob. We need to find them fast, so we can officially announce our intentions to beat the Prophet at his own game."

"What with all the erroneous news reports recently, he may already have that idea," Cassie walked into the common room with Denevik, after hearing our discussion.

"I thought you were asleep," I stopped short of accusing her of not resting.

"I'm good. We're on the way to the kitchen for something cold and icy."

"Sounds like a good idea," Vik said. "Trips to split-time always dry me out."

"Where are Travis, Trent, Rajeon, Lyr and Rob?" Cassie asked.

"Checking on the investigators," George replied. "I've been relaying information on their latest known whereabouts from my comp-vid," he held up the device.

"Anything new on that front?" Denevik asked.

"Nothing yet."

"We did learn that the Prophet wasn't directly responsible for spreading his disease on the hover-way," Vik informed Cassie.

"How did he do it?"

"He infected grass seed and water, somehow," I answered. "Gillen Wilker showed up with a box of grass seed and a jug of dirty water. The moment he opened both I was nearly knocked down by the Prophet's stench."

"Does this mean he hasn't been the source of those false news releases?" Denevik mused.

"I still can't say that for certain. Besides, who else would do that? The proximity of this theft to the media company responsible for the latest false news report can't be mere coincidence."

"No idea who else could do that—or who would even want to. Want us to bring drinks for you?"

"Let's take this to the kitchen; we need a break anyway," I said.

∽

*Travis*

"Are you sure this is a good idea?" I asked Rob, who currently had his fingers dipped into the potting soil of a house plant belonging to one Urell Vealdt, crime investigator for the city of Portal.

"Yes, I feel it," he nodded, pulling his fingers from the pot and brushing dirt off his hands. "Urell has emptied his water glasses on the plant, to conserve water," Rob said. "The plant and the soil now have the beginnings of the Prophet's poison in them."

"Fucking hell," Rajeon swore. "He has a wife. No doubt she's infected, too."

"I'd say they're all infected," Rob advised. "Anyone who was anywhere near that site is infected."

"They need to be quarantined," Trent said.

"How many other sites are we talking about?" Rob lifted an eyebrow at me.

"Too many," I said. "Way too many."

"We have to put Teeg on notice—we'll have to devise some way of removing these people from their duties—unless Randl wants to track down the petty criminal and publicize this to the Prophet—that he can find any or all of his minions if he wants."

"I say hold off on that until we have more criminals captured and the investigators pegged as carriers," Rajeon advised.

"If we put all our resources into this, we may be able to do it in a few weeks," I said. "It means sending almost everybody into the field, but it can be done."

"I think we ought to get on it fast, before the Prophet decides to move all his minions," Rob suggested. "We may not have weeks to accomplish this."

"Rob's right," Rajeon said. "If the Prophet discovers we're on to him, he'll move all of his petty thieves in a blink."

"We'll have to work out how to get as many teams as we can into the field at once," Trent said. "Let's go—Urell could be back any time."

I folded all of us back to the safe house, where we found Randl and the others discussing similar problems in the kitchen.

*BlackWing X*

*Sabrina*

I'd sent three messages to Travis and Trent, and still hadn't heard from either one of them. Maybe it was too soon.

Maybe it wasn't. I had no idea where they were—Perri's reply to the message I sent to her was *they're on assignment*. Nothing more than that—not even a civil *how are you.*

# CHAPTER 13

*Unnamed Dwarf Planet*
   *Griffin*

"Now that Geeva has been snatched away, who will you go after?" My father asked as he scraped scrambled eggs out of a skillet onto our plates.

"You believe that media claptrap?" I frowned at Wylend.

"You think the Prophet has her and her bunch?"

"I have no idea who the Prophet might have," I replied. "But, since you asked, Dorlent is next on my list."

"Dorlent—that murderer?"

"That's the one. He has a stable of assassins who are just as nasty as he is. If the Prophet gets his hands on him, nobody may be safe."

"Good luck with that one," Dad made a face. "I'm a Fifth-level warlock, and even I'd have second thoughts about going after him. Erland calls him a ninja, he's so deadly."

"I used to fight Ra'Ak, remember? Besides, Dorlent has the third largest space fleet, after Laddus and Geeva. The Prophet wants ships —remember that, too?"

"I remember. Just be careful, all right?"

"I'm always careful. Things happen anyway, sometimes."

"What's your first move, then?"

"I'll let Teeg know that Dorlent is my next target."

"Is that wise?"

"Do you think I have an answer?"

"I can see this is a touchy discussion. We'll talk about something else."

"Thank you."

*G'margis*

*V'dar*

"Who is next on the list?" I asked W'dell.

"Dorlent, my lord."

"Good. An assassin and his stable of killers will be as useful to me as his fleet of star cruisers. Do what you can to track him; I'll put all resources I have into his location."

"As you will it, my lord."

"Good. Very good. Don't forget to track Randl Gage, too. You know I want his death more than anything."

"I'll put every effort into locating him as well."

"Keep me advised. Even if I am sleeping, I wish to know of vital discoveries immediately."

"Of course, my lord."

*Founder's Palace, Campiaa*

*Teeg San Gerxon*

"Dorlent? Do you know how many agents—good ones—we've lost to that prick?" I stared at Griffin. "It's a suicide mission just to mention his name at the CSD."

"He's too much of a threat to leave alone; if the Prophet finds him first, you know what will happen afterward." Griffin waved away Wyatt's offer of a drink.

"We may have located one of the smaller minions in the Prophet's arsenal," I said. "We've discovered, too, that the Prophet can spread his poison in seeds and tainted water."

"How did you learn of that?" Griffin's forehead furrowed in a deep frown.

"After he had the stuff dumped in a particular place, it infected the ground and the grasses around it. I feel the Prophet is waiting for the unsuspecting to come along. Randl's team is tracing possible victims infected by it already."

"Will you tell me where?"

"I'd prefer not to release that information."

"Suit yourself. I'm hunting Dorlent, now. I doubt I'll cross paths with Randl."

"Good. I expect to be kept informed."

"Of course you do." He didn't discuss the matter further; he folded away instead.

"It's always a dance with him, isn't it?" Wyatt poured a glass of bourbon and set it in front of me.

"Every fucking time," I agreed and tossed back the bourbon in a single swallow.

❧

*D'margis*

*Randl*

"You are now the hub," I told Barry and George. "Since you've helped us narrow down the locations of all the food thefts, you'll be the ones to inform me of the largest to smallest of them, so I can assign teams to investigate."

"We can also narrow our search for certain words or phrases occurring around those locations," Barry said. "This will allow us to do several things at once."

"If anything important crops up, let me know right away," I told them. "Even the slightest thing could hold a great deal of significance."

"We understand, Commander," George said. "Our system is set to alert us, even when we are sleeping."

"Good. Communication is key in this; I feel it."

"We are on the job already," Barry confirmed. "Thank you for allowing us to work in the field, too."

"You like that, eh? We'll see if we can send you out on other investigations, then. George, I have something for you—it was delivered this morning."

"You have a gift for me? Thank you."

"Don't thank me—this is from Zaria." I handed him the small box containing his medallion.

"George," Barry turned the puzzled android in his direction. "If you ever doubt your worth—or whether your existence is justified and blessed, it resides in that medallion," Barry whispered reverently. "Put it on and never take it off."

"Who is Zaria?" George asked as he removed the medallion from its box and settled it over his head.

"Think of her as the Queen of Larentii," I smiled at him.

"A Larentii? I never thought to see or know one."

"I think I can arrange a meeting," I told him. "If she doesn't appear beside you at some unexpected moment before then."

"Please, thank her for this gift," George said.

"I will."

*Portal, Havek*

*Cassie*

"According to Barry and George, these three locations are the most likely ones where Wilz Brak may be holed up," Rob pointed out the three locations on his comp-vid map. "All three are populated, so he's hiding in plain sight, somehow."

"Could be underground," Denevik suggested. "I've seen it done before—put a perfectly normal house or houses above ground, with innocuous inhabitants, who, in turn, hide the tunnels and shafts leading down to the lair."

"I hate tunnels and shafts," Zephyr complained. She, Blaze and Ebb had been sent to help us, while Barry and George had gone back to D'margis.

"Those are my domain," Rob gave her a smile. "You don't have to go."

"We don't know yet if there are any tunnels and shafts," Trent pointed out. "We'll have to scout the areas, first."

"A small lake is here," Ebb pointed at the second location. "Do you suppose they could be hiding there, under water?"

"Anything is possible, especially if the Prophet doesn't want us to find them," Travis observed.

*If it will eliminate a servant of the Prophet, I will go wherever I must,* Lyr sent, a determined expression on his face.

Lyr was slight of build with thick, red hair, but underneath, he was made of sterner stuff. I could see he was more than focused on his mission to destroy the Prophet, even if he only hid the rest of us from his prying mind while we did what was necessary.

Like the rest of us, he, too, wore one of Zaria's medallions.

"Which one should we check first?" Rob asked.

"Let's go with the waterfront property first—that's a more upscale neighborhood, with larger plots capable of hiding someone either underground or underwater," Travis made the decision with a firm nod. "Then we'll go with this one, because it's the closest, and that one last," he pointed at the one farthest away. "Let's go."

～

*Klerz (A Non-Alliance World)*
  *Korvus Katergáris*

"I must say, your offer was so intriguing, I almost disregarded it," Dorlent toyed with his comp-vid. I'd offered a monarch's ransom in credits, just to meet with me and hear me out.

I had work for him—most certainly. No doubt, too, several of his assassins had come with him to this wharf-side pub on the eastern edge of Klerz's largest city. Dorlent wouldn't appear in public without backup in case the meeting was a set-up or became too dangerous to continue.

Dorlent's talents were shrouded in myths and legends. Many said he could disappear in a crowd of one, he was so skilled at his work. In this dimly-lit ale house, smelling of sweat, saltwater and beer, it was nearing the midnight hour. When Dorlent took the bench across from mine and I got my first look at him, I had no doubt he could vanish faster than a mouse into a hole.

"I assume you have a target?" A dark eyebrow lifted as I pushed a box containing unregistered credit squares toward him. As promised, forty million untraceable credits, just for a meeting.

"Several targets, actually," I replied.

"A price will be levied per head per location," he replied while the box of credits vanished from the table with a quick swipe of his hand.

"What if I said they'd all be in the same location at the same time? It will prove easier than snatching fish from a bowl."

"Then there must be some difficulty attached to these targets. Are they heavily armed? Warlocks, perhaps? Why would you contact me if this would be so simple?"

"Because I wish to keep my hand out of this, you understand, and, when you accomplish this feat, your prowess will endure until the end of time."

"Again, you intrigue me," he said. "Tell me about the targets."

"Here," I slid my comp-vid toward him so he could read it. I watched subtle eye movements, telling me he'd read through it twice.

"You're sure of this?" The eyebrow lifted again as his eyes searched my face. "Your targets will be at this location during this time?"

"Absolutely. Handle this as deftly as I know you can, and many will die. That will, indeed, please me and be worthy of the one-billion credits I'll pay for your services."

"One third up front is standard," he said.

"I anticipated as much." Lifting the larger box by my side, I set it on the table. "See for yourself that it is there," I offered.

Lifting the lid, he glanced briefly at the credit chips inside, all in large denominations. "Ah. Very good. Shall we meet here again, on the day after?" He shut the lid on the credits box and locked it.

"Same time," I agreed. "Do this and your reputation will never suffer tarnish."

"I can see that for myself. Thank you for this opportunity, Mr. Katergáris. I will put my very best on this project, and I, myself, will deliver the hardest blow of all."

"I'm counting on it," I told him.

*Portal, Havek*

*Cassie*

"There is something down there," Ebb informed us after dunking his head in the lake for several minutes. "I felt it—it's not natural, so I assume it is crafted by humanoids."

"How big is it?" I asked.

All of us stood in a secluded section of the lakeshore, beneath a willow-type tree whose tendrils hung around us, hiding us from the prying eyes of residents. Homes were scattered around the lake; prime property for the wealthiest in the neighborhood.

"It's not that big, but it could be connected to the rest of Brak's compound," Ebb replied.

"An emergency entrance or exit?" Travis considered Ebb's description.

"Possibly," Ebb conceded. "I can go down to investigate."

"Nobody goes alone," Travis warned. "If you go in, we all go in. It's why we brought our breathing masks."

"At least Ebb can sense it—I've found nothing by *Looking*," Trent said.

"It's how the water acts—I can sense when it is forced to move around something, and whether the obstacle is natural," Ebb told him.

"That's a fine detection system you have, then," Rajeon said.

"Put your masks on," Travis instructed. "We're going in and Ebb will lead the way."

*I do not need a mask,* Lyr sent, pulling off his jacket and pants before changing into his other form. I watched as he formed scales over his body and webs and fins on hands, toes, arms and legs.

"Sirenali are formidable in the water," Rajeon nodded his approval at Lyr's transformation. Lyr stuffed his clothing into a small bag, then tied its cords around his waist. When he nodded his readiness, the rest of us pulled on our masks and followed Ebb into the cold lake.

*D'margis*

*Randl*

"I'd like you to head up this investigation," I handed a comp-vid to Vik, showing the location of the second-largest frozen food theft. "Choose a team and take them in."

"How are Travis and Trent doing?" he asked as he scrolled through the information.

"Right now, they're swimming in a lake to find out if the construction Ebb sensed is a hidden entrance into Wilz Brak's lair."

"Sounds like fun," Vik grimaced. "I hate murky water."

"You may end up doing the same thing, you know."

"Understood."

"I'll come with you initially; we may have to go into split-time to witness the theft, like last time."

"If I could have, I'd have reached out and crushed Gillen Wilker's throat; he couldn't do a thing to stop me, either."

"You know we can't interfere like that; we've been warned about changing the past. I pushed the envelope when I helped my mother," I didn't attempt to hide the bitterness in my voice. "At least Zaria says it was something that happened anyway, so there wasn't much harm done."

"Yeah. Too bad you couldn't kill V'dar then."

"We don't know whether something worse would have taken his place."

"Don't depress me, okay? Every time we seem to have the upper hand with him, he grows stronger. Liron planned for every fucking scenario, didn't he?"

"It sure feels that way." I lifted the water glass on my desk, rose from my chair and went to pour the contents onto Esmeralda. She needed a drink; I didn't.

"How's Esmeralda doing?" Vik asked after watching me.

"She's fine. The sunlamp is doing its job, and I think she's grown three inches since she got here. Perri says it's because she's happy."

"I'm glad somebody's happy. I'd like to take Perri and Zanfield with me, if that's all right. Jincus, too. He's antsy and wants to get his hands dirty."

"I'm good with that. Dori may want to sharpen her claws, actually."

"No problem. Dave will want to go."

"Of course. I'll find a Sirenali investigator to go with you."

"Thanks. When do we leave?"

"Tonight, so put your team on alert and coordinate with Barry and George."

"Will do, boss."

～

*Portal, Havek*

*Cassie*

*There are two guards there,* Ebb reported.

He was right; when the murky water cleared enough for us to see the underwater pod, there were two armed guards standing inside it. Behind them, leading farther below the lake bottom, was a door into a tunnel.

*Now what?* Rob asked. He was uncomfortable in the water; that was more than obvious.

*I can break the bubble and take care of the guards,* Rajeon offered. *The rest of you will have to swim into that tunnel until you find where it leads.*

*Could be a trap*, Denevik observed.

*Then let me go first*, I replied. *My fire isn't held back by water.*

*Denevik, if I send you and Cassie in first, I trust you can clear the way for the rest of us?* Travis asked.

*You can count on it*, Denevik replied.

*Good. Rajeon, you go first. Get this first obstacle out of our way. Cassie, Denevik—once Rajeon destroys the bubble, you head into that tunnel first. Everyone else, we wait three ticks and go in after them. Is that clear?*

*We're clear*, Ebb agreed.

The giant octopus that Rajeon became would have scared the pants off anyone. The moment his massive tentacles slapped onto the bubble and began to squeeze, both guards opened fire.

The bubble blew outward with the force of the air inside it, sucking both men into the water. Two of Rajeon's tentacles snatched both men and squeezed.

Blood filled the water now gushing into the bubble's unprotected doorway; Denevik gripped my arm and *skipped* us toward it. The tunnel was so dark, I had to go to prelim and light my hands to see what was ahead.

Muck, water plants and mud washed in after us, blurring our vision further—until a shining pool of light appeared before us.

*They'll be waiting with weapons*, Denevik warned.

*Then it's time, I suppose.*

*Yes. I'm turning now. Do it, Cassie.*

*And so I did.*

D'margis

*Travis*

Had Cassie not released her fire when she did, then all of Brak's minions would have fired upon us while Brak and his warlock escaped. But, with Denevik being at her side and immune to her fire as she burned everything around her, the warlock's power was neutralized.

Wilz Brak was burned so badly he was barely alive; his warlock had died attempting to run from us.

Trent and I followed Brak's gurney-bot as it wheeled into the med unit at the compound on D'margis—we didn't want him to die before Randl could get a good look at him. "I'm here; where are the others?" Randl appeared inside the med unit.

"Back at the safe house—we sent them there," Trent replied.

"Ah, Wilz, we meet at last," Randl looked down at our guest. "Yes, I see that you're obsessed—that's at least one question answered."

"Anything else there?" I asked.

"No, but Vik and I can go into split-time, now that we know the location."

"If the Prophet doesn't know we were responsible for this, he will soon," Trent advised.

"I know. We have to work on getting the other locations dealt with quickly."

Wilz Brak's eyes had turned glassy. "He's gone," I checked the life support readings on the gurney-bot's side panel.

"I'll deliver the body to the CSD infirmary on Campiaa," I said. "Teeg can make the announcement in a few days that Brak has been eliminated from the most-wanted lists."

"Good idea. If the Prophet doesn't figure this out, then we have a little time to get to the others," I said. "How much damage is left in Portal?"

"One of those lakeside mansions is nothing but a burned pile of rubble," Trent shrugged. "Nobody inside it survived, once we pulled Brak out of there."

"I'll ask Teeg to do damage control," Randl said. "A bomb or two going off in a criminal's lair ought to do the trick."

"Commander?" Zanfield walked into the med unit with hesitation, a comp-vid gripped tightly in his hands.

I went cold at what I saw in him. Already, there was a new report from the media, rightfully blaming the BlackWing Pirates for the destruction of Wilz Brak's lair on Havek.

"Give it to me," I held out a hand.

"How?" Zanfield shook his head in confusion.

"No idea. This was less than an hour ago. If the Prophet knew, why didn't he come after the team I sent to Havek?"

"There's another media report? About the attack on Havek?" Travis demanded.

"Yes. Come with me; we'll take the body to Campiaa, then have a conversation with Teeg. Zanfield, call Vik; I want him with me."

We ended up taking Travis' team from Havek, too; Teeg wanted to speak with all of us. We sat in his library, which held enough seats for all of us around his conference table.

"I cleansed everything that Ebb and Robb told me was contaminated," Cassie replied to Teeg's question. "The lake is black from all the burning, and the ah, water level is down maybe two or three feet. The mansion is a total loss."

"As it should be. We don't need more of the Prophet's filth getting passed around," Teeg nodded at her. "At least there are no images released of what happened—yet. Was there anything that could be seen of you in all that?" His gazed moved from Cassie to Denevik and back again.

"I imagine all anyone would see was a massive fire," Denevik answered, his voice calm. "I stood near the center of it, and as tall as my Full Thifilathi is, the fire was much taller."

"I've already asked for images submitted to local news media," Teeg waved a hand. "Nothing has come in, yet, not even from individuals in the area."

"Here's something—but it only shows fuzzy fire," Wyatt slid his comp-vid toward Teeg.

"That's odd—the images become blurry the moment the fire explodes in the mansion," Teeg scrolled back and forth through the recording.

"Do you suppose the heat had anything to do with it?" Travis asked. "I'm surprised none of the surrounding homes didn't suffer heat damage, it was so intense."

"I kept it within a certain radius, or tried to," Cassie defended herself.

"This isn't a point to argue—I'm glad of the damaged images, actually. All I can see from this is a huge fire. It could easily be explained away with a bomb or another incendiary device."

"With an *inconclusive cause* determination at the end, submitted by the investigators," I sighed. "Let's hope that's it, anyway."

"We're back to how the Prophet got the information so fast and didn't attempt to fight back, or whether there's a third party involved," Teeg said. "I want answers, and I want them now. Is the Prophet the only enemy the BlackWing Pirates have made?"

"I doubt it—with so many crimes conveniently laid at our feet," I told him. "This, though—if it is a third party, it has to be a very powerful one, or one who's gotten extremely lucky this time around."

"I'm in the extremely lucky camp, myself," Teeg admitted. "If the Prophet had any idea of your whereabouts, or that of any of your people, he'd have shown up to deal with this himself, rather than pointing information after the fact to a local news agency."

"I'm of that opinion myself," Denevik agreed. "If he'd had any idea where we were," he didn't finish.

Nobody could see it, but I knew he was gripping Cassie's hand tightly beneath the table. I had no idea whether either of them would survive a meeting with the Prophet—I doubted it. Denevik did, too.

"As of now, you're finished on Havek," Teeg said. "I'll have Griffin put a team together to look for those others affected by the Prophet's disease. We have several names already—we can watch them closely and remove them from their jobs discreetly if their actions warrant it. Where are you headed next?"

"Stixx," I said.

"Proceed with caution. At the first sign of anything going wrong, abandon the investigation, I beg you."

"We will certainly bear that in mind," I dipped my head in a nod as I rose. "Does anyone have to use the bathroom before we leave?" Wyatt snickered at the joke.

*One more thing,* Teeg sent as I walked toward Vik.

*What's that?*

*The ball to celebrate the founding of the Campiaan Alliance is in two days. If you wouldn't mind, I'd like to borrow some of your crew as extra security. Disguised, of course.*

*Which ones?*

*Cassie, Denevik, Rajeon, Vik, Travis and Trent. Anyone else you think might be useful. You're invited as a guest, if you'd like to come.*

*I'll make them available to you and ask Dori if she'd like to get dressed up.*

*Thank you.*

~

G'margis

   V'dar

If I hadn't seen the news feed, I wouldn't have known about the attack on Brak's domain. A phrase came to me as I read the article released with the vid—*losing it*. I should have felt it when the attack came.

I should have known that someone or something had burned the area where my obsessive disease was growing.

*Why hadn't I felt it? Had Randl Gage gained power, as I'd gained power?* Fury burned in my chest; Where were Alken and Je'Dik? I hadn't heard from them in several days. *What were they doing?*

~

Krelk Homeworld

   Alken Wilker

Je'Dik's persuasion was strong. I found myself unwilling to argue with any of his decisions. Therefore, we'd gone to his childhood home to meet with his foster parents. The Prophet had ordered us to hunt Randl Gage; I found myself sitting down to breakfast inside a modified cave.

Built into a cliff face, the cave faced the morning sun. Outside the glass-surrounded front door, many steps led downward to a communal courtyard. It should have been quite primitive, as the Krelk were a relatively young race.

Instead, the hollowed-out stone dwelling contained every modern convenience his foster mother, Cha'Riz, desired.

Still, though, the race preferred to dress in the skins of animals rather than weaving cloth. They hunted those animals, of course—it was a desired tradition among the males.

As for their language, I didn't understand most of it. Je'Dik translated anything his foster parents wished to say to me.

They also didn't wear goggles as Je'Dik did and didn't appear to mind that he did wear them. I didn't ask about them, either. I also didn't ask when or if we were planning to hunt Randl Gage again.

Je'Dik wouldn't face the Prophet's wrath as I would. In all his servants, the Prophet worked around any of Je'Dik's failures, as if he'd been instructed to do so. The rest of us, however, could die at any moment if the Prophet were angry enough.

Still, I couldn't bring myself to argue that point with my companion. His will was foremost at the moment, and he wished to spend time with family.

"Eat," Je'Dik ordered as I stared at eggs and meat of unknown origins on my plate. "The others will be here, soon."

"Others?"

The frown aimed in my direction let me know Je'Dik was done answering questions. Frankly, I didn't have long to wait; I'd barely finished half my meal when the first one arrived.

A shiver went through me as another Krelk entered the dwelling, wearing identical goggles. He dipped his head to Je'Dik and spoke a single word.

Moments later, another arrived, also wearing goggles. Then another came, and another, until there were twelve goggle-wearers crowded in the family's living space. Each one spoke the same word when greeting Je'Dik, then all settled onto chairs and began to talk in their language, while Je'Dik's foster mother served tea and pastries.

The conversation went on and on; eventually I stepped onto the stone balcony outside the door and gazed about. This particular rocky formation held many similar dwellings, up and down its tall cliff face.

In the distance lay a forest, and beyond that, a large lake. From this height, I could see the sun shining on the water far away.

*Where are you?* the Prophet's voice shouted into my mind, startling me so much I almost tumbled down the steps. Catching myself in time and breathing with difficulty, I was about to answer when I heard Je'Dik's mindspeech.

*I am tending to my father's business*, he snapped back.

He had foster parents—why was that? *Who* was *Je'Dik's father?*

# CHAPTER 14

 *'margis*
*Randl*

"We're putting the petty criminals on hold for a few days," I announced in the central courtyard. "Teeg asked us to provide additional security for a function two days from now. I know that's not what we're about," I held up a hand to stop any grumbling. "But the moment he mentioned it I knew we had to go. Something about this unsettles me, and I believe our help is needed."

"What kind of function?" Denevik asked.

"One that all the important people in the Campiaan Alliance will attend. There will also be foreign dignitaries, royalty, presidents and other world leaders from the Reth Alliance present."

"Will we be in uniform?" Vik asked.

"No. You'll be dressed as guests, so you have two days to find appropriate evening wear. Make sure it's suitable for fighting."

*Cassie*

"You can wear that black dress you're hiding in the closet,"

Denevik's breath against my ear sent a shiver through me. "I'll find some jewelry to go with it."

"But," I turned toward him to argue.

"Don't worry," he smiled at me. "I think you'll approve."

I still wanted to argue with him but didn't; he wore a very determined expression, and I understood this was important to him.

"All right. Do you have something to wear?"

"I don't. Would you like to come with me to help?"

"Of course. Where and when?"

"Well, it's almost time for lunch right now on Kifirin, and I'd like to take my lady for a nice meal and shopping if she's available."

"You going to Kifirin?" Vik sidled up to us, followed by Ocenosek and Cudworth.

"We are. Want to come with us?" Denevik grinned.

"I was hoping we could have lunch with Reah," Vik said.

"There's a thought," Denevik agreed. "I wanted to talk to my granddaughter anyway."

"She's one of the Queens scheduled to come to the ball, since she's married to Teeg," Vik shrugged.

"And to you," Denevik leveled a pointed gaze at Vik.

"And a bunch of other people. I was going to ask her to bring Farzi and Nenzi with her," Vik sighed.

"I think that's an excellent idea," Cudworth agreed. "If protection is needed, those three can certainly defend themselves."

"Mom will be there, too, and she can take care of herself," Vik went on.

"Who's coming with her?" Denevik asked.

"No idea. Winkler doesn't mind these things; Gavin hates them unless he gets to dance, Drake and Drew would come, Rigo would certainly come—he has more experience at these things than anybody else I know."

"I'm sure she could bring the entire herd and nobody would mind," Ocenosek observed dryly.

"Ry will come, representing Karathia," Vik said. "I haven't seen him in a while. Maybe we can catch up while watching the crowd."

"Well, then, are we ready to go? Have you contacted Reah about lunch?" Denevik asked Vik.

"She says come on; they're holding the soup course for us."

I may have squeaked when Denevik grabbed me around my waist and *skipped* us to Kifirin. I'm certain my mouth was open, but any sound I made was left behind on D'margis as we landed in the great hall of the High Demon palace.

∼

*High Demon Palace, Kifirin*
*Queen Reah*

The moment I saw them together, I knew. My grandfather arrived with an arm around her, and she glowed with tamped and unexplored power. I didn't have the talent that Zaria or Breanne did to see through someone to their parentage, but surely there was tremendous power in this one's roots.

I'd never seen Denevik this happy before; his joy at bringing this woman to his ancestral home fairly radiated about him. And, out of all my great-grandfather's descendants, Denevik had been the one to father the mother of a true Queen to sit the throne of Kifirin. His sister, Glindarok, had the capability, but she'd given her authority to Jaydevik Rath and his brother, Gardevik.

Then, they'd succumbed to invasive, outside forces and almost allowed the destruction of the High Demon planet. Had Lexsi, Kory and Zaria not stood beside me, it would have been destroyed.

Both Jayd and Garde were dead, now, and Glinda was barely a shell of her former self. She still held my other daughters in thrall, however, and it was difficult finding sympathy for her.

"Avilepha," Vik stepped toward me and kissed my cheek.

"I've missed you," I told him.

"I'm going to Teeg's ball—I was hoping to have some time to talk to you and Ry while we're there."

"Teeg invited you? What about your work?" I asked.

"He wants extra security, so I'll be there for that," he shrugged, tucking my hand in the crook of his arm. "I heard lunch was ready. Is that true?"

"It is and you know it," I slapped his arm with my free hand. "Come on, I can see you're about to expire from starvation. Besides, the palace tour is scheduled to come through here any moment."

I led the procession toward the end of the hall, the others following. We'd almost reached the passage leading to the dining hall, when I heard the tour enter from the opposite end.

It was the usual noise, people walking, shoes clacking on marble floors, hushed voices echoing as they took in the life-sized statues of High Demon Kings lining the hall.

I didn't hesitate in our exit—until someone shrieked.

I felt as well as heard the fear in that scream. Someone was being threatened.

"Queen Reah," someone shouted. "I have your tour guide hostage."

Tory's hand gripped my arm; if he hadn't, I probably would have *skipped* to the tour group. He was right to hold me back—I looked and saw that the ranos pistol pressed against the woman's head ensured she'd be dead in moments no matter what I did.

"What do you want?" I turned slowly to face this new enemy.

"Untraceable credits and a way off this gods-forsaken planet," he snapped. The woman he held wept as the pistol was shoved harder against her temple. He was taller than she, and madness shone in his eyes.

*Let me handle this*, Cassie's sending was quite calm.

*Can you save Keeli?*

*I think I can.*

The rest of the tour group had backed away and were now huddled against a wall, terrified and silent. If the fool understood how powerful a ranos pistol was, he could fire into the ceiling and bring the roof down on all of them.

*Then do it*, I responded to Cassie's offer.

I thought she'd missed at first; she'd swiftly raised a hand and shot a stream of fire so thin and deadly it surprised me.

The second stream of fire, however, pierced the assailant's

forehead neater than any projectile I'd ever seen.

We watched as he crumbled to the floor, much like a building toppled by a bomb planted at its base. The timing between Cassie's firings was minute, and with such deadly accuracy on the second one, I wondered that she'd missed with the first.

Until Denevik explained it to me.

*She sealed the barrel and the trigger on the ranos pistol. He couldn't have reflexively fired the weapon as he died,* my grandfather informed me.

*How did you know what I was thinking?*

*You have a familiar frown on your face. Come, let's clean up this mess and get our visitors taken care of.*

By that time, palace security had arrived. I ordered an immediate investigation into how someone armed with a ranos pistol had gotten into the palace and had the visitors' credits refunded and then treated to a meal and drinks at an outside restaurant.

"Cassie, thank you," I told her after I'd gotten the housekeeping staff to clear away what little blood had fallen to the floor. Cassie's fire had seared the wound, so there wasn't much evidence left behind.

As for damage control, the tour wasn't close enough to see that Cassie didn't actually have a weapon in her hand—they assumed it, rather, and that was the best outcome in my opinion.

"Are we still hungry?" I asked my group.

"I think so," Vik grinned at me. "Come on, let's eat. You can ask Cassie questions over lunch."

"Well, I was thinking about doing just that."

"Good. Wanna race?"

I laughed and it felt good.

*I gave the kidnapper's image to Quin,* Lissa sent as we had our lunch.

*What did she say about him?*

*Obsessed, so whoever placed the obsession also provided the weapon, in my estimation.*

*I'm still working on how he got into the palace with a weapon. Everybody has to pass the weapons detectors.*

*Do you have images of the group and the palace staff manning the entrances? Send them to me and I'll get them to Quin.*

*I can do that. If there's nothing there, then somebody folded or* skipped *him in,* I replied.

*Yeah. That worries me, too. If they can get past your shields, well, that leaves the rest of us vulnerable, doesn't it?*

*Yes. Yes it does.*

*I'd like to see the images of Cassie taking him down—if you have time.*

*I'll come to you tonight and recreate them.*

*Thanks. Want dinner?*

*Of course. And a few drinks, too.*

*I'm on it,* she said.

~

Cassie

"He was obsessed, so somebody was going to die, no matter what," Queen Reah told me. "I sent his image to Lissa, who gave it to Quin. Quin says he was obsessed, so whoever placed the obsession probably gave him the weapon."

"Thank you. I just felt an overwhelming sense that he was going to try to kill everybody in the tour group if we didn't stop him," I said.

"You're probably right," Reah agreed with me. "I was afraid he'd shoot the ceiling and bring the roof down on all of them."

"That's possible," Vik agreed as he dipped into his dessert. "I didn't even consider that. A ranos pistol would be powerful enough to do it."

"I was afraid to turn and go after him," Denevik admitted. "Anything could have set him off."

"Same here," Vik nodded. "Even if I *skipped* down there, he could have gotten at least one shot off. Too many things could go wrong in that scenario."

"We were prepared to protect the Queen and her party," Cudworth stirred honey into a fresh cup of tea and drank. "I'm grateful it wasn't necessary."

"Why do your names not reflect your High Demon heritage?" Reah asked Cudworth and Ocenosek. "I meant to ask you that when we worked together before, but changing events and the disappearances of Vik and Denevik pushed it out of my mind."

"We've worked here and there as security before, and the -*vik* at the end of our names gave us away every time. The element of surprise is sometimes the best defense anyone can have, and an enemy certainly wouldn't take us for High Demons if our names didn't fit. That's why we changed them legally in both Alliances."

"Interesting," Reah said thoughtfully. "And wise, too, I suppose, if one is determined to work off-planet. You work for Randl, now?"

"Yes. We have his approval, as well as Zaria's," Ocenosek said.

"We're fortunate to have them," Denevik told Reah.

"If you didn't work for Randl, I'd offer positions here," Reah smiled. "I have that much confidence in both of you."

"Our Queen is most kind," Cudworth dipped his head to her. "Thank you."

❧

Not long after we finished lunch, we went shopping at a high-end tailor's shop. "I have just the thing," the clerk told Denevik and the others.

"We don't want to be twins—or quadruplets," Vik teased, since Ocenosek and Cudworth wanted suits, too.

"Of course not. This way," the humanoid tailor waved off the joke and walked toward the back of the store. "I have this in black, and this one in charcoal," he pointed out two formal sets of clothing. "We also have these in white, a lighter gray and dark blue."

"Which one do you like?" Denevik turned toward me.

"I like the charcoal," I stepped forward and fingered the fabric. "Nice. Very nice," I turned back to Denevik. "I think you'd look great in this."

"I think it'll be charcoal for me, then," Denevik grinned.

That day, I watched as three High Demons were fitted in black suits by an alterations-bot, while the fourth was dressed in charcoal, black dress shoes and a tie.

Haircuts for all were next on the list. Denevik was quite happy about getting a trim, I could tell.

"One more thing on the list," he told me as I admired his haircut.

"What's that?"

"Reah wants to show you something."

"Oh. Okay." I had no idea what was going on. I thought he wanted to take me to a jewelry store. A part of me felt relief; another part was disappointed.

Denevik *skipped* me back to the palace, but to a part I hadn't seen before. Reah was already there, waiting for us.

"This is the royal vault," Reah said, nodding to two High Demon guards who stood outside it. An eye scan and fingerprint DNA opened the door for her.

I should have known—I didn't.

"This is my great-grandmother's jewelry collection," Reah led us toward a set of slender drawers to the left. "I'll shut the vault on my way out—Denevik can *skip* you out when you're ready."

"Thank you," Denevik told her. She smiled and lifted a hand in farewell on her way out. Once the locking mechanisms engaged on the vault, Denevik turned back to the drawers.

"My mother's jewelry is here," Denevik smiled down at me. "Some of the pieces she left to any of her sons who married. I'm the only son left," his voice held regret. "Here," he pulled out a drawer. "She loved these," he said reverently as the drawer revealed a necklace of small gold squares set with black opals. Matching earrings and a bracelet lay next to it. "This will go perfectly with your dress."

"Denny, no," I breathed. "This is so beautiful. What if I lose it?"

"We'll find it," he told me. "It's just stuff. You are the true jewel."

I didn't realize I was crying until a tear dripped off my cheek and onto my hand.

"Avilepha, these are for you," Denevik breathed, lifting the necklace and settling it around my neck. The bracelet and earrings came next. Then, he lifted my left hand and kissed it.

"One day, if you allow it, I will put something suiting your beauty and your fire on a finger," he added, before pulling me close. My arms went around his neck; he laid a kiss on my temple before holding me away.

"I've never given you a proper kiss," he hesitated for a moment. "High Demon males ah, mark their mates," he hesitated again. "I was never pulled to do it with my deceased wife—she was humanoid. You, however—my Thifilathi roars for it at times."

"I ah," I hesitated this time. "Queen Lissa showed me her claiming marks," I sounded flustered. "But you don't know how my kind of demon does—well, this is awkward," I rubbed moisture from my cheeks.

"How your kind does what?"

"Uh, we can have uh, sex the regular way—if our partner is human, as you say. With another demon, we uh, go to prelim and ah, it's better if there's a demon hollow nearby."

"What?"

"It means I could set everything around us on fire if we don't take precautions," I explained in a rush.

"Is that what I saw when you turned in the lake before hitting Wilz Brak's hideout? You call it your *prelim?*"

"Yes. It's an intermediate version of me, between this," I tapped my chest, "and the full fire demon. It's roughly the size of your smaller Thifilathi."

"Interesting," Denevik's eyes widened.

"Yeah. If this puts you off, please tell me now."

"It does quite the opposite, actually."

"There may be some uh, rolling around, destroying the ground or rocks beneath during the ah, intercourse," I clarified. "It doesn't hurt when I'm like that. It takes a lot to hurt any of my kind when we're like that, actually."

"This is—intriguing. Why have I not heard this before?" he asked.

"It's embarrassing." I hung my head.

"I don't see it that way. Come, we should go back. The jewels look lovely on you, avilepha."

Denevik *skipped* us to D'margis while I was still trying to deal with my embarrassment. I had no idea whether Denevik and I were compatible in a sexual way, and that turned my embarrassment into worry.

~

*Randl*

"Reah is taking care of the aftermath," Denevik explained. I'd called him and Cassie into my study shortly after their return to D'margis. "There are no recorded images; guests aren't allowed to carry comp-vids or cameras of any kind into the palace. Cassie was too far away for them to know she didn't hold a weapon."

"Vik says the same thing," I leaned back in my chair with a sigh. "Cassie, you did the right thing—but I still worry that word of your talent will get out and the Prophet will target you specifically, right along with me."

"Quin said the man was obsessed. Should we be investigating that?" Cassie studied me intently.

"For now, Reah and Lissa will be looking into that, with help from some of their mates. If they find anything that connects this to us, they'll let me know."

*I would like to be informed if Cassie is in danger*, Denevik sent.

*Understood. I'll keep you in the loop.* "Do you need anything, Cassie? We have a counselor on call," I offered aloud.

"No, there was nothing else that could be done for that man; he was dead the moment he was obsessed," Cassie shifted in her chair. "The others in the tour group may need the counselor, Commander."

"Reah will take care of it," Denevik reached out to pat her hand. "She is good at what she does."

"You have a theory about this, don't you?" I frowned at Cassie. I had a theory, too; I merely waited to see whether hers aligned with mine.

"I think the one who obsessed that man was testing the security in Reah's palace," Cassie said. "Somehow, they had a connection to him that would break the moment he died. Somebody wants to invade the most impenetrable palaces and seats of governments—perhaps in both Alliances. I think every planetary leader should be put on notice —especially the ones who hold power."

"That is exactly what I thought," I said. "I've had a conversation with Teeg, but he'd already talked to Reah and Lissa. They all reached the same conclusion. I hope the short amount of time that passed between the hostage taking and the obsessed man's death will make the one responsible rethink his plans."

"Or convince him to up his game," Cassie sighed.

"That concerns me, too," I admitted. Cassie's parentage was revealed in her skill to size up a situation so quickly. Reah, in our recent conversation, told me that Cassie had talents she wasn't aware of, as yet. I wondered how long those who knew of it would delay before informing Cassie of her full heritage.

"I suppose this means we have to be more than vigilant at Teeg's ball, then," Denevik shook his head. "I was hoping to dance with Cassie."

"We'll try to make that happen at least once," I said. "Hold onto that hope for now. Go get some rest; you both look tired."

"We'll stop by the kitchen, first," Denevik rose and held out his hand to Cassie. "We haven't had dinner, yet."

"Neither have I," I said. "Mind if I join you?"

"Let's go," Cassie smiled at me.

*Krelk Homeworld*

*Alken Wilker*

I finally got tired of listening to a group of twelve discuss something in a language I couldn't understand. At one point, however, one of the twelve shouted something and the others went still, waiting.

Until the one shouting looked as if he'd collapsed upon himself.

Somehow, that was quite disappointing to the others, and it

worried me. For a moment, I considered reporting everything to the Prophet, and then decided I didn't want a verbal tongue lashing from him over something that I didn't control.

Instead, I left the room and went to the kitchen for a cup of tea. I'd go outside again and breathe air that wasn't filled with loud, rapid speech, punctuated by much growling and grumbling.

∿

*G'margis*

*V'dar*

Father had played me in this, just as he'd played others in my favor. Still, it angered me. *I* took precedence. *I* was in charge.

*Except where Je'Dik and his brothers were concerned.* I'd been instructed to step back whenever they had their own assignments to deal with. At this moment, with my anger so hot against Randl Gage, it infuriated me to follow that command.

"Where are we on our search for Dorlent," I spoke aloud to my rogues. Lately, they'd been asleep within me, as I hadn't heard from any of them.

*Tracking*, one informed me. *You will know when we have a lock on his location.*

"Make sure it isn't like last time," I snapped.

*We will make sure.*

"Good. Someone fetch W'dell for me," I shouted to anyone listening.

∿

*D'margis*

*Cassie*

We found Barry and Beverly having a late dinner in the kitchen. Beverly smiled at us and rose to get more plates.

"No, we can do this for ourselves," I told her.

"Then hurry it up; we need to talk to you," she said.

"Well, all right, then," I teased before following Denevik and Randl to the sideboard, where leftovers waited for us.

"What's on your mind?" I asked Beverly and Barry as I set a plate with a roast beef sandwich on the table and pulled out a chair.

"Barry and George may have picked up on something," Beverly said right away. Across the table, Randl perked up immediately as he settled on his seat.

"What's that?" Randl asked.

"You know we have all the locations for those food thefts," Barry began. "Since the blow up on Havek, there has been some chatter going back and forth between those locations containing some of the same key words and phrases. None of which make any sense," he added.

"Which is what you were looking for," Randl prompted.

"Yes. We have to cut through a bunch of systems to pin down exact locations, but we're working on it. When George was forced to stop and sleep-charge, I took a break for dinner."

"You're saying the messages are going around and around, before getting to their final destination?"

"Like extremely long spaghetti," Barry nodded.

"You need to stop for the night and sleep," Beverly scolded. "You can't follow those messages if you're too tired."

"I know."

"Take Beverly's advice," Randl agreed. "You'll be better at this when you're rested. George will be ready to go again soon enough; he can hold down the fort until you get back."

"I'm not arguing," Barry gave him a tired grin. "I know I need to sleep."

"Now, you," Beverly turned toward me. "I heard some rumors about what you were up to today. You can't let that interfere with your sleep, either. You need to be on your toes for that wingding tomorrow night."

"Is there anybody who doesn't know more about this than I do?" I pointed a disgruntled frown at Randl. He gave a noncommittal shrug in reply.

*Founder's Palace, Campiaa*
  *Wyatt*

"It took less than a minute, total," Dad pointed out. Reah had asked Nefrigar, her Larentii mate, to recreate the scene at the High Demon palace from earlier in the day. Griffin, he and I watched the images on the screen opposite Dad's desk.

"Thirty-nine seconds," Griffin frowned, then used the power he had to play the scene again. We watched it from the perspective of the tourists, cowering against the far wall while the hostage-taker held the woman against him, a ranos pistol pressed against her temple.

In the distance, down the long hallway, with life-sized statues of High Demon Kings in Full Thifilathi overlooking the scene, my mother, Queen Reah, and those with her looked tiny in comparison.

"You can't tell that the woman wasn't armed," Dad said, "Unless you zoom in on the image."

"Yes," Griffin tapped his chin thoughtfully before freezing the image. He'd chosen the moment when the slenderest, first thread of fire made its way toward the perpetrator. "Amazing that she targeted the pistol, first, rendering it useless. Its own safety system would have recognized the inability to fire and shut itself down."

"That, in itself, reduced the man to a simple target. If you move the images forward slightly, you'll see the second shot of fire. Cool-headed she was, the entire time," Dad breathed in admiration.

"That is something we certainly agree on," Griffin turned back to face Dad. "I'm sure this concerns you—regarding your security tomorrow night."

"It does."

"Good. I'll bring in extra guards."

"Thank you. Make sure they remain discreet."

"Of course." With a nod, Griffin folded away.

"Why didn't you tell him we have extras coming, too?"

"Because I didn't want him to know," Dad replied.

∾

*Queen's Palace, Le-Ath Veronis*

*Lissa*

"Winkler, if you and Rigo will stay with me tomorrow night, then the rest of you can disappear into the crowd. Just keep looking for something similar to the attacker at Reah's palace earlier."

I spoke to the full complement of my mates, who'd gathered in my library to discuss the Campiian Alliance Founder's ball. "If that fool had known to aim his pistol at the ceiling, it would have turned out a lot worse than it did."

"The next one may correct that mistake," Rigo spoke quietly.

"We know," I told him. "That's why several of us will have a shield around the entire building—to hold it up if somebody tries that."

"At least it's at a casino ballroom, rather than the Founder's palace," Erland noted.

"We all have our assignments," I said. "Dress is formal. Our goal is to make sure everybody is alive at the end."

"We'll do it, and we'll look good while we do it, too," Drake grinned. He and Drew slapped palms in a Falchani version of a high-five.

∾

*New-Fangled Bar and Grill, Lissia*

*Wisdom*

I'd asked them to meet me here; I found the couple sitting at the end of the bar as requested.

His dark eyes followed me with a deep frown as I made my way toward them.

"You have something to say?" he accused.

"I'm afraid it's worse than that," I admitted. "I have a confession to make."

# CHAPTER 15

'margis
    *Randl*

"Non-alcoholic drinks if possible. For those of you who can, neutralize the alcohol in your drinks," I told the assembled crew. All of them were dressed for a ball; I'd asked Zanfield and Perri to do away with the flashy colors for the night.

They looked so nice together this way, but I knew they'd both be happier as their normal, extraordinary selves.

All of us would be disguised to anyone else; only those who know us would see our true faces. "Tomorrow, we will go back to hunting the Prophet's petty criminals, so be ready for that. Tonight, we stand guard for both Alliances."

With that, I folded all of us to a prearranged ballroom in a neighboring casino. From there, we'd be ferried a few at a time to the venue, as arriving guests. Teeg had left nothing to chance in this endeavor; all of us would be admitted by our identity chips.

"Ready for this, my love?" I took Dori's hand and tucked it in the crook of my arm. She was stunning in a royal blue gown with silver trim that hugged her waist and hips before flaring at the bottom.

Silver shoes peeked from beneath the hem; I had no idea how she'd found the time to put the outfit together.

"Someday, let's do this just for the fun of it," she smiled at me.

"Whenever you want, just say the word," I agreed, leaning down to kiss her.

◇

*Campiaa City*

*Cassie*

"I don't have proper words to describe how beautiful you are," Denevik whispered as we waited for the hover-limo to pick us up. The early evening in Campiaa City, with a fresh, light breeze blowing off the waters of the bay, was perfect.

"I would give anything if this were a real ball, and all we had to do was dance, drink and talk," I told him. "And thank you for the compliment. You look very handsome—and not only in a fancy suit."

He smiled down at me as our courtesy vehicle stopped and the driver came around to open the door for us.

Denevik helped me into the back seat, then sat beside me. The driver closed our door and trotted around to slide into the driver's seat. "Only a short drive," he announced before engaging the hover-drive and pulling away.

*Let me know if you sense anything unusual,* Denevik sent.

*If you'll do the same.*

*Don't worry,* he replied. *We have to stay together in this.*

*Agreed.*

◇

*BlackWing X*

*Sabrina*

I'd seen the communication by accident; Randl sent it to Jett, and he'd forgotten to wipe the screen before leaving the bridge for a moment.

Travis and Trent, along with the others, were going to the Founder's ball on Campiaa. Yes, they were providing security, but so was the rest of Randl's crew—except me and the others aboard BlackWing X.

At first, I was furious as I stalked away from the bridge and took the trans-vator to my quarters.

Then, the anger turned to sadness, and the sadness to self-pity. Why didn't Travis and Trent ask me to go with them? *Why?*

I stared at my image in the mirror when I shouldn't have. A former friend would have called it ugly crying. She was right—I felt ugly inside and out. Something had to be done. *I* had to *do something.* I didn't want to feel like this again.

*Ever.*

I slumped onto my bed and ran through my options. I'd have to choose one, after all, to achieve my goal.

~

*Founder's Ball, Campiaa*
    *Randl*
I could see why Teeg wanted extra security. There were so many dignitaries, queens, kings, presidents and other important people, that the ballroom was overflowing into a second ballroom down the hall. He'd arranged for both, and had a third ballroom waiting, just in case.

Food, drinks and music were available in the first ballroom, while music and dancing occurred in the second. That's how Dori, Cassie, Denevik and I ended up guarding the second ballroom; Dori and Denevik wanted a dance with their partners.

*We will help you watch,* Kev'Ril informed me. *We will send out tendrils of our sensors, searching for anything that doesn't feel right.*

*Thank you,* I told my Chief R'pex. *I will do the same.*

*Ildevar has come,* Teeg informed me, letting me know that as of now, both Founders were in the same location. *He never replies to invitations; he comes or he doesn't—it's to fool anyone who may be watching for his scheduled appearance at events.*

*Where is he?* I replied.

*For now, he is with Queen Lissa and me, and is well guarded. Some of his High Council have come with him, dressed as normal bodyguards.*

*If you need assistance from us, let me know.*

*I will.*

*Heads up,* I sent to all my people. *Ildevar Wyyld is here with Teeg. Stay sharp; we can't lose even one Founder. Both Founders would send the Alliances reeling.*

*We have them in our sights,* Travis and Trent replied.

*Denevik and I will join Travis and Trent after we finish our dance,* Cassie informed me. Others let me know they'd keep watch on everyone else.

*Thank you,* I told all of them. *If anything happens, we may be the deciding factor in the outcome.*

*Ildevar is not helpless,* Bennall observed.

*I know what he is,* I told her. *Still, one can be caught unaware and that could spell doom, no matter how powerful one is.*

*That is true. We are watching with you tonight for that very reason,* Kev'Ril responded. *All are vulnerable, under the proper circumstances.*

"Shall we dance?" I held out my hand to Dori, whose eyes lit with pleasure as she accepted.

～

*Lissa*

*Eyes, ears and nose on alert,* Winkler reported in. He'd gone to speak with Lukas, Grand Master of Harifa Edus. They'd become very close friends; Winkler often went to join the full-moon hunts at Lukas' standing invitation.

*I wish Quin were here,* Reah sent. *If any of these people are obsessed, she'd know right away.*

Quin and Justis had declined the invitation—their wings were a huge curiosity to humanoids, and being bombarded with questions wearied them greatly. There was someone else who had the same talent, however—two someones, actually—Breanne and Zaria.

*Bree, what are you doing right now?* I sent. I had no idea whether she'd reply.

*Contemplating the state of the universes,* she replied.

*Feel like attending a party?*

*Not particularly. Is there a reason I should?*

*Did you hear about the attack on Reah's palace earlier?*

*I did.*

*I'm concerned we may be dealing with the same thing tonight. Besides, Teeg and Ildevar are both in attendance at the Founder's ball.*

*Are the BlackWing Pirates there as security?*

*Several of them.* I was beginning to lose hope that she'd come.

*Hank and I will come,* she replied, surprising me.

*When?*

*We're here, now, walking in the door. I'll let you know if I see anyone who's obsessed.*

*Thank you.* My sending conveyed the relief I felt by her appearance. As for Hank, his handsome face could be a chick-magnet at first, but his glower at approaching women would probably put them off.

If he started blowing smoke, they'd run away screaming, no doubt.

Wyatt

Jayna and I stood on the opposite side of the ballroom, watching the crowd between us and Dad, who was on the other side, having a conversation with Ildevar Wyyld.

*Your Aunt Bree is here, looking for anyone who's obsessed,* Gran sent.

*Thank goodness. I thought she didn't like these things,* I returned.

*She doesn't—I was surprised she agreed to come when I asked.*

*Should we be concerned because she agreed to come?*

*I thought the same thing,* Gran said. *Be on your toes, honey. I'm more worried now than I was earlier.*

*Me, too,* I admitted. *And it's deafening in here, with so many talking.*

*Can you filter it? If not, I might be able to filter some of it for you.*

*You mean potential threatening from non-threatening?*

*Sort of. Hold on, I'll come to you.*

Gran can slither through crowds as well as any lion snake I know. As a Queen vampire, she had talents few others did, since turning to mist and disappearing from one side of a crowded ballroom, only to appear in another, would frighten the more mundane among us.

"Here we go," Gran was at my side and smiling at me, before touching my face briefly. The reduction in noise was immediate and welcome.

"Thanks, Gran, you're a life saver," I grinned at her.

"Let's hope that's not a literal requirement before the night's over," she said. "Parties are supposed to be fun. This one has turned into anything but. Jayna, you look lovely tonight. Wyatt, you should ask your partner for a dance."

Jayna smiled at the suggestion. "I think that's a great idea," I said. "Shall we?" I offered Jayna my arm. She accepted immediately.

*Keep me posted if anything feels off,* Gran said as Jayna and I made our way toward the doorway and the hall beyond.

*You'll be the first to know,* I told her.

～

*Cassie*

*Reah just told me that Li'Neruh Rath is here with Breanne,* Denevik said as we made our way into the other ballroom.

*Who is that?*

*The god of Kifirin,* Denevik replied. *And a strict one, too. I'll tell you what I know of the history of Kifirin, both the planet and the god, when we have time and a bottle of whiskey available.*

*Is he mean and nasty, too?*

*I wouldn't say that—he's very unforgiving if somebody deliberately breaks the laws, though. He was quite angered when the former King and his Prime Minister refused to see sense or reason. Their misdeeds resulted in a war for the control of Kifirin and brought Reah to the throne after their defeat.*

*Sounds scary,* I shivered.

*You should have nothing to worry about, avilepha. Besides, he only rules over High Demons. No other races come under his direct command.*

*Where I lived before, gods didn't walk among us—not openly, anyway,* I said.

*Few in the Alliances know of them and wouldn't recognize most of them even if they introduced themselves,* Denevik patted my arm with his free hand. *Would you like something to drink?* We'd arrived in the other ballroom, where waitstaff with trays worked their way through the crowded room.

*Water or fruit juice?* I asked.

*We'll find it for you.* Denevik's grip on my arm tightened as we strode into the crowd.

Lissa

"Is that?" Gavin, who stood beside me, frowned in the distance. He was tall enough to see over most of the crowd; I wasn't.

"What?" I demanded.

"Zanfield Staggs—in all his former glory," Gavin said.

*There's an imposter here,* Randl's mindspeech interrupted. *The real Zanfield is in disguise in the other room.*

*Bree, do you have eyes on him?* I sent.

*Give me a second—now I do. He isn't obsessed, but he also doesn't belong here.*

*Just a party crasher, or something else?* Teeg demanded.

*A party crasher shouldn't have gotten in on his own,* Bree snipped at Teeg. *I think he may be an unaware distraction. Somebody else got him in, but I can't see past that simple fact.*

*Everyone on alert,* Randl sent. *We have a Zanfield impersonator, who is acting as a distraction.*

*Is he armed?* I asked Breanne.

*If he is, he doesn't know it.*

*Great. Who wants to go get him?*

*I can have Cassie and Denevik escort him out*, Randl offered.

*Tell them to be careful. We'll be watching the rest of the crowd*, Teeg replied. *I'll have house security arrest him outside the casino.*

*Cassie*

"Well, hello Zanfield," Denevik took the imposter's arm. When he tried to pull away, Denevik's grip tightened and he said, loud enough for those around us to hear, "You promised us a drink at the bar down the street, remember?"

"Go quietly or we'll arrest you here," I hissed in the man's ear. He went still, knowing immediately that we were security in disguise.

"Let's go get that drink," the man agreed, walking with Denevik toward the exit.

*Keep your guard up*, Lissa sent.

*We will*, I replied.

The man was quite willing to leave the ballroom with us and didn't argue when Denevik pointed him toward the main entrance of the casino. He didn't balk until we reached the outer doors to walk outside.

I could see three members of house security waiting outside to take him prisoner; farther past, casino guests wandered up and down the sidewalk adjoining the roadway, and Campiaa Bay beyond that.

Only the slightest flash of hover-vehicle lights on the eyewear of a pedestrian warned me; *get down*, I shouted mentally to everyone who could hear. Then I folded space outside and became a wall of fire as weapons discharged in my direction.

*Randl*

*The enemy is firing at us*, Denevik sent from outside the casino. Inside the ballroom, the scene was just as chaotic, as an army, dressed as casino employees, had stormed the room after appearing from nowhere.

Cassie's mindshout to get down, echoed by Kev'Ril's warning of the attack, had sent almost every ballroom guest to the floor. I wasn't the only one to put up a shield, either. I felt at least six others blooming alongside mine, as the powerful made their presence known to protect Teeg's guests from harm.

While ranos blasts bounced off the shields, many casino guests and employees had died when the attackers first arrived.

*They're all obsessed*, Breanne's voice sounded in my head.

That angered me. Someone else was pulling these puppets' strings without endangering himself. Was this the work of the Prophet, or another deranged criminal?

Purposely, I strode toward the edge of the shields that protected the ballroom. Once there, I walked straight through them, causing a few behind me to gasp or shout for me to return.

Pulling power into myself while deflecting ranos pistol blasts, I released a surge of energy so lethal, it destroyed the attackers' bodies and weapons in a single explosion. A few walls were destroyed, too, but the beams held, keeping the roof from falling on the crowd.

If the Prophet was behind this, I'd just announced my presence to him.

I waited for his appearance there in the hallway outside the ballroom, breathing hard and cursing under my breath.

*Cassie's taken down the outside threat*, Denevik reported. *Twelve shooters armed with ranos rifles.*

*Good. I've taken care of the ones who came inside*, I responded.

*We have a few casualties outside.*

*We have some here, too.*

*Randl, I need to talk to you—and Barry*, Cassie sent.

*About what?*

*About the one who almost destroyed Earth IV, where and when I came from.*

*Cassie*

Denevik couldn't hear what I needed to say, so I didn't have his strength to lean on as I told Randl and a room filled with powerful people what I knew. Barry knew more than I did, though, since he'd seen Ver'Dak in the flesh.

"You saw what?" Lissa asked.

"Ver'Dak wore goggles. He never took them off," Barry explained. "And I believe there were others like him, although I only heard him mention one name."

What name was that?" Randl asked.

"Je'Dik. He said it like it was almost holy or something," Barry replied. "I can still feel the evil radiating off that creature."

"Creature?" Teeg frowned.

"Not human," I said. "Barry can probably give you an electronic image of Ver'Dak."

"This means we have another enemy to worry about," Reah shook her head. "No doubt, it was the same one testing my palace security earlier."

"Do we know if Je'Dik and Ver'Dak are separate from the Prophet?"

"We don't know that, but if they are connected, they worked independently of him tonight," Randl said. "If the Prophet knew I was here, he'd have come himself for a showdown."

"True enough," Ildevar Wyyld breathed a troubled sigh. "We certainly weren't prepared for that scenario, either."

"Here," Barry handed his comp-vid to Randl. "This is an image of Ver'Dak."

"Krelk," Lissa said immediately, after looking at the comp-vid Randl held out to her. "Or mostly so," Breanne agreed as she glanced at the screen.

"Not much fashion sense, either," Lissa nodded at Breanne's assessment.

"Griffin is complaining that he wasn't included in this meeting," Teeg announced. "I'll go pacify my CSD Director. If there's anything else?"

"That's it for now," I said. "If Barry and I think of anything else, we'll let Randl know."

"We expect updates," Lissa told him.

"You'll know as soon as I do," he promised.

Barry and I let the others walk out first before following them out of the small meeting room Teeg secured for us. As he said, Griffin waited outside and launched into a swift conversation about dead guests and employees, along with the bodies of those who'd been obsessed to attack us.

"I can give you names," Breanne's voice had turned frosty as she spoke with Griffin. There was a connection there—one that she didn't appreciate. Lissa, too, moved away from Griffin deliberately.

*Denny?* I sent.

*Here in the ballroom,* he replied.

*I'll come find you.*

*I'll meet you halfway.*

"Drake, Drew and Teeg's warlocks protected the people inside the second ballroom, with help from Perri, Cudworth and Ocenosek," Denevik explained. "Travis and Trent *Pulled* in their blades, folded outside the shield and removed heads while Zanfield and the others worked to calm the crowd. Actually, Ocenosek and Cudworth changed and stared down anybody who thought about running out the door."

"That must have been a daunting sight." I tried to hide a smile.

"I'm sure it was. I'm more worried about the wall of fire that shot outward to take down specific targets," he told me.

"I'm just glad I found something to wear when I let the fire go. I feel awful about my dress. Oh, Denny—the jewelry," my hand went to my throat, where the necklace had lain until I became fire.

"It's just stuff," he repeated firmly. "You did what was necessary, avilepha. I will carry the picture of you, dressed as you were tonight, forever in my heart."

His words were meant to console, but I felt guilt and remorse. I should have refused to wear such precious things in a potentially hazardous situation.

"Cassie, we're having a meeting with Teeg before we go home," Zanfield and Perri came to find us. "He's having food brought in if you want something."

"Yeah. I could eat," I admitted.

"The meeting is in his library. Ildevar is there, too. Come on." Without hesitation, she folded us to Teeg's library inside his palace.

*Randl*

Griffin, disapproval in every aspect of his expression and posture, leaned against the library wall rather than joining us at the table. Food was brought in as casualties were counted and names of both victims and attackers were disseminated.

Breanne was the one to give names. She sat beside Li'Neruh Rath, whom she called Hank, who sat quietly, his gaze thoughtful as he glanced from one to another at the table.

I had no desire to check in with the media and what they might be saying about the entire debacle. At least we'd done our job, keeping Teeg's invited guests safe. It was those outside the ballrooms who suffered the consequences.

"Forty-seven employees and casino guests, and another twenty-six attackers who were obsessed?" Teeg stared at the list on his comp-vid. "That's a total of seventy-three. Have all the guests been escorted to their rooms or their ships?"

"All of them are safe and where they wished to go," Griffin confirmed. "I've arranged for counselors and other medical personnel to be available if needed. Guards have been assigned if they're staying on Campiaa. Also, any food items or drinks they order are complimentary."

"Good. Thank you."

"This was a disaster, but it could have been so much worse," Reah laid out what everyone else was thinking. "If any world leader or ambassador had died—I shudder at the thought. Teeg, you'll need to do damage control."

"I know. We'll have to provide explanations on how the ballrooms were protected, too. Everybody here knew they were somehow shielded from ranos blasts; they just don't know how."

"Warlocks?" Perri suggested. "That would be my guess, if I didn't know better."

"You did have four warlocks with you," Stellan Starr pointed out. "We shielded the guests in the second ballroom, with Drake and Drew's help."

"I'll claim Ocenosek and Cudworth as my personal guards," Reah offered. "I just don't know how to explain, well," she shrugged and looked in Cassie's direction.

"A talented wall of fire, you mean?" Breanne offered.

"Exactly," Reah agreed.

"Warlocks," Perri shrugged. "I'm telling you, just say warlocks or wizards and you're covered."

"Except that every warlock I know will be asking how to perform that particular spell," Lissa said. "They can do fire, no doubt about that, but to hold it and manipulate it like that—I have no good explanation."

"Just call it an experiment," King Rylend offered. "I can say it's something we've been working on, but it's so potent that the spell is protected by the Crown of Karathia."

"Good, because I'll have to explain that to the media for sure," Teeg said. "Who else needs another drink?"

Drinks were brought for nearly everyone in the room, while Teeg and Griffin walked out to talk to the waiting media.

*Cassie*

*I wouldn't want that job,* I told Denevik when Teeg and Griffin walked out of the library to speak with the media.

*I believe the phrase,* under investigation, *may be key in this interview,* Denevik replied.

"Have you always been able to become fire?" Li'Neruh Rath asked, making me jump.

"It's all right—you're among friends," Lissa told me.

"I don't really know," I told him. His eyes were nearly as black as night as he listened intently to everything I said. "When I was younger, my mother and then Aunt Shelbie warned me against turning. Most other elemental demons are forced to turn on the full moon after a certain age. It's never been that way with me."

"Has it always been that strong?" he continued.

"I can't say that it was—I sort of had to die to get to this point."

"What?" Breanne was the one who spoke, and she sounded outraged.

"On Earth IV, in order to defeat the Shakkor Agdah, a wizard would choose a fire demon to cast a spell upon, so they could destroy a multitude of the enemy at once. Present Shakkor Agdah company excepted," I nodded at Barry, who nodded back.

"A wizard tried to kill you?"

"I felt myself die, I think, but then I woke up in a crypt in New Orleans, where he'd stuffed my body, waiting for me to wake up again. I'm still pissed about the whole thing. After that, though, the fire came easily and I found I could make it as big and hot as I wanted, and I could manipulate it any way I chose."

"She almost defeated—well, I shouldn't say," Barry offered.

"We take your meaning," Breanne told him gently.

"She did destroy the rogue Shakkor Agdah," he added. "They left the path of wisdom long ago."

"Or were led astray," Randl suggested. "Similar to the ones earlier tonight—only the choice wasn't theirs to make."

"I assume a few missing persons reports will be resolved after tonight?" Lissa asked Breanne.

"Yes. Their families will be devastated. Most had no criminal record before tonight."

"Where did they come from?"

"This is where it gets interesting," Breanne said. "And I didn't see this in them since they were obsessed. I had to take their likenesses and compare them to missing persons reports. Zaria and Nefrigar were a huge help, making it possible to get the information in no time. All the attackers can be traced to a single convergence two months ago. They were all on the same shuttle from Campiaa City to the spaceport. All traveled back to their homeworlds across both Alliances, and then disappeared within a three-day period, the last one going missing six days ago."

"So the obsession was planned in advance," Lissa shook her head. "Whoever did this, they came to Campiaa to scout the locations, then chose a shuttle full of people on the way out."

"That's what I believe, yes," Breanne confirmed. "Since none of them were from the same general location, nobody thought to check into whether there was any connection."

"There wasn't a reason to do that. It made no sense to look at it that way," Wyatt said.

"This makes for a more solid theory that the Prophet wasn't involved in this. He tends to send out those he's obsessed and filled with his disease after capture," Randl said. "I didn't get a whiff of the Prophet from any of those who were here. They weren't infected."

"Then we definitely have a second faction inviting themselves to this party; a faction that may or may not have ties to the Prophet, but is acting outside his knowledge or guidance," Lissa summed everything up for us.

"That's my opinion as well," Randl confirmed. "If he finds they've been operating outside his guidelines, I'll be interested to see what he does about it."

"We may not want it to get that far," Breanne warned. "Look at it this way—if this faction is strong enough to go out on its own without his knowing—and do this kind of damage, a war between them could prove disastrous."

"I have a question," I interrupted the ensuing silence.

"What is it, Cassie?" Breanne turned toward me.

"Could this second faction be behind all the news releases, real and imagined, about the BlackWing Pirates? Or, could it be a third faction we haven't seen yet?"

"That's—terrifying," Li'Neruh Rath breathed, plumes of smoke accompanying his words.

"For now, we can't rule out either possibility," Randl nodded at me. "We've fallen behind in this race, without realizing it. It's as if the air around us has grown thick and forced us to move in slow motion."

"If the second faction is indeed the ones mentioned earlier, then we ought to look into that," Reah said. "I'd like Randl and anyone else who might help to go over the recordings of the attack at my palace. That event has to be connected to this one. They're testing us—to find our weak spots."

"And perhaps our strong ones, too," Randl observed. "If they sort out who can be attacked versus those who cannot, that means any state house, palace or high seat belonging to the non-powerful can be taken or controlled."

"We've seen some of that already," Lissa pointed out. "In the battle for the hub worlds."

"True enough," Teeg said as he and Griffin returned to the library. "We just left a dissatisfied group of journalists who are shouting for more information. If the one who has disseminated faulty information to the media decides to place blame for this debacle, I have no idea what to do about it."

*This is a nightmare,* Denevik sent to me.

*One I'd really like to wake up from,* I replied.

"I need to debate this with the High Council," Ildevar rose from his seat. "I'd like to be kept informed whenever anything new is discovered or discussed, and a full recording of your press conference would be appreciated. On another note, everyone here needs to be accompanied by others when returning home. Breanne, if you, Lissa and Li'Neruh Rath will come with me, I'd like a private word."

"Griffin, escort them to Ildevar's palace," Teeg ordered. "You can give him the full particulars on the press conference so he can coordinate his answers with ours. Come back here afterward, so we can plan our follow-up."

"I'd like the information from the follow-up, too, when you have it," Ildevar dipped his head to Teeg.

"You'll have it, of course."

"Very well. Shall we?" Ildevar nodded to the others, who folded away together.

*Lissa*

I have moments in my memory, and no matter how old they are or will become, those memories will never fade.

Most of them are not good memories.

The moment an arrow pierced Glen's eye, killing Winkler's werewolf guard before he fell to the floor at a recycling business in Albuquerque, will haunt me forever. The day I begged René to stay with me as he lay dying of an arrow wound in a field on Merrill's property in England, still brings tears.

I will also never forget the moment we landed in the rotunda of Ildevar's palace, where fifteen assassins appeared from nowhere. All were dressed in black leather, many of them carrying bows to shoot modified broadhead arrows that can kill by exploding on impact.

They were prepared to kill a vampire, and I was the likely target, being the Vampire Queen.

Our shields went up quickly, as we drew together to combat this new threat. With all our eyes focused outward at our attackers, Breanne raised her hands to separate particles. The rest of us, like fools, watched and waited for her to deal with them.

The final assassin was cleverer than all of us, perhaps. He was a vampire turned to mist above us, but still within our shield when he dropped down behind Griffin, claws out, to take his head. Only a hiss sounded, alerting us to his presence as Griffin's body collapsed.

Ildevar was faster than I on this night, as a stunned numbness overcame me; his Ra'Ak bit the vampire in half before he could return to mist. Ildevar's teeth—long, sharp and poison-filled, killed in an instant. Ildevar swallowed the vampire's head and shoulders, while the rest of the body disintegrated into black ash.

A dusting of that ash fell across Griffin's face, forcing a strangled "No," from my lips.

*Mom?* Travis' wobbling, mental voice interrupted as I gaped at Griffin's separated head and body, the precious blood of the first and oldest Saa Thalarr pooling on the marble floor of Ildevar's rotunda.

*Travis?* How had he known this had happened?

He didn't.

*Mom, Jett found Sabrina. She killed herself,* he wept.

# CHAPTER 16

*Queen's Palace, Le-Ath Veronis*
*Lissa*

There was no argument over whether Bree ought to *Change What Was* for Griffin. It was his time and that was that. As for Sabrina—this was the second time in as many lifetimes that she'd resorted to suicide.

Bree confirmed that Dorlent had taken Griffin's head with his deadly vampire claws before Ildevar bit him in half and swallowed the upper half of his body. She separated the particles of the other assassins before they could run from her afterward.

"Somebody paid to have this done," I blinked morosely at Merrill, who sat across from me at the kitchen island. The grim set of his mouth told me he had mixed feelings about Griffin's death, just as I did.

As for Sabrina and the impact her suicide had on Travis and Trent —both were currently with their fathers on Falchan, banging swords until they exhausted themselves enough to grieve.

Jett accepted assistance from Randl and Zaria to take Sabrina's body to the state morgue in Campiaa City; Teeg had the regrettable duty of informing her parents of her death.

I had a question for Zaria, however, when she was able to come see me. Sabrina had one of Zaria's medallions. Why hadn't it protected her?

"My medallions won't interfere in personal choices," Zaria arrived, looking as weary and worn as I felt. "Sabrina, unfortunately, made a personal choice."

"I can see how that could be too much interference," I said, while Merrill poured a cup of tea for Zaria and pushed out a chair for her to join us. "We're having a fest of mixed feelings over Griffin," I added.

"Yeah. I feel the same," she admitted. "It's difficult to know that I had a grandfather such as he. By the way, Wylend will arrive any minute."

"How do you know that?"

"He just sent mindspeech, asking me if you were here."

"Lissa?" Wylend appeared nearby, looking as if he would collapse at any moment. "He was hunting for Dorlent. Do you suppose Dorlent found out about that?"

"I have no idea," I told him. "Here, sit down. I'll get tea or something stronger if you want it."

"I'll take something stronger," he said. Zaria pushed out a chair for him; he took it and scooted it forward with power, his hands shaking as they gripped the edge of the granite countertop.

"No man should outlive his child," Wylend wiped his face. I *Pulled* in a bottle of Scotch and a glass, pouring it half full for him. He looked as if he needed it.

He was right—Roff, when he'd heard the news of Sabrina's death, had left the palace and gone to his brother's home to grieve. He'd lost his child twice, and in the same way each time.

"It's a curse at times to be immortal, or mostly so," Wylend said after downing half his Scotch. "I've seen my grandson die and be reborn as someone else's child. Will I see Griffin reborn to another? Why are things never the same?"

I hadn't seen my grandfather break down before, but he did, then. I rose from my chair and went to put my arms around him as he wept, his body shaking so hard I was forced to use vampire strength to hold him.

"It's a curse to have things be the same," Zaria said softly. She would know, having gotten the Lyristolyi drug twice. "It's a choice between your suffering or theirs. Let them have the gift of peace and a clean slate, Great-grandfather."

"Aunt Lissa?" Kyler's tear-filled voice interrupted.

"Honey?" I pulled away from Wylend, who also turned to look. Kyler and Cleo had come; this death had hit both hard, but Kyler most of all, as Griffin had helped raise her when she was young.

"Come here, Great-granddaughters," Wylend held out a hand. Cleo and Kyler were pulled into his embrace as all three wept.

Zaria and I exchanged glances. In her eyes I saw regretful acceptance and realized that I felt the same. *Will you come with me to see Roff?* I sent.

*Of course. He needs to know that this is not his fault in any way. Sabrina never knew he was her parent in a former life. The deep-felt pain of a child's loss exists as long as the parent does, and Roff has twice the burden to bear.*

*Merrill, we'll be back,* I sent to him.

*All right. I'll take care of things while you're gone.*

*Ask Winkler and Rigo to help if you need it.*

With that, I folded Zaria to Roff's brother's home, which wasn't far from their winery.

"Roff?" I whispered. Roff' sat in his brother's study, body leaning forward, his head down, wings folded tight against his back and hands hanging loosely between his knees, as if he no longer knew what to do with them. I knelt in front of him and took his face in my hands.

The well of pain in the dark depths of his eyes filled me with pain, too.

"Will you let me help you?" Zaria asked as she knelt beside me.

"Can you?" Roff asked, his words labored, his voice trembling and filled with unshed tears.

"I can try," Zaria offered, before putting a hand on each of us and closing her eyes.

She truly was Breanne's daughter—she gave us such a wave of love it filled our souls with light and hope, before sending me into Roff's arms in the tightest of embraces.

She left us there, too, going who knew where. I hoped she'd find solace for herself, wherever that was.

~

*Klerz*

*Korvus Katergáris*

The credits I'd paid to Dorlent were easy enough to find. I intended to collect from his many other stashes, too—to add to my already considerable wealth.

Dorlent had done me a favor, killing the new Director of the CSD and getting himself and his best assassins killed at the same time. I'd been hoping for such a positive outcome and wasn't disappointed in the least.

Now it was time to create even more havoc and animosity between the two major players I'd pitted myself against; the Prophet and his nemeses, Randl Gage and the BlackWing Pirates.

With a hefty amount of credits floating in a large chest beside me, I took a seat at Dorlent's desk in a former hideaway to consider my next move.

~

*D'margis*

*Randl*

"I don't understand this at all," Dori sat on the edge of my desk, her face toward me, one foot swinging in nervous anxiety. "The Sabrina I met in the beginning would never have considered this."

"I certainly didn't get that from her, either," I agreed. "What changed? I couldn't predict for even a minute that she'd go this direction."

"Travis and Trent only had eyes for her—I have no idea why she was so jealous of Cassie."

"That makes no sense to me, either," I confessed. "It was like she'd closed herself off to all of us and went in a direction nobody expected."

"I—just feel at loose ends—like a boat that broke away from its moorings and now floats wherever the waves take it."

"A good analogy," I sighed. "Like reality has ceased to exist for just a moment, with disastrous results."

"Um, Randl?" Zanfield tapped on my study door, a comp-vid in his hand. His hair had been spelled to resemble the whitest color imaginable—the color of mourning where he was from. It matched the white uniform and boots he wore.

Without a reply, I held out my hand. It wouldn't be good news; I could see it in Zanfield's eyes. "Teeg hasn't even made the announcement, yet," Zanfield whispered as he strode forward to set the comp-vid in my hand.

I was forced to read the media headline twice before it registered. *BlackWing Pirates Contract Dorlent's Services to Murder CSD Director Arden*, it read. *Dorlent dies in subsequent altercation with Ildevar Wyyld's guards*, the subheading continued.

"How would anyone even know this?" I blinked at Zanfield. "Ildevar would certainly keep his name out of this at all costs."

"I don't know. I'm going to have a drink with Vik and Dave, if you want to come."

"Yeah. Let's go. Dori?" I stood and held out my hand.

"I could use a drink," she agreed and placed her hand in mine. "At least nobody pointed out that the god of Love, the god of War and the Vampire Queen were Ildevar's guards," she leaned her head on my shoulder as we walked out the door. "And of those three, the god of Love is the one who killed Dorlent's assassins. Ildevar himself took care of Dorlent."

"If they knew the other stuff, why didn't they know that, too?" Zanfield asked as we walked toward the trans-vator.

"It's hard to know things about them," I pointed out. "Which brings us back to the question, how did anyone know of this before anybody said anything about it?"

"The only good thing to come of this is that it put the attack on Campiaa in second place as a news story," Zanfield observed.

"Yeah. It did that, all right."

～

*Krelk Homeworld*

*Alken Wilker*

Je'Dik's gloved hand jerked upward, warning me against asking questions, so I didn't. Rather, I followed him when he stalked out of his foster parents' home. "Take us to Klerz," he ordered. "I have business there."

Without a word, I transported him to the largest city on the planet. The wharf was a good place to land—plenty of shadows in the early morning and nobody asking questions, because their business was as shifty as ours.

"Feel like a drink?" Je'Dik asked, without expecting a reply. I wasn't particularly in the mood for a drink, but I'd heard stories about Klerz. For a price, a young prostitute could be procured.

Quite young, if the credits were sufficient. One had only to ask the proper question of the proper proprietor.

"Here," Je'Dik led me into a bar that smelled of vomit and beer. Would the owner agree to pay for a cleaning spell? It would benefit me as much as the bar; the place stank worse than a pigsty.

Je'Dik chose a table in the corner, where he could see everyone coming in and out of the place. Eventually, someone new walked in and headed immediately for our table—*as if he knew who we were.*

"If you don't like the smell, I'm sure you can put a spell together to mask or purify the air you breathe," a cloaked man growled as he pulled out a chair opposite mine.

His skin was reddish and swarthy; I hadn't seen that complexion since I'd last seen someone from Berouk, seventy years earlier. His face, the recognizable square shape of that people, bore no trace that a smile had ever appeared there. The only thing different about him was his eyes—instead of the usual brown, they were a pale blue. I wanted to squirm uncomfortably under his gaze.

Berouki were nomads, who gathered in clans and warred with one another, although their weapons had upgraded since I'd seen them last. This one had blood other than Berouki running through his veins, although blue eyes could indicate any number of races.

"I brought payment, Korvus," Je'Dik slid a pouch he pulled from a pocket toward our guest. "Nice work on getting Arden out of the way, and your information on the protections surrounding certain ah, governments, proved to be spot-on. The credits are all there, and you can do whatever you like with the warlock."

"What warlock?" I asked, puzzled.

Gillen often accused me of being slow on the uptake. Would things have turned out differently had I been faster in my realization?

No.

He was far stronger than I, and I was unable to fling even the smallest spell in his direction in my defense.

"I'll take these, then," he said. I blinked in horror as a set of testicles appeared on the table, their severed skin neatly seared shut so there was no blood.

"And this," the one called Korvus smiled at me, belying my presumption that he'd never done so in his life.

I confess, I didn't start screaming until my power was completely destroyed and the pain of my testicles having been ripped away from my bleeding body hit me harder than a thick, rocky wall traveling at light speed.

Je'Dik nodded to Korvus, then both folded space, leaving me doubled over in pain inside the foulest smelling bar in existence.

~

*Queen's Palace, Le-Ath Veronis*
*Lissa*

"Where's Wylend?" I'd brought Roff back to the palace; he was now in bed in his suite after Karzac placed a healing sleep.

"He got news just a few minutes ago, from Rylend," Merrill said as I walked into the kitchen, expecting to find him and my nieces there. All were now gone.

"What news?" I asked.

"Alken Wilker was just handed over to some of Ry's guards on Klerz. It appears that someone removed his power and his testicles for him."

"You know neither of those things breaks my heart," I said.

"I know." Merrill rose from his seat and pulled me into his arms. "I sent word to Randl—he can let Perri know when the time is right."

"I'd tell Zanfield first, and let him help in that decision," I buried my face against Merrill's shoulder. "Thank you for being here," I muffled against his shirt.

"Why don't you come spend time at NorthStar?" he spoke gently against my hair before laying a kiss there. "Bring whomever you want with you."

"I'll see if Roff wants to come when he wakes," I pulled away from Merrill. "Where should we scatter Griffin's ashes?" I asked the question that had bothered me for several hours.

"Are you sure you don't want the Larentii to separate his particles?" Merrill's dark eyes locked with mine. For the moment, Griffin's body occupied a slab in Ildevar's capital city. No coroner was allowed to touch the body, by Ildevar's order and by the shield placed around it.

"I thought maybe he said something to you in the past about that—you know, if the worst happened."

"He never mentioned it. Perhaps we should scatter them on his homeworld—they've built a shrine to all the vampires tortured to death in the past. He'd have died there, too, if he hadn't been selected to become the first Saa Thalarr."

"What did they see in him?" I asked.

"I don't know. Perhaps you should ask Belen that question—or the Larentii Wise Ones."

"It doesn't matter," I turned away. "He's dead and not coming back."

"Lissa, come to us at NorthStar. Please. Let us take care of you. You need time to heal."

"I think we all do."

"Yes. Definitely yes."

❧

*G'margis*

*V'dar*

"After I hear that Randl Gage not only killed the CSD Director, you're saying he also killed Alken?" I wanted to burn Je'Dik to a stump of his former self but was prevented by my father's order years ago.

"Yes," Je'Dik shrugged, as if I should have known about it already. Since I couldn't see the fool's eyes, I had to take his word for it. As Je'Dik was a lesser son, surely Father had instructed him not to lie to me, and I had to take comfort in that.

"I trust you will not lose Gillen so easily, if I send him with you?"

"You can depend upon it."

"Go find him, then find Randl Gage. I command it."

"As you will it."

❧

*Gillen Wilker*

"I don't care that Alken's dead," Qatti sniffed. "All those spoils of war belong only to us, now."

"Always the mercenary, eh?" I frowned at her. No, Alken's death didn't bother me so much, either, but it aggravated me that Qatti would take my feelings so lightly—or not at all.

*Gillen,* Je'Dik's mindspeech interrupted my thoughts. *The Prophet orders us to find Randl Gage. Be ready to go in an hour.*

*All right,* I replied.

"You'll be here by yourself soon," I informed Qatti. "Try not to get yourself killed."

"Where are you going?" she demanded.

"To avenge my brother with Je'Dik," I invited her to argue with me. "Don't sneak into the gardens to get warm; the Prophet won't like it."

227

"Go fuck yourself *and* your dead brother," Qatti spat at me.

"Whatever you say, dear, and fuck you, too." I folded away from her before she could get the last word.

*King's Palace, Karathia*
*Zaria*

Ry had sent mindspeech, asking for my help in dispatching Alken Wilker. I wanted to see him first, to understand who or what had removed his power, and whether he had any information to give us regarding the Prophet.

As for doing away with the raping pedophile, I'd brought help for that. After all, Perri and Pauly were both members of the Ironsmith family, now, and I left it to Ilya to deliver justice.

*He brought both blades.*

"He's inside a powerlight cage in the dungeon, although Dad calls the cage overkill. Alken couldn't swat a fly with power and a rolled-up newspaper right now," Ry informed us.

"Have you ever read a newspaper?" I asked, teasing my half-brother.

"No, but Mom always said she needed a newspaper to swat flies," he grinned.

"Remind me to take you back in time, so you can get an actual newspaper," I told him. "Shall we get this over with? I think Ilya wants to get this done."

"So do I," Ry nodded at Ilya. "Come on, I'll get us down there."

"I had to put a sound dampening spell on him; he wouldn't stop yelling," Ry said, crossing arms over his chest as we observed Alken Wilker. With arms waving wildly, Alken was cursing all of us, but Ry's spell prevented us from hearing the words.

"I had to sear his wound closed," Ry continued. "Somebody removed his balls along with his power."

"I can see that," I nodded as I studied Alken and everything I could read from him. "He has an obsession not to reveal the Prophet's location or anything else about him," I said. "But there are other things I can see—important things."

"Such as?"

"The one who arranged for Griffin's death—for payment, and the one who paid him, although the image isn't a good one. I think Cassie had the right idea," I shook my head in amazement.

"Do you have everything you need?" Ilya turned toward me, an eyebrow lifted in curiosity.

"I got everything I could from him that's useful," I said. "I had to ignore —well, you probably know what I had to ignore. He's all yours, now."

"I'll remove the cage," Ry said, and lifted his hand to cancel the spell.

Ilya's hands moved in a blur. His first bladestroke removed Alken's head; the second bisected the body perfectly before it crumpled to the floor.

Ry performed a containment spell to keep the blood from staining the floor. "Will you take care of that?" Ry turned toward me.

"Absolutely," I said and separated Alken's particles, as if he'd never been. "For Perri and Pauly Ironsmith," I nodded in satisfaction. "And for too many others whose lives he ruined. Ry, will you ask Teeg, Ildevar, Randl and anyone else of importance to a meeting? I need to tell them what I saw."

～

*Queen's Palace, Le-Ath Veronis*

*Lissa*

"I didn't see Je'Dik Dis'rai's name in Alken—he was obsessed against it. I saw it in Korvus. Je'Dik paid Korvus to kill Griffin. Korvus paid Dorlent to do the job. He was quite pleased with himself that

Dorlent was killed afterward—he reclaimed the payment after Dorlent's death," Zaria explained.

My library was full of people, all of whom were impacted by Griffin's death or who needed to know about our newest enemies—Je'Dik Dis'rai and Korvus, last name unknown.

Zaria had images of both floating at the center of our crowd, so everyone could get a good look at them. "Je'Dik, with help from one or two others, is responsible for many assassinations across both Alliances—some of which were attributed to Dorlent," Zaria went on. "I saw all this in Korvus—somehow, he knew of it."

"Here's my question," Randl began. "Does the Prophet know of Korvus? Are they working together?"

"No," Zaria said. "This arrangement was between Je'Dik and Korvus only. Je'Dik has kept things from the Prophet before—I also saw that in Korvus. He knew things, and I have no idea *how* he knew them."

"Could you see his beginnings? Who and what he is?" I asked.

"He has talent and power—much of that was compartmentalized, I believe. I'd have to see him face-to-face rather than through another man's memories to get to that," Zaria replied. "As for his outer image—you can see for yourself that he looks of mixed race. Barouki, perhaps, with something else."

"The term Korvus, in Latin, means raven," Merrill pointed out, "although the spelling may be different. It could also have several other meanings, depending upon the language employed."

"Korvus is a common name on Wil-Wil," Ildevar offered. "There, it means *of true purpose*."

"Blue eyes are common among those people," Pheligar offered.

"How would there be a meeting between two from such opposite worlds?" Rigo asked.

"Stranger things have happened," Tybus said. He'd come with Teeg, so both could hear what Zaria had to say.

"Stranger things, indeed," Nefrigar agreed. "My question is this; how do you intend to proceed with this new-found information?"

"Putting out wanted posters for Je'Dik could push the Prophet in a good or bad direction, depending on his mood," Randl said. "I'm not sure we ought to play that card right now."

"We can certainly release Korvus' image to everybody, though, and let it be known that he was ultimately responsible for Griffin's death —by hiring Dorlent," Merrill suggested.

"But we know nothing else about him, and there will be plenty of questions from the media and those they serve," Teeg countered. "We've already suffered hits to our credibility lately, as you know."

"We are sure that Je'Dik and those like him are responsible for the attack in Campiaa City," I pointed at Teeg. "If we're not releasing that information, maybe we ought to hold onto the rest of it, too."

"We probably should keep it inside this room," Ry suggested. "Is there anyone here who wants to take up the cause of hunting down Korvus?"

"I'm willing," Bel Erland raised his hand.

"I'd go with Bel Erland, with Dad's permission," Wyatt nodded at his half-brother. "Jayna may want to go with us."

"Kory and I can go," Lexsi raised her hand.

"Do you understand how dangerous this is?" Ry frowned at Bel Erland.

"More dangerous than the Prophet?" Bel Erland leveled his gaze on his father.

"I suppose not," Ry admitted. "Fine, but every scrap of information comes back here—to all of us. Understood?"

"Sounds good to me," Wyatt agreed. "Dad?" He turned to Teeg.

"Go ahead but tread lightly. This one managed to destroy a Saa Thalarr. Never forget that, son."

"Where will you start?" I asked.

"No idea," Lexsi said. "Any thoughts?"

"I suggest you start on Klerz—that's where Je'Dik met with Korvus," Zaria interjected. "Never hurts to work your way backward. Just one word of warning—any hint of the Prophet, you drop everything and run."

"Then we'll start on Klerz," Bel Erland said. "If we don't fold back to Gran's to eat or sleep, we'll let you know where we are," he nodded to me. "This is our headquarters for hunting Korvus."

"If you don't check in, we'll start the hunt—for you," I warned.

"We know. Thanks, Gran."

*D'margis*

*Randl*

Zaria and Ilya traveled to D'margis with me, to speak with Zanfield. He was still awake and talking with Vik and David in the kitchen when we arrived. Perri had gone to bed, as had most of the crew.

"Zanfield, we have news that concerns Perri," I told him. Zaria, Ilya and I took seats at the table.

"What news?"

His shock of gleaming white hair shone brightly in the dimly-lit galley—Perri had placed a glow-spell on it when she changed the color.

"Alken Wilker is dead," Ilya said. "I executed him earlier today."

Zanfield went still for a moment before replying. "I hope his death wasn't an easy one," he breathed, lowering his eyes.

"Zan, somebody else made sure he suffered before we got to him," Zaria said. "That particular person removed Alken's testicles and his power. After that, somebody on Klerz turned him in for the bounty on his head—while he was still bleeding."

Zanfield's eyes were red-rimmed when he lifted them to gaze at Zaria. "Perri suffered so much from that filth," he leaned back in his chair with a troubled sigh. "Who knows how many others suffered the same? If Quin hadn't offered healing," he spread his hands on the table.

"Perri would still be having nightmares," Zaria finished for him.

"Yes. Even now, I must proceed with caution and patience," he grimaced at the memory.

"Zan, I can give you the names of the others," Zaria said softly.

"I want the names of those who still need help. I want them to get the best care available," he said. "Funds will be provided—anonymously, of course."

"I think Quin will be happy to assist with that," Zaria told him. "Your money can help them in other ways, I'm sure."

"Give me the information, then, and I'll have my people take care of it."

"You'll have it in a few days, after Quin and I are done."

"Have I ever told you that you are the best sister anyone could ask for, even if we aren't related by blood?" Zanfield allowed himself a small smile.

"Right there with you," Zaria grinned at him, extending her arm for a fist bump. "You're the one who has to figure out how to tell Perri the news. I really don't want to upset her in any way with this."

"I'll tread lightly, no worries," he promised.

"I'll leave you two off the roster for tomorrow, then," I said. "The others are going out to hunt more petty criminals belonging to the Prophet."

"I'll look forward to it," Vik told me. "Unless you have something else in mind."

"I considered going split-time to Klerz, but that would be useless," I shrugged. "Zaria saw as much as she could from that encounter."

"I'll be keeping tabs on the ones who are going there tomorrow," Zaria said.

"Stay and have a drink with me," I invited as she and Ilya began to rise.

"I'd take a drink," Ilya said, settling on his chair again.

"I'm with him," Zaria nodded at Ilya. He chuckled and put an arm around her shoulders. Of all her mates, there was a special place in her heart for this one.

"Want Scotch?" Vik asked.

"I think we do," Zaria confirmed.

# CHAPTER 17

*D*'margis
    *Cassie*

"Denevik, I'm putting you and Cassie in charge of hunting A'bil," Randl told us at a breakfast meeting the following day. "Barry and George believe he may be on Ja'kel."

Under ordinary circumstances, he'd have placed Travis or Trent in command, but both were still on bereavement leave.

Something about Sabrina's death felt off to me, but I didn't know her as well as the others and kept my mouth shut on the subject. I also had residual feelings of guilt in the matter, although my logical side kept telling me it was foolishness.

"Do we have a place to stay on Ja'kel?" Denevik asked.

"No. Actually, BlackWing X is in the area; you'll use it as a base while you're investigating," Randl replied. "I hesitate to put any of you in a safe house, now that we have other factions who may be hunting us—namely, Je'Dik and his cohorts, plus Korvus. Jett and his crew will help keep you safe," he added.

I couldn't stop the shiver as he told us we'd stay aboard X; I couldn't say why, other than I hoped we wouldn't be anywhere near Sabrina's cabin.

"Vik, you and Rajeon will be in charge of the investigation on Skyrock; you'll be searching for Vilst," Randl went on. "I've arranged for BlackWing VI to act as your command base. All of you, stay in contact with Barry and George, and choose your teams wisely. Any conflicts in your selections, see me."

"We'll take the sprites," I said.

"No argument from us," Vik agreed.

"Take Lyr with you, too," Randl advised. "Vik, you can take Horris," he named another Sirenali investigator.

"Sounds good," Vik acknowledged. "We'll take Dave, Chazi, Bekzi and Darzi, too."

"I agree with your choices," Randl nodded at Vik. "Be ready for transport in an hour. Pack your bags for at least a week."

*Randl*

"Perri wasn't at breakfast this morning," I said as I passed Zanfield on the way to my office.

"Beverly sent food to her suite," Zanfield said. "We talked last night. I think Perri's taking this well enough—but she needs some time to adjust. Are we needed anywhere?"

"If she's up to it, you can join Vik and Rajeon tomorrow," I said.

"I'll ask and let you know."

"I'm going to send Cudworth with Vik and Ocenosek with Denevik—they work well together, and that'll give everybody a decent crew—if Perri isn't ready by tomorrow, I'll find two others to send. Maybe Star and Annie." I named two of Barry's fellow Shakkor Agdah.

"I think Perri will be good to go tomorrow—she's working on letting go of her anger."

"Understood," I acknowledged. "Keep me informed."

*BlackWing X*

*Cassie*

"Susan, how are you?" Denevik asked after we landed in the galley with our companions. Susan had volunteered to serve as a cook for Jett and his crew; I'd yet to see the hen she could become, although stories regarding her fearlessness were legendary among the crew.

"I'm good. Want something to drink? Lunch will be served in two hours."

"How about we settle in first, then come back for lunch. We'll discuss our plan of action over food," Denevik grinned at her.

"There are enough berths down the port side, if some of you double up," Susan said. She didn't say it, but Sabrina's cabin was on the starboard side.

"I think we can manage," Denevik replied. "Come on, let's go figure out where we're sleeping," he said, leading the way out of the galley.

"I'm glad you're here," Susan said, patting my shoulder as I went past. "Everybody has been so down, lately. We need cheering up."

"You know, I think I do want a cup of tea," I told her, breaking away from Denevik's wake.

"Come with me," Susan smiled and led me toward a table.

*I'll catch up,* I sent to Denevik.

*Take your time,* he returned.

~

"So. A Buff Orpington?" I held my mug in both hands and sipped tea while talking with Susan.

"You know what a Buff Orpington is?"

"I grew up in Alabama," I said. "Went to school with someone whose parents raised prize-winning chickens. I know about Silkies, Sebrights, Polish, Cochins, Frizzled Cochin bantams, Sussex, Wyandottes—the list is long," I said.

"We chicks need to stick together," she laughed.

"Right on," I said, making her laugh again.

"I have a question for you," I said, working up the courage to ask.

"You want to know if anybody has ill feelings against you," she said, guessing what I was about to say.

"Well, yes."

"The answer is no. The Sabrina that was onboard this time—that was somebody I didn't recognize. I have no idea what happened with her, but something was off. Now, I can't say for sure, but I believe she was headed for a cliff, no matter what. Even Nari and Tiri felt something was wrong, because Sabrina started snapping at them, too, and they get along with everybody."

"What the hell happened, then?" I sighed. "This sounds so odd—no matter which side you examine."

"No idea. I've had conversations with Jett about it, and neither of us can find the source of the problem. At the core of it is this, though —we've lost a brilliant mind. I have no idea where this feeling of inadequacy originated."

"I read her biography on Denny's comp-vid," I confessed. "Why in all the worlds would she feel jealous of me?"

"It doesn't make sense, and that makes the mystery more confusing. If she needed help, I'm not sure why she wasn't getting it."

"People have a tendency to ignore it if they're in the middle of it," I admitted. "I wasn't in the best frame of mind after I died."

"What?"

"I came back," I said, "although I'm still a bit hazy as to how that happened. Somebody told me later that my anger was normal under the circumstances, and that helped a lot."

"Anger at?"

"The wizard who killed me," I shrugged and sipped more tea.

"It's in times like these that I wish Cliff were here," Rob sighed as we stood at the edge of what looked like a forest—in the middle of other forests. Wealthy people owned multiple plots of land, and they'd planted them full of trees to hide their homes from anyone passing by.

Barry and George had traced messages from A'bil to the large estate we'd walked to—on a public trail. We'd stopped after reaching the property's edge; Rob informed us that there were electronic sensors buried in the ground, which would alert the residents if we walked onto the property.

All the property in the area was protected—by invisible electronics designed to give a mild shock for passing the boundary, and increasingly harmful shocks if an invader proceeded farther toward the massive homes in the neighborhood.

Others not only took that precaution, but also paid enormous amounts to wizards or warlocks to back up the mundane systems with other nasty surprises for would-be trespassers.

The only safe way to get to the house was through a gate, where we'd be forced to announce our presence before said gate would open.

"Yeah, Cliff could sniff around for signs of A'bil," I agreed. "Zephyr will have to check things out for us instead—and we have to hope A'bil isn't disguised."

"Or, we could wait until nightfall and fly over, to check on things," Ocenosek suggested.

He was right—he and Denevik had wings in Thifilathi form.

"I can still go in now," Zephyr offered.

"I think it may be safer for us to go in; we're immune to spells of any kind," Denevik said.

"That means we have to go back to the ship and wait until dark," Rob mused.

"We'll come back after dinner—and dress better for the task at hand," Ocenosek said.

"All in favor?" Denevik asked.

"I guess we're in favor," Rob agreed.

"Good. Let's go; we can have another meeting over dinner, if you want," Denevik said, although I could tell he wanted just the opposite.

*No meeting*, Lyr replied, making me snicker.

*Skyrock*

*Vik*

"This doesn't look promising," Rajeon frowned. He and I stared at the overgrown area hiding the compound we'd gone to investigate.

"They've run into something similar on Ja'kel," I sighed. "It'll take a machete and three weeks to get through that jungle."

"We get through, easy," Bekzi informed me.

"You want to try that?" I turned to him and his brothers.

*Electronic sensors activate by weight*, Horris sent. *A lion snake's weight is spread out, rather than being in a relatively small location. I doubt they'd trip the alarm or activate the shockers.*

"Good point," I told him. "If you're sure you want to risk it," I turned to Bekzi, Chazi and Darzi. "Any sign of trouble, get out of there fast."

"We fold out if trouble comes," Chazi acknowledged. "We send what we find."

"Don't spook anybody," Rajeon warned. "Do you want me to come with you?"

He could turn into anything—a lion snake would be no problem.

"You not fold," Bekzi pointed out the biggest problem with Rajeon's offer. "We best choice."

"Fine. If you need help, though," Rajeon replied.

Without a response, Bekzi, Chazi and Darzi turned, then slithered across the boundary of what Barry considered Vilst's property. I hoped we'd know soon enough whether that were true and if the petty criminal was in residence.

Once we had that information and a better knowledge of the layout of the compound, we could formulate our plan to deal with Vilst and his horde, then dismantle the place.

"I'll take you in if we're needed," Cudworth's hand dropped onto Rajeon's shoulder.

"I wish we had Rob here to stick his toes in the dirt," Rajeon breathed as we watched three lion snakes crawl through thick brush and disappear from sight.

"That has come in handy," I confirmed. "I wasn't even aware that his kind existed, and only on Earth IV of all places."

"Plenty of unique races exist on Earth IV," Cudworth agreed. "Elemental sprites and elemental demons are the biggest ones. Cassie is certainly an eye-opener."

"Randl says she's extraordinary among her own kind. I think there's something other than elemental demon in her. That's just conjecture, though, because Randl clams up about it if I ask."

*Small box above ground. Concrete*, Bekzi sent. *Rest underground, maybe? We come back, now.*

"Just what I was afraid of," I said aloud. "Bekzi says he thinks most of the compound is below ground. They're on their way back."

"You think we can borrow Rob's services?" Rajeon asked.

"We can ask."

~

*BlackWing X*
*Cassie*

"Just heard from Vik—he wants to borrow Rob for a few hours," Denevik said, handing me a brownie and a fresh mug of tea. He'd found me in my cabin, where I'd gone to take a nap, before discovering I was too restless to sleep.

"If Rob wants to go," I began. "Thanks for the treat."

"You're welcome, and all the sprites want to go, as does Ocenosek. I gave them the okay; Ocenosek is taking them to Skyrock."

"I hope they stay out of trouble."

"There's enough strength there that they shouldn't have a problem," Denevik said. "Jett asked me to the Captain's cubby to have tea. I'll check in with you later."

"Okay. Have fun discussing guy things," I told him as he walked out the door and shut it behind him.

Lifting the brownie, I took a bite out of it. Susan made excellent brownies, I concluded as the taste of dense, moist chocolate hit my tongue. I was going to savor every bite of it, I decided, chewing slowly.

Instead, I dropped it on the floor, and the mug of tea followed when Sabrina's apparition appeared in my cabin.

"Help me," she begged, holding out a ghostly hand.

I meant to say *what?* I'm sure—my mouth moved, certainly, but no sound came out.

"Please help me," her spirit wept. "I know you can." She stretched her hand out farther, trying to reach me.

I'll never know why I held out my hand to her—but once I did we connected, and a shock of fear and power went through me. Together, Sabrina and I were quickly sucked through time, although I didn't understand how it happened until afterward.

*Skyrock*

*Robin Newbourne*

"It's underground, all right, and there are plenty of nasty things around it, for protection," I explained after pulling my toes from the soil.

"Underground entrances or exits?" Vik asked.

"Yes. Two. I have no idea whether Vilst is home, or how many are currently inside the bunker," I said.

"We don't have Cassie with us this time," Cudworth warned.

"You have lion snakes and a pod'l-morph," Rajeon pointed out.

"We also have High Demons and sprites," Blaze said. "While I can't do what Cassie does, I can burn just about anything."

"As High Demons, we tend to fry people," Ocenosek cocked his head at Vik.

"True," Vik considered what we had to work with. "If Vilst isn't in there, though, he'll hole up somewhere and we may never find him. Damn the bone dust he's used to cover his property."

"Need mister," Bekzi suggested.

"Yeah. We do," Vik agreed. "Let me see if Mom is busy."

"There's no need to bother her," Cudworth began.

"If she can't come, maybe she can send another mister," Vik argued.

Turning his back, I understood he was contacting his mother in mindspeech.

～

*NorthStar, Avendor*

    *Lissa*

I'd taken Merrill's advice; Rigo, Winkler, Roff and I had come to NorthStar to take a few days for ourselves. Actually, Roff and I did; Rigo and Winkler came to make sure we ate and slept properly.

Gavin had gone to Campiaa—he didn't say it, but he was worried about Gavril. Losing an employee could be tricky, especially if the employee in question was related. Wyatt, Bel Erland and the others had dutifully checked in with Tony and Aurelius, who were keeping me informed of their progress.

I was very surprised to hear from Vik, who was currently on Skyrock.

*Mom, we need a mister,* he said after I answered his mindspeech.

*For?*

*We may have located Vilst, but his compound is a hole in the ground that's protected against almost everything. Before we go busting in, I need to know whether he's actually in there or not.*

*That's it?*

*Yeah. We can take care of the rest.*

*I'm not sure I can leave here without Winkler and Rigo,* I told him.

*Not a problem—bring them with you.*

*Be there in a few.*

*Thanks, Mom.*

Before I could leave NorthStar, I not only had Winkler and Rigo with me, but Merrill, Kiarra, Adam and Pheligar, too. All of them wanted to see Skyrock, which sounded so much prettier than it actually was.

～

*BlackWing X*

  *Cassie*

I wanted to scream at her. Sabrina's ghost had disappeared, leaving me standing beside her body three days earlier, immediately after she'd shot herself with a laser pistol. Blood pooled around my feet— I'd be leaving footprints behind. *How the hell was I going to explain that?*

I started to panic; all the movies I'd seen where an innocent shows up after the murder, only to be accused of said murder flitted through a brain nearly paralyzed by fear.

And then, somehow, I understood. She'd left her life thinking she was alone—that nobody cared.

"Sabrina," I knelt beside her body, taking her hands in mine. "I don't know what happened to you, or why. In another life, maybe we could have been friends. You left so much love behind you—people are grieving. If I could, I'd give your life back to you, so you could see it for yourself. If you're still here somewhere and can hear me, I would show you that love."

A wave of emotion washed over me—one I couldn't stop or hold back. Somehow, too, I understood that it wasn't only Sabrina who needed help. I reached out with my power.

When everything turned so bright it nearly blinded me, I fainted.

*Skyrock*

  *Lissa*

"Who wants to go in with me?" I asked.

Everybody raised their hands, including Pheligar. "You know, this makes me think of a hotel in Chicago, a long time ago," I frowned at the crowd gathered around me.

"If I take you, you may see things you weren't expecting," I went on. A couple having sex was one of the things everybody inside my mist saw that day.

"I read about that," Pheligar wore a thoughtful expression.

"What?" My hands were on my hips in indignation. That schmuck had read my diaries. I glared at Pheligar, who didn't even blink.

"My brother is in charge of the Archives," he said. "Larentii are free to read anything kept there."

"Unbelievable," I shook my head. "Fine. Fucking fine. Let's go and get this over with."

Gathering the crowd inside my mist, I headed for the underground bunker. I didn't bother trying to go around the tangle of trees, brush, thorny vines and everything else that grew on the property; it gave my tagalongs a close-up view of everything we passed through.

Until I began to feel dread every time we rushed through more of that tangle—the closer we came to the concrete bunker, the worse the dread became, until the realization hit me.

Was it already too late? I hadn't shielded anyone, and had no idea who might be affected, or when.

These were no ordinary thorns.

No.

These were designed to poison anyone coming in contact with them—some sooner than others.

*Get out*, a voice shouted in my head.

Just before things went crazy.

# CHAPTER 18

*B*lackWing X
      *Cassie*

"Cassie? Wake up. Please wake up." Those words, followed by a vigorous shaking of my shoulder, made me groan. I felt as if a mountain had dropped on me, and for a while, I couldn't recall where, when or why I was.

Until I realized who was shaking me.

"Eeep," I squeaked before crabbing backward until I hit the wall —*of Sabrina's cabin.*

"Cassie—I," Sabrina looked as if she'd been crying, the laser pistol she'd used lay on the floor nearby.

With a swipe of my hand, I sent it flying under her bunk. "Sabrina, what?" I began, waving a hand as if that would improve my thinking process and bring the proper words to mind.

"Thank you. Thank you so much. I don't know what came over me," she started crying again. "I just didn't feel right—like I was sick and didn't know I was sick," she scrubbed tears off her face.

I thought about telling her that Travis and Trent loved her and were distraught over her death. That too many people were devastated by her loss. *Why hadn't someone followed up on what was wrong with her?*

"Come here," I held out my arms. She slid over so I could hold her while she cried. "It's okay, now," I soothed.

*Except I had no idea how things had gotten that way.*

～

*Skyrock*

*Lissa*

I'd never seen the inside of a *Changing of What Was*. I'm sure it looked to me like the way traveling through poisonous vines looked to those with me.

A rewinding of time, so fast it was a blur, as I and my passengers were thrown out of that briar trap so quickly, I barely understood what was happening.

I may not have believed it, either, except Merrill, Adam, Kiarra and Pheligar understood it, too.

"What the fuck just happened?" Vik demanded, as I reformed and everyone else fell away from my mist, just as we were before our journey started.

"Those vines—I will take a shielded cutting and transport them to the Archives," Pheligar sounded ruffled, and Larentii were never ruffled.

"What are they?" Rajeon breathed. "I felt—bad."

"The Prophet has found a way to affect us mentally," Kiarra snapped. "Fucking hell, take a U-turn and fucking hell again."

"That doesn't sound good," Vik mumbled.

"Honey, it's not good. Tell Randl to meet us at NorthStar. We have to put a shield over this mess and then discuss it."

"I'll take the cutting to the Archives," Pheligar nodded and disappeared.

"I hope they can figure that out fast," Winkler growled. He wanted to become wolf in the worst way possible.

"Bekzi," I turned toward him and his brothers. "Were any of you in contact with those thorns when you went in earlier?"

"They grow higher up than snake crawl," Bekzi lowered his hand to show the approximate height the thorns grew on the bushes. "We not touch."

"All right. Good," I breathed a sigh. "Let's go to NorthStar and start sorting this out." *Thank you*, I sent to Breanne. *We'd be in trouble if you hadn't helped.*

*What are you talking about?*

*Changing What Was.*

*I didn't Change What Was.*

*Zaria? Did you Change What Was for us?*

*I didn't Change What Was*, she replied. *What's going on?*

*A U-turn into hell*, I replied. *Can you meet us at NorthStar? We have a new development.*

～

*BlackWing X*

*Denevik*

"We're ordered to stand down," Jett informed me. "Randl says nobody goes looking for more petty criminals—that's on hold. He's in a meeting at NorthStar, which may move to SouthStar. The Three will need this information."

"What happened?" I asked.

"The Prophet has found a new way to destroy us. It appears that power may no longer protect us from his machinations."

"How is that possible?"

"He can infect our minds—in ways we can't detect as yet."

"I think I'd like to attend that meeting at SouthStar," I rumbled.

"I'll ask if we can come. If they allow it, then bring Cassie, too."

"I'll go wake her."

～

*Cassie*

*Cassie?* Denevik's mindspeech sounded frantic.

*I'm here,* I replied.

*Here where?*

*Wait—I'll uh, come to you. Where are you?*

*In your cabin.*

*Okay. Uh, don't be shocked, all right?*

*About what?*

*Um, about who.*

*Cassie, where are you?* His mental voice became more insistent.

"Here," I said after folding into my cabin while supporting a swaying Sabrina with both arms.

I'd never seen Denevik speechless before. His mouth worked, but no words came out.

"I don't have an explanation for this," I whispered as he stared, wide-eyed, at Sabrina and me.

*NorthStar*

*Lissa*

*Mom, Sabrina's body has disappeared from the morgue, and the staff is acting like it was never there,* Gavril reported. *Dad and I can't figure this out.*

*Get Tybus to fill in and come to NorthStar,* I said. *There are new developments. A missing body is almost irrelevant at this point. Hurry if you can; I've asked others to come and time may be short.*

"We'll move the meeting to SouthStar as soon as they get here," Ashe appeared as if he'd been called. Charles arrived seconds behind Ashe, and then Bree and Hank arrived.

All of them looked a bit disheveled—if this were any indication, our new discovery was turning out to be worse than I thought.

"That's not the whole of it," Bree came forward to give me a hug.

"What else is there?" I asked as she pulled away.

"You'll see soon enough."

I did, and almost went to my knees with the shock of it. Jett, Denevik and Cassie arrived—*with Sabrina*.

~

*D'margis*

*Randl*

"Both of you are welcome to come with me," I told Barry and George. "Beverly is coming."

"We'll go," George replied immediately.

Somehow, he viewed Beverly as a surrogate mother, too, and she treated him as one of her adopted children.

"I'm here," Beverly walked into my study, followed closely by Dori, Zanfield and Perri.

"Let's go, then. Be prepared—Queen Lissa says the news isn't good."

*The news is logical*, Bennall informed me.

*And inevitable*, Kev'Ril added. The hair on my arms rose. I had the feeling that I wasn't going to like what I learned at this meeting —*at all*.

~

*G'margis*

*V'dar*

The groves and the gardens were my sanctuary, now—they were the only place I felt comfortable. A message on my comp-vid from W'dell stopped me from opening the door and going inside, creating irritation. If the fool didn't stop bothering me, I'd slice him precisely in half myself.

"My Lord," W'dell's voice sounded tiny coming through the device. "I found irregularities on Skyrock."

"What irregularities?"

"There have been no replies from Vilst. I have sent three messages, as instructed, and he has failed to respond."

"Damnation. What is he playing at?" I demanded. "Those vials need to be distributed."

"I have told him that in all three messages. I've attempted to reach his second-in-command, and received no reply."

"Send Qatti to find out what the fool is doing. If he's refusing to obey orders, have her eliminate him."

"I will relay that order, my lord."

"See that you do, and don't disturb me for the next hour."

"Yes, my lord."

I'd rather send Gillen, but he and Je'Dik were handling other business. I'd fry Qatti myself if she failed me.

Opening the sealed door into the groves, I breathed in the scent and warmth that flowed outward. "Ah. Such wonder," I breathed as I closed the door behind me. It wasn't evident at first—until I found the body of an attendant.

He'd died at the hand of another, who lay nearby, the handles of the sharp pruning shears still in his hands. That one had committed suicide after killing his fellow worker. Cursing, I kicked the body in my path out of the way, only to find another as I walked to the end of a row of trees and turned the corner.

Shouting for attendants to come to me, my voice echoed within the massive, artificially-lit cavern.

There were no replies.

Fury encompassed my mind, sending rogue gods scattering from my body.

They were terrified of my anger.

*As they should be.*

～

*Cedar Falls, Falchan*

*Travis*

"I don't know what Mom wants—she just said it was important," I pulled on a shirt. Trent was doing the same; Mom interrupted our afternoon sparring—it had to be important.

For three days, Trent and I'd crossed blades until we were too tired to stand. It was all that kept us sane after—well, *after*.

Dad forced us to clean up rather than going as we were—there was knowledge in his eyes, but he didn't share what he knew.

He and Uncle Drew were coming with us; they'd been called just as Trent and I were. We'd land at NorthStar before being transported to SouthStar. That in itself told me how important this was.

*This sounds really bad, doesn't it?* Trent sent as he pulled on socks and boots.

*Yeah. Mom wouldn't ask us to come otherwise.*

"Ready?" Uncle Drew poked his head inside our shared bedroom.

"Ready," Trent scrambled to his feet. I couldn't recall the last time I'd seen him move so awkwardly.

We were folded away from Falchan, landing in the massive kitchen at NorthStar. Mom waited for us there, as did Kiarra, Cassie and —*Sabrina*.

~

SouthStar
  Lissa

"I don't know," Cassie said. Dragon asked her about Sabrina's miraculous recovery. He'd skirted what we all suspected—the *Changing of What Was*.

"When I went back to my cabin, Sabrina's ghost was there, begging me to help her," Cassie continued.

"You saw her ghost?" Drake asked. Travis and Trent were somewhere in SouthStar's groves, walking and talking with Sabrina, who remembered little of what happened to her.

"I saw and heard her ghost. She asked me for help. When she reached out a hand, I sort of—took it."

"You touched a ghost?" Merrill asked.

"That's what pulled me back to her body. In her cabin. Right after she'd—well. There was blood everywhere. It was on my shoes."

"Then what happened?" Breanne coaxed gently.

"I wanted Sabrina to know that she was loved, and she wasn't alone. When I touched her body, I saw—she wasn't the only one who needed help."

"Who else needed help?" Hank prompted.

"Vik. Rajeon. Queen Lissa. Others." Cassie's voice began to tremble —she thought she was in trouble.

"Did you see why we needed help?" I asked.

"I saw—thorns. Thousands of deadly thorns. I knew they were deadly, but I didn't know how. Then, everything got so bright, I must've fainted. Everything went black and I didn't wake up until Sabrina started shaking me."

"What's the first thing you did when you woke?" Breanne asked.

"I knocked Sabrina's laser pistol under her bed, so she couldn't reach it."

"Is it still in her cabin?"

"I guess so. Denny called me and said we needed to go. It slipped my mind. I'll get rid of it the second I get back, I promise."

"You're not in trouble, Cassie," I told her. "Someone else will take care of the pistol, all right?"

"What's this about, then?" I admired the courage it took for her to ask.

"What do you remember about your mother?" Breanne asked.

"Little things. Watching her cook. Helping her in the flower garden. Listening to her and Aunt Shelbie talk."

"The fire demon was on her side, wasn't it?" Hank asked.

"Yes. I've felt for a long time that my father wasn't my father, but that may be wishful thinking. The ice demon my mother married was an awful, awful man."

"I think we can lay your fears to rest on that quarter," Breanne stated. "Morton King was sterile. Neither you nor your sister are related to him."

"I ah," Cassie began.

"Don't worry, we'll help you sort it all out," Breanne held up a hand. "We're just putting the chain of events together to explain how things happened, that's all. Now, we have to turn our attention to those thorns—and what they're capable of doing, and where and how they came to be."

"They have their beginnings with the Prophet, and his disease," Charles took up where Breanne left off. "I've had word from Nefrigar and Pheligar. The best Larentii scientists and the Wise Ones went back in time to study the cutting Pheligar took; the plants were infused with power—from the Prophet and from P'loxett, the planetary spirit. No doubt, the rogue gods have had a hand in this, too."

"Which tells us what, exactly?" Ashe crossed arms over his chest.

"It tells us that the Prophet expended a great deal of power on common trees and plants. After that, it was only a matter of time before they accelerated their own evolution. We're dealing with sentient trees and plants, and they're far from happy with anything on two legs. They took the Prophet's disease and morphed it into something that affects the brain of anyone coming in contact with it. We believe that's what changed Sabrina—she may have been the weakest link among the BlackWing Pirates, but somehow, somewhere, she'd had contact with a sentient plant."

"Which, in turn, caused her to commit suicide," Kiarra nodded.

"A question to the R'pexi," Charles turned to Randl. "In the past, with the god who always comes at the end, was this particular option explored—to create a disease to spread through trees and plants?"

"Kev'Ril says no," Randl replied. "They say what you already know —that power accelerated the evolution in these experimental plants and trees. The outcome is both terrible and logical at the same time."

The truth, as fatal as it could become, was now clear to all of us. Without understanding what the repercussions were, the Prophet had doomed us all.

*Had he also doomed himself?*

Those of us in the Hierarchy would still exist, but our bodies would become poisoned and fall away. I doubted than any physical body would remain if the spread of these plants went unchecked. They held power, now, and eventually, they'd grow strong enough to kill even the best of us.

"What the hell are we going to do?" Adam demanded. He'd reached the same conclusion I had.

"We have to see if any of the other locations we've pinpointed have the vines or something similar growing on the property," George rose to speak. "We need Cassie to cleanse all of it—including the seeds and roots. We have to find the Prophet's gardens and do the same to them. If this continues, even the animals and insects will die."

"It's either that or we attempt to communicate with them," Corent said.

Until then, I hadn't realized he'd come with Gavin and Gavril.

"Corent, that would be too dangerous," Breanne said. "This is like creating your death and thinking, awww, it's so cute as a baby."

"There is another way," Charles leaned against the door jamb of Ashe's massive library.

"What's that?" I asked.

"Get rid of the Prophet, then *Change What Was*."

"Right. Because we've been so successful getting rid of him so far," Vik snapped.

"Uh, I hate to interrupt things," Zanfield held up a comp-vid.

"What now?" Randl buried his face in both hands.

"See for yourself," Zanfield rose and walked to Randl's chair.

"*BlackWing Pirates create deadly, plant-based disease*," Zanfield announced before laying the comp-vid on the arm of Randl's chair. "*Disease can cause suicidal or murderous thoughts*, and it just—goes on from there," Zanfield shook his head.

"How the fucking hell does anybody know about this? We just found out about it," Kiarra cursed.

"Somebody's been playing us all along," Randl lifted his head and sighed. "One step ahead, whether it's truth or a lie. Even split-time tells me nothing."

"Do you suppose Korvus had anything to do with this?" Zaria asked. "He knew about Je'Dik. What else does he know? His brain is so compartmentalized, I could only touch the surface of it when I saw his image."

"If this is him, why is he blaming me for all of this?" Randl demanded.

"Perhaps to distract the Prophet? You notice he hasn't focused on killing innocents or raising dead armies lately," Pheligar suggested. "Instead, I believe he's focused all his energy on you and the BlackWing Pirates. He has petty criminals under his thrall already. He's been searching for criminals who can give him ships and influence over their territories. With the credit going to you regarding the worst of those, he will be angry. Nefrigar believes that if we can be affected by the plants and trees V'dar has created, then he can also be affected."

"We've dealt with diseases among the powerful before," I said. "Remember the Ra'Ak who were physically and mentally ill?"

"That wasn't the best of times," Merrill growled softly.

"Korvus' interference is only speculation at this point. My question is this—where has he been and why has he not interfered before?" Adam asked.

"No idea," Randl said. "I'm usually not at such a loss, but even Kev'Ril and Bennall know nothing of this one."

"Has he surrounded himself with bone dust? Is that why we can't find anything by *Looking*?" Kiarra frowned.

"Good question," I nodded at Kiarra. "Did you see anything like that?" I turned toward Zaria.

"Nothing that would indicate it, but as I said, he's very compartmentalized and there wasn't much on the surface for me to read."

"Larentii can compartmentalize easily," Pheligar pointed out.

"I doubt this one has ever seen a Larentii," Merrill stated. "If Korvus is a criminal, no Larentii would make themselves known to him."

"That is generally true," Pheligar agreed with Merrill. "There are no records in the Archives referring to such a one as Korvus, so no Larentii has made note of him before. Nefrigar is currently putting files together of what we know so far."

"No records in the databases of either Alliance on him," Gavril confirmed. "Either by name or by talent or association with other criminals."

"If he paid Dorlent for Griffin's death, he's not poor," Rigo observed. "One third up front would have been frighteningly expensive."

"We've tried to pinpoint credit transfers and such, but found nothing so far," Gavril said. I understood then that he'd been searching diligently to find the one responsible for his grandfather's death—and Gavin was helping him. No doubt Wyatt was communicating regularly on what he and the others turned up in their search. For now, that hadn't been much.

"Where do we go from here?" I asked, voicing the latest concern on everybody's mind.

"Perhaps the next move belongs to the Prophet," Charles suggested. "If he has been affected by this disease, he may reveal himself."

"You're suggesting we sit back and wait?" Ashe asked. I understood that Strength was demanding an answer from Wisdom. Breanne—Love, looked from one to the other, waiting for a response.

"If the Prophet is going to react, I feel it won't take long," Wisdom said. "I've been wrong before, but he has proven himself to be somewhat impetuous before—especially if he wants revenge."

"You mean he doesn't want anyone else taking credit for what he did? He's been silent on the subject in the past," Vik interjected.

"But this—it's his crowning achievement, although he has no idea how dangerous it has become. With the madness that comes from his plants and trees, can we not expect irrational behavior?"

"I can't decide whether that would be a good or bad thing," Randl said. "If he moves quickly, we could be caught unprepared."

"Then prepare yourselves," Wisdom replied. "A final battle is coming. If he wins, he will still destroy himself with his own short-sightedness. If we win, we must destroy his garden and *Change What Was* if necessary, to be rid of these malevolent, fabricated plants and trees."

"What about Je'Dik and his kind?" Cassie asked.

"One thing at a time, young one," Hank turned to her. "Your help in this will be invaluable, I believe. For now, the Prophet is the bigger threat. We will set our sights on Je'Dik and the others afterward, if it is still necessary."

"We've seen that Je'Dik has managed to separate himself from the Prophet when it suits him," Zaria pointed out. "I agree with Cassie—Je'Dik and his kind will also be a problem for us, but as Hanlekidus says, the Prophet and his poisons are currently the greater threat. My medallions are made to let me know if the wearer is threatened. I received no such warning for Sabrina, and we know now that something did bring harm to her," Zaria hesitated. I understood that she and Breanne were having a silent conversation before speaking again.

"I will work to modify the medallions," she went on. "That work will be accomplished soon, with help from volunteers." She nodded to Breanne and Hank.

Since Breanne was one of her mothers, I wasn't completely surprised. Hank had worked in the medical field in the past, so I understood his offer to assist.

"Is there anything else to discuss?" Charles asked.

"I say we keep the lines of communication open," I suggested. "This way, we're all informed and can act accordingly."

"I'll get my people ready," Randl rose first. Cassie, Vik, Jett and the other BlackWing Pirates gathered around him. Ashe stood and transported them to D'margis.

"Lissa, can we have a private meeting at your palace?" Breanne and Hank approached me.

"Sure," I said. "We can have food brought to the arboretum if you want."

"That sounds great," Hank agreed, his eyes hooded. I understood that I was about to get information I didn't have already. With my curiosity growing, I allowed Breanne to fold us to Le-Ath Veronis.

*D'margis*

*Randl*

"Hold onto the information you've gathered on petty criminals; we'll need that to cleanse the grounds," I told Barry and George.

"Should we still search for key words and contacts?" Barry asked.

"Yes. If the Prophet and his people are losing sanity and becoming suicidal and murderous, they may increase their communications. It can't hurt to keep searching, in case someone slips. If you detect any variation of the Prophet, or V'dar, let me know immediately."

"You think they'd be that stupid, Boss?" Vik asked.

He, Jett, Cassie, Denevik and I had met with Barry and George inside my office. "We can't discount anything right now," I pointed out. "Sabrina—she was affected and did things she wouldn't have done otherwise, including outing us in public. You think some of V'dar's conscripts are much stronger than that?"

"Probably not," Jett agreed. "He prefers the weak-willed, in my experience."

"Do you think the poisonous plants can overcome his obsessions?" Cassie blinked at me.

"I think it's possible."

"Damn," Vik breathed.

"What will we do about all the locations we've designated?" George asked. "Anyone who gets close to them could be affected."

"True. I'll send a message to Zaria. She may be working on it already. If not, I'll figure out how to place shields around them so no plant materials go in or out."

"We've taken care of it," Zaria appeared with two Larentii beside her. "Only plant material will be filtered from moving away from those locations. All of them have thorns growing, although none as extensive as Skyrock. I'm concerned that all of the Prophet's small-time criminal minions may be dead. There's no evidence that anyone's been in or out in days."

"They've killed themselves?" Vik frowned at Zaria.

"Or each other," she told him. "At this point, it doesn't matter. Dead is dead. Something else you should know," she turned back to me. "You no longer need to worry about those carrying the Prophet's disease on Havek—they're dead. A few took others out with them, but they're dead. Now, for everyone's safety and peace of mind, I need to see Rob."

"Because he stuck his toes in the dirt in several places," I nodded my understanding. "I'll get him now."

A few minutes later, after I sent mindspeech, Rob rushed in the door. I hadn't told him what the problem was, only that it was an emergency.

"Cassie?" Zaria turned toward her. "You're the one who detected the danger last time. Will you put your hands on Rob to see whether you feel the same thing again?"

"With Rob's permission," Cassie said.

"Cassie can touch me anytime," Rob agreed. He was beginning to understand our worry.

"All right." Cassie moved toward Rob, before settling her hands on his shoulders. The light came so fast, it registered on the back of my skull and stayed for several seconds. At least I was blind and only saw it in my mind; the others (except for Zaria) were rubbing their eyes in pain.

"Rob, you no longer have a problem," Zaria sounded grimly pleased. Cassie had proven to Zaria that she really could *Change What Was.*

*How?* I sent to Zaria.

*You understand who her father is. Understand that she is also related to me. More details will be revealed later, no doubt.*

*After she is told—gently, I presume?*

*I certainly hope so. She knows Morton King wasn't her or her sister's father. Still, this must be approached carefully.*

*Does her sister have the same father?*

*No. That information will come later.*

I hadn't seen her sister—not when and where I was. Perhaps I'd know more if I met Destiny; Barry thought she was wonderful. If we survived the inevitable battle with the Prophet, I wondered what she'd think about George, because Barry would introduce them.

*Do you suppose that her father understood the need for Cassie to be born when and where she was?*

*I think it's more likely that someone her father and other mother knows was the one who recognized the need and made it happen.*

*With their knowledge?*

*Nope.*

"Not the first time that's happened," Zaria spoke aloud. "May not be the last, either." *It's tough on the ones born from that, but it works out better for everybody else,* she added in mindspeech.

*Cassie didn't have an easy time of it,* I confirmed Zaria's words.

*I understand that completely.*

Zaria didn't have an easy time of it, either. Both were, as Salidar Deluca would say, made of sterner stuff—with iron wills and a refusal to back away from doing the right thing, no matter how hard it became.

"People," I began, addressing the others in my office. "We have a Prophet to destroy. Barry, George, you did amazing work tracking down those petty criminals. Go back now and check all their recent communications. Maybe we can intercept something from the Prophet."

"We'll work on that now," Barry nodded. He and George almost ran out the door.

"Would it hurt to go ahead and cleanse the grounds on Skyrock?" Cassie asked. "I think the time for worrying about the Prophet discovering us is past—we need to get this over with and destroying those plants could be a good place to start."

"One more thing," Rob said.

"What's that?"

"Is anyone working on a vaccine for this? Surely it's possible."

Zaria exchanged glances with the Larentii who stood beside her. "I will take our findings to Karzac and Renegar," one of them spoke. "If there is a way to protect against this, they will be the ones most capable of creating a vaccine."

"Ask them to bend time if it's necessary," Zaria suggested.

"We will." All three disappeared, leaving the rest of us alone.

"Cassie, do you think you and Denevik can go to Skyrock by yourselves, or do you want others with you?"

"We'll go," Denevik answered. "If anything appears out of the ordinary, we'll send mindspeech."

"I'll come with you, and bring Ocenosek and Cudworth," Vik offered.

"Good," I said. "The five of you ought to be safe enough. I need to check in with Travis, Trent and Sabrina."

"On our way," Denevik said, and *skipped* away with Cassie and Vik.

*G'margis*

   *V'dar*

Harming the trees and plants was the only thing that kept me from destroying the entire garden, just to get rid of the mess of it.

I despised mess and here, bloody, mutilated bodies were everywhere. That's when Qatti came running in to find me.

"They're all dead on Skyrock," she said, breathing hard from the effort of dodging bodies while racing toward me. "Just like—this," she turned and swept her hand to indicate the closest pile of lumpy carnage. She hugged herself, rubbing her arms as if she were freezing. It wasn't freezing where we were.

"You found no information—no evidence?" I snarled at her.

"I found a comp-vid." She pulled it from a pocket and offered it to me. "It was the only one that wasn't smashed."

"Did someone else kill them?"

"No. I did a scry—they did this to themselves."

Fury overcame me at that moment—with a desire to destroy foremost on my mind. I blasted the stupid witch in front of me before she had the opportunity to scream.

That wasn't enough, however. I folded space to other parts of my compound. I'd kill anyone who stood in my way, then threaten the gods who'd deserted me at the first sign of trouble.

I'd kill them, too, if they refused to return.

# CHAPTER 19

*S*kyrock
        *Cassie*

"I can feel Zaria's shield, but it won't keep us out," I told Denevik when he asked. "It won't keep my fire out, either."

"How can you know that?" Ocenosek asked.

"It told me," I shrugged. In reality, I'd been just as skeptical as he, but then Zaria's mindspeech came to me from the shield itself. She'd allowed for my intervention, it appeared. "There's enough space for me to stand inside and release my fire," I added. "I'll keep it inside the shield. If the fire department shows up, it's your job to fend them off." I grinned at Denny.

"We can handle the fire department," Cudworth chuckled. "Go do your thing."

While my companions held back, I stepped through Zaria's barrier. "You're toast, now, evil thorns," I whispered, before releasing the hottest fireball I could form inside the shield.

~

*McAlester, Oklahoma*

*Korvus Katergáris*

"Hello Grandfather. I see you've made improvements to this clock." I lifted the antique cuckoo clock and examined it carefully.

"It works now." He smiled at me, knowing I understood completely *how* he'd made it work.

"You couldn't find parts?"

"Not unless I manufactured them."

"Ah." His eyes, dark as opposed to my Grandmother's hazel, held a light I recognized. "Your talents must remain hidden here," I cautioned.

"I know. I fixed that for your grandmother. She's clearing wall space to hang it up."

"Good. How's your neighbor, Barbara?"

"Doing well. She brought brownies over yesterday. There may be one or two left in the kitchen."

"Good with coffee?"

"The best."

"Let's go, then." We walked through the back door into the house, where Grandmother was wiping down the kitchen counters.

"Korvus wants a brownie and coffee," Grandfather smiled at her.

"He's lucky we still have three left," she set her cleaning cloth aside and pulled a foil-covered baking dish from the island. "Sit down, I'll have coffee and brownies ready in a minute."

"Your neighbor brought an entire dish of brownies?" I asked.

"She's very generous, and we love brownies. Plus, we give her all the pecans that grow on our backyard trees. What have you been up to, lately?" Grandmother pulled a serving spatula from a drawer.

"Creating havoc," I sighed. "But it's for a worthy cause."

"You always say that," Grandmother turned to me with a smile.

"Because it's always true. I have people trying to follow me, but they'll find nothing of importance."

"You sound worried, just the same."

"These aren't people who can be disposed of," I shifted on my chair as Grandmother set a brownie and a cup of coffee in front of me.

"Why is that?" Grandfather asked, after thanking Grandmother for his brownie and coffee.

"They're important."

"In their world?"

"And to all of us."

"Ah." He didn't ask more questions; instead, he bit into his brownie with a sigh of satisfaction.

"Damn, these are good," I said after my first bite.

"I told you they were," Grandfather laughed as I bit into the brownie again.

~

*Queen's Palace, Le-Ath Veronis*

*Lissa*

"A few people remember seeing someone that fits his description, but they didn't know who he was or where he went," Lexsi flopped onto the sofa in my study with a frustrated sigh. Kory sat beside her, in the center.

"It's like he appears from nothing, then disappears into nothing," Wyatt complained, taking a nearby chair. He patted his knee, silently telling Jayna she could sit with him.

"I performed a scrying spell at that seedy pub, and absolutely nothing showed up on him," Bel Erland shook his head before taking the other end of the sofa. "I did make the place less stinky, though."

"We could barely sit there while he worked," Kory agreed. "It was a favor to us."

"Did you find anything on the other two?"

"There was a block on Alken Wilker," Bel Erland replied. "Also a block on Je'Dik."

"But we did find something on Dorlent," Bel Erland grinned suddenly. "Korvus met Dorlent in the same bar, only a few days before Griffin was killed."

"We found where he kept his local stash of money, but Korvus already cleaned them out," Wyatt sounded disappointed. "We did find a few weapons, though. Sent those to Dad so the CSD could match assassinations against the weapons used. He says he'll give what he can't reconcile to the ASD, so they can do the same."

"At least it wasn't a total bust," I said. "Any more leads to track?"

"We want to talk to Randl and his comp-guy, Barry," Bel Erland said. "If he can find those petty criminals belonging to the Prophet, then he should be able to trace any electronic communications from Korvus."

"Well, you'll have to ask Randl about that—I'm sure they're hunting the Prophet as hard as they can."

"I guess the Prophet is still the bigger threat," Wyatt nodded his agreement. "This, though—who can outsmart us this easily? Where did Korvus come from? Nothing about this makes sense—from a practical point of view."

"Ah, Lissa," Karzac appeared in my study, only to find all my guest seating occupied.

"What's up?" I asked.

"Renegar and I have a very promising version of a vaccine," Karzac smiled. If he was smiling, then it was more than promising.

"How long did it take?"

"Two years, but that's beside the point."

"You're at the trial phase?"

"Yes. If you'd approach Randl, I believe he may be interested in getting his people vaccinated."

"I'll let him know immediately."

"Is that the vaccine against the mutated Prophet's disease?" Wyatt asked when Karzac disappeared.

"Yes. Now keep that to yourselves; we don't need widespread panic or a demand for something that may not be readily available to the public."

"How long before the vaccine takes effect?" Bel Erland was more than curious.

"I don't know; I'll ask Karzac. A trip back in time may be necessary. I'll go find him—you need to find dinner."

"Mom invited us to eat with her," Lexsi said.

"Dad is meeting us there," Wyatt and Bel Erland spoke at the same time.

"Lexsi, honey, what about your dad?"

"He's on a special assignment. He says he'll try to be there when it's done."

"Did he mention where?"

"No. I was afraid to ask. He did say he may bring a few others with him."

"That means Cassie and Denevik. Maybe Ocenosek and Cudworth, too," Bel Erland grinned. "It's nice to see Denevik so full of life."

"It is," I agreed. "Who'd-a-thunk?"

*Skyrock*

*Cassie*

"Well, that ought to do it," Cudworth stared at the circle of black, crusted ground inside Zaria's shield. "And we didn't even have to fend off the fire department."

In the center of the destruction, where I'd spent extra time and effort, there was a large sinkhole where a former lair had been. Now, it was nothing but ash and black dust. The remains of nearly twenty bodies were now blending with the rest of the cleansed grounds.

No plant or thorn survived—I made sure of that.

"There were no vehicles, so they had another way out," I noted.

"Wizard or warlock," Ocenosek guessed.

"My thoughts exactly," Denevik nodded. "My question is this—is he dead, or did he get away before the blood started flying? If he did, he's carrying the disease with him, and that, combined with power, spells disaster."

"Who would know about that? Other than the Prophet?" I asked.

"Alken Wilker might know, but he's dead."

"Do you suppose his brother would know?"

"Gillen? That asshole? Where would we look for him?"

"No idea, but he ought to start worrying—if he has any idea this is what the Prophet's machinations are coming to—and hopefully before he goes off the deep end. He's a Fifth-level. Alken was a Four."

"How about we go ask Alken—before he's sliced and diced," Zaria appeared. "Before that happens, I'll take you by D'margis—we'll ask Perri if there's anything she wants to say to the asshole before he dies."

"Or if she has a message to send," Ocenosek looked thoughtful.

"I'll bet Zanfield has a message for him," I said, before thinking.

"I'll bet he does," Zaria turned a bright smile in my direction. "Let's go get 'em."

In less than a second, we were at the compound on D'margis, where we found Travis, Trent, Sabrina, Randl, Perri and Zanfield at a table in the dining hall, having tea and snacks.

"I hope we're not interrupting anything," Zaria smiled at them. "But we have a proposition for Perri and Zanfield."

"What proposition?" Perri asked.

"Well, I need to go back and look into another small matter before Alken Wilker meets his end," she replied. "If you want to say anything before that happens, here's your chance."

"I want to say something to him," Zanfield growled.

"I'd like to go so Zan can have his say, and then leave before—well," Perri looked down.

"Of course you can," Zaria replied. "Whatever you want."

"Then yes," Perri agreed, as Zanfield reached for her hand under the table.

"Do you want to come?" she asked Randl.

"I don't need to—I'm sure all of you can handle things just fine. We're working things out for Sabrina, going forward."

"All right. Have fun. We'll be back." Zaria waited until Zanfield and Perri stood and joined our group before bending time.

My first visit to the royal palace on Karathia landed me in its dungeon. There, we found Alken Wilker inside what Denevik described as a powerlight cage.

The fool didn't even have the decency to look ashamed when he saw Perri was there with us. I didn't realize I'd begun to smoke while tongues of flame traveled up and down my arms until Denevik cleared his throat, making me jump.

"Sorry. I just want to fry his ass so bad," I whispered.

*Ilya will take care of him in a bit,* Zaria sent.

*Thank you,* I replied.

"Come to gloat?" Alken spat at Perri.

"I did," she snapped back. "Look at you now—acting tough inside a powerlight cage. Oh, and I forgot, somebody took your balls, didn't they? Tell me, why was that? Did Korvus know what you were?"

"Shut up," he snarled.

"Oh, no," Zanfield held up a hand. "You have no hold over her anymore. Remember—you sold her brother to me. You thought I wanted him for some sick reason, and you did it anyway. Too bad you didn't know I was determined to save his life instead. By the way, we removed that filthy spell you put on him, too, and he now has the finest tutors available to help him catch up with his studies."

"He's still a null," Alken accused.

"As if that's worse than what you are," Zanfield hissed. "Oh, and your power—didn't it disappear the same time your testicles were ripped off?"

"Get the fuck away from me," Alken shouted.

"No," Zanfield said pleasantly. "But I do have a question. If you answer it, I can guarantee a swift execution. Refuse to answer and I'll let my friend Cassie slowly burn you to death."

"You think she can get fire past a powerlight cage?" Alken taunted.

"Go ahead. Burn a kneecap," Zaria turned toward me.

"Thank you," I said and stepped forward, allowing fire to form around my right hand. Alken laughed.

He shouldn't have done that.

My laser-burst of fire connected with his left knee so fast he didn't feel the pain for a moment—in fact, the scent of his burned clothing came to him before he shrieked and fell to the floor.

"Want to answer that question now?" Zanfield examined his fingernails. "Cassie can burn a hand, next."

"What the fuck do you want?" Alken sounded close to tears.

"Did the compound on Skyrock have a wizard or warlock? Is that how they got in and out of the place?"

"Phestre," Alken called out when I made a threatening move with my hand.

"Third-level, with dozens of warrants against him," Zaria supplied. "Thank you, Alken. I'll remove the pain, but not the burn. I'm taking these home, but I'll be back—with the King and your executioner."

"Don't trouble yourself," Alken sniffed as the pain left him.

"It's no trouble."

～

"If we can change clothes really fast, we won't be late for dinner at Reah's palace," Vik grinned when we landed in the common area of our compound. "She'll love hearing what we just found out."

"We'll pass," Zanfield waved off the invitation, before he and Perri folded space.

"We're going to dinner?" I looked up at Denevik, who smiled.

"I guess we're going to dinner, then," I told Vik, who grinned. "We'll hurry."

Denevik *skipped* us back to our suites, which were side-by-side. In five minutes, we were outside, dressed well enough for dinner with the High Demon Queen.

"Shall we?" Denevik offered his arm. He *skipped* us to Kifirin, where Reah and several others waited for us.

～

*That is Glindarok, the former Queen of Kifirin*, Denevik informed me as he walked me toward a cluster of people surrounding Reah. They

269

were waiting for us just outside the formal dining room. *The others are Reah's older daughters and their husbands,* Denevik continued.

*Why are they hovering around Glindarok instead of Reah, then?* I asked.

*Long, tragic story,* Denevik said. I didn't miss the curl of smoke that escaped his nostrils, either. *Glindarok is my sister, and yet she and Jaydevik did wrong in this.*

"Hey, Great-grandfather," Lexsi joined us, taking Denevik's other arm.

"Are you trying to make me feel old?" He beamed down at her.

"She makes *me* feel old," Kordevik Weth, Lexsi's husband, stepped in beside Lexsi.

"You're only as old as you feel," I pointed out.

"Well, that can go either way, then," Kory laughed.

"Depends on the day," Denevik agreed.

"With me, it depends on how much coffee I've had," I teased. For a moment, Cliff's image appeared in my mind—he'd have said the same thing. All those mornings I found him in the kitchen, a mug of coffee in his hand as he stared out the window.

He was one of the bravest I'd ever met, and he'd given his life to save another.

"You have a sad look," Denevik's finger came under my chin.

"Just thinking about an old friend who was killed in the big dust-up back home," I sighed. "He was like an adopted werewolf uncle, who died a hero."

"Then we'll raise a glass to him tonight," Denevik said.

"We're here, finally," Vik, Ocenosek and Cudworth arrived, followed closely by Wyatt, Jayna and Bel Erland.

"Shall we?" Reah called out, inviting us into the dining room. We followed her inside.

~

*D'margis*
*Randl*

"How am I going to face everyone?" Sabrina asked.

"They understand," I told her. "They know that wasn't you."

"*Now* they do," she covered her face with both hands. "I can barely face Travis and Trent."

They'd left so I could talk to Sabrina alone.

"They know what happened. Would they blame you if you got wasting disease?"

"No."

"Then stop worrying about this. At least we—Cassie—was able to turn things around."

"I can't believe what she did for me," Sabrina wiped tears off her cheeks. "I—what she gave me—it felt like pure love."

That's when I knew how Cassie was related to Zaria, but I didn't say anything to Sabrina. "You are worth it," I said gently. "Don't ever believe otherwise."

"I guess I owe her—a lot."

"I think she'll say you don't owe her anything."

"I want to do something nice for her, though."

"I'll get back to you on that," I tapped the table, indicating we were done. "Go have a beer with the others while you can. We have a lot to do and not much time to do it."

*Campiaa City, Campiaa*

*Korvus*

I found Phestre at a casino bar, pouring drinks down his throat as if something had left a terrible taste in his mouth.

*Not far from the truth*, I surmised.

"I'll buy the next round," I said, slapping him on the back and pulling up the barstool next to his.

"Who the hell are you?" His eyes narrowed in anger, while a bit of spittle left over from his last drink marred a corner of his mouth.

Phestre wasn't the ugliest I'd seen—not outwardly, anyway. Inside his mind was a nest of venomous snakes, any of which could strike randomly and with a great deal of destruction.

"Korvus," I slapped him on the back again—hard enough to leave a stinging mark. He took a moment, while his body wobbled in the opposite direction of his head.

"Huh?"

"I see you've had enough," I pulled him off the barstool as if I were his best friend, intent on getting him to a room where he could sleep off the drunkenness.

"Still want those drinks?" the bartender asked.

"No, but take this for your trouble," I tossed a generous casino chip onto the bar.

"Thanks," the bartender swiped the chip off the bar and pocketed it.

"No worries. I'll get this one home."

Forcing a man to walk who was already dead of lion snake poisoning wasn't the worst thing I'd ever done in my life, but it was still distasteful. The puncture marks on his back would look like a real bite when I deposited the body in an alley for security to find.

At least the fool had enough sense to disguise himself while he sat at the bar, drinking. I'd make sure his face was recognizable from all the wanted posters available. Someone would receive a generous reward for finding the thieving, murderous creep.

No evidence that he died in any other way than snakebite would be present, and several people would breathe easier, knowing a threat was destroyed.

Soon enough, the *coup de grâce* would be delivered, and Randl Gage would reap his reward.

*I looked forward to it.*

∿

*High Demon Palace, Kifirin*
*Cassie*

Dinner was winding down, with dessert plates sitting in front of us and everyone leaning back with a satisfied sigh.

That's when Teeg San Gerxon arrived with news. "Phestre's body was found earlier in an alley outside a casino," he reported as Reah invited him to sit and ordered a dessert and drink for him.

"That happened fast," Denevik rumbled. "How did he die?"

"Lion snake bite," Teeg said. "Baffling case, too—we generally don't have lion snakes on Campiaa—unless it's someone I know personally, and none of them are responsible."

"One less thing to worry about," Ocenosek laid his napkin beside his plate.

"I came to ask for Cassie's help in disposing of the body," Teeg admitted. "If she can cleanse anything the body's touched, I'd feel better about that, too—since we don't know whether the disease can be transferred from one to another."

"Isn't it funny how we've almost stopped worrying about the Prophet's disease, in favor of this new threat?" Wyatt said.

"The Prophet's disease requires the Prophet to activate it. This one —it can infect indiscriminately," Cudworth responded.

"Denny and I can go back with you to take care of the problem," I told Teeg.

"Good. We'll leave after I have cake."

Half an hour later, Denevik and I followed Teeg as he led us into the CSD Forensics Lab and Morgue, where Phestre's body was. He'd been quarantined from all others, a hazardous materials warning flashed above the door and a crew was standing by to sterilize everything after I was done.

"It's okay if you melt the table," Teeg said, pointing toward the body lying on a steel gurney at the room's center.

"It won't be necessary," I told him. "You should leave now."

"Turn your eyes away and don't watch through the window," Denevik said softly as Teeg moved toward the door. Teeg hesitated for only a moment before nodding and walking away.

Once the door was shut, I went to work. Only the finest particles of ash drifted about the room when I was done. It would take a few hours to cool the room down enough for the cleaning crew to do their work.

~

"I suppose we ought to just start carrying extra outfits for you wherever you go," Denevik sighed as we sat at a casino bar later, having a drink.

"Yeah."

I was dressed in something that belonged to Jayna; one of Teeg's servants had pulled it from her closet and offered a bathroom where I could get dressed.

"We were told where you were," Ocenosek and Cudworth joined us at the bar. "A drink sounded good," Ocenosek said pulling out a barstool next to Denevik's.

"Two drinks sounded better," Cudworth added, sitting beside his brother.

"Two whiskeys to start," Denevik told the bartender, pointing his thumb in our friends' direction.

"It was hard seeing Glinda there," Cudworth shook his head. "Hadn't seen her since before she abdicated."

"You can't say the old days are the better days, though," Ocenosek tossed back the whiskey he was served. "Reah's done a better job than anyone I've seen in the palace."

"It's a wrench to admit that, but it's true," Cudworth sighed heavily.

"Too many important things went unnoticed in the past," Denevik agreed, tossing back his shot of whiskey. "Lord Weth tried to warn the palace, but his words fell on deaf ears, most of the time."

"Some might be offended by that comment," Cudworth said, emptying his glass and shoving it forward for another pour. "We know better, now."

"You can say that again," Ocenosek clinked his refilled glass against his brother's. "Hard work and being forced to make your own way can do that to you. I'm glad my brother was with me all this time—even if we've had our arguments."

"Here's to not taking anything for granted," I lifted my glass of whiskey and soda.

"Absolutely," Cudworth agreed. "We're stronger together, whether we like it or not."

Denevik's arm came around me, then, and he leaned in to plant a kiss on my temple. *We are stronger together,* he sent. *You make me feel young again, avilepha.*

~

*BlackWing X*
  *Jett Riffler*

"We shouldn't come too close to D'margis," I warned Sela, my pilot. "Go farther down the scale. I'll let Randl know we're in the vicinity, but I doubt we'll find anything in this string of planets."

"On course for H'margis, Captain," she responded.

"Good enough. I'll let Nari and Tiri know so they can begin their work."

"It's tiring, isn't it?"

"Yes, it is. We've been too many places, and they've all blended together. The only thing noted in the logs is *nothing found.*"

"It's always in the last place you look," she nodded, holding back a smile.

"That it is," I agreed. "I'll go see my treasure hunters, now. The bridge is yours."

"I'll take good care of it, Captain."

~

*Ja'kel*
  *Gillen Wilker*

Je'Dik refused to go with me to Ja'kel to check on A'bil's stronghold after Qatti warned me about Vilst's demise on Skyrock.

*Qatti?* I sent as I stood amidst the worst carnage I'd seen in a century. A'bil's thieves had cut one another to shreds, scattering blood and gore everywhere, including the walls and ceiling.

*Qatti?* I sent again. *A'bil and his pack are all dead. Qatti? Did you hear me?*

Still no answer. She'd sounded frightened earlier; it was the only reason I'd left Je'Dik on the Krelk homeworld and went to check on A'bil by myself.

After getting no answer yet again, I decided to contact the Prophet. *My lord*, I sent, *A'bil and all of his servants are dead.*

*As is your wife*, the Prophet's sending was accompanied by cackling laughter. *Come to me, Gillen. I can make you dead, too.*

I folded space to get away, but it was already too late. The Prophet had latched onto me like a dog connected to a leash. Rather than rejoining Je'Dik, I was thrown to a cold, rocky floor in the G'margis tunnels, where the Prophet stood, his crazed eyes locked on me as I lay helpless before him.

My death should have come, then, but an enormous explosion at the other end of the tunnel drew the Prophet's attention, compelling him to turn away swiftly.

A door opened nearby; hands grasped one of my boots and pulled me forward as the Prophet, his back to me now, swayed in indecision.

"Get in here!" W'dell's sharp hiss jerked me out of a near-trance. He grunted with effort as he dragged me into his comp-lab and shut the door. When I began to protest, W'dell's response was soft and angry. "Hush, you fool. He's trying to kill us all."

*D'margis*

*Randl*

Something was wrong—I could feel it. Fear and anger warred with one another, but those emotions came *to* me, not *from* me. *Kev'Ril?* I sent.

*I feel it, too, as do the others*, he replied. *But the source is beyond us, still.*

*It only strengthens as time passes*, he added. *Can it be?* My chief R'pexi hesitated.

"Commander," Barry ran into the central hall, where I stood. George was right behind him. "We have a message," Barry waved a comp-vid aloft. "Someone is asking for help. He says the Prophet is trying to murder him."

"Where is this coming from?" I demanded, snatching the comp-vid from Barry's hand.

"Nearby. We haven't pinpointed the exact location, but we're working on it. Something is holding us back from getting through. That's not normal."

*Everyone on alert*, I shouted mentally at my crew. *Scramble!*

In moments, they began to assemble in the central hall, dressed for battle and bearing weapons.

Last to appear were Cassie, Denevik, Ocenosek and Cudworth. The High Demons were in Full Thifilathi, roaring a challenge. Somehow, Barry had already told Cassie what he and George discovered, so they arrived together and battle-ready.

"Stronger together," Cassie shouted, raising a fire-engulfed fist. Vik joined the other High Demons in a roared reply.

*Randl, G'margis*, Jett shouted in my mind. *Akrinn and Lorvis have reanimated; Nari and Tiri have a hit on the Prophet's gold!*

"G'margis," I bellowed at my assembled crew. "We've found the Prophet."

# CHAPTER 20

*'margis*
  *Randl*

If I'd had thoughts that this would be an immediate confrontation with the Prophet, that idea was quickly eradicated. Nari and Tiri had pinpointed the Prophet's stash of gold. We'd landed there, then separated into three groups to explore three tunnels leading toward a central, common area.

The Prophet had certainly designed this warren; the walls and floors we passed and walked upon were polished smooth as glass. Doorways were fashioned of perfectly-aligned angles—he'd left nothing to chance.

Eerie silence met us as we stumbled through these dim, frigid tunnels, where spilled blood had swiftly frozen over. No wonder he'd stolen so much frozen food; the planet itself would store it properly. *Anybody affected by the cold needs to leave now*, I warned in mindspeech. *Everyone else, send mindspeech if you see or hear anything.*

Vik, Cassie and the other High Demons had taken a third of the crew down an adjoining tunnel to explore, Travis and Trent, with another third, had taken the last. Dori, who'd turned to her ocelot and padded beside me, breathed out puffs of freezing mist as she sniffed the air, searching for something alive as we passed mangled bodies of V'dar's crew.

*I'm here—with Travis and Trent's crew,* Zaria informed me. *The medallions will keep everyone from freezing. They're also re-keyed to prevent the spread of the new disease.*

*The Prophet has gone nuts, thanks to that disease,* I responded, stepping over a body cut in thirds with laser-like precision.

*Definitely V'dar's work.*

*Barry, do you have a lock on that signal, yet?* I sent to him.

*George and I are working on it,* he replied. *Something—like static—keeps interfering.*

*Keep me advised.*

*Yes, Commander.*

*No lock on the signal, yet,* I sent to Vik, Zaria and Travis. *Tread lightly.*

*All these bodies haven't been dead long,* Vik reported. *Keep your weapons at the ready,* he sent to everyone.

*Any sign of the trees and plants?* Trent asked.

*Nothing so far,* I returned.

*Trees and plants need heat and light to survive,* Cassie interjected.

*They're probably in one place, to conserve both those things,* Zaria agreed.

G'margis shuddered mightily beneath our feet, nearly knocking me down.

*Was that an earthquake?* Vik demanded.

*No,* I hissed into his mind. *That was V'dar.*

*Korvus Katergáris*

How simple it was to fool the unsuspecting. I now wore the guise of Jincus, one of Randl Gage's least capable, power-wise. I was the rearguard, carrying a ranos rifle at the back of Randl's pod. Those ahead of me were focused on what was before them, rather than behind.

*Perfect.*

I wasn't surprised when the Prophet caused the planet to shake; he wanted the entire thing to crumble at that point, I'm sure. He'd been captured by a mutation in his own devices, and the small piece of his brain that was still aware didn't like that in the least.

I'd already begun to tease away V'dar's and Randl's shields—they were melting into the rock at their feet without their knowing. That particular trick was something I learned at an early age, and I'd used it to my advantage many times.

*It won't be long, now*—a surge of joy almost erupted into laughter. I squelched it, shifted my ranos rifle into a more comfortable position and stepped around yet another precisely sliced body.

*Randl*

*His power feels stronger, the closer we get to the open space ahead,* I sent.

*We're not there, yet,* Travis informed me. *I can't see it.*

*I'll hold back until you do,* I said. *I can see the light of it in the distance. Vik, what's your position?*

*I haven't seen it yet, either—our tunnel curved significantly, and we've found sleeping quarters along the way. Half were filled with the Prophet's victims.*

*Take nothing for granted,* I ordered. *Keep checking every room you encounter. We can't have survivors attacking from behind.*

*Understood.*

Everyone following me halted when I did; Dori stood beside me, growling softly. *I know he's up there,* I told her. *If he finds us, the others will have to fold space quickly to come in behind him. I doubt he wants to fall into a trap like that.*

*If he's smart, he'll wait until we're in the open,* Dori responded. *He'll choose the best position for himself—if he still has functioning brain cells. Check the ceiling and any upper caverns. This place is beginning to smell like a tomb.*

*A really cold tomb,* I agreed. *Damn; I can't believe he forced his people to live like this.*

*A horrible place to die, but then none of them were innocent, most likely.*

*Not after he got his obsessive-compulsive claws into them.*

*Yeah. Nothing like a megalomaniac who can place obsession.* Dori's ocelot sat back on its haunches.

*No matter what happens, remember I love you,* I said. *If something happens—well, follow Cassie and Zaria out of here, okay?*

*You think they aren't meant to die here, don't you?*

*Yes.*

*What if I refuse to leave without you?*

*My love, I'm trying to avoid that. Please calm my heart and say you'll do as I ask.*

*Randl, what do you know that I don't?*

*I—just feel strange,* I said. *Dearest, V'dar is my brother. Our mother was the same.*

*You're nothing like him, so stop scaring me. We have to kill him and do it quickly. Strike first; worry about the fallout later.*

*I intend to do that, if at all possible. I have no qualms about destroying him.*

*Then stop with the weird shit.* A soft growl accompanied her sending.

*Just remember what I said about Cassie and Zaria.*

*I can see the opening,* Travis reported.

*We're in sight of it, too,* Vik confirmed.

*Move forward with caution,* I sent. My pod fell in softly behind me.

Queen's Palace, Le-Ath Veronis
Lissa

"You'll have to ask Quin if there are any large spheres left," I told my sister. "Or Zaria—she probably knows." Breanne and Ashe had come to visit, with a very strange request.

"Zaria is occupied at the moment; will you take us to Quin?" Bree asked.

So far, Ashe hadn't spoken but he looked a bit pale to me. This was important and here I was, delaying things. "Let's go," I said, folding the three of us to Avii Castle.

"We need a large sphere, if you have one," Bree sounded desperate as she spoke to Quin.

"I have two; one is slightly smaller," Quin replied. We'd found her and Deena on the royal balcony, having tea.

"We'll take the big one, but we need a favor from you," Ashe said.

"What do you need?" Quin rose and shook out her wings.

"We need you to place a call into the sphere—the strongest one you can do, to draw the servants of Liron into it."

*They've found the Prophet?* I sent, feeling a sudden need to sit down.

*We have to hurry, and we have to bend time,* Bree replied. *Then we have to figure out how to place the damn thing in the right spot without the Prophet knowing, or we're screwed.*

*Where?* I asked.

*In a really cold place,* Ashe replied.

"I know someone who can help you," Wisdom appeared. This wasn't the Charles I'd met in the past; he seldom wore that disguise any longer. Tall, dark-haired and dressed as if he were ready to plead a case before the Supreme Court, he sounded like he was in a hurry, too.

"Who can help them?" I asked, my voice sharp.

"An ice demon, of course. Get the sphere and let's go."

"An ice demon?" Quin was puzzled. She almost jumped when a sphere the size of a bowling ball appeared in Bree's hands.

"You'll know more as time goes by," Charles explained. "Place the call. We have to go."

Bree handed the sphere to Quin. Light gathered around the Avii Queen, illuminating even her red feathers as she held the stone close to her mouth to whisper the calling into its depths.

Wisdom pulled the sphere away the moment Quin was done, then he, Ashe and Bree disappeared.

∼

*G'margis*

*V'dar*

They were coming; I could feel it—I could feel *him*, deep in my bones. Why was I getting this information now? I should have felt it in the past.

Was something wrong?

My shields—had I forgotten to raise them?

I didn't want to raise them, now; I was getting juicy information from the lack of shielding. Something about him called to me, like a seductive touch. The song that I heard in my head told me to allow his approach.

He and I—we were a part of the same.

*How?*

Where were my people? I needed them to do things for me.

*Oh.*

All dead, except for that whiner, Je'Dik. I hadn't seen him when I'd killed Gillen and that fool, W'dell. I'd shut off their call for help, too—probably why I had uninvited guests.

Randl Gage was one of them. Did he think himself strong enough?

Where were my rogues?

I swung around, catching my reflection in a patch of ice formed by moisture on a cavern wall.

Was that my reflection? My hair was untidy, my clothing torn and dirty. That wasn't me. Couldn't be.

I ignored the one making that reflection. He sneered at me in return.

"You're the one caught in the ice," I pointed out. He laughed at me.

*Had I ever been drunk?* The voice I heard sounded that way.

No matter.

*He* was coming.

*Randl.* I found his name again after fumbling for several moments.

Yes.

He was going to be dead.

How were we connected?

What was that strange pull I felt? No matter—it would all be over soon. *Return to me now,* I commanded my rogues. *My father ordered you to obey me. Come. You are needed.*

Extending my power, I felt them rushing toward me.

*Randl*

I almost stumbled when I felt it—the rush of power heading toward us.

*The rogues are coming,* Zaria shouted into our minds. *We have to kill the Prophet before they get here.*

*Fold space,* I sent to those who could. *The Prophet is ahead, and we must reach him first.*

Actually, *I* needed to reach him first, or he'd kill all of us. I stepped into split-time to get there before the others, leaving Dori's ocelot yowling angrily behind me.

*V'dar*

Randl's stench arrived the moment he did, and somehow, he'd frozen time around us as we faced one another.

Still, a part of me recognized him. How had this been hidden from me? Why couldn't I do what he'd just done, to step back in time and suspend it?

For these short moments the madness had left me, and I understood that's what it was. How had my own genius turned against me and mine? It had forced my rogues away from me; I could see them in the periphery of my vision, trying to reach me through this bubble of frozen time.

Yes—I should have been able to do what Randl did; *we were brothers.*

"I see you recognize me now," Randl spoke.

"But do you?" I countered. A part of him knew we were connected

—but had he understood how *well* we were connected? "If our witch of a mother weren't dead already, I'd kill her for this," I hissed at him.

"Do not insult my mother," he hissed as blades appeared in each of his hands. "I promised my father I'd kill you myself for what you did to her."

"Your father? How funny and tiring at the same time," I laughed humorlessly. "Get this, Randl Gage—I can see it now. Our father is the same."

"You lie." He leveled a blade at me as he took a step closer.

"You think a blade will stop me?"

"You think you can stop *me*? I carry the R'pexi from many worlds. All have sworn to do battle against the god who always comes at the last."

"Then you carry your own death with you," I laughed with genuine humor this time. "Can't you see it? Two eggs, rather than one. Both fertilized. She held one back, hiding it because both of us, unleashed upon the worlds, would end it in half the time. I imagine that's what took her strength and eventually destroyed her—trying to make you into something you weren't."

"Fuck you, V'dar. I don't care if Liron was my father. I don't care that you're my brother. I still intend to bring you down." Randl's anger showed in his face and his posture; he was about to launch himself at me.

"Kill me, and those rogues waiting outside this bubble will come straight to you," I pointed out. "You won't be able to deny them; they intend to carry on with our father's plans. You will become what you despise, Randl Gage, and nobody will be able to stop it. You think those R'pexi will be able to withstand my rogues? They'll be subverted, just as P'loxett was subverted—to serve me."

*Cassie*

We were motionless; helpless to do anything as we were frozen in time. Inside the bubble at the center of the illuminated common area, Randl faced off against the Prophet.

*Don't move,* Zaria cautioned me.

*But,* I began.

*You can break away from the paralysis if you want. Don't.*

Realization came. The stage was set; if anyone moved, it could force the outcome to go one way or another. We couldn't intervene or everything would be destroyed. I couldn't say how I knew that, but I did.

In this, things had to happen as they would.

*Yeah,* I returned. *I get it.*

*Randl*

Every cell in my brain screamed that V'dar's words were a lie.

*Except they made far too much sense.* Neither my mother nor my pap had the power and talent I did.

Nobody in their families did, either.

There was only one place it could have come from—one source.

*As long as you remain in the light, we will be with you,* Kev'Ril soothed.

*If I go dark, then kill me if you can,* I told him. *I expect nothing less.*

*We know this—we chose an honorable god,* he replied. *We will do as you ask, if it is necessary and we are strong enough. Remember; if you die, everything dies, because we also will die with you.*

*My worry is the rogues,* I said.

*Ours as well.*

*Let's get this over with, then.*

*It will be as you say, Reviendus.*

*Korvus Katergáris*

I'd walked through split-time before—now I would do it for perhaps the last time. Hefting the ranos rifle to a firing position, I shielded myself and entered the bubble of split-time Randl Gage devised—where he and his brother now held a conversation, delaying the inevitable.

Time to intervene, as I had so many times before. A ranos rifle on its own wouldn't be sufficiently effective.

With the power I intended to add, perhaps it would.

*Yes.* I smiled as I considered the amount of power to contribute.

*It should be more than sufficient.*

*V'dar*

Randl Gage was ready to strike; I understood that. Within this bubble of frozen time, I was myself again. I could strike back, but without my rogues, would I win?

Once this time interruption was gone, the madness would return. Would I carry on our father's work when the madness ruled my every decision? How would I know it? I'd just murdered every servant I had, except Je'Dik and his brothers.

Would I kill them, too, although father forbade it?

I studied Randl, who'd hesitated for a moment before leveling his most powerful blast in my direction.

Would *he* carry on our father's work?

That was the command I had from our father; the work—the goals —above all else. One of us needed to continue the work and force all worlds to obey.

*What if we were one?*

Randl shouted as I allowed the sack of skin and bones I wore to crumple. That brain was infected with madness, so I'd left it behind.

Randl shrieked as my spirit entered his body—we should have been one in the beginning.

Now we were one again. *Hello, Randl,* I greeted him in mindspeech.

*What? Get out,* he ordered, forcefully attempting to expel me.

*Sorry, we're together now, as we always should have been. You're stuck with me from now on. Let the barrier down, brother. Our rogues wish to join us.*

He squirmed; I could hear his scream as he attempted to separate us.

I dug in deeper. There would be no division between us now, I decreed it. His R'pexi struggled to move away from my spirit, as if I'd taint them by association.

Which was exactly what I desired. All of them—all the worlds—would bow to my commands. Something had placed a barrier between them and me; I struggled to destroy it. Where was that power coming from?

From outside the bubble.

Visions swam in my senses. Strength from many other medallions was flooding into a medallion Randl wore, to keep the R'pexi away from my grasp. I turned my power toward the medallion, to destroy that link. All the worlds would answer to me, once that occurred.

No—they would answer to *us; I merely had to destroy the medallion and subdue Randl Gage.*

*Wait—who was that?*

Someone stepped out of nothing to confront us, drawing my attention away from the medallion.

I laughed; he only held a ranos rifle. I lifted Randl's left hand to blast him.

"Korvus, no," Randl's voice sounded as he held up his right hand, while he and I warred with one another for control.

*No,* I heard someone else's anguished, mental voice.

A female voice.

The blast that hit us tore Randl's body apart. A mental shriek tore away from me as I rushed toward my abandoned body. Another ranos blast was fired, destroying that body before I could reach its safety.

As darkness came, everything began to shake and crumble.

Realization came as I faded; the R'pexi were dead, as Randl was dead—and the universes would implode without their presence. *I'd achieved Father's goals after all.*

~

*Cassie*

Time moved again. Rogue gods dived in as the planet began to shake. Outside G'margis, I could hear stars exploding. Rogues shrieked as their destination, the Prophet's abandoned body, was destroyed by the same one who'd killed Randl.

*Korvus.*

"Fucking asshole," I screamed as I leveled the strongest laser-blast of fire I could create at him.

I was close enough to see the hole I'd pierced through his chest; Korvus fell as if in slow motion. One of his strange, blue eyes shut before the other, in a ghostly wink. It sickened me.

Several things happened then—things that didn't make sense until later.

A sphere the sized of a bowling ball bounced across the rock floor, sucking rogue gods into its depths—against their will as they screamed in anguish and terror.

Then, three shining gods appeared from nothing, while the ground continued to shake and disintegrate. Somehow, in all the confusion, Destiny ran toward me to hug me tightly as she trembled in fear.

*How had my sister gotten here, and why?*

The light that flashed from the three who'd arrived blinded me, rendering me unconscious.

# CHAPTER 21

*vii Castle*
    *Cassie*

When I woke, I found Destiny, Barry and George standing beside my bed. Barry's arms were wrapped around Destiny, and I wasn't surprised in the least.

"I thought I saw you," I croaked. "On G'margis." My mouth was dry and raspy; I suddenly realized how thirsty I was.

"Water," George held out a glass.

"Does this mean I'm not in the past anymore?" I asked.

"We're out of the past and back where we were before all that mess started," Beverly walked into the room. "What are you doing—can't you see Cassie needs help sitting up?" she frowned at Barry.

"I'm not sure what happened," I mumbled as Barry let go of Destiny and helped me sit up in bed. I took the glass of water from George and nearly emptied it.

"Nobody knew Korvus was going to explode when you blasted him," Beverly soothed. "You've been awarded medals by the Founders of both Alliances for killing him."

"But," I began. Korvus hadn't exploded. What did they think happened on G'margis?

"Cassie needs rest," Zaria walked into the room. "She has a headache," Zaria added.

"How did you know about the headache?" I touched my temple, which was throbbing.

"I'll take care of this," Zaria shooed everybody out of the room, including Destiny. Once they were gone, she sat on the side of my bed and put her hands on my temples. The headache disappeared immediately.

"You and I remember things differently," she spoke softly. "Everyone else only recalls what they are supposed to remember. I'll fill you in on that later—Randl can help."

"Randl died. I saw it," I breathed.

"Our mother can *Change What Was*—it's why we can do it, too," Zaria said, smiling at me. "She did it to bring Randl and the R'pexi back and removed all taint of Liron and V'dar from him. He and all his R'pexi are doing fine. Quin's sphere that Destiny released at just the right moment caught the rogue gods, and now they've been sent into the time where they didn't exist."

"Destiny doesn't remember being there?"

"She doesn't. Later, that memory may be restored. It's up to the Three to decide."

"What do all the others remember?" I demanded.

"They remember that Randl killed V'dar, and that you killed Korvus when he tried to kill Randl. They think Korvus exploded."

"What about all the trees and plants?"

"That's another thing the Three took care of—it was something that should never have been, so all of it was destroyed."

"Why did they get involved in this at the end?" I asked. "It doesn't make sense."

"Well, they're allowed to act if their kids are in trouble."

"Right. Okay. Which kids? Who are they?"

"Come with me," she said, holding out a hand. "They're waiting."

～

*Queen's Palace, Le-Ath Veronis*
   *Lissa*

"This arrived five years ago, with the request that we watch it together today," Breanne handed a memory chip to me. She'd come to find me in my private study, where I was going over the boring small print of proposed legislation.

"Thank goodness; I was about to fall asleep," I took the memory chip from her hand and set it on my comp-pad.

I almost jumped off my chair when the image of Griffin loaded up.

"I'm dead—it's the only reason you're watching this recording," Griffin's voice was flat, without inflection. "I know how you feel about me, and I deserve all of it. I won't try to cover my acts with apologies —there's too much history between us to make any of it right.

"What I do want to do is this; at the end of this recording are account numbers, and names assigned to each. Those accounts hold funds I've put together over the years, and I'd like them distributed to you, Amara, my grandchildren, my father and a few others I've named. You'll understand about the delay in getting this recording when you see some of the names I've assigned.

"While I understand that forgiveness will not come my way and should not come my way, there is one final gift that I want to give to you.

"You can find them at this address on this date." Both flashed onscreen under his image. "I hope you love them as much as I did. Good-bye, Lissa. You always made me proud."

I turned my eyes to Breanne, whose mouth had dropped open as her eyes widened in understanding. Before I could stop her, she'd grasped my arm, then bent time and folded space.

We landed on the edge of a tidy lawn surrounding a small, cottage-style house. Next door, a black poodle frolicked around a woman watering flowers around her porch.

"They're home," the woman called out when we hesitated.

That's when the door opened, and a man and woman stepped outside. The breeze caught their scent and brought it to me. Both hands flew to my mouth as I stifled a scream of excitement.

"Great-grandmother, Great-grandfather," I shouted as I ran toward them. Bree was only a blink behind me. We fell into welcoming arms. Griffin had done something he shouldn't, and I'd thank him to my dying day for it.

Here were Narissa's parents, alive and well. He'd saved them from his mother's murderous intentions and allowed them to live the simple life they'd chosen for themselves.

*Narissa was so short-sighted, to call our great-grandfather a traveler,* Bree sent as we switched great-grandparents for more hugs.

I'd known that from his scent; she'd known it from looking at him. Quendes Grey hadn't aged one bit, it appeared. He held much of his Larentii ancestor in his genes.

Winifred, my great-grandmother and Quendes' wife, held me away from her and smiled through happy tears. "Brenten said you'd come when the time was right," she told me. "You and Breanne, too. He told me we have great-great grandchildren."

"And great-great-great-grandchildren," Bree said, hugging Quendes again.

*You saw him in the past; why didn't you know this?* I sent.

*Because this happened long after,* Bree replied. *I can see all of it, now. He hasn't wandered once since he and Winifred met.*

"We'd like to visit our family, if that's all right," Winifred told me.

"Gran, I'll build you a fucking mansion if you want one," I told her.

"She is plain-spoken," Winifred turned to Quendes.

"Brenten said you were," Quendes grinned. "Let me lock up the house and we'll go."

*Cassie*

"Where are we?" I asked Zaria.

"This is the house Wisdom built for Love," Zaria said. She and I stood before a massive window overlooking a sea so blue-green and beautiful it took my breath away. "There's room here for Love and all her mates, Wisdom and Strength included.

"Why are we here, then?" I asked. "I don't feel important enough to be here."

"You'll know soon enough that you have as much right to be here as anyone."

"I felt the same way, the first time I was brought here," Randl appeared beside me. I was so happy to see him, I hugged him on the spot. He chuckled when I awkwardly let him go.

"Does Dori know—what really happened on G'margis?" I asked.

"She doesn't. None of them do," Randl sighed, then he visibly shuddered. "I'll never forget how oily it felt, having V'dar inside me."

"He's gone," Zaria reached around to pat his back. "Gone for good. Now, all we have to worry about is the rest of Liron's half-Krelk brood."

"There you are," Breanne said behind us. We turned; Love stood there, surrounded by Wisdom and Strength. Nearby was Hanlekidus Frebell, or Hank, as Breanne and Lissa called him.

"You're the last one we have to tell," Breanne said. "Zaria and Randl already know."

"Know what?"

"Who your parents are," Breanne smiled.

"I'm Zaria's father," Wisdom announced. "Breanne, Lissa and one other are her mothers, who are also known as Love, Hope and Determination."

"When Breanne *Changed What Was* for Randl and the R'pexi," Ashe Evans, who was Strength, began, "I lent her power because it was a daunting task, stripping away everything that was from Liron, yet preserving all of Randl's talents and restoring all his world spirits to life and health. As a result, Randl is now more closely related to us than anyone else. Therefore, Love and Strength are his parents."

"My pap will always be my pap—the one who raised, loved and taught me," Randl sighed. "I just have extras, now. We're figuring it out. Your mom will always be your mom—the one who bore and raised you," he added. "That won't ever change."

"I still don't understand," I said, wondering why I'd been brought here yet again.

"Your mother is Love," Hank told me. "Zaria and Randl are your brother and sister, because Breanne is your mother. Your father, strangely enough, is called War."

"Don't let that fool you," Breanne said. "Hank is far more than War. He is Karma, Vengeance and Justice, too."

I must have looked as dumbstruck as I felt. "It's normal," Hank folded to me and gripped my arms gently. "I was numb when I learned I had a daughter. I hope you'll come to tolerate me, if nothing else."

"Well," I breathed a shaky sigh. "I'm grateful I no longer have to call that murderous asshole Morton King my father."

"It'll be all right," Hank folded me in a warm embrace. "You'll see."

I hoped he was right.

Really.

~

*Private Planet*

*Wisdom*

Only three others know where my private hideaway is; the Shining Ones—the Eye, the Ear, and the Voice, who is also known as the Mouth.

Only I know that the Eye was once part of me, the Ear part of Strength, and the Voice a part of Love.

The Eye sat next to my desk, toying with a gadget I'd purloined from a monk's cubicle after his monastery was devastated by plague. The books I'd also taken were now in the Larentii Archives.

"You can have that if you want," I looked up from my writing.

"I'll leave it here—I can play with it whenever you call me in."

"So, no roots, eh? No choosing a place to call home?"

"Not right now. That could change eventually, I suppose."

"You did more than well," I told him after finishing a sentence and closing the book. "You don't look happy," I added, studying his face.

"Should I?"

"Perhaps not. Blame me if you want; I gave this assignment to you."

"I took it willingly."

"You didn't understand how long—or how hard it would be, though," I said what he was thinking.

"True enough. I lied when I shouldn't have been able; acted when I shouldn't have been strong enough. Interfered when nobody else would have," he hesitated. "I reopened gates that should have remained closed, to distract the BlackWing Pirates so we could test the Prophet's reaction to our taunting."

"Because I asked it of you," I agreed. "You never failed me once, even when I asked you to infect a shipment of seeds and trees with a mutation that would react with the Prophet's disease and spread quickly to others. It was the only way to reduce V'dar's power so he could be defeated. Now, thousands upon thousands of graveyards and mausoleums the Prophet claimed will lie in peace, since their desecrator is dead."

"Yes, but the list of people I did fail is extensive. I pushed the one called Sabrina toward suicide—twice." He set the gadget aside and looked away. "My daughters, my son, my grandchildren, my wife and my friends? Do you know how hard it was for me to sacrifice Lissa? To deny Breanne to her face? To watch Wyatt die?"

I flexed my hands, attempting to come up with a suitable reply. "Is there some way I can compensate for that?" I asked, understanding the hollowness of the offer after the words left my mouth.

"If there's one thing I've learned during this lengthy assignment, it's that the loss of love cannot be compensated." When he turned back to me, his eyes held tears. "They've all moved on and left me behind, to deal with this pain on my own. Mortals are reborn and will find that love again. I am immortal and there is nothing for me, now."

"There must be something," I said, although a part of me understood his misery.

"There is. Never call me Griffin or Korvus again."

He left me, then, before I could tell him that because of his actions —his sense of duty and self-sacrifice, that the universes would now have a chance to live, rather than dying once again in an endless, senseless repetition.

*I owe you*, I sent to him. *All of us do.*

# EPILOGUE

*Summer Palace, Le-Ath Veronis*
*Lissa*

They didn't want a formal dinner, a ball or anything like it. Quendes and Winifred asked for a family picnic instead.

Pavilions were now set up on my private beach, and tables set beneath them were filled with food and drinks. Today, while the sun shone even into the night on this side of the planet, Glendes Grey would find his father still alive and waiting to see him again.

Great-grandfather Quendes explained things to me like this; he'd married the woman chosen by his father and done his duty for Grey House by producing a child. The lack of love in the relationship troubled him, causing him to make several poor choices.

Once he met Winifred, however, as he wandered the fields on Refizan one spring day, he understood what love was. It was then a matter of careful planning and timing to fool his family into thinking him dead.

He didn't recall that he and Wini had been attacked by Narissa—Griffin muted that memory in them.

"These crab puffs are delicious," Quendes arrived at my side with a plate half-covered with the petite delights.

"Reah makes those," I said. "She and Lexsi put the menu together."

"This beach is perfect," Wini joined us. "I don't know why you don't spend all your time here."

"Well, I have work to do and Council meetings to attend," I said. "It's not all fun and games being Queen of the Vampires."

"Look, Quendes, it's Breanne, and she has so many men following her," Wini exclaimed.

"Those are her mates," I said. "Behind them, you can see Quin and Justis, Queen and King of the Avii, landing with their guards."

"Oh my goodness, they have wings," Wini gushed. "Are we related to them?"

"You're related to Quin through Breanne and Zaria," I said.

"We're related to royalty," Wini smiled at Quendes.

"Many times over," I agreed. "You are kin to the Queen of Le-Ath Veronis, the Queen of the Avii, the Queen of Kifirin, the King of Karathia and the Founder of the Campiaan Alliance."

"Grey House has arrived," Quendes said softly, his voice trembling. He had no idea how Glendes would react.

Glendes wore the black robes of his office as the Head of Grey House. He and Lira walked together, arm-in-arm. Behind them walked all the Division Heads and First-levels, dressed in their traditional colors. That including Raffian, Shadow, Cleo, Kyler and Nissa, dressed in the blue of the K'shoufa jewelers. Toff and Trik flanked Nissa; they wouldn't allow her to wander far from their sight as she was pregnant again.

"I hope he's not thinking this is a Grey House monthly dinner," Quendes sighed.

"It'll be all right," I patted his shoulder.

The Grey House contingent continued to walk toward us, their robes flowing about their feet, their steps measured as if treading in ceremonial rhythm.

"I'm in trouble," Great-grandfather moaned, and then he blinked.

Beginning at the back of that procession, things began to change. Formal robes changed colors.

Transformed.

Even I was surprised as robes became brightly-colored Hawaiian shirts, and trousers became shorts. Shoes disappeared altogether, leaving bare feet to plant impressions in the sand.

"Papa?" Glendes hesitated as he came close.

"Glenny?" Quendes whispered.

"Papa." Glendes folded himself into Quendes' arms, and all was right with the world.

*Cassie*

"Don't worry, dearest, you will be welcomed as warmly as anyone else," Zarigar smiled at me. Denevik had worked most of the day to convince me of the same thing. I was still trying to come to terms with this universe and my place in it.

Even Destiny was having an easier time of it, but then she hadn't had an entirely new parentage thrust upon her. Breanne and Hank weren't crowding me; far from it. They offered to help me if I needed it, but I couldn't decide whether I wanted or needed help.

In the few weeks that had passed since the Prophet's demise, war had broken out on several planets. Small wars on other worlds were now much larger in scale and threatening to go global.

*Je'Dik's work, and those of his kind*, Randl said. He and the rest of the Formidables were now turning their gaze upon that last of Liron's brood. Soon enough, Lissa said, the Alliances would begin to call for mandatory conscriptions beyond the normal, peacetime numbers.

At least the Prophet no longer existed, but we were left wondering just how much damage Je'Dik and his kind could inflict.

"We have something for you, dearest," Zarigar interrupted my thoughts, which had wandered.

"What's that?" I asked.

"This." Denevik held out a jewelry case.

"But," I began.

"The Wise Ones are also capable of *Changing What Was*, dearest," Zarigar breathed as I opened the case to find the black opal jewelry I'd destroyed on Campiaa.

"The dress is hanging in your closet—for when we go dancing again," Denevik grinned.

"I love you," I flung myself into Denevik's arms. "You, too," I said, turning to offer a hug to Zarigar.

"A gift well-deserved," Zarigar kissed my temple. "Come. You will wear these with pride as we attend the family picnic."

"Come on before they eat it all," Rob arrived to complain.

He waited patiently while Zarigar placed the jewelry around my neck, in my ears and on my wrist.

We walked toward the thick crowd of people, most of whom, I'd learned recently, were related, somehow.

I had a large family—something I'd never dreamed possible.

"I think this will be fun," I said as we reached the edge of the crowd.

"Hey, cousin Cassie," Vik called out, holding up a glass of champagne. "You're behind on your drinking already."

"Says who?" I retorted and made my way through the crowd to take the glass he offered.

∼

*Harifa Edus*

I ate.

I slept.

I hunted.

Something important—crucial—tugged urgently at my memory, but I chose to ignore it. Game was plentiful—especially deer. I often heard other wolves howling in the distance, but I ignored them and didn't howl back.

Perhaps I could have joined them, but for now, I didn't feel the need. I was satisfied with how things were and had little desire to change anything. It felt good not to have anything other than my own survival pressing upon me.

Sometimes, I wondered what those troubling, crucial things could be, before tossing them away with a shake of my fur and trotting down game trails in search of wild creatures—known and unknown.

Until another wolf came looking for me.

Something about the scent informed me that I knew him, and, as he approached me in a friendly way, I didn't growl.

"Time to come back to the real world," the wolf transformed into a man, although his scent was still familiar.

I chuffed my answer, then sneezed at him. He laughed. "Come on, Cliff. I told you I'd introduce you to Lissa, and there's a picnic waiting. You've had six months to yourself. Time to decide what you want to do with the rest of your life."

"Well, hell." I rose on two feet and my fur disappeared, leaving me naked as I glared at Winkler.

I remembered, now.

Somehow, someone had pulled me away from that infernal mountain in Georgia just as I was shot. I'd yelped—I remembered that, too, as pain bloomed in my chest and everything went dark.

I didn't recall much after that; I'd ended up here, where I could be wolf for a while with no other worries.

"Here." Shorts and a polo appeared in Winkler's hand; I accepted them reluctantly. The moment I pulled them on, he transported me elsewhere. I found myself on a beach, where a crowd had gathered and the scent of delicious food tickled my nostrils.

The crowd parted, as if they understood what needed to happen. At the center, two people were revealed. Both had gone still and silent when they noticed me.

"Cliff," Rob's shout was one of pure joy. Cassie's shriek closely followed as they ran toward me.

Had I not been a strong, sturdy werewolf, I might have fallen when both leapt into my arms. A booming sound came; I didn't recognize it as my own laughter for several moments.

It had been a long time since I'd laughed with such delight.

*A gift for three heroes*, Randl Gage's voice informed me softly. *And well-deserved.*

The End